Queen City
A Novel
Edward Crosby Wells

Cover photo by MK M Riddell

To Ronald L. Perkins
for the journey of a lifetime

~BY THE AUTHOR~

NOVELS
Queen City
Gnarled Pines

PLAYS (Full Length)
3 Guys in Drag Selling Their Stuff
Desert Devils
Flowers Out Of Season
In The Venus Arms
Poet's Wake
Streets of Old New York (Musical)
Tales of Darkest Suburbia
The Moon Away
The Proctologist's Daughter
Thor's Day
Wait A Minute!
West Texas Massacre

PLAYS (30 to 60 minutes)
20th Century Sketches
Empire (40-minutes)
Slow Boat to China (30-minutes)
Tough Cookies (60-minutes)

PLAYS (under 30-minutes)

21 Today (monologue)
Civil Unionized
Cornered
Dick and Jane Meet Barry Manilow
Harry the Chair
Leaving Tampa
Missing Baggage
Next
Pedaling to Paradise
Pink Gin for the Blues (monologue)
Road Kill
Samson and Delilah
Sisters of Little Mercy
Vampyre Holiday
Whiskers

COLLECTIONS

A Baker's Dozen
19 One-Acts, Monologs & Short Plays
6 Full-Length Plays, Volume ONE
6 Full-Length Plays, Volume TWO
Bananas
Lavender Ink

SCREENPLAY

Road Kill

CHAPTERS

1. the other side of wonderland
2. tea time at shady sanctum
3. jesus and the devil walk into a bar
4. too much public television
5. the obligatory book
6. a night in snow white's crotch
7. may I put my hands on her
8. robbery, villainy, insanity, and cardinal sins
9. origin, orgies, and the color of magic
10. better call fuzzlbum
11. frackers, buzzards, and real live mormons
12. shitty tits, made in china
13. gnomenclature for unconscious dimensions
14. what's a gingrich, birthing and a beautiful thing
15. there goes the neighborhood
16. coming home to roost
17. lunchtime at shady sanctum
18. on the road, a woman with a dick, and rolly stomps on it
19. hitler's ego, and monsanto's bad seeds
20. lock and load and risky pleasures
21. party like it's the end of the world
22. back to sphincter island
23. welcome to wonderland

ONE
the other side of wonderland

Queen City, Colorado began as a commingling of settlers, speculators, alchemists and prospectors who gave up their every attachment—wives, children, mothers and creditors—to stake claims to Rocky Mountain mines of silver and gold in pursuit of the miraculous mother-load that will, they think, fulfill their every dream. Well, at least it got them out of the house.

Drifters and grifters from just about everywhere came looking for something. Some weren't sure what that something was, but some were sure they would find it in the Queen City of the Plains. They came and they settled, putting down roots into mile-high ground situated against the majestic Rocky Mountains to the West that inspired, to one degree or less, the white kinda-mountainous roof of maybe-snow-capped peaks rising over Queen City International Airport. Eastward are the barren plains and the flatlands of Kansas—*the dead zone.*

Much like America, equality, and democracy, Queen City is an idea—*an enchanting idea.* It evolves while yet maintaining infinite dimensions of its past: Gothic, Modern, Victorian, Post-Modern, Contemporary, Quaint, Bold, Steampunk, Deco, Pretentious, and a hodgepodge out of time and ahead of its time at once. No one can easily stick a label to it. It is neither fish, fowl, nor Rocky Mountain oyster. Welcome to the other side of Wonderland—*Queen City.*

* * *

Some of the most atypical individuals live in the Capitol Hill district of Queen City. Carla Bean is one of many of those unconventional residents who live on Capitol Hill.

Carla Bean, once known as Carlos Martinez, owns who-the-fuck-can-figure-it-out La Bean Hacienda; a converted stable that consumes two extra large lots. *"A wonder to behold, but not to be believed. A gaudy mismatch of everything,"* was the sum-total of what the Asshole Princess of Self-Focused Critics wrote regarding La Bean Hacienda for *Architectural Digest*. The Demon Critic proceeded to slobber her unbearable euphemisms and similes, her unspeakable grammar, doublespeak, and an endless parade of repetitions across two slick pages. That blatantly egregious reference to La Bean Hacienda was simply used as an example of the antithesis of, "...that gringo rattrap in Cherry Creek..." bemoaned Carla Bean, "...a prefab owned by carpetbaggers from Dallas, Los Angeles or some other woe-worthy place." Carla was heartbroken, for a short while anyway, until another side of her arose from the suburbs of Hell to come to her rescue suggesting a vendetta.

She began her vendetta with a barrage of poison-pen letters handwritten to the editor and to the "sick bitch gonzo writer" herself. Every single day two letters were written in purple ink from a tortoiseshell fountain pen. As her vitriol grew daily, her diminutive handwriting became mean and jagged stabbings as large as fingernails. No one from *Architectural Digest* ever replied. She felt abused, hurt, unnoticed. She was thrown into a tailspin which headed straight into a deep and hate-filled depression, which she felt disposed to parcel out among her friends and anyone else who gets in her way. When Carla is unhappy she dragoons those around her to be the same.

The daily missives and telephone calls, the angry outbursts, pretending to be a lawyer threatening to sue their collective asses, became more unbalanced by the day. Once she screamed into the phone, "I know where you live, fucker!" followed by a barrage of ear-piercing shrieks. After a month of menace she made one last, regrettable, most unwise, phone call, "There's a bomb hidden in your building!"

After an hour of her bullying interrogation, she finally let the Men in Black Suits have their say. After another hour of explaining the situation *ad infinitum*, interspersed with her sobbing and contriteness, the Men in Black Suits confessed their surprise that she and La Bean Hacienda were treated, *"...so shockingly, so shabbily."* Carla Bean entertained the Men in Black Suits with her coquettish, sensuous, woman-girl persona. She turned into a purring kitten with a come hither smile, "Anytime you boys are in town be sure to come see me. *Ohh*, and since we all agree that this was nothing but nonsense you may leave now. Ya'll have a pleasant day, ya hear?" The Men in Black Suits bowed and walked backwards toward the front doors and let themselves out, smiling as though they just had the fuck of their lives; and, perhaps they had.

The following day a computer generated legal document arrived via certified mail. The document was complete with two unreadable notarized signatures from the magazine's attorneys. If the Men in Black Suits hadn't helped her to turn over a new leaf, the *"cease and desist"* order scared the bejesus out of her with threats that, unlike Carla's own threats, could in fact be carried out. She *ceased* and she *desisted*. After a month without a word from anyone at *Architectural Digest*, she felt assured that would be the end of it. And it was. She never heard from the magazine again. And, of course, she did not renew her subscription.

Carla Bean, once a slight man, was now a slight woman, a natural beauty, a mature woman shrouded in mystery. Her dyed-black hair is cut into a strikingly asymmetrical shape that suits her face and temperament perfectly.

When Carla first saw Mister Bean, Mister Bean saw her as a vagina, a lovely vagina, but a vagina nonetheless. When she wasn't a vagina she was a piece of arm candy—a trophy he could fuck. She saw him for what he was; a sad man with a shitload of money. They both knew full-well that their living together was simply an arrangement. When Carla told Mister Bean that she was a transexual, he was captivated and stimulated—not the response Carla anticipated. After a few months they found the best in each other. The vibes they shared were positively intoxicating, so Mister Bean asked his vagina to marry him and, without any hesitation, his vagina said yes. Mister Bean loved the idea that Carla's vagina was once a penis, and the thought of it always gave him an erection. Their's was a match made in somewhere otherworldly: a strip joint on Colfax Avenue where Carla gave her future husband a lap dance.

Carla was happily married right up until Mister Bean died from eating a moldy baloney sandwich while sleepwalking. It took Carla nearly an entire year before she could put on a face, an attitude, get out of the mansion, get her hair and her wigs done, get a waxing down under, and have a bit of fun. And, boy-o-boy, did Carla Bean know how to have fun—and a lot of it!

On either side of the north entrance to La Bean Hacienda, rising two stories high, two marble Ionic columns stood attached to nothing. "It's a wonder they haven't toppled. Must be some kind of gravity or magnetic thing or something," those who saw it were heard to say.

The frieze below the cornice of each column depicted naked Greek soldiers with spears, shields and unreasonable stiffies. Some nights the columns prowl around the grounds. One night, while wading in the outdoor pool, the south pillar fell and chipped its cornice. The north pillar helped it up and out before the sun rose and they managed to wobble their way back to their places where they stood guard at the north entrance to La Bean Hacienda.

Neighbors gathered daily with binoculars and cellphone cameras to catch anything they could see over the dull yellow stucco wall. Did either of the columns appear askew? Minnie Beach swears the columns switched places. Others swear that they had noticed something odd about them, but they were never crystal clear about what that something was. When they try to remember, they suffer unbearable migraine headaches.

* * *

There are Keepers of Count among the Capitol Hill bunch. As an example: The Keepers of Count keep count of the kinds of flowers their neighbors plant or intend to plant, how well their choices of colors will coordinate, what kinds of insects might they attract, who was watering their yard on no-watering days, and who was getting suspicious-appearing deliveries from Amazon? Things of little consequence populated the minuscule dimension of gossip within a galaxy of doomed machinations, performed from a sense of insignificance, trapped them in the mire of their discontent. The Keepers of Count kept count.

The Capitol Hill coterie appeared conspicuously in coffee houses and sidewalk cafés. They provided an advantageous viewpoint to do what comes naturally; observe those whom they know, then dig for lethal information that may come in handy, whenever and wherever it could possibly be needed sometime in the future. Information was the coinage exchanged during the duration of their social intercourse.

* * *

The excitement and the scent of sublimity that had wafted through Queen City's early morning air, ended in a gathering of clouds, gray and mournful, in the late afternoon sky when the FEA field trip came to an abrupt finale when their chartered bus, more than an hour late, returned with neither Victoria Aires, who banged and marched to her own drum, nor her wife Lily Nettles, who heard V's drum, but didn't march to it, were missing. *Oops.* They had arranged the entire adventure, they were founding members of the Friends of Erotic Artifacts, they were looked up-to by some and not so by others; in either case, their being abandoned was seen as an astonishing oversight.

Professor Hans von Mummi, of whom most on the bus had, at one time or another, wondered from where the "von" came; or if it were simply an abused preposition, was on the bus. Before taking an early retirement, Professor von Mummi, alone in the night while playing with his chemistry set, blew-up and destroyed the entire applied sciences building where he headed the chemistry department at Queen City University. After returning home from a month in Queen City General, and another month in Utah getting plastic surgery, von Mummi looked right as rain. Better than rain, in fact. Still, he needed something to occupy his mind. So, he decided to write an opera.

His opera, *Snuff in the Tropics*, based on the Jonestown Massacre, had a free public reading at the Uranus Café in Queen City's LoDo district; a pretentious throwback to the Beat 1950s' cafés that populated New York's Greenwich Village. However and unfortunately, the cast was so large that the small avant-garde coffee house could not accommodate an audience in excess of twelve. Besides, who wants to listen to a "reading" of an opera? Surely, something is bound to be lost in transliteration.

Prof. Hans von Mummi's wife, Helga, an environmental artist, accompanied him on the FEA field trip. Helga's claim to notoriety was papering the trees and grass of Cheesman Park in Queen City's Capitol Hill territory with pink crepe paper. But moments after she had completed the installation, a torrential rain came and the paper soaked into the lawn, dying the entire park pink as it disintegrated. Apparently, crepe paper wasn't such a great idea. It took several mowings before the park returned to green. Helga then restricted herself, at the request of the City Council, to the interiors of shopping malls. Parenthetically and oddly enough, the sunny day following her crepe paper washout, the Gay Pride Parade assembled in the pink park causing some to think it a message from God.

Also on the bus was Eddy Spaghetti. Eddy moved to Queen City from New York City a few years earlier. He was a jolly plump queen, quick-witted, sometimes sarcastic, yet always had an empathetic shoulder to cry on. Eddy Spaghetti had the ability to see into the future; so far into the future, in fact, that he saw Manhattan underwater, which he presumed was due to global warming; so, after researching the topography, the mountains and the plaines; the meteorology, the number of sunny days, and, of course, the fagnometer, the city's percentage of gay people; he found everything he was looking for, and more, in Queen City, Colorado. He was in the Wild West—a childhood dream of his—a mile high above the Pacific and Atlantic oceans, reasonably safe from death by drowning, and he loved Queen City. Eddy Spaghetti, a black man born in Harlem, a former window decorator for Bloomingdale's on 59th and Lexington in Manhattan, worked at Queen City's Neiman Marcus doing the same. Now in his mid-forties he had, in his late teens and early twenties, sashayed through four years in the Navy—a queen's paradise.

Mikey and Mercy Pentcist, proprietors of The Prometheus Society LLC, were on the bus. The Pentcists specialized in removing the bodies of loved ones, turning them into ashes before scooping them into hand-crafted boxes before return delivery. They make all the arrangements as well as the boxes. The mourner is free of worries and stress. Should one want a quiet no-questions-asked cremation, no frills, one instantly forgotten, a never-happened cremation, the Pentcists were thrilled to accommodate their "special" clients in their time of distress—for a significant economic windfall. The Prometheus Society LLC is a cottage industry owned and operated by the Pentcists from their very own cottage.

Mikey Pentcist was once a grandiose pontificator perpetually certain that he knew better than anyone within the sound of his voice. His friends and acquaintances found him a boring buffoon. Since his quarrelsome certitude intimidated any attempt to disagree with him, Mikey the Pontificator quickly and drastically limited his sales ability; as well as his friends. That said, about a year before today's FEA field trip, he suddenly became a quiet person, a submissive person, an introspective man—he became Mikey the Ordinary. What happened? Everybody noticed, but none could figure a motive for the change. It was as though Mikey wasn't there anymore; which brought to the minds of many, *The Body Snatchers*. Some went so far as to check their cellars for pods. Those who hadn't cellars scoured the bushes.

Mercy Pentcist is a champion when it comes to selling insurance for a low maintenance funeral. The secret to her success is her studied illusion of empathy and her uncanny ability to secure down payments from people who could never afford the monthly installments, and so, they would eventually default. Not Mercy's fault. *Ut-ahh*. Mercy convinced herself that helping the poor buy into the American Dream of dying with dignity, with a quick and quiet departure, with neither inconvenience, nor stress to the survivors for whom she was doing God's work. Clearly, it was not her responsibility that *"...some who hadn't thought about the consequences of their signed-commitments, who forfeited years of their payments because they should have known better and paid their policies on time."* It certainly wasn't the fault of Mercy that *"…they'll soon find themselves in a black hole and covered with lye."* The Pentcists were not nice people.

Nelson Beach, the lawyer who had managed to squirm free from disbarment after Sara Hookerbee, a lady with a heart of lead accused him of sexual harassment, was on the bus, in the last row, thinking herself unseen. Sara Hookerbee, his newly hired secretary, settled on an undisclosed under-the-table payment. She dropped the charges and Nelson raised her rank from secretary to executive assistant. He thought that he could then remain close to her without needing to pay for her personal and especial services, but with Executive Assistant Hookerbee, everything is negotiable.

Nelson Beach sat on a narrow bus seat next to his wife Minnie; plus-sized, resembling a blond Rhine maiden, who was a woman with a kind heart and a gentle disposition. Her husband's indifference left her to create the illusion of the bus seat being more narrow than it ought. Minnie made jovial remarks meant to amuse, but they were never thought through far enough to anticipate how some might misinterpret her meaning. Poor thing. Minnie stayed home mostly and did nothing as far as anybody knew, other than housewifery—and suffer her husband's abuse.

Carla Bean, along with her current inamorato, a hot young and hung Greek houseguest, were on the bus sitting near Billy Butts the entertainment and society reporter for *Out And Beyond*.

Moving on, the bus finally returned to Queen City with the Friends of Erotic Artifacts *sans* Victoria Aires—whom everybody knew as V—and Lily Nettles, who nobody noticed missing until long after the bus was on its way home; a fact that V would find unimaginably insulting and Lily would find it a just-goes-to-show-you lesson learned.

Going back to when the chartered bus was nearly halfway home from Dead Squeezer's Caverns, Carla Bean's Greek house guest inquired, "Lady with hat no come back?" of the whereabouts of V who had worn her mauve fedora, about which Minnie Beach had fallen flat upon her own petard with one of her lackluster attempts at wit which was obviously well beyond her grasp, by pointing out earlier that day to everybody within a block of the bus station, "I love your hat, Vicky. Maybe I should go to the thrift store with you next time." Minnie Beach reminded one of a roly-poly toy that uprights every time it is knocked over.

"You do that," V said, balefully. "...and my name isn't Vicky! Call me that again and I'll flog you like a piñata!"

Though it was Minnie's overblown desire to be quick-witted, she would settle for funny, even amusing; however, she was regrettably disadvantaged by a shortsighted sense of humor. She gave the occasional dinner party designed to reinforce her friendship with others, although they never worked out quite the way she had planned. Her last dinner party resulted in four of her guests coming down with ptomaine poisoning from her matzo ball soup. "It wasn't my fault. Queen Soopers sold me old rancid matzo meal."

V rarely paid Minnie Beach much mind since the time Minnie tried to get away with claiming that that thing hanging from the second floor balustrade in her Georgian prefabrication was a rubbing of the Cardiff giant that she had rubbed in a circus sideshow tent when she was still young, slender, and unmarried. Furthermore, Minnie went on to declare how she nearly got herself trampled, maimed and quite possibly killed when three bull elephants objected to her crossing the circus grounds in the dead of night while on her way to the egress along with three charcoaled bed sheets flapping in the wind of an impending tornado. *Pah-lees. Really? Too much!* She was rescued, she claims, by a big, beautiful, blond, blue-eyed aerialist named Claus who happened along just in time to sweep her out from under Bosco the Brute, the biggest of the three bull elephants. *"Bull"* was certainly the name for it, according to just about everybody to whom she told that story. Although, everybody thought it highly imaginative and somewhat revealing; still, nobody was about to believe a word of it. Lily Nettles almost did. Perhaps she wanted to believe. Yet even she, with her trusting nature, always trying to make the best of everything, soon thought better of it. Besides, the Cardiff giant was discovered to be a hoax a long time ago, so a rubbing of it was an irony twice removed. To this day, Minnie Beach refuses to change her tune, although Claus elicits a refrain of "the man on the flying trapeze" when her philandering husband is within earshot.

Minnie Beach was made to suffer. No matter how painful the slings and arrows of her outrageous misfortunes, she suffered them in silence. In silence she found a stronger self: a self who could manage her own reconstruction. Her friends would never know how deeply the stabs of their disbelief had penetrated. Minnie Beach could never, ever, take her friends, those doubting Thomases, too very much to heart ever again, but she did; time and time again.

Minnie was made to endure misfortune. She knew "friends" would only break her heart beyond complete repair one day; as if it were a piece of fine china, like her mended teacup that once broken could never be all together mended. No matter how delicately adhered with unseeable fractures held tightly back together, Minnie would always know it was damaged. She could not help but feel guilt and chagrin every time she caught a glimpse of the blameless teacup. What a dreadful humiliation befalls her whenever she serves that rehabilitated teacup. She came to realize that she did not much like her friends because time and time again they would chip or break her porcelain heart.

Sir Geoffrey Hemphill retired, but from what nobody knew, was on the bus. He was a natty gentleman who suffered an aura of sadness and confusion. Sir Geoffrey was amazingly short, a hundred pounds wet, dressed smartly in a safari suit with a pith helmet covering the combover that he dyed, along with his goatee, coal-black; causing him to appear startlingly like a lawn gnome. *(Lawn gnomes were a growing danger in Queen City. Since they lost their appetite for small furry things, they began biting, bruising and eating people's feet. The smart folk take along baseball bats when going outside in the dark.)*

Sir Geoffrey had tried to persuade the bus driver to go back to pick up "the girls" since, feared he, "Were left waiting in the dust of the bus, rejected and forlorn." Getting no satisfaction from the driver, Sir Geoffrey, in a fit of rage, withdrew his mighty Swiss Army knife and threatened the driver to within an inch of his life, so to speak, with the first blade he could manage to pull out which happened to be an inch long bottle opener; causing a bit of excitement and general chaos in his attempt to demonstrate his chivalry and the degree to which he was willing to go to retrieve V and her actress friend Lily, whom he saw as a barrier to V's surrendering herself to him in his attempts to court her for her hand in marriage. He never got a clue from V and, for that matter, from himself. He wanted her as a beard and she wanted him to come out of the closet and be a honest friend. Besides, her hand in marriage was no longer available since she had already given her hand to Lily the very first day marriage to same sex couples became legal. Poor Sir Geoffrey suffered from selective hearing and never gave up his courting ritual.

When the bus pulled off and stopped along the side of the road, somewhere where one could look and see only miles of nothing and nowhere, the driver informed Sir Geoffrey that he was merely moonlighting as a bus driver on weekends and that he was a member of Queen City's Finest. It took a bit of time for Sir Geoffrey to let that sink in, but by the time it did he was being handcuffed and informed of his rights. Coincidently, the driver/policeman mysteriously disappeared the following day; leaving behind a pregnant Chihuahua and a wife who never noticed him missing, although the Chihuahua seemed to, every now and again.

So, when the chartered bus had finally come home to a full stop, all aboard were eager to disembark. Some were worried over the whereabouts of V and Lily. Some were not. Billy Butts was preoccupied with weightier matters such as himself and what wonderful company he must have been for all on the bus. Billy really should have been an entertainer; a talkshow host; a grifter. He had the gift of gab and a wealth of talent yet to be mined.

* * *

FEA field trip Saturday started on a high note and, by all accounts, it seemed a glorious morning.

"What a glorious morning," Lily mused.

"Not so glorious, Lily. It's hot, it's dry and if Minnie Beach says one more word about my hat I am going to hand it to her!"

"So much for a glorious morning. I don't see how that will gain you anything, V. You did buy that hat in a thrift store. I was with you," glibly said.

"Get off it, Lily!" snapped V who had already moved on to visions of Minnie Beach getting run over by a shopping cart in Queen Soopers, although that might be impossible given the size of Minnie vis-a-vie the cart's wheels; or, perhaps, slipping on a jar of mayonnaise, but upon a second thought, came another vision where Minnie wouldn't be hurt by any glass, or any other object; just her pride and her butt. V was a fair-minded person who simply wanted justice and little more, though it's the little more that could get worrisome, yet deliciously satisfying.

"I'm sure she meant well," said Lily, trying to be of comfort.

However, V took no comfort from Lily's words, nor their tone, and so she simply said through an undignified sneer, *"Meant well indeed, Lily."*

"You don't really care about stuff like that," Lily said, or asked—it seemed more a question than a statement, but too ambiguous to tell.

"What kind of stuff?"

"Revenge."

"Revenge? What kind of revenge?"

"What other kind is there? The kind that hurts people, V."

"Then, of course I do not really want revenge. And I certainly do not want to harm the poor soul. Nevertheless, I am not going to stifle my imagination from having visions designed to amuse myself. So I shop in thrift stores. So what? Who doesn't? Lily, you do not happen to know if mayonnaise comes in plastic or glass jars, do you?"

"I'd say some are and some aren't, but I think more plastic than glass. There must be a glut of oil, or a shortness of sand. What do you think, V?"

V feigned a shudder, "I refuse to think about it."

They all boarded the bus in relative silence. Nothing of any consequence took place. Just a measurable lull. Perhaps they were waiting for the air conditioning to kick in and provide them with a greater degree of comfort. At least, enough to break the silence.

Nelson Beach the Philanderer and Sonofabitch split a buttered crescent with Minnie while Sir Geoffrey, whom everybody referred to as "Sir," yet nobody knew whether or not he was actually knighted, and if so, for what and by whom, forged ahead to get the aisle seat across from V, knocking against the seat occupied by Mikey and Mercy Pentcist in their high lacquered hairdos more suited to drag queens, causing them to drop their magnetic checkers just as they put the last checker in place. Helga von Mummi leaned forward blocking her husband from being seen by Carla Bean whom she imagined staring at his crotch as he was busily arranging himself in his new white linen slacks. He was a well-endowed man and mighty grateful for it. Carla did catch the action, but she was too busy trying to disengage Billy Butts who was kneeling, facing backwards in his seat in front of her, looking like a balding gray haired elf; talking about Jackie O and how they had a great many friends in common who came to The Studio where he had been a club boy while going through his trust fund during his glory days in New York City before joining AA after several hospital incarcerations, was drooling all over Carla's Greek who didn't seem to mind at all. The Greek nodded and smiled showing his pristine white teeth and, though not knowing most of what Billy Butts was saying, he didn't need to understand any of the words to get the gist of what Billy had in mind. The Greek did not discourage. Soon the Friends of Erotic Artifacts were rolling along their merry way towards their long awaited FEA field trip to Dead Squeezer's Caverns.

TWO

tea time at shady sanctum

Maxfield Talbot, a burly man, appearing to be in his seventies, sat on a beanbag watching natives beautiful black women glistening rainbows banana skirts dripping fruit flies naked beady-eyes behind shrubbery wearing Campbell's tomato soup cans paying constant attention they throw off the cans where manhood stands Jesus naked whips snap where are you the Vatican everything out of order does it matter not really look at the mess you've created you need more self-control keep jumps shorter remember order by secret signs learn to read envision pay attention believe it you're doing good yes believe it keep jumps short and simple try harder stop messing with time did we switch points of view with time no they are all yours listen to yourself we are in the mind always in the mind listen LISTEN! AWAKE! Max awoke and mumbled, "Where was I there...where is here where am I now?" Max wriggled out from under his bed while trying to remember yesterday, or if there actually was a yesterday, and if there actually was, would it come again tomorrow?

The especially tall pine legs of Maxfield's bed, made by one of his sister's husbands to accommodate his "portly proportions," heightening the bed to allow him to remain a robust figure without going on one of V's torturous vegetarian diets. Max believed himself to be completely invisible while under his magical bed; and, maybe he was.

Maxfield's hallucinations are inexplicable, if indeed they are hallucinations. However one might try, there are no words, not one single word, to capture a nano-fraction of his disjointed reality, or an essence of his drug-induced visions, if they are drug-induced —the inexplicable Maxfield Talbot.

* * *

Another time, in the parlor of Shady Sanctum, Victoria, Maxfield's niece, was having "another one" of her anxiety attacks.

Whenever others disagreed with her, however slight, it added more anxiety which caused her to be anxious about anxiety itself. V's mantra to escape and forget about those who did not think as she, was to smoke a doobie; it helped to see her fault-finders, lamentable and pitiful as they were, in a better light. She abhorred disagreement, and she was enraged when her opinions were challenged.

The visions and ideas V conjured for the sake of others, in an effort to save them, never came to fruition, since she was never quite sure what exactly needed saving. Nothing ever came to mind in that regard. V told herself that she had every reason to be anxious. She was diagnosed bipolar, which she found quite depressing. V was prescribed enough drugs to put a person of lesser tolerance into a persistent vegetative state. But visions fade and melt. They disappear and stream towards their source. Time becomes entangled. Memories become taunting devils, impossible bullies who come from nothingness and disappear into nothingness; leaving a sadness and a desire to try to become acquainted with the subconscious, or at least to learn to listen to its advice. *"After all, it is the home of my conscience, is it not?"* V said to herself. *"Love this new prescription. Is it me, or is it Lamotrigine?"*

V desired to be an ageless woman, a natural woman of grace and mystery. V was also a woman hellbent on leaving an indelible mark in history. Her anxieties had anxieties of their own. Each passing day became more insufferable. *"More psychotropics, Doctor Goody."* For V, anxiety has always been well-traveled, carefully surveyed, and familiar territory.

"Who is that sitting at the kitchen table, Lily?"

"He looks a lot like a satyr."

"Nonsense. You are suffering some kind of LSD flashback."

"I never took LSD, V. That was you."

"Are you sure?"

"I am certain. There is a satyr sitting at the kitchen table writing something in a spiral notebook. He looks pretty real to me."

"I never doubted he was real, Lily. I have known several satyrs in my day."

"You're full of it! Take your damn pills," her wife advised.

"They give me dry-mouth," V sighed.

"But they make you more…"

"What?"

Lily was reluctant to get it out, but she managed, "…normal."

"What in hell is 'normal,' *Lillian?*

"Sorry, just saying."

"Please, try not to say 'just saying' to me. I am not one of your Facebook friends. How about you go see what he is writing. When a satyr takes notes it is a sign of something historical about to happen, and we are somehow involved."

"How do you know that?"

"I read it once."

"V, he just disappeared."

"That's a satyr for you. They come and then *poof,* they're gone."

V, bright red hair, pale white skin, attractive, freckles, though not enough to be a distraction, never wears make-up, well-groomed, eccentric, writes with a fountain pen, only in green ink, claims to be "close to forty," with the understanding that fifty is also close to forty in the grand scheme of things. She is known for her fashionable hat collection to cover those bad hair days, to avoid the ravages of sunlight, but mainly because she finds hats simply fabulous. If you want to be a woman of mystery wear a hat, the bigger the better. If you are a black woman on Sunday morning wear a hat ornate with muted colors, pink, purple and lilac petals shimmering in the slightest breeze or the turn of a head. If you are the Queen of England wear the same thing. Cowgirls wear a hat. If you need to hide a hole in your head you wear a hat. For the love of haberdashers everywhere, wear a hat!

V claims not to give a "rat's ass" about what others think of her, but that is most certainly, in every respect, not true, fake news. If anything, she gives too much of the rat's ass for what others think.

V owns a prodigious red stone Victorian mansion—a beautiful example of late nineteenth century architecture—that her father left to her after his "mysterious death."

Her passion for going against the untangling evolution of time and fashion became part, but not parcel, of her persona. She had a good act, and she liked herself for it. Most of her *haute couture* came from yard sales and thrift stores. She knew how to create the eye-popping illusion of opulence on a dime.

V saw herself as a "theatre person" and all her friends would agree. Most thought of V as a drama queen, but the fear of her unexpected screeds of literary maleficence, should anyone speak out of turn, or out of place, elevated the consciousness of her friends to an undesired level of agreeability. Bipolar people leave little to the expectations of others.

V held a high opinion of herself as an artist. She knew she had a natural flair for directing. She daydreamed of having her own little theatre where she could show off her talents. Without quarrel, few would dispute what had become fact, that her talents and directing skills went far beyond the four walls of Theatre. V challenges herself to create and perform her own life with *joie de vivre*, a brava performance indeed, until she gets bored. When she is bored, V sharpens her directing skills on the lives of others to the dissatisfaction of friends and foes alike. Although, distinguishing friend from foe needed a great deal of effort, and appreciable skill. Once, V had a mercurial epiphany, *"Perhaps I am a bit overbearing."* Then she forgot about it.

Once, Sir Geoffrey Hemphill pleaded, "Will you marry me, Miss Aires?" She replied with, "Oh, Sir Geoffrey, I might if I were not already married, but I would think about a life with nothing to do after dark and change my mind." V performed a spirited rendition of shy with a touch of coy and a whole lot of no. Poor Sir Geoffrey; he really was a lot of fun, looking spiffy in his white linen suit, pale blue shirt, dark blue with yellow diagonally-striped tie, and vibrant yellow socks that poured into his brown and beige saddle shoes—dressed to the nines and all for V. The slightest thought of "coming out," making himself visible, frightened Poor Sir Geoffrey beyond description. *"A life in the closet may not be living, but it's safe,"* he thought. After his proposal to V, she smartly rose and said as the actress she never was, "You are so cute," then left the room at warp speed.

Feelings of shame, anger, sadness and self-hatred with suicidal tendencies are often exacerbated in the wake of unrequited love. *"It's not about love, kiddo, and you know it."* Poor Sir Geoffrey wouldn't listen to his higher self. So, he felt himself doleful, witless, a man of little consequence, as he sat dreaming he was still awake in the parlor with Maxfield, who had recently returned from safari in Africa, and so he borrowed Sir Geoffrey's ear well into the night to relive it.

Cruelty would certainly be one of the many last things to enter V's mind, but when people pose a question they ought to know why they asked and what it is they want to do with the answer. Do they want some truth, or do they want to postpone the inevitable by going on a long and arduous expedition through the maze of V's rhetoric? *Poor Sir Geoffrey.*

V's father, The Late Reverend Aires, once a man of the cloth, probably synthetic and made in China, became a radical disciple of an unknown Roman Catholic denomination that he had founded himself, and whose teachings had absolutely nothing to do with Jesus, nor the amelioration of Humanity: "Rose colored glasses are for the flock to view the Good Shepherd, not for the Good Shepherd to view the flock," the Good Shepherd often told his Little Princess Victoria before sending her off to pass the collection plate. With the restrained smile of a sad, starving, disconsolate, but hopeful, orphan, V created a short piece of theatre impeccably played. Those who looked into her watery crestfallen eyes, who sat and waited for the end of their world, dropped more cash into the collection plate than they could otherwise afford. The Little Princess had an affect on folks, which left many worshippers feeling guilty for their own poverty. The late Reverend had also gained considerable recognition from his missionary work which took him around the world converting to whatever, saving whomever, however, for a price. Jesus can be an expensive business. While still in her teens, the Little Princess had become a world-class traveler. When the Little Princess reached her closer-to-fifty birthday—another over-priced regenerating cream reason for supplemental anxiety—she made up her mind to leave for posterity a certain and indelible contribution, which now only left her to settle upon exactly what that contribution might be; yet further cause for anxiety.

V is not quite the controlling, argumentative creature that some have mistakenly mis-thought. She can be those things, of course, but it is not one of her full-time personas. V learned the long and hard way, that it is no longer beneficial for her sense of wellbeing to make confrontational choices, or to take unnecessary chances; a lesson learned with maturity. V is unquestionably smart, intuitive, often overreaching, overbearing, rarely knows what is good for her own good. Psychotropics helped her regain some of her bearing. V has an inexplicable desire for lasting fame which she disguises as, "leaving something for posterity." Sometimes intelligence is a terrible burden especially for women—men often find it troublesome.

V is easily bored and she does not suffer fools willingly; evidenced by those who have exited her life only to find themselves transformed into the walking wounded, limping back to their zombiehood. Before the medications, V was perceived as a bitch. That's not to say she was or she wasn't; it's all a matter of degree and interpretation. Now, through the magic of chemistry, V could be more deliberate, thoughtful and carefully rehearsed before launching into anything that could be deemed provocative. V does gain a great deal of satisfaction from her supposition that the multiple levels of her rhetoric avoids instant provocation; she has the knack to send her victims merrily on their way without their realizing her villainy, until it is too unreasonably late for a counterattack.

V rarely goes out into the world at large unless it is necessary, or there is the promise of fun, or she simply must get out for no apparent reason. Her switch to isolationism came after she recognized that, "On balance, the heavy side of the scales snores with sleeping people who have chosen their ignorance, their lies, their deceptive euphemisms born of prejudice, hypocrisy, and rampaging hatred. People, generally speaking, cannot be easily trusted, or trusted at all. No way, no how, no one except Lily, of course. There was always Lily, trustworthy and predictable." Maybe V's darker moods were simply passing clouds of negatively-charged particles of self-consuming acridity. Or, a psychotropic glitch.

Oftentimes, V sincerely thinks herself far too complicated for most mortals to grasp for more than twenty seconds, or so. There are moments in her days, sometimes entire days, when she believes herself a genius. Then, time persists and she finds herself in a *Ground Hog Day* sort of way. "There must be something better! Days should not be indistinguishable nor interchangeable with the day before, or the day before that," V pouted in a world-weary, muted outrage. "Who am I kidding? I'm not a genius; never was and never will be. But then again...."

It should be pointed out that after V dropped out of community college she never stopped educating herself. V is one of Gertrude Stein's biggest fans. All of Stein's books fill the top shelf of her bedroom bookcase. Once that shelf was filled with Ayn Rand, but when Ayn Rand began to smell like Monday's fish on Thursday, V tossed her Fascist greedy ass into dumpster-hell along with a copy of *The Art of the Deal,* for which she paid a quarter in a yard sale, to make room for Gertrude Stein. She credits Stein with teaching her the ever-interesting elements of subtext. How to read, basically. V has been using what she believes to be education in sublimity ever since; to mystify with seemingly never-ending layers of indirection and subtext which she claims, "...should not be mistaken for ambiguity." V told this to the man seated next to her at one of Minnie Beach's dispiriting dinner parties. When the man barked in return, "I don't get it!" V smugly accused, "That is because you are short of imagination! You must have exchanged it for a degree in who the fuck cares!" The following day V learned that the man who had been seated next to her was a Nobel Prize winning nano-scientist working on a government project in Colorado Springs. *"So friggin' what!"* V remarked to herself when she learned of her ignorance.

V's father died from an oversized Africanized honey bee attack. Strangely odd, since the killer bee should not be able to survive as far north as Colorado. Maybe, its faulty navigation had something to do with hotter and heavier air from global warming. In whatever case, V was left to pay the astronomical taxes on the mansion known as Shady Sanctum. Maxfield Talbot, her father's step brother, helps out with his royalties from several books—*An Entomological Study Of Washington DC, How To Think Like An Ant Before The Rapture, Don't Kill Our Friends The Bedbugs,* and *For The Love Of Dung Beetles*. His foray into the field of etymology produced his first book on the subject, *Conversations With Insects*, but he soon returned to his entomological roots due to a royalty dispute; one does not pay interviewees! There is also Max's Social Security which helps to keep Shady Sanctum in the family. There is little left in the Talbot coffers after paying for all those pounds of illicit drugs, his traveling expenses before he learned to fold space—although he still has much to learn in that regard—his latest trip to Haiti on bug business, and all those epicurean escapades in Morocco.

Maxfield has made it his life's work to study arthropods which led to his earning a rather widespread reputation from his knowledge of the practical implementation of gene splicing. His lectures on the ins-and-outs of entomology were a hit on the university circuit. Any knowledge of his surreptitious experiments in insect husbandry—not quite the Doctor Mengele of the insect world—were restricted to a few handpicked peers. One of them was Doctor Fleischmann, an old Queen City University chum who now lived on an obscure island in the Coral Sea.

Doctor Fleischmann was released from prison after five years for not living up to his oath as a doctor of medicine, causing the death of a wildly popular pop singer which, in turn, made Fleischmann a wildly unpopular pariah. So, he sequestered himself on a small island east of New Caledonia and northeast of Australia known as Sphincter Island. While working for the late pop star Fleischmann bought the island with cold hard cash. That was before he murdered his cash cow; the King of Pop.

The last time Max saw Fleischmann they spent their time together reminiscing about the old days. They entertained themselves having a bit of fun for auld lang syne—manipulating DNA. Maxfield and Fleischmann went to work manipulating the DNA of a New Caledonian scorpion with the DNA of an African cockroach. The result was a super-sized cockroach with an unnerving-sized scorpion stinger like a rat's tail. The thrill of creation! The ecstasy and the rapture from ejaculating without touching yourself was overwhelming. *Work was good.* Then it happened, Murphy's Law, the thing they never anticipated; their creation quickly duplicated itself and the duplication began to duplicate exponentially like a virus. Their little monsters had quickly become problematic.

The morning after their venerable accomplishment, Max awoke to observe several cockpions crawling up the windowpane. He imagined they were looking for a chink in the window. In a blink of his eye, the cockpions paired-up and began dancing the tango, the dangerous kind, razor-sharp angles, quick turns around the surface of the glass and all the while their stingers stood ready, but for what, or whom? "It's time to boogie," Max said out loud to no one but himself.

There was a huge abandoned hospital on the island that had been the home to hundreds of terminally ill patients from around the world; a place to rest and wait. When whispers and rumors of Doctor Sphincter's experimentations with body parts, especially fresh organs removed from his patients, both dead and alive, for his clandestine work to create a super-subspecies of Man, it all came to a complete halt when the authorities discovered his true vocation; he was then murdered on the spot by subhumans with brooms and pitchforks. The sanatorium was closed permanently. The Island of Doctor Sphincter was abandoned sometime in the 1950s and remained so until Doctor Fleischmann took-up residence in the early 2000s. Serving as doctor to the biggest rock star in the world paid unnecessarily well.

"Thank you Maxfield, you've been a good friend."

"You *do* know what will happen sooner than later?"

"I do. There is nowhere else for me to go. I am a pariah, you know."

"I do," mumbled Max. "Big time."

Doctor Fleischmann and Max walked in silence to the edge of the cliff on the far side of the island. They hugged one last goodbye before Max jumped from the cliff and disappeared into somewhere in the future, leaving only sparks of light that were soon extinguished by the ocean below. Maxfield reappeared under his bed. "Boy-o- boy, I'm getting pretty good at this!" Max, as he occasionally does, gleeked.

Sphincter Island was no longer habitable by humankind, nor mammals of any kind; only the pariah was left behind, tucked away from society. The huge cockpions were discovered to be cannibals that survived solely by eating one another. After every meal, they became even more ferociously hungry. Their lust for devouring one another was insatiable.

The cockpions split like giant amoebas, infesting the island. Doctor Fleischmann knew that he could no longer endure his unique predicament. He could not live with himself for the rest of his life—which he knew would be a short one. *"For Pete's sake! I really liked his music, his dancing—"* He then chose the largest cockpion from those slowly circling him, he picked it up and held it in the palm of his hand, *"This is for you, Mikey."* Fleischmann waited until he felt the devil's sting. As he lay dying, his last spoken words were, "This is it and that's that," and then he was cockpion food.

Max is rarely invited to speak at universities, nor take all-expense paid trips to study bugs as he once did. When he briefly taught entomology at Queen City University, his students referred to him as "A giant in his field," then they giggled and Max would humbly thank them. It took Max two years after his fleeting stint at QCU to become conscious of what they meant. His short tenure in academia came to an abrupt end in a university men's room. Max and three of his students were caught smoking marijuana; pre-legalization in Colorado. He was conducting an experiment into the nature of memory loss. *"Who the devil knows why academics are so damn incredulous!?"* Maxfield seemed insane to some, to others he was simply an old hippy drug addict, but to a brave few, Professor Doctor Maxfield Talbot PhD was a master and guide into the creative powers hidden within the vast unending universe of the Self—the magical, mystical place of creation. Some thought Professor Talbot, *The* Master. However, *The* or not, Master or not, following him was a trip down a rabbit's hole—something to ponder before jumping in.

The late Missus Reverend Aires died while giving birth to V, so naturally she had fulfilled any debt to that which posterity could possibly hold claim. V's mother was remembered by V's great uncles and aunts (all gone to a better place, except for Maxfield) as a ferocious force of nature with a fun wit. The late Missus Aires was clearly demented, or as some proclaimed, "possessed." She loved acting in little theatres around Queen City until, while playing Ophelia in Hamlet—the devil knows what got into her—she broke-out into song and danced the cooch across the stage. What a memorable farewell performance! She gave birth to V nine months later and died, but not until every last drop of her spirit found its way into her newborn, Victoria. Whenever conversations turned to family history, especially involving the late Missus Aires, amazingly, no one recalled a thing. When relatives turned their memories to Maxfield, they could not remember his ever looking younger than he appeared to them now. Fifty year old memories and yet Maxfield has always appeared seventy-*ish*. They chalk it up to the tricks of memory.

Gert Aires-Birdsall, V's father's sister, along with her

husband Charlie, established a retreat near Lake Titicaca in Peru for clairvoyants, spiritualists, astral projectionists, space and time folders, and intergalactic surfers who rode gravitational waves through spacetime just for kicks.

Puerto Nostradamus, highly praised in several esoteric journals, enjoyed a fashionable reputation as the favored watering hole for celebrated Internationalists and the usual perennial variety of *nouveau riche*. The glossy brochure made Puerto Nostradamus appear an attractive destination for those who would or could develop their psychic abilities. *"Hidden potentials that lay sleeping within the initiate are carefully nurtured at Puerto Nostradamus,"* was written at the top of the brochure.

Their brochure was filled with sepia-toned photographs of well known psychics, including Shirley MacLaine and Nancy Reagan. There were quotes endorsing Gert and Charlie's hospitality. Madonna said, "A miraculous experience," and the Jersey Governor Crispy Crapp bragged about having lost one-hundred pounds, *"I lost 100 pounds."* However, what is meant to be will be, the Governor regained every ounce and then some in less than two months. There were pictures of natives rowing across Lake Titicaca, guests riding on several domesticated llamas and a visiting dignitary helping Charlie hold down an alpaca while Gert was busy sheering it. Another photo was of Gert all alone in the garden tending to her coffee plants, while a rather dark and dirty-looking family rested beneath a cacao tree in the background, to the left of Gert's bonnet. All this was beguiling, yet V had serious doubts about that sort of thing which, consequently, kept her from visiting Aunt Gertrude. Although, V did recommend Puerto Nostradamus to a good many of her ex-friends. It sounded devilish even without having any idea where it was, what it was, or anything about it. The very name of Puerto Nostradamus conjured something other than a place for spiritual enlightenment.

Then, there is Cousin Harriet, Maxfield's younger sister, who found the word "Aunt" much too matronly for her taste and, therefore, insisted she be called "Cousin" Harriet. Cousin Harriet disappeared before the courts waived her privilege to enjoy the company of three husbands while two of them were still alive. As a result, the four of them took flight from Queen City International Airport for Gotham City from where they booked passage on a Norwegian freighter and haven't been heard from since. Cousin Harriet, in her own small and special way, achieved a certain amount of local, however infamous, notoriety.

"Why shouldn't I enjoy a bit of recognition?" V asked Lily.

"What have you done for it?" Lily answered by asking.

"You're being provocative, dear heart." V had already arrived at an acerbic edge by the time she got to "dear heart." She hated questions that led to self-incrimination. "Sometimes you beg the question, Lily. No one gives a rat's ass about me. I have nothing. I am nobody. Just a buttload of unfulfilled dreams." Even V, herself, had trouble believing what she just said.

"*Boo-hoo.* Give me a break! You're being silly and you don't believe a single word of it. By this time tomorrow, today's anxiety will have morphed into your usual arrogance of genius, and then you'll hate yourself, think you're stupid and then *voila!* you're a genius again. That's the bipolar cycle. I'm used to it."

"I would not have used the words 'arrogance' and 'usual' in the same sentence," V pouted.

"People love you, V. You host the Ladies' Grecian Culture Study Group once a month, Friends of Erotic Artifacts bimonthly, and you're a Capitol Hill fixture, a celebrity. You are the woman around whom the world revolves."

"Really? Do you really think so?"

"There might be a few who wouldn't agree with the revolving world stuff, but you're still The King to me."

"There's always a few out to get me. It is always best to know who they are. Who are they, Lily?"

"How would I know, V?

"Exactly. Maybe I should forget about it."

"Forget about what, V?"

"*Posterity.* Maybe I should forget about posterity and say

fuck it!"

"That's the spirit. Fuck it!" Lily had finally found something with which to agree, as she offered up her empty teacup for refilling. By coincidental happenstance the cup and the subject were dropped.

Pudgy Penny and Piggy Peter came barging through the bird's eye maple double doors that entered into the parlor. These custom-made doors were adorned with naked smiling cherubs bearing shields and swords, anchors intertwined with hexagons and rhombi, roses and ribbons of leaves, and most ornate is the three-foot tall dancing Dionysos that splits in two whenever the doors are slid open. Shady Sanctum was, after all, the residency of the late Reverend Kirby Victor Aires. The late reverend knew the worth, just short of pompous, of a pious atmosphere.

The twins Penny and Peter were a last minute gift to Maxfield from Cousin Harriet the night she decided to fly the coop, as it were, with her three husbands—Jacques, Sean and Bonito. The twins were twelve years old when Cousin Harriet gave them to Max nearly ten years ago, and they haven't aged a day since. No one was really sure where Harriet had picked them up; one day she just showed up with them and said she had found them. "I found them. Here. They're yours." And, though the twins were not identical, they were similar. Pudgy was noticeably fatter than her brother Piggy whose pumpkin-red Buster Brown was cut not quite so butchly as Pudgy's.

The twins returned early that morning from Haiti together with their Uncle Max who folded spacetime in order to spend five weeks—only a day in Queen City time—with a mulatto family to study dark migratory short-horned locusts. The twins entered the parlor wearing an assortment of beads, trinkets and, *"Oh my god are those human teeth?"*

"Auntie Vickie!"

"What now, Peter?"

"Is there any way of getting in the basement, if say Penny and me was locked out 'cause somebody went and bolted the door from inside or something like that so there's no way to get down there if say somebody wanted to so what would you say to that?"

"*Yeah*, what do you say to that, Auntie?" Pudgy Penny asked with unremarkable indifference.

"I would say don't call me Auntie," V twisted an indecipherable smile and added, "Coal slide, I imagine."

"So did we," grinned Pudgy Penny, looking like a jack-o-lantern stuck atop four and one half feet of coagulated gelatin. "What else," continued the irritatingly impatient Pudgy Penny, "would you say?"

"I would say that's it, kiddos," answered V.

"We're not kiddos!" Piggy Peter shouted.

"Of course not," V snickered, "but it was the kindest thing I could think of to say."

All the while, Lily sat and watched quietly. She would not look directly—as a blackbird flies—at the children. Lily made it a point to keep her glances as short as possible for fear of frightening the twins with her brutal thoughts; of which she was certain the twins could read.

"Can we have it?" Pudgy Penny asked while fingering her beads and human teeth. "It's dark. It's damp. It's dirty, it's moldy and it's smelly."

"It's just perfect," chimed Piggy Peter. "Will you give it to us?"

"Oh, my," sighed Lily, *sotto voce*, from behind her hand covering her mouth and nose.

"Hello, Auntie Lily."

"Hello, children..." then begrudgingly added, using four or five syllables to squeeze it out, "...welcome home."

"We're not children!" Piggy Peter corrected.

"Well, you're home anyway. How wonderful." If there were ever sarcasm in Lily's tone, this was it; and that was as far as Lily's interest could take her. She thought better of asking them how their trip had been—she didn't want them in her head. Lily did not much care for anything about anything having a single thing to do with the children. To her, the twins were a mutant virus; one of life's calamities—like floods, famine, pestilence and death.

"Well, are you going to give it to us or what!?"

"What...."

"The basement! Weren't you listening?" Pudgy Penny took an annoying air that smacked of condescension diluted with a lethal amount of exasperation.

"Nobody uses it anyway," added Piggy Peter, no less gelatinous than his sister, peering through two narrow slits beneath the red bangs of his slithery hair. "Since Uncle Kirby went over and out and all those goof balls who used to meet down there took a hike, it ain't used for nothing no more." Piggy Peter never met Kirby nor his goof balls, since he was dead long before the twins arrived. They didn't know the man, just bits and pieces cobbled together from overheard and, most likely, misheard conversations. But they learned to fake a sense of solemnity by not disturbing the seldom talked about memories of V's father, whose interest in matters theologically paranormal took him and his small circle of illuminati to the basement where he kept a most impressive library of old and rare books that have long since disappeared. There was a worktable where he wrote his psalm books; publishing and selling them himself. Much of Kirby's personal income had come from the sale of sacred relics. The genesis of those sacred relics remain a mystery, as does the nature of their sanctity.

Before Kirby Victor Aires met and married V's mother, and before he became the renegade high priest of his own theologically incorrect, surreptitious cult—The Brotherhood of Solar Agnation —Brother Kirby had decoded ancient and forbidden books in one of the sub-basements beneath the Vatican Palace. Brother Kirby was the pet of the Cardinals, and he was considered Cardinal material by the Pope, until Brother Kirby had an epiphany.

Things don't always work out the way we imagine they should, as proven by Brother Kirby who instigated a heated argument with His Holiness over the existence of God vis-a-vie the ability of the individual to become their own God. *"I am God!"* he yelled at the Pope.

"You are an idiot!" Arshmann shouted back, but not in his usual shriveling old man voice. It was certainly not the Pope's voice that boomed with ungodly hatred from deep within the pit of Hell. Maybe, there are many pits in Hell. Like Dante's, perhaps. Surely, it wasn't the voice of God, unless, this God was unique to Arshmann himself; which only goes to reinforce Kirby's point.

The encounter ended with the Pope on the floor holding a burning candle in his clenched fist while Brother Kirby held a brass candlestick over the skull of His Holiness.

"I curse and excommunicate you!" proclaimed Pope Arshmann.

"Big fucking deal," said the former Roman Catholic Brother.

The following day Kirby was escorted off the sacred Vatican grounds by an attachment of Swiss Guards. Never again would Kirby acknowledge the infallibility of the Pope, that self-important German Nazi, the bitter ideologue who had memorized the party lines. Moreover, he was stupid. *Stupid, stupid, stupid!* Brother Kirby was out the gate and on the street. Soon afterward, Brother Kirby started his own anti-Catholic Brotherhood of Solar Agnation with the book he walked off with from the Vatican's immense storehouse of misappropriated loot, and the largest known collection of the world's treasures. The late Reverend hid the book in the back of his trousers. As the Swiss Guards escorted him off Vatican property, one of the guards observed, "That man has the squarest ass I've ever seen."

"Well? Will you give us the basement, or must we seize it by force?" Pudgy Penny challenged.

"If the two of you want it take it. You're driving me crazy!"

"You're already crazy, Auntie Vickie," chimed the twins in unison.

"Come, Drusilla," said Piggy to Pudgy.

"I will, O Zeus, my brother," swooned a pensive Pudgy to Piggy.

Then they were gone, down the hall and well out of earshot by the time V finished refilling Lily's replacement teacup; a black mug imprinted with I'VE BEEN TO THE ZOO in gold lettering.

"You gave away the basement?" Lily sounded perplexed, puzzled and careworn.

"Only for a week or two. Then they will trade it in for something else. The attic maybe. By the way, Zeus I know, but I seem to have forgotten who Drusilla was?"

"Caligula's sister."

"Oh yes, of course," said a weary V, rolling her eyes while pouring herself another cup of Earl Grey from her Dresden china teapot cracked here and cracked there and covered with the tea cozy Lily crocheted the time she came down with a foot infection; a reaction to a bite or sting from a source unknown. To that day Lily still suspects it was from one of the spiders that were given sanctuary in the house ever since V had declared that any attempt at killing them was *verboten*. Or, it may have been one of the black centipedes that are occasionally seen scurrying across the parlor floor, racing between the legs of V and Lily as the *"little fuckers"* headed to their den hidden somewhere within the walls.

"They could be poisonous! I better Google," Lily told herself.

"Which reminds me," continued V, "next Saturday is our FEA field trip, is it not?"

"It is," Lily confirmed, remembering something. "That is, unless Carla Bean forgets to take her meds and pulls another one of her stunts."

"I don't think so, Lily. Her last one was less than two weeks ago and, knowing her, she wouldn't chance another scene quite so soon; especially after taking in that new boarder. She's a stickler for making a good first impression, particularly for new conquests, after that she doesn't give a rat's ass. La Bean certainly made a mess of things; insulting Poor Minnie's buffet before dropping her emerald ring into the punch bowl, polluting the poor thing's Georgian Ambrosia punch with the heavy scent and bile taste of Gardenia Bold. Made by some French faggot, according to Carla. Anyway, as she fished about in the peach-colored brine, its tide rose midway to her elbows before she nearly drowned herself in shock from seeing the disturbingly distorted faces of everyone there. As you know, all that cleaning-up after her vile tantrum left me exhausted. And poor raving Billy Butts! Will he never learn to shut the fuck up long enough to take a breath? I guess it was her attempt to strangle him with her peach-tinted hands that brought the evening's festivities to an abrupt conclusion." V paused to sip tea while waiting for the right words. She didn't need to wait too very long before, "Nope, not so soon as Saturday, Lily. She keeps her new boarder in the Paisley Room; the room that nice fellow papered for her. You know, the one you always liked with the mysterious eyebrows you thought Arabesque. I detected his eyebrows were carefully plucked and that he didn't align the paisleys quite right. Carla has always been quite practical in utilizing her inamoratos. I wonder whatever happened to him? Billy Butts certainly couldn't restrain his lust, but I think Mister Arabesque was all one way about that sort of thing. With him—the inamorato—when the time came to choose, the choice came down to Carla with all her prurient interests and a seemingly endless amount of money, or Billy with matching interests, but far less money, Carla won, if not hands-down, certainly by a nose. Anyway, this newest boarder had been a tourist guide in Athens. Apparently, he has all the attributes which make for success: tall, tan, piercing black eyes, wide infectious smile, perfectly even white teeth, and not an original thought in his lovely head. He doesn't speak a lick of English, but Carla said he is willing to help her learn Greek in exchange for room and board, and, or whatever else. Although, the idea of teaching one without a lick of English by one without a lick of Greek does sound intriguing." Sometimes, V's breezy, affected manner can get so protracted one would need a surveyor's level to measure its boundaries. This was one of those times. Despite being someone whose life was riddled with missed opportunities, *"I keep feeling I am here for something. Something good. Something better. Something. But what?"*

V was an avid collector of *objets d'art* and, unless eclecticism is a specialty uniquely to itself, V had no especial field of interest other than her splendid collection of erotic artifacts that she had gathered at one time or another, one place or another. "Something from just about every period in art history—nay, Human history," V assured doubters in what must have been a case of inflated exaggeration, a little white lie with shades of gray. *"I do not lie—I hyperbolate!"* Easy to mistake the difference.

"The Queen City Art Museum refused my donation. For free! For fucking free! No interest in the history of sex toys dating back to the Roman Empire, maybe one or two of them were up an Emperor's ass. Imagine that? Back before that cult of one-godders brought down the Roman Empire. Shows what they knew."

"Who knew? The Romans or the one-godders?" Lily asked with no real interest.

"I don't remember."

"Get out the bong and take a few good tokes, V. You'll feel better in no time."

"Suppose I do not want to feel better?"

"*Hmm.* I think there's some kind of existential thing going on here, V."

As regards the subject of Art, V's only requisite was that she be "moved" by it and would continue being moved long after she brought her precious piece of Art home; provided the price was right. What more should one ask of Art?

V holds strong opinions, not only about Art, but pretty much about everything. She is careful about what she puts into her brain. For example: V reads only books considered intellectual, some of which she had no idea what she was reading, but she knew that one day the wisdom contained in those books would surface with clarity, engendering a positive shift in her point of view. She could not say how she knew she knew, though she knew with unwavering certitude that she simply knew, period. Ergo, damn the empirical. Full speed ahead!

"A matter of maturation and saturation, Lily."

"Really?"

"I don't know. I don't even know what 'existential' means, other than it is *au courant,* over-used and certainly mis-used. Who wants reality anymore anyway? Do you really want what's outside that window—needs cleaning by the way. Do you really want what is out there, Lily?" V asked with all sincerity. By the by, the next day V might extoll, with all the same sincerity, an opposing point of view.

"It sucks, V, but you can't remain inside forever."

Easygoing Lily prefers listening while leaving V to do pretty much all the talking. Lily did not want to interrupt and spoil the elation V enjoys from hearing the sound of her own whisky voice.

Lily shares many of V's qualities, although Lily is more relaxed, more confident, and not bipolar. Lily does suffer a fear of death, but only for short durations and they are always from the same source; just before her entrance—stage right, left, or upstage—when she's certain that she has forgotten every one of her lines, when she wants to run, when her heart gets stuck in her throat; yet, she goes on without missing a beat, without dropping a word; reborn onstage, and with an audience.

The long list of characters that Lily had performed, were all prequel to her arrival in Queen City. Since then, little of note.

THREE
jesus and the devil walk into a bar

What in blue blazes are you doing Maxfield the future is out of sync you were warned about folding spacetime with dough gum I know you know I just thought if I tried new things untested things to save the planet it's too late you don't listen you don't use your best judgement too many bad choices how do you plan to correct this mess I don't stop messing with universal spacetime I'm sorry but no but you've been messing around for centuries what will help what to do you tell me nope it's up to you don't freeze going numb afraid don't go back to Sphincter Island I don't want are you crazy the cockpions nope I won't go back there but you do you go there in your dreams and every time you do you're messing with the universe kahbluey off-kilter off-balance put an end to it or create your own my own alternate universe can I do that WAKE UP.

* * *

One of the Colfax Avenue hookers, the one they call Paradise, the two-hundred pound black woman wearing a stringy blue and red wig, two gold front teeth, the funny one, the jokester, the good-natured, the notorious one who wears the same tight black faux-leather halter that squeezed her tits so tightly together they became a yin-yang symbol, not an easy feat for sure, causing them to appear ludicrously erotic, a bit disturbing, held in with just enough black faux-leather not to be arrested for doing what Paradise knew instinctively to do; to have and to give sweet diversions and one helluva good time! She levitated over the bystanders, wearing her usual black faux-leather cummerbund, to match her halter, that barely covered her hoo-hah. Spandex carefully sewn on the back of the cummerbund to accommodate the girth of Paradise, provided ample stretching room. Her hot pink rubber flip-flops with multi-colored sequins, meticulously applied by Paradise herself one sequin at a time, covered every exposed nano-inch of her flip-flops, reflecting the sun spotlighting where

Paradise stood on the air above anyone's reach.

"I am beautiful!" Paradise declared as she removed her wig and tossed it to a lucky member of her audience. Her audience, a collection of Colfax regulars, fell to its knees. Except for a few who tried to take selfies with her in the background, but they were out of luck in the light of the blinding sun. "I am beautiful! I am the Black Madonna!" Paradise rose higher.

Her audience shouted, "You are beautiful! You are the Black Madonna!"

Paradise kicked her flip-flops off into waiting hands.

"You are beautiful," the crowd chanted.

Paradise removed her cummerbund and let it drop into eager arms. Two-hundred pounds of naked Paradise undulated with amazing grace upon the air. She raised her arms and slowly danced her dance of Salome on the corner of Uinta Street and Colfax Avenue. Cars parked in the middle of the street. Folks stood on car roofs to get a closer look, while other folks lined blocks to watch Paradise levitate higher and higher above the street, out of reach, over the traffic lights. Her hands and arms swayed to unheard music. The faster Paradise moved her arms to the Music of the Spheres—perhaps—the higher she rose over Colfax Avenue and the louder the crowd cheered. They succumbed to the pleasure of the Black Madonna's enchantment as she spread her come-hither arms, smiled with two gold front teeth sparkling, turned and danced the light fantastic into the sun; challenging science and mystifying religious leaders and their flocks: The Black Madonna of Colfax Avenue.

As one student astronomer from Queen City University explained it, "The phenomenon is caused by the gravitational effect of something huge. Maybe gravitational waves, or perhaps global warming has reached its point of hopelessness; or maybe something from outer space is coming! *It's coming for you! Ha, ha, ha! Damn it, Janet!* Just joking." No one thought him humorous, nor particularly informative.

The entire touring company of *Cats*, currently running in

Queen City for the umpteenth time, fell victim to spontaneous laryngitis; consequently, the actors gave an exemplary performance in mime. The electricity of the audience sparkled. The audience was seduced by it. Something new. Something happened. Something they'd never seen before. Even those who didn't love it, or thought the dwarf from England ruined American Theatre, were amazed. Tremendous applause broke the evening's silence. In unison, the entire audience rose to their feet and gave bravos to *"...a stunning new re-interpretation of a tired old thingy...theatre is born again!"*

As irregular incidents continued to mount in Queen City there was possibly, though highly improbable, enough evidence to suggest that Queen City was overrun by malevolent spirits. Some suggested that Queen City was the epicenter for all the wicked spirits in the world, and that they were escaping into the world from out the cracks ripping Queen City streets and causing new overpriced pressed board houses to snap, crackle and pop.

Panic, exaggerated, overacted, badly acted and mostly self-focused, filled the streets of Queen City. Throngs of screaming humanity climbed one over the other to beg forgiveness from the invisible. They sat in bars where all drinks were on the house, although one would need to step over passed-out drunks just to get into the house. Soothsayers predicted the end of the world. Even those who never spoke sooth saw it coming. The sidewalks were inflamed with anger and incredulity from those who were trying to find a way out of the wreckage. Some huddled and cried with friends and relatives, even those friends and relatives they hated. Some stood frozen staring at cracks that continued to grow. Some felt the Earth moving under their feet. Some removed their shoes to experience the sensation. Streets and sidewalks rolled with the rumble of an earthquake, buildings swayed and fell, cracks continued to splinter and tear apart Queen City, Colorado.

* * *

Alarmed, Lily cried out, *"What's happening!?"* while leaning over the porch balustrade that was covered with two layers of chipped paint, green on the surface and white lead paint beneath. "Gawd! Look at that! The entire street, V." V was speechless as she, too, leaned over the porch balustrade next to Lily; so Lily questioned herself, "An explosion? An earthquake? What?"

"Frackers!" V overcame her speechlessness. "Goddamned motherfucking frackers!"

"Really?"

"You can go to the bank with it."

In silence, both V and Lily gave the scene below their full attention. Squirrels gathered catalpa bean pods, small green peaches and marble-sized crabapples. They take bites, tiny bites, tentative bites, and then they spit them out and throw their spoils to the trembling streets and sidewalks. They fly through trees that line the streets like handsome, well-groomed, green soldiers. They leap without hesitation from treetop to treetop. They fly through their urban forest, flying from one side of the street to the other. They know they can and that's all it takes—the knowing. They do, and once they do, they never stop flying—the squirrels. Folks pour from out their homes. Some stare in disbelief. Some hesitantly patrol the streets, surveying the damages from slashes in cement and blacktop. In the middle of the street, directly in front of Shady Sanctum, a sinkhole appears that seemingly could lead to China. Neighbors run back inside their homes to watch the news, hoping for information about this extraordinary phenomenon. Unless it is on the news, it didn't happen.

"Was it a bomb? Did it come from Russia? Is it radioactive? Mister Death takes his time, slowly and horribly, when it's a nuke."

"Frackers!" V repeated, "Goddamned motherfucking frackers!"

V and Lily sighed in unison from their watch over the balustrade.

* * *

That didn't happen there is no sinkhole but there will be yes in their future it will be their future for the first time Maxfield you were warned that wasn't on purpose what was that it just happened that's all nothing just happens it does sometimes it does but the sink hole that's later like Sphincter Island is later I don't want to go back you will I may have nodded off from the dough gum you think I suppose pull yourself together Max stop with the dough gum or you could cause serious damage for the future of the planet you've got to be joking no I'm not it's just a quick nap that's all WAKE UP!

* * *

Eons from Earth, Sumer (a.k.a. planet X), the largest planet in the solar system, was approaching the closest it ever comes to Earth in its orbit around the fringe of the solar system, taking sixty-six thousand, six hundred and sixty-six Earth-years to complete a single day. All those sixes. Co-incidental numerology; or purposely planned by the Universe to scare off mathematicians and cave dwellers?

Sunlight does not reach Sumer directly. Reflective quixelite crystals float near the edge of Sumer's atmosphere, collecting the faintest of light from distant stars, magnifying them by trillions, which then provides the illusion of direct sunlight needed to grow the lush patches of food and foliage that color and perfume the scenic landscape of Sumer. It is the illusion of sunlight that matters. No one questions its reality. Without quixelite, Sumer would be an ice covered rock whirling in space.

The quadrillions of quixelite crystals that float at the edge of Sumer's atmosphere are each an individual conscious entity. They can also will themselves together as a single consciousness. As One, they can open and close ranks to allow for outgoing and incoming ships; or form an impenetrable shield against meteors or any other known threats to Sumer. The crystals provide every bit of energy needed to serve the needs of the entire planet without depleting a single non-renewable resource. Also, the nanoscale crystals that fill Sumer's atmosphere nourish the soul, deepening and widening an understanding of the essence of Nature, of Self, of Consciousness, of Overlords, of the Oversoul of all there is, was, and will ever be. The crystals also granted wishes.

"If you were born in a holodeck, lived your entire life and died in that holodeck, holograms would be your reality," a cunning red monkey said. He goes by the name of Kafka the Red, who sings arias from classic Italian and French operas acapella, and the seldom performed lost opera written by Gertrude Stein that Kafka the Red found stuffed inside a dried baguette. Kafka the Red performs on a diminutive stage bordered with gold and quixelite filigree. A single red curtain draped with especial care given to each velvet fold of levitating plush scarlet plunging to one side of the stage and held back by a thick gold cord with tassels in a vape bar in Sumer City, known as KAFKA'S LAST STAND—owned and operated by the red monkey himself.

Three young satyrs could not control their outbursts of ear-piercing laughter, until Lucifer had had enough of it and asked them civilly (for Lucifer) to quiet down. Satyrs do not respond well to being told what to do, civilly or otherwise; especially by Lucifer, an employee of the Underlord.

"Tell it to Dionysus, bonehead!"

"Well," Lucifer whispered to Jesus, "I see that being nice to disruptive satyrs will get us nowhere. It's a dead end."

The devil-twins were strolling—spying really—when they heard Lucifer called a "bonehead" by a satyr who hadn't even earned his horns yet. The twins began giggling until they turned into sparks of hot quixelite and vanished. They are only allowed fifteen minutes a rotation. Remember all those sixes? That is a single rotation. One would be dazed by the amount of wreckage the twins can do in only fifteen Earth minutes. But, since the father of the children is Mad Monsanto the King of the Underworld, the twins were privileged to do whatever the hell pleased them, as long as they limited themselves to fifteen minutes per rotation.

"There go the twins again. I swear by all the black matter in the universe I'd put them on a spit over the fires of Hell, but they'd probably love it! There they go. Back to Hell," Lucifer said, then burst into laughter.

"Earth?" Jesus winced.

"Yes, planet Earth. That's Hell enough, isn't it? You would know something about that, wouldn't you? Still in pain, dearest?"

A longish uncomfortable silence befell the two as they inhaled from their vape whips. Lucifer drew hard on his whip and inhaled the quixelite vapors. "My beautiful friend," began Lucifer after exhaling, "we all know who took the blame for every sin in the world. *Me*. You think that felt good, my friend? Do you think it didn't sting?"

"Of course it did, I'm sure. But you wanted the role, didn't you? It was your choice, wasn't it?" Jesus asked Lucifer, already knowing his answer.

"And so did you!" bellowed Lucifer. "You brought them something you call love and they killed you. At least, they didn't succeed in the larger scheme of things 'cause, lo and behold, here you are, Jesus."

"Yes, here I am."

"You knew your lines. Every one of them. Forwards and backwards. Humans are a lost cause, dearest one. You should play another role next time. How many seasons have you played your tired old Jesus character?"

"I don't remember, Lu."

"I'm sure you do, Jeez. You know we both freely chose our roles. I work for the Underlord and you work for the Overlord. We both had the same goal: to help humans to become humane. A noble cause for both of us."

"It is the order of things."

"Jesus! You chose the 'order of things!' Sorry for shouting. I sometimes think that the Lords don't exist? I already know you believe in yours, but don't you think *your* Overlord is all about what to do and what not to do; emphasis on the not?"

"Lu, that *is* the order of things."

"What a fool you can be, Jeez. Be a hairdresser next time you go down there." Jesus finds that funny and laughs. Lucifer continues, "Why do you suppose the masses throughout history personified their Gods?"

Jesus shrugged and did not respond. He knew he was about to get himself embroiled in a conversation that he has had with his friend, Lucifer, countless times over millennia. Jesus folded his arms, leaned back in the comfort of his vape bar chair and waited for Lucifer's tired old grousing and pontificating to begin. He didn't need to wait long for what usually starts with, "You know I love you, man."

"And I love you, Lu."

"So don't be offended—"

"It is impossible to offend me."

"One day I will bet you on that. Anyway, here goes: You cannot talk to the unconscious and assume they are going to understand you; much less, that they could possibly grasp any idea for what you said…any idea for all the real and constructive love, or whatever you want to call that thing you offered them. They hear what they want to hear and they're deaf to everything else, everyone else. You gave them something to sooth their mortal fears; something to look forward to. You were a port in the storm, dearest. Anyone who promises life everlasting is going to be on their hit parade—a big seller. Do you want to hear what I would have done, Jeez?"

Of course, that was the last thing Jesus wanted to hear, much less, answer. He slowly inhaled before answering, "Naturally, I suppose."

"I would not have given the rabble so much credit. You said yourself that they didn't know how awful they were."

"Something like that. I believe I said that they didn't know what they were doing. I prayed for their forgiveness."

"They threw your prayers on the ground, in the dirt. The fact is, they don't know a thing and they don't care to open themselves to learning new realities. There are so many alternate realities, and yet they limit themselves by choosing ignorance and mumbo-jumbo. It makes them comfortable. They do not create, explore, take risks, nor use their imagination. They see their reality one dimensionally. A dimension they can accept and agree upon, and they call it reality. A world-weary system built upon a false premise. Threaten anything within their bubble and they will destroy you. If you really look at it, Jeez, you might as well bang your head on the wall until you knock some sense into your head."

Jesus pouted. "They didn't know better, Lu! They were victims of innocence."

"Ignorance, Jeez. *Ignorance.*"

"Call it what you will, Lu; but it isn't their fault. Innocence is their original sin. They haven't been on Earth long enough to know something better; to choose what to ignore or what not to ignore. Sometime's, Lu, you really try my patience!"

"Sometimes, my dearest friend, you try mine, too. Humans do, indeed, choose their own ignorance. *Period.* Subject closed. They choose it and they choose badly," the devil pronounced.

"You don't crush a sapling because it doesn't bear fruit; you protect it until it does. It needs time to grow."

"Sometimes, Jeez, when the tree can't grow, when it folds back onto itself and withers from unexpected realizations in the shadows of false starts, disappointments, misdirections, too much compromise, withering into resignation, back into dust—you are obliged to put it out of its misery. Play another role next time. Take a rest. Take responsibility for the actions of your followers, as well. Christ! You should have been a hairdresser."

"Lu! Are you going to continue beating this dead horse?"

"Tell me, Jeez, how do you do it? Is it your amazingly divine good looks? Or your annoying goodliness? Or, maybe your deliciously edible ideas? Which is it? One? Two out of three? All of them?"

"Give me a break, Lu."

"I love you, Jeez, and you know it! But, you should stop being a sapling and grow up! After all, we are brothers from different sides of the same coin, so to speak."

"I took the role of their Savior," Jesus stated with a mixture of defiance and regret, "because I thought I actually had something to offer."

"*Yeah.* You added more dark matter to an atmosphere already suffering from too much of it. Not only was the idea of Believers and Non-believers bad enough, it created Right and Wrong and that was the cause of many wars, still is; a flesh and blood war over the invisible—the unknowable. How sad is that?"

"I'm aware, Lu. It is sad and it pains me. Please. I'm tired. Give it a rest."

"A rest? Wake up, Jesus!"

"I used myself as an example. I gave them visions for more dimensions yet to come. I gave them something to look forward to, something real, something to ease their material suffering."

"But, they didn't get it; therefore, you gave them nothing. You are an amazingly funny, stupid, yet loving man." Lucifer slowly exhaled a thick protracted stream of vapor that rose to make curlycues in the air above the head of Jesus. The curlycues twisted one over the other. Lucifer jocularly accused, "You got in their way. Souls must change themselves—by themselves. That was the point of their creation." Lucifer's vapor stream descended over the head of Jesus, turned into a golden halo, annoying Jesus.

"Stop that! Get rid of that damned thing."

"As you say, merchant of illusions and myths! Perhaps, lies?"

The halo vanished. "Never lies. My character never lied, Lu. I spoke only truth. I genuinely wanted to be of help. To show them the Miraculous. They chose the text over the subtext. Missing the subtle, the ethereal. Something transporting, transcending. I tried to show them the power of Will. It is the greatest power given to Man and yet they let it atrophy because they don't know how to use it. I tried to teach them, Lu, but everything went *meshugge*." Jesus was visibly unnerved.

"And you see what that got you. Surely, you must agree that it is impossible to communicate truth, unless they already know it for themselves."

"Everybody knows the truth when they hear it."

"In that case, what they needed was confirmation, my dear beautiful spirit, but you wove the truth into riddles, parables, ambiguity...your own ambivalence. Even until this day on Earth they still take you literally. *Now* tell me everyone knows the truth when they hear it."

"Not my fault!"

"There you go again, Jeez. Of course it was your fault. The fruit of your tree, dear boy, has rotted to the core."

"Thank you for that; since you feel a need to state the obvious. Besides, I will not do another performance. Once should have been more than enough for me."

"But it wasn't, was it? You took many names other than Jesus."

"Never again. I leave it to their nature."

"Not a bad idea, Jeez"

"Lu? Maybe you should go this time. You'd make a terrific Jesus."

"Me? The Evil One with horns and a pitchfork? Although, I would like a makeover. Alexander the Great might be an enjoyable experience. Or Al Capone. Fun roles. Maybe a Broadway musical superstar. I want to live and have fun without restrictions and without your pitiful guilt. *Lady Gaga!* Now I could do that."

Jesus pretended to listen to Lucifer, trying to figure why he was sitting in the best vape bar in Sumer City listening to Lu's accusations from seasons ago. How much guilt must one Messiah bear? "Lucifer, I have a question for you."

"Shoot, kiddo."

"Why must all the world suffer the atrocities of others? Must they accept their misfortunes silently, stoically, alone? Why shouldn't I care? Why shouldn't I try?"

"I don't know, kiddo. Your mitzvah, I suppose. Most atrocities are committed in the Overlord's name! I will give your question more thought, if you will think about how that cushy bed of Faith and Belief is leading your followers to their own apathetic demise. Jesus the Christ! I hate do-gooders!" Lucifer reached into the air, smiled, held his hand out to Jesus and said, "Here it is: So they can deflect and delegate all responsibility away from themselves and place it into the hands of the invisible. There it is: My final answer."

"What are you talking about?" Jesus asked.

"The personification of the God."

"I don't see his point," Gertrude Stein said with a boozy smirk, "I would certainly know the point were I stuck inside a holodeck!"

"You think?" Plato asked, although it sounded more like a challenge. "One day, perhaps, you will learn the nature of reality and the reality of nature. Give it time, Gertrude."

"*Shh,*" Gertrude Stein snarled. "I want to hear the monkey sing. He promised to do my best opera."

"Which one is your best one?" Plato asked.

"My last one, of course. One's last one should always be one's best one."

Once upon a time, Sumer was the fourth planet from the sun. Then a Herculean meteor sped between it and Earth, causing them to collide. The collision generated enough energy for Sumer to carve off half of the planet Earth and incorporate it into itself. Consequently, Earth, now half its former size, was knocked closer to Mars. Sumer, along with its added mass of Earth—containing deoxyribonucleic acid, the main constituent of chromosomes and genetic information—was catapulted into an orbit well-nigh out of the solar system. Sumer revolves around the sun from the farthest edge of the solar system, beyond the ice planets. This will be the fourth rotation the Sumerians will visit Earth. They knew of the name change from New Sumer to Earth and, considering the terrible things that have been evolving on the planet, they gladly welcomed the change since they no longer want to be associated with it. Earth is monitored regularly from impossible distances, but once every rotation the planet Sumer is in position for physical

contact. The contact port is due to open shortly.
.

FOUR

too much public television

Lily Nettles is an unemployed middle-aged actor with a practical wash and dry cut. Once a natural strawberry blond, she is now in need of regular touching-up to keep the omnipresence of strawberry. Lily is, as is V, in that middle-age agelessness that dares the hazard of guessing; to guess could lead to an existential crisis. To guess too high could be interpreted as an inexcusable insult. To guess too low could sound suspiciously patronizing, untruthful and definitely unnecessary. Best to never bring the subject into the light of day.

Another life ago, when Lily Nettles, aka Lilith Champagne, played the ingenue in the French Provincial 'B' touring company of Andy Webber's *Ben Hur, the Musical*, she was beguiled by an absolutely perfect stranger who took her into the tombs beneath Orléans. He was a hottie, twenty-ish, with the face and body of a god named Philippe le Hottie. Philippe le Hottie waited impatiently outside the actors' exit, chewing on the corner of his playbill, shivering in the hot summer night with anticipation and excitement to get Mademoiselle Champagne's autograph. Philippe le Hottie spoke no English to speak of, so he mustered his courage to gain her attention by removing his shirt and showing off his abs. A streamlet of warm saltwater meandered through muscled ridges meeting, ever so briefly, where they gathered into the small pool in his navel, before pouring rivulets of sweat that wandered through the heat and humidity in the dark maze of his curly love trail. Philippe stood glistening under the alley streetlights on that hot summer evening, catching the attention of everybody in the cast and crew as they exited from their final performance of *Ben Hur, the Musical*, he blessed himself and prayed to Saint Joan of Arc for the famous Mademoiselle Lilith Champagne from America to notice him.

The Mademoiselle nearly fell over herself going down the three cast-iron steps outside the stage door and almost toppled onto the cobblestone alleyway that led to the parking lot. Fortunately, with the grace of Saint Joan, Philippe le Hottie reached out to help her regain her balance. Lily grabbed onto him. He was holding the playbill for her autograph, but dropped it when she, spontaneously and uncontrollably, gave her French god an arousing, blazing French kiss. He asked Lily if she'd like to see his hung meat and cheese. That was all her Albuquerque high school French could make of it. Surely she had misunderstood, but she was helplessly enthralled as she obediently took his hand. Spontaneously, hand-in-hand they strolled the few blocks to the *Viande et le Fromage Boutique*, Philippe's family business. Her wishful thinking vanished from the embarrassment of her fallacious translation.

Philippe and Lily pushed aside the cheeses and meats that hung in the backroom. They came to a spot where muted music came from below. Philippe opened a trapdoor in the floor covering a staircase that led down into the catacombs of Orléans.

The impatient lovers maneuvered through yet more cheeses and meats. As the music grew louder, projections of spiraling colors splashed across cold dank walls and spilled over human bones. It was a *Happening!* A hundred or more young French men and women in cowboy get-ups, under hats measured in gallons, doing a Texas line dance to the music of a fiddler with a seeing-eye dog, was a jubilant surprise at a *Happening* in a tomb under Orléans with a god named Philippe le Hottie. *"Holy merde! Am I dreaming?"* It was a wet dream come true; actually, Lily had never dreamt that particular wet dream, but she will—oftentimes.

The following morning, after Lily found herself between Philippe and a wheel of stinky cheese, they walked arm-in-arm along the way to the waiting buses that would take Lilith Champagne, along with the cast and crew of *Ben Hur, the Musical*, to the airport. They stopped and shopped and fondled each other like playful puppies; nearly forgetting they were on their way to their final *au revoir*.

It was during that never-forgotten spree, in another life, where Lily acquired her impressive assortment of Magdalenian bone and ivory implements of unknown usage. The common consensus divided them into three possible ways in which they could have been intended: for making war, for eating, or as sex toys. Imagine the things one can find in a *magasin d'aubaines à Orléans,* which is something like a Salvation Army thrift store.

Lily is a hoarder. She is a dedicated saver of the useless. Lily the Packrat saved everything that tickled her fancy, utilitarian or not. She, also, enjoys window shopping; everything is free.

V discovered Lily in the Gunnysack Players' Performing Garage in downtown Queen City. Their production of *The Trojan Women* made Lily's performance of a man playing a woman playing a man remarkable. Sort of like *Victor/Victoria* without Julie Andrews—and requiring far less talent.

Talthybius, the herald (Lily), made all the pronouncements. An important role which sometimes required adding *woes* to those of the Chorus: *woe, woe, woe to the boy-child Astyanax,* whom Lily snatched from out the hairy arms of Andromache, his mother, when soldiers in black leather tunics entered, two on motorcycles and one on a motorized bicycle, to demand the boy-child's death. They performed hideous choreography hideously (which may have made it better), before whisking Lily off the stage sidesaddle. Then Menelaus and Helen had a little speech, but nobody paid much attention to it. Lily entered with a bundle of broken doll's parts which were supposed to be the severed remains of Astyanax. Finally, after Hecuba rolled out a *papier mâché* toilet bowl painted red, white and blue for Lily to throw the bundle of pieces of Astyanax into, to the *woe, woe, woes* of the Chorus who waved red streamers to signify the burning of Troy, the set cleverly folded and toppled over hitting nobody. That was really about all V could make of it.

The critics were split. Babs DeVos of *The Queen City Post* loved it, but she had trouble telling her readers why. She has always been appreciatively vague without actually saying anything real, or otherwise. Maybe she never learned how. She certainly knew nothing of sentence construction. Bianca Purge of *Westword* did not like it and she had no trouble telling her readers the depth to which Theatre had sunken that night. And, then there was Billy Butts who wrote for *Out and Beyond,* a monthly Queen City throwaway tabloid found mostly at the entrances to gay bars, bath houses, and just about every establishment frequented by the LGBT and sometimes Q community. Butts took an unusual position on *The Trojan Women* by *not* taking a position. Instead, he wrote about how he had been to Troy, New York, his position in society and brief, but highly personal, bits of information about those who were in attendance. Being a middle-aged gadfly in Queen City's society Blue Book, knowing everybody who was in it, and being a trust fund baby with an abundance of idle time and the means to fill it, should have made Butts a happy man, but he fell short of it and blamed it on his mother.

On the evening V attended that dubious performance, she might have said out loud, *"Even a pole vaulter couldn't throw this shit high enough to reach the gutter."* V hoped that she hadn't said that out loud, but if she had, *"Fuck it"* That was how excruciatingly awful the entire evening was.

Afterwards, a wine and cheese affair for the audience to acquaint itself with the members of the cast. Especially with one black-leathered soldier who was the playwright, director, producer and manager of the Gunnysack Players' Performing Garage, Stanley Oliver Sugarloaf, or S.O.S. to his eclectic collection of misfits. It was there, under those circumstances, when V took notice of Ms. Champagne who later turned out to be Lily Nettles formerly of Albuquerque, New Mexico. Lily was the only person in the theater who V found sincerely interesting, who wasn't self-absorbed, or preoccupied with keeping an eye on the door; they became the closest of friends and lovers. When same sex marriage became legal, they were married.

Lily swallowed the last of a candied cherry. "You might not settle the matter for posterity at all because you'll change your mind more times than it takes to commit yourself to it. Imagine your anxiety then," Lily sounded with positive conviction while remaining matter-of-factly.

V stiffened, her mouth fell open, her greenish eyes widened, then closed into two narrow slits that appeared quite sinister. Her ears flew back like a startled jackrabbit. V was poised to capture the spirit behind what she heard while listening to its echo. It's not complicated: V disdained small talk. V stared blankly into the vast space a few inches above Lily's head before she could any longer remain silent and uttered in what many have called, that whiskey voice of hers, "You think I cannot commit myself to my choices, do you?"

"I do," replied Lily. "Sometimes. I sometimes wonder if those Libra scales might be the root of your anxiety?"

"I need," began V, making certain to establish direct and wide-eyed contact with Lily, who now was mustering every ounce of her attention, and carefully aiming it towards where she felt it might do the most good. "I need," V began again, "to know that when I am dead, gone and done with..." she paused to take some slack from the tautness of the moment's tension, sighed, wrinkled her upper lip and continued, "...that it wasn't all for nothing!"

"It?" a cautious Lily inquired.

"My life. My goddamn life! I need to know, Lily," V sighed before adding with fierce intensity, "I need to know something better!" It was a chilling wind that filled the sails of her rhetoric.

"Well," said Lily, resigned, "I don't think your life has been all for nothing."

"That's what an Aquarian would think: *what will be will be.* Think of something better. I cannot go on and go out as though I were never here; as though I had never been."

"Why not? People do it every day. They come and they go and who remembers them? Or cares? Nobody cares and everybody forgets sooner or later; when they are dead long enough. Hardly worth the time consumed with anxiety about the inevitable."

None of this, of course, sounded vaguely like anything V wanted to hear. Sometimes truth is like an unwanted growth behind one's ear, out of sight, invisible, but always felt. She then conjured a familiar refrain which began with, "I refuse to believe..." but was stopped short when Max appeared quite suddenly, surprising them both. "There's no getting into the basement. *'Zeus refuses, Papa Max!'* That's it. All. Nothing more. Just a voice from out the lower depths, *'Zeus refuses, Papa Max!'* How dare they, Victoria?"

"You know them better than I. Did you try the coal slide?"

"Nailed. I should have sold them last year in Morocco when I had the chance. Top dollar. A man with gold teeth and a perpetual hard-on offered me two goats and a box of condoms. Essentially agricultural, you know."

"The children?" Lily asked, incredulously.

"You needn't playact for me, Lily. One day I shall show you outrage. Without 'the method'! Just pure and simple outrage. I too have walked the boards once or twice, Miss Champagne. Yes, of course the children! Besides, they're not children. Not really. Never were. Never will be. Throwbacks! Recycled genes. Objects of discordant chaos. Is that possible? Harriet hated me because...well, whatever her reason, misguided as it was, she saw herself fit to drag home from the pit of Hell the Golem and the Golemess! They're not human, V. They're not and that's the truth! Have you noticed that they don't age? They've been here, what? It feels like they've been here forever and they haven't aged a day. They're the children of the Lord of the Underworld. And that's a fact."

"Really, Max, how you carry on. *Tea?*"

"Thank you, V, but I must decline. I'm way too upset." Maxfield stood by the doorway looking nervously about. "He isn't Zeus, you know."

"Peter?"

"Caligula. He is Caligula convinced he is Zeus."

"Peter?"

"Lost. Forgot he was playing Caligula when Caligula started playing Zeus. Too much public television, if you ask me. *Ahh,* you should have been there. Nothing like you'll ever see on PBS, I can tell you that. Drums tom-tomming. The scent of mystery in the steamy night. The sweet taste of conch stew. The sweaty dancers writhing on the soggy soil beneath the banana trees."

"Soggy soil? Writhing?" V gasped.

"Sweaty dancers? Banana trees?" Lily gasped.

"Public Television?" V and Lily gasped together.

"*Ah!* The rites of...I need a hat pin!"

"There must be a dozen or more hat pins in the attic in with Cousin Harriet's old hats," V offered.

"Yes. Of course. My little miss nasty sister was always big on hats. Maybe she got that from you, Victoria, or you got that from her. Did you know that it was the sizing used to make hats that made the hatters mad? I learned that from public television. Mercury vapors, an occupational hazard. I suspect Harriet might be the victim of a milliner. Those creatures are locked in the basement; Mad Harriet's rejects, the children of the damned. They're not from Earth. You should know that by now, don't you? I know where they're from. I've been there. I'm from there. Nice place. *Except for them.* I know you don't believe me. You don't happen to have a hat pin, do you?"

"I told you where to find some."

"I don't fit on the stairway to the attic, Victoria."

"You've lost everything I've let you borrow, Max." Max scornfully winced, tightened his lips and appeared as if he were holding something back that he badly wanted to say, but couldn't. "Come and sit down, Max. You've been chewing on those roots again, haven't you? I worry about you, Max. One day you'll find yourself missing." V exhaled.

"No. Not at all, Victoria. It's impossible to find yourself missing. Leaves. Leaves from the Haitian highlands. First you boil them until they make a mush. Then you squeeze it all up into a tight ball. After it's cool, of course. Then you dig it up after you've buried it at least two feet deep for no less than five days, then you unwrap the cheese cloth, pinch off a tiny piece the size of a pea, pop it in your mouth and chew slowly. Those Mexican shrooms don't come close."

"One day they'll come and take you away," Lily prophesied, while chewing on a candied cherry.

Max sneered, "One day pigs will seed the clouds with excrement and it won't be right as rain."

V blindly patted the arm of the Ravenna Bishop's chair suggesting he sit. Instead, Max continued to stand in the doorway shifting his bearish weight from one foot to the other in a nervous and nerve-racking way. "*Zeus refuses.* Beelzebub! What I need is a hat pin!"

"Voodoo, Maxfield?"

"Lily, when in Rome carry a cross. In Haiti, a hat pin. Don't wear one around your neck unless you have it encased. I've got to pin down a short-horned migratory locust. There's a rare hopper for you. They eat everything in sight. Miles and miles of pastures and plains eaten to the bone. Never underestimate the appetite of things that hop."

Startled, Lily yelped! She had not noticed Max approaching, thinking him still standing in the doorway, when he mistook her finger for a candied cherry as they simultaneously reached for the last one.

"No. You go right ahead, Lily."

Lily wasted no time and ate the last candy before inquiring, "Maxfield, how many hoppers do you suppose it takes to level a neighbor's unkempt yard? More than a few hundred?"

"I should say so. Thousands, Lily. There are far worse things than the short-horned migratory locust," Max magnified his factual, informative, professorial tone, which had the effect of taking his inquisitor aside and into an unuttered sense of commitment to a confidence about to be bestowed, or betrayed; one could never figure which. "Dutch elm disease for one. Caused by a fungus. Devastating. A yellowing of the foliage. Defoliation. Death. I need a hat pin!"

Lily was bothering with something to the side of her chair when she asked, "Must it be a hat pin? Will a long sewing needle do?" Lily was holding a sewing needle extracted from her pink wicker sewing basket given to her by V for Christmas several years earlier. Neither put much stock into Christmas anymore. They celebrated the Winter Solstice for a couple years with two diesel dykes with whom they are no longer friends, Peter O'Toole and Billy Butts. And then, traditional commemorations became "too tedious" for V. The sewing basket was a joke gift, but Lily loved it and quickly discovered that she actually did enjoy refurbishing thrift store apparel.

"Of course. Absolutely. Thank you." Max quickly snatched the needle from Lily, leaving her with V to worry and sort through a quandary of misgivings, not the least of which is how Max disappeared.

"One day they will come and take him away. It is inevitable. Mark my words," V knowingly stated, with the benefit of magical thinking and her far-reaching foresight, that enabled her to see foregone conclusions.

"Maybe not."

"*Hmm*...maybe not. Anyway, where were we?"

Without missing a beat, Lily answered, "Something about your goddamned life and you should know better."

"Wow," V exclaimed. "You are good." Lily smiled. However V pouted, sighed and said, "So much for posterity," feeling a pity party coming on.

Anxiety, from V's sense of a wasted life, filled with false starts and half-baked exercises in the profundity of the useless, filled her wasted hours. *It must change.*

FIVE

the obligatory book

Outside the hamlet of Squeezer, after two uneventful hours, the FEA field trip chartered bus turned onto a scenic dirt road; that is, if rock-strewn red dirt and giant red monolithic boulders that rose from out dry red clay, piercing the blue Colorado sky, along their way to the summit of the steep bluff can seen as scenic. At road's end stood the picnic tepee and souvenir stand where tickets were sold to descend the shaft leading down into the caverns and, of especial interest, the Wall of Delights—the *pièce de résistance* for the Friends of Erotic Artifacts.

All were quick to disembark when the bus finally rolled up in front of the tepee and made an abrupt stop nearly hitting a man in lederhosen who was foolish enough to stand wide-eyed and frozen as umpteen tons of metal and humanity came barreling towards him. The near fatality could easily be attributed to the bus driver's auto-asphyxiation from taking those bumpy and torturous backroads, causing him to bounce continuously, generating more noxious emissions to add to the greenhouse effect. As the passengers disembarked they were greeted by "Rocky Mountain High" song by John Denver, pouring out from a boom box held on the shoulders of the lederhosen clad tourist who still stood on the spot where he narrowly escaped becoming German roadkill.

The Friends of Erotic Artifacts were greeted by the Wall of Delights which began their journey into the depths of Dead Squeezer's Caverns. There were faded petroglyphs along the entrance walls and they were stunningly etched into the stone by, conceivably, artisans of an ancient civilization. The friezes of frenzy suggested an orgy of monumental proportions. This was what they came to see and it was already the most titillating FEA field trip since their jaunt to Aspen to spot and photograph retired celebrities. Today's adventure had just begun; and it was already destined to be the most unforgettable escapade to date.

Carla Bean, whose imagination held her Greek paramour's interest—for the moment—was overwhelmed by the sheer magnitude of the versatility and virtuosity of those ancient artisans. She clung tightly to her tall dark man, pressing into him while making mental notes of all the arousing positions on the Wall of Delights. Parenthetically, Carla's copy of the *Kama Sutra* had been long lost, along with her favorite dildo, and she doesn't remember where she might have left them, or to whom she might have lent them. They could be with anyone, anywhere across the United States—except Utah—Europe, Asia, or the Mediterranean.

The tour continued along the great rocky corridor with its bulging walls covered with copulating stick figures. *The lust! The hedonism! The licentiousness! The rapture!* A lascivious experience beyond mere mortal ability to put into words—so, best left to one's imagination. After pausing for Minnie Beach to finish a rendering in her sketch pad, the tour moved on.

"When old man Squeezer opened these here caverns to regular people he made his fortune," the guide explained, "and fame he never knew he wanted until he got it. Ain't that always the way? He was a simple sheep farmer; a shepherd who lost his sheep and didn't know where to find them. Just like Little Bo Peep." The guide paused and waited for Mercy, Minnie and a curiously unattractive, dark-faced, narrow-eyed man to catch-up before resuming his tedious homily. The narrow-eyed man let escape a *tee-hee*. "As you may already know, those lost sheep later led old man Squeezer to discover these here caverns...." The guide went on and on; and the narrow-eyed man *tee-heed*.

In short, the story goes, there had been a *baa-baaing* heard from under a little oasis set aside in the pastures surrounding a neat row of evergreens where the tepee now stands. The ring of evergreens were planted to keep the sheep from eating flowers and doing their "duty" around the headstones of the families Squeezer, Higgins, Slatterly, and a few bastard Bartles, and also from attracting too much attention from neighboring ranchers. Not a single soul connected the *baa-baaing* with Squeezer's missing sheep, since most of the citizens of Squeezer had been occupied by practicing their own *baa-baaing* for the annual sheep calling competition and barbecue. The sheep had been missing for six days when Digger Beetle, a local grave robber of gold teeth, watches, rings, and whatever treasure lay six feet under, was arrested without evidence, found guilty and promptly hung that very same day for sheep rustling. Despite that, the spirit of irony would have its way. On the seventh day of the sheep disappearance mystery, old Ida Slatterly, while placing flowers on Hank Slatterly's grave, who was her wicked former husband, felt the Earth go "aquilk with demonic lamentations aquaking the body and soul." Exactly what she meant by "aquilk" nobody knew. "Aquake" had already been well established years earlier to describe the sensation of shivers to the bone. She had invented many a word in her day, such as "idioddity" which is used to this day by the residents of Squeezer to describe a tourist or out-of-towner. "*There goes another idioddity getting gasoline over at Lou's.*" Idioddity would also apply to the entire busload of the Friends of Erotic Artifacts.

    Moving on: the guide continued to explain how all the local farmers were missing something; chickens, geese, ducks, goats, cats, dogs, cows, more sheep, a mule, and children. The aquilking of the ground over Hank Slatterly's final resting place was now the entrance to the caverns next to the souvenir stand, and also where the ground had opened and swallowed poor old Ida Slatterly. When the hole that was then Hank's grave was finally discovered, Digger was accused of being up to his old shenanigans. The townsfolk got out their ropes, but that was to no avail since he had already been hung the day before. In any event, poor old Ida had fallen and landed on the top of Hank's skeleton, not twenty feet from the Wall of Delights. She managed to live long enough in the menagerie of children and farm animals to tell her horrifying story to Harry the Barber, one of the volunteers who came to her rescue during those last minutes of her life. Harry the Barber was there to witness her account as she gazed upon the fornicating figures etched along the cavern's walls and her impassioned smile as her eyes blinked and shut for the very last time. All the animals and most of the children were rescued shortly after her unfortunate death. That's the gist of it.

"Now, as we round this here bend," continued the guide, "you will notice to your left the Grotto of the Green Guernsey. This natural formation of limestone took thousands of years to evolve into what is clearly one of nature's wonders, teats and all. You can see the slight discoloration marking her darker patches...."

"Oh! Get a picture of that!" Minnie screamed to her husband Nelson the Philanderer just as he was about to snap one anyway. She jarred him so much with her scream, the picture came out upside down. Nelson the Philanderer's executive assistant, Sara Hookerbee, followed in the shadows, disguised with a wide-brimmed straw hat with dangling tassels, large sunglasses in a white frame, and a bustier corset that threw her tits almost to her chin. Minnie pretended not to see the bitch, but she could not avoid seeing her, and she did not care anymore.

* * *

Shady Sanctum loomed over its neighboring homes in the heat and shadows of early afternoon, offering a full view of the Colorado State Capitol building with its genuine gold leaf dome. A profusion of rose gardens lay along both sides of the street. Roses were always very fashionable in the Capitol Hill neighborhood where fashion itself was quite fashionable for its own sake. The sheer abundance of roses, of every sort and color, and paired with lesser known perennials, were a Mulligan stew for amateur horticulturalists.

Old Pansy Hedgeworth, who didn't live on the same street as Shady Sanctum, shared the alley with Shady Sanctum. She hosted the bravest assortment of roses. Since the roses were within her fence where nobody could reach them, many thought they were plastic. They were, however, discovered by V and Lily not to be plastic, when V helped boost Lily up and over Old Pansy's fence to grab a rose. The verdict came in—the roses were painfully real. Lily found herself in agony, trapped in Old Pansy's triffids, unable to climb back over the fence, disheveled and covered with scratches as though she had tangled with a thirty-pound cat.

When Lily finally did disentangle herself, she slowly limped her way around to the front yard and made her escape through the entrance gate followed by two yapping, ferocious Chihuahuas sprinting after her. Lily was still running down the block when she heard police sirens on their way to Old Pansy's. Out of breath, she ran faster. When Lily finally returned to Shady Sanctum, by the long way, visibly suffering from lack of oxygen, she simply stared at V before stomping upstairs, slamming the bedroom door, and began to remove rose thorns from her arms, legs and her yellow Capri pants covered with light orange dots the size of dimes. Lily will need to hit the thrift stores next half-priced Tuesday. There were a few folk on the Hill who were deadpan-faced serious when they spoke of Old Pansy Hedgeworth. They were certain that she ate children, and who knows what else?

Red, pink, yellow, ivory and white raged and burst with great thorny merriment into a confusion of unequaled splendor upon Old Pansy Hedgeworth's corner. Blushers and Beauties, haughty and scarlet, mixed in among prickly and pink ramblers spilling from whitewashed trellises, strangling and nearly burying what few yellow hybrids managed to survive in Old Pansy's yard, now three feet deep with flattened roses.

"This is the work o' those mangey-ass Bernards what belong to the queers next door. Those hairy beasts are always tryin' ta do somethin' nasty in the rose bushes with my little boys," Old Pansy told the good-looking young postman who delivered her Golden Age magazine with a photo of Baby Trump on its cover. Old Pansy quickly closed the front door and masturbated with the TV remote while lounging in her faded and timeworn red velvet armchair.

To the chagrin of neighbors, Shady Sanctum hosted not a single rose; front or backyard. Instead, the front yard was a horticultural act of dissidence—peonies, pansies, daylilies, daisies and a raspberry bush added to the colorful collage. Max was watching an army of black ants busily about their business with a peony. It was a tricky situation trying to adjust the magnifying glass into sharp focus without setting the subjects of his inquiry ablaze, nor did he wish to harm the peony.

"Damnation," moaned Max as he watched two black ants turn into specks of charcoal.

Meanwhile, not a sound was coming from out the basement and this disturbed the atypical world of Maxfield Talbot immensely. Shortly after V and Lily had gone to the bus station, the twins went into the basement, nailing the door shut behind them. Not a peep had been heard since.

"Beelzebub!" This time three black soldiers curled-up in a puff of smoke. Max slipped the magnifying glass into his back pocket and disappeared around the corner of Shady Sanctum. Moments later, he reappeared chewing a piece of Haitian dough gum and carrying a claw hammer which he soon put to use extracting nails from the wooden slats barring the entrance to the coal slide. After removing the last nail, Max carefully lifted the windowed door. With the unwieldy bulk of him leaning into the basement, barely fitting through the coal slide's door, adjusting his eyes to the gloom of it, his nose to the scent, Max went sailing down the chute head first landing on top, and nearly crushing to death, a naked Penny who was straddling an equally naked Peter who, after letting out a great deal of air under the weight and sudden impact of Maxfield's raid upon their privacy, began screaming and yelling for him to *"get the fuck off."*

"How could you? You ought to be ashamed of yourself! Have you no sense of decency?" Those words might have been defensible had they come from Max. However, they did not. Instead, the outrage was that of Pudgy Penny.

"How could you? You of all people!" sneered Piggy Peter. "Come, Drusilla. We are betrayed."

"I'll say, Zeus," proclaimed his outraged sister, squeezing into her bibbed overalls.

"You shall be assassinated," Max informed them rather casually, "Brutally. Without mercy. A bloody mess. You'll be stretched out on cold marble, knives slashing, splashing, oozing pools of thick red life, bleeding, pleading for your wretched lives, arms raised with your fingers clawing for one last breath of air. *Arghh! Arghh! Arghh!* And poor Drusilla! Dead as a door nail! Or is it a knob? One of those. Dead anyway. Done in by her loving brother. Runs in the family, you know. Bad blood, tainted like inbred show dogs. Prissy little fuckers! Snapping Pomeranians! *Arf! Arf! Arf!* Out of their skulls with incestuous insanity, best put to sleep. Now that's an euphemism for you: SLEEP. You little hellions want to be put to SLEEP? *Stab! Plunge! Arghh! Arghh! Arghh!* Know what I mean?"

And then a ray of hope twinkled in the eyes of Piggy Peter, "Zeus cannot be assassinated! You do know you are bat shit crazy, right?"

"I know," Maxfield agreed. "I also know that Zeus suffers from horrid, odious, and painful convulsions. Like the time silly Harriet got a fish bone caught in her throat kind of convulsion. *Jupiter!* Wasn't that a mess!? PLOP. Right off Olympus and into the Aegean. And then the Dark Ages, children. Catholics ran the whole kit and caboodle; a bloody bunch, you know, back then; the Catholics. Blood splashed and bubbled like an Exxon oil spill. I genuflect to their knack for mass killing. A wet blanket of ignorance covered the land and it's a long wait for Michelangelo, Kiddos."

"Let's get out of here, Pen. He's off his nut."

"I am not off my nut!" Maxfield whined.

"You're a silly old drug addict!"

"Yeah, and your off your nut," added Pudgy Penny.

"Am not!" Perplexed, Max shook his head wondering why children were so blatantly provocative? *"But then, they're not children, are they? They're not even human!"* Max said to himself. *"Spawn of Satan!"*

The twins dashed up the coal slide and locked the entrance window behind them before hearing Max moan, *"Beelzebub!"* while trying to chew, with great deliberation, the bitter dough gum, which his nearly extinct sense of taste instructed his brain to envision as something reminiscent of Amazonian roach paste. He swallowed hard and shuddered. Then, something strange happened. Max leaned against a wooden pole, one of several used to reinforce an unusually high ceiling for a basement—or an unusually low floor—braced himself against it and waited for the pandemonium of a dispirited stomach to quiet down. Slowly the pole began to move, giving Max the sudden jolt of a realization that he may be about to topple over. He checked himself and, with balance intact, shifted his attention to the source of the grating rumbling noise—and this time it wasn't his stomach.

His accelerated imagination conjured a vision concerning a hitherto unknown door that inched its way ajar, exposing an equally unknown chamber used, no doubt, for an array of unimaginable unknowns. His mind, a mentor to itself, refused to be more specific. As it happened, his imagined vision and the reality of the moment were fairly well synchronized. Behind the boxes of potatoes with their sprouts desperately groping the air for some hint as to which direction next to take, a panel did indeed open into a room Max never suspected nor wondered about the possibility of its actually being there, but nonetheless, there it was, just beyond the sprouts. It was more or less a large closet; a veritable treasure trove for the curious and adventurous mind of Maxfield Talbot, amplified by the introduction of Haitian dough gum. Indescribable projections for fantastical possibilities and things one found reason to hide or, in the least, obscure from inquiring minds, entered his mental quagmire. One had to be there in the thick of his brain to see it. Nothing could compete with Maxfield's brilliantly lit and vivid mind, overly anxious and too often misunderstood, balanced somewhere between neurotic and psychotic; here, there and nowhere, at once. *"What could it be?"* He was about to find out. There was hidden contraband waiting be snatched and brought into the light of day. Chili sauce? Raspberry preserves? This was, after all, the former sanctuary for the Brotherhood of Solar Agnation, so maybe there were esoteric documents containing secret rituals.

Full-bearded and burly, Max appeared like an enormous bug-eyed hairy Hobbit, as he stumbled over the box of potatoes en route to his destination with unyielding determination. The closer he came to that hidden chamber, the more he salivated. Wiping his beard dry with a frayed red bandanna, his free hand came to rest on a large dust-covered book that he assumed had something to do with his brother-in-law's Brotherhood of Solar Agnation. The book's cover glistened with the new color. *A new color.* "Hmm," Max mumbled to himself. "a *new color? I know this book. Duh. This is made of quixelite."*

There was nothing else in the secret hiding place. Aside for some pickled eggs, a few jams and jellies, the book was all the treasure in the trove: A bulky book of a new color with peculiar writing on its cover that moved and changed as Maxfield stared at it. He was shivering with excitement, which might be called *aquaking* in the town of Squeezer. The light of divine cognition flashed upon his consciousness, went out, then flashed again. Strange lettering rose from off the book, 3D without the glasses, momentarily blinding Max with laser-sharp white light before collapsing back onto its cover. This was, for Maxfield, a matter concerning the infinite connections which bridge the keen workings of his mind, flashing on and off like fireflies, delivering glimpses of the workings of both celestial mechanics and quantum physics, and all from the radiance of himself. There was a moment or two of doubt when he questioned whether the light which shone upon his insight was waxing, or on the wane. Apparently, it was on the wane, since a bank of fog rushed in to obscure his quickly vanishing understanding. Epiphanies and moments of peak awareness are generally that way; one minute of bathing in the light of total understanding, and the next minute left dripping wet and standing in the dark totally mindless. Max was beside himself and, though he felt himself the very best of company, he bit off another piece of Haitian dough gum, *"just in case something goes south."*

Maxfield stood tottering on the brink of a new dimension that he was certain had nothing to do with the dough gum. He never gives the dough gum credit for anything, unless it's disagreeable. Maxfield questioned the overpowering wisdom that he believed he had; was it the result of old age, maturation, or the result of his sheer abandon to the moment, to the sensation discovery imparts? Maybe all of the aforementioned. Maxfield chewed the piece of dough gum tirelessly, telling himself that his sense of wellbeing had nothing to do with anything. Max's understanding of what he thought he understood, and the reality of what is, left a gap so wide that civil engineers would need years to ponder the expanse of that unconstructed bridge before daring to cross it. Nevertheless, that has yet to stop Max from traveling upon an unsubstantiated edifice.

With hands literally quivering with excitement, Max held the book to his hairy man-boobs. Slowly, he began to become vaguely aware of a long lost state of being, accompanied by an inordinate sense of *déjà vu*. He took the book with the new color to the old worktable at the opposite end of the basement. There he sat upon the very same stool that Brother Kirby sat upon for hours, doing his sacred relic mountings. Beneath a lit bare bulb Max once again looked at the book's cover wondering when and where he had last seen it. Alphabetical characters rose from off the cover of the book spelling out IDIOT in bright red neon. This didn't faze Max one bit. He always had the dough gum to blame for anything that was out of the ordinary. Out of the ordinary, for Maxfield, is relative. The neon IDIOT vanished. And, HELLO, MAX. LONG TIME NO SEE. He slowly moved his fingers over the book's cover and the words that greeted him fell back into its cover. It was soft as silk to the touch. *"Whoa. When was the last time I saw this book? Hmm. It's always about a book, isn't it? Why not a lampshade or a pomegranate? But no, it's another mumbo-jumbo book that must save the world; the derivative cliche of cliches. Holy cow and filthy knickers! I've been an idiot! This book can't save the world. I had a book just like this when I was a child—eons ago."* Maxfield opened the book and disappeared into an alternate dimension.

"Hello, old friend."

* * *

Deep within Dead Squeezer's Caverns, the spirit of

discovery was most evident in the Hall of Giant Mushrooms.

"Symbolic. Yes, I should say symbolic. They remind one of a phallic symbol. Wouldn't you say phallic symbolism?" Helga Mummi quizzed no one in particular. After it became painfully clear to her that she was to receive no answer from anyone, she surmised that their taciturnity was the result of bad hearing, or perhaps a reticence created by the party's brimming hostility from boredom; stupefied by their guide's narrative concerning calcium carbonate deposits forming stalagmites in the form of giant mushrooms, scattered here and there across the cave's floor, conjuring in Helga's mind strangely exciting images complete with accompanying shivers—*aquaking* again. Helga realized there would be no engaging anybody, so she proceeded to answer herself, *"Quite right. A phallic symbol and that's all there is to say. Phallic. Phallic, phallic, phallic...."* as her eyes shifted from stalagmite to stalagmite.

"Now, let's go into the Chamber of Little People with Big Heads," the guide droned on. "This is not to be confused with the Chamber of Dwarfs. We'll be getting to there as soon as we enter the next room."

Single file, the group moved along the narrow passageway which connects the Hall of Giant Mushrooms to the Chamber of Little People with Big Heads.

"The heads are so big, you wonder why they don't topple over."

"Some do, V," Lily said, pointing to the cracked heads strewn about the chamber's floor.

"They are not only a danger to themselves, they endanger all within their toppling zone. Best not get too close. There is a severe danger in noticeably speaking metaphorically. It is existentially disturbing, Lily."

"*Ah hah.* I will remember that in case it ever becomes handy. I've actually known people with mighty big heads."

"I'm sure, Lily. What with being in the theatre, and all."

"Oh, look!" exclaimed Mercy Pentcist to her husband

Mikey. "Can you see the little beady eyes and the nose?"

"Yeah," Mikey replied, "but I don't see a mouth."

"I suppose," V intruded, "eyes and noses are enough when the head is that big." Followed by a ponderous silence.

Meanwhile, the strange and mysterious narrow-eyed fellow lurked in the shadows, while keeping a dark and squinty gaze on V.

"Would you take a look at him," Billy Butts whispered to V. "I bet he's somebody's guru."

"Take a look at who, Billy?" V seemed exasperated.

"That guru-looking person. Wearing a burnoose. I think he's cruising me. Older men have always been attracted to me. That one in the burnoose, I'm sure he's hot for me."

"For God's sake, Billy! What are you carrying on about? You're over fifty. You *are* an older man. Get a grip! I don't see anybody in a burnoose, anyway."

"Well, he was there a moment ago, V. It looked like a burnoose. I went to a Halloween party with the Duchess a few years ago at Too-Much and Mad Michael's. Eddy Spaghetti was there. He covered his face with white greasepaint and came as a greedy Capitalist white man. That was before he threw Too-Much out because he thought he was cheating but it turned out he was only taking evening pottery classes. But it was too late. Too-Much moved on to live in Shady Sanctum with you guys. Did you know that Tommy Too-Much is in the Blue Book? Not by that name of course. He's always been Tommy Too-Much to everybody. It costs sixty-five dollars a year to get yourself in the Blue Book. I know. I've been in it forever."

Tommy Too-Much had lived in a spare room in Shady Sanctum, adding another resident to the household; Lily, V, Max, Cousin Harriet, Pudgy Penny and Piggy Peter. Too-Much remained an entire year. He found a part-time job in a warehouse, sorting and stealing DVDs from Netflix. This afforded him the money to go to hairdressing school, to get his first hairdressing gig, and to move out of Shady Sanctum into an apartment of his own.

"There were two people wearing burnooses," Billy raved on. "Or is it burni? I wore my monk's robe and the Duchess went as Gertrude Stein which was a wildly strange choice since she already looks like Gertrude Stein even when it's not Halloween. Maybe I should have gone as Alice B. Toklas with a tray of brownies? Is it a bad thing for a black man to wear whiteface? Maybe not. What do you think?"

"I think...."

"I love my monk's robe," Billy interrupted any answer that might be coming his way, "...and since I only get to wear it once or twice a year, I thought Alice B. Toklas wasn't a necessary companion to Sylvia's Gertrude Stein. Why should I take away her thunder? You do know about Alice's brownies, don't you?"

Eddy Spaghetti stepped out from behind one of the little people with big heads and said to Billy Butts, "*Girrrl*, I went to a party in Harlem dressed as Queen Elizabeth. She didn't seem to mind."

"I didn't think it was a bad thing, I mean the whiteface and all. Eddie, do they have gurus in Tangier? By the way, I was thinking about interviewing Carla's new friend. I might even run a feature on him. *Hot, hot, hot. Out and Beyond* is always interested in fresh meat; especially Greek meat. Know what I mean?"

"*Girrrl*, I never know what you mean." Eddy grinned.

"Especially when *you* don't know what you mean. Were I you," V warned, "I would keep my distance from Carla's new acquisition."

"At least," Lily offered, "until Carla's done with him and finds herself a shiny new toy."

"I wonder what she'll do with him after she's done with him." Eddy pursed his lips. "I don't mind a secondhand Greek...or, for that matter...."

"If you will look to your right," said the guide, "you will see why we call this room the Chamber of Little People with Big Heads."

"I don't see it. Everything looks the same as in the Hall of Giant Mushrooms," Minnie observed. "Only smaller."

"You've got to squint, my dear." Carla instructed.

Squinting, Minnie said, "Oh, yes! I see it. Would you look at that. Absolutely stunning."

"If you are seeing it now," said Carla in her sweet vermouth mixed with a large portion of bitters demeanor, "Your vision is quite extraordinary, since you are looking in the wrong direction."

V, upon hearing this perked up, smiled, and felt that wondrous sensation one gets from seeing another's pain from embarrassment, when it is a well-earned comeuppance. "The next time, Lily, Minnie Beach will think twice before showing her stupidity in my presence, especially when it's about me."

It was the mysterious stranger wearing the burnoose with the pointed hood whom Minnie had mistaken for one of the bigheaded little people that, when Billy shouted in his high-pitched voice, that has been heard over the din in restaurants, noisy parties, busy bus stations, artillery ranges, anywhere and everywhere; including an audience of one; *"Hello there."* The enigmatic stranger had nowhere to hide nor run as Billy ingratiated himself upon a new victim. "My name is Billy Butts. What's yours?"

"Yours?"

"Name."

He took his time sizing up the creature. "Faakhir."

"Excuse me?"

"Faakhir."

Billy thought he smelled a hint of curry. "Nice to meet you, Mr. Keer."

"Faakhir," he corrected.

"Kerr," said Billy and then paused a few seconds before exclaiming with great delight, "Keir Dullea is one of my favorite actors. Met him once at The Studio, back in my clubbing days. That was me, a club boy."

After taking his time to figure out what he had in front of

him, he decided the creature was harmless enough, "Is one word. *Faakhir.*"

"That's fabulous! You're like Cher, or Madonna. That's really neat. *Faakhir.*"

"I do not understand."

"Oh, I'm sorry. You are from someplace else, aren't you?"

"Yes. Someplace else."

"Are you a guru? Give good advice? You look like a guru. Do gurus have crystal balls?"

"Guru? Guru. Yes. Me guru. No crystal balls. Sorry."

"I knew it! I just knew it! Oh, how exciting!" Billy hollered across the Chamber of Little People with Big Heads as the rest of the party were about to enter the Chamber of Dwarfs. "V! Lily! Wait till you see what I found." Billy then turned back to Faakhir and said, "Come, come. I want you to meet two very dear friends of mine. Victoria Aires lives in Queen City in a big Victorian mansion that her father left her. She's my best friend. She likes to be called V. Lily Nettles is an actress who also lives in the mansion. They call it Shady Sanctum. The two of them are married. To each other. I wish I were married." Billy, not too quickly, realized that Faakhir had vanished, muttered, *"What did I say? The man was an apparition."* This was not Billy's first encounter with beings of no substance, so he didn't seem particularly challenged in any way by this revelation. Then Faakhir reappeared from behind a stalagmite. Billy went giddy when he materialized. "Will you follow me? Come. Right next to me. I want to introduce you. You are real, aren't you?"

"Yes. If you promise not to blow in my ear," Faakhir whispered. Billy asked himself, if he had heard rightly.

They were standing next to V and Lily, when Billy said with affection and a stiff upper lip, "Oh my darlings, V and Lily, this is my new friend Faakhir the guru. Faakhir is just one word. Isn't that clever? Like Beyoncé and Geronimo."

"Is my pleasure to meet, ladies."

"Thank you," V said, while sizing-up the little squinty-eyed man.

Eddy Spaghetti whispered into Billy's ear, "*Girrrl,* he's wearing a dress."

Lily, exhausted from walking and looking at nothing but rocks, with barely enough enthusiasm to float the words the three feet needed to reach Faakhir said, "Glad to know you."

Wearing his pith helmet, Poor Sir Geoffrey came over to see what he could see and what he saw seemed of little consequence, so he returned his attention to the guide who was saying, "Now if you will follow me into the Chamber of Dwarfs you will see Sleepy, Dopey and Bashful doing something to Snow White which is probably best left unsaid."

SIX

a night in snow white's crotch

The phone rang and rang and rang. *Where were V and Lily?* And rang and rang and went into voicemail. Had someone been there to answer the phone they would have known it was Peter O'Toole, who had just returned from London's world premiere of two one-act plays written by himself, *The Naked & The Depraved.*

Peter O'Toole, playwright, poet, philosopher, general man-about-town, *bon vivant*, is the only son of the late Roxanne Cox-O'Toole and the late Toots O'Toole; and not related in any way to the actor of the same name other than they both share a common redundancy.

Toots O'Toole, while crossing a busy Philadelphia street after parking his Packard some blocks from the hospital where Peter was due to arrive at any minute, was run over and killed by a Volkswagen bus filled with nuns singing "Dominique" while on their way to a prayer retreat and a 24-hour bingo marathon in Hackensack, New Jersey. When Peter's mother was informed of her husband's death she flipped-out, grabbed her breakfast tray and began beating Peter with it, "I hate you! I hate you! You little sonofabitch! You did this! Wait until I get you home, you little fucker! I'll drown you, you piece of shit!" And, the infant Peter hadn't yet been born!

It took two nurses, a doctor and the janitor who was carelessly mopping her room, to pin her down long enough to sedate her. As Roxie O'Toole fell asleep, Peter was born and Roxie was wheeled to a locked ward on the dreaded eighth floor. Peter's mother died shortly thereafter from internal hemorrhaging from beating him with the breakfast tray before he was born. Baby Peter disappeared a few days later. It was suspected that the nuns in the Volkswagen kidnapped him, but there was never an investigation, so it was anybody's guess. After Peter graduated from Saint Somebody's college near Philadelphia, he met the *"love of his life"* and followed him to Queen City. Unfortunately, the love of his life was a short-lived affair, when *"the bastard!"* took off for Los Angeles with a new love of his life, leaving Peter to reinvent himself in Queen City, Colorado.

Peter O'Toole, tired from his flight back from London, finished unpacking, changed into his silk blue paisley robe and tried to relax with a dirty martini, but there was no relaxing. Peter was too excited to tell the ladies all about his *"...glorious night, not too awfully far from London's West End."* It was, in fact, sort of an Off-Off-Off and down-down-down a dark alley kind of West End. The one and only review was dull to hostile, but Peter convinced himself that it was not a negative review, since the English critics understate everything and they never gush. They do not use words in the same way as Americans, who overstate everything. So, what Peter will eventually tell V and Lily is, "*The reviews were shamelessly gratuitous, my dears, lavishing praise upon this humble playwright from the other side of the pond. Our side, that is. I was a hit with the Brits."* His lies, entrenched in insecurity, would have to wait until one of "the ladies" was there to pick up the phone. In any case, after he did get around to delivering his well-rehearsed white lie to the girls, V would Google and discover from the one review she could find, that *The Naked & The Depraved* was a complete disaster. In any event, the phone rang and rang and rang and went into voicemail.

Peter the Playwright falls into the 'intellectual' category. His studied words, intermingled with pieces of outspoken thoughts, said in his highly-practiced fluid tone, never worked in real life as well as they appeared on paper. He is, arguably, an excellent playwright. Peter had written several well-received plays that have been produced worldwide. Still, there is bound to be the occasional "experimental" flop. His one-acts, *The Naked & The Depraved*, are two of his occasional "experimental" endeavors. When Peter suffers malicious reviews, his face-saving response is generally, "Oh well, it was just an experimental nothing-much play anyway." But, he took it personally and painfully. Peter's thin skin was his Achilles heel.

A hour later he tried calling the ladies again and this time he received an answer. It was Pudgy Penny.

"I don't know," Penny sneered. "The bus is late. Tried her cell. Got nothing. We're hungry. Maybe she's underground."

"Underground?"

"Yeah, a cave."

"So that's why it kept rolling over to voice mail."

"*Duh.* We're hot and hungry. Stupid old Max up and disappeared."

"To where?"

"I don't know and I don't care. We're starving. Send pizza. Two pizzas."

"I could, but I think it best you wait until your Aunt V returns."

"*I don't!* If we don't get something to eat soon, the devil knows what we'll do."

"Well, Peter, I don't know what to tell you."

"This isn't Peter, fuckturd! Peter's on the pot."

"Sorry. Jet lag effects my hearing, dearest Penny."

"*Yeah, whatevah.* You want us to tell 'em you called. I get it. But, she better hurry 'cause I could eat a horse, or a cat."

O'Toole wasn't sure if that was the plea of the famished, or a threat against the life of Mercury, Lily's Russian Blue. "Penny, darling, you wouldn't really eat sweet little Mercury, would you?"

"*Condescending fuckturd!*" And the sound of Penny hanging up the landline was Peter's only answer.

O'Toole decided to get dressed and go down to the bus station and wait for the girls. Thirty minutes later he arrived just in time to catch Poor Sir Geoffrey handcuffed and being loaded into a Denver squad car. Billy Butts caught sight of O'Toole and came gushing forward, tripping over himself, after first bouncing off Minnie Beach in one of his artless maneuvers.

"Peter, Peter, Peter! It's Billy! Billy Butts!"

"Billy, Billy, Billy. It could be none other," he chuckled.

"I've something to tell you," said an out of breath Billy.

"I've no doubt. Shall it require boots and sunglasses?"

As usual, Billy exercised selective hearing when he did not want to *'go there,'* or didn't understand, said, "You'll never guess what happened."

"You're probably right, Billy."

"I'm in love," blurted Billy.

"With somebody else?" Peter asked, rather sharply.

"Carla's newest. His name is Al. He's got a longer name, but it's impossible to say. Unless you're Greek, of course. He's going to sneak out tonight after Carla goes to sleep. Isn't that exciting?"

"Not for Carla."

"He doesn't speak English good."

"Neither do you. No one cares when one either speaks or does not speak English *good*, but I'd go with 'speaks English well,' were I you."

"He's making fun of me, isn't he? Maybe not," Billy said to himself.

Peter continued, "However did you manage to arrange the tryst, Billy?"

"Hand signals. I guess they're what they call the universal alphabet. And what else? Oh! I guess you saw them carting off Poor Sir Geoffrey."

"I did indeed."

"He tried to hijack the bus."

"Do tell."

"I think it was a machete," Billy said. "Or, something like that. I didn't see it. I was busy at the time."

"With hand signals, no doubt."

"That's a good one, Peter."

"I aim to please. So tell me the story of Sir Geoffrey's incarceration."

Talking with Butts was a constant test of patience, for anyone. But, for Peter O'Toole, it was not his patience on trial—it was his civility. Like a human cactus, Butts pierced him with little pricks of his being.

"We left V and Lily back at the caves. Everybody was in such a hurry to get home, I guess nobody noticed, or everybody forgot about them, or everybody noticed and nobody cared. Although that's not likely, is it? Sir Geoffrey wanted to go back to the caves and pick V and Lily up, but the bus driver didn't. That's when Sir Geoffrey pulled out the machete from his pocket."

"You can't put a machete in your pocket, and you can't pull one out of it, either, Billy."

"*Whatevah*. Some sort of knife, or corkscrew. I don't remember. That's all I know. Don't ask. Gotta go. What do you wear to meet a Greek in the middle of the night?"

"Something with feta, I suppose." Peter was nonplused.

* * *

Dionysos ripped asunder for V as she entered the parlor where O'Toole sat in his favorite chair; an original bent steel van der Rohe, which V treasures and sees as a perfect example of functional art. Peter was enthralled while reading about himself in the foreword to *Angels Fall Upward*, "*...many have said, is his best. O'toole's Roman Catholic background—and a short stint in a Seminary—is apparent with his brave use of imagery and symbolism. Tense and profound...*"

Peter stopped reading when he heard V's entrance as she said, with dramatic flair, "Quoting others to support ones assertions seems a terrible waste of time, don't you think, dear Peter? One should know enough, or one should learn enough, to quote themselves. I assume you agree. You certainly must, mustn't you? It is the lazy mind that cannot support its own weight. Of course you agree."

"At best, I have only an ill-defined idea for what the hell

you are talking about. And how are you, dearest V?"

"You really don't want to know. You must tell me all about *The Naked & The Depraved*. The reviews; sensational, I trust. Of course they were. And dear old London—did you tell my favorite city how I miss it so? No silly indignant Irish Catholic bombings, I trust. When I was there last, a bomb went off not three blocks away. Close enough to scare the bejesus out of me."

"They don't do that anymore, dear heart. Too tedious and the Irish finally got tired of strapping bombs on themselves, I imagine."

"Oh, no. The Irish would never strap a bomb on themselves. They leave it in a corner and run. Peter, have you seen Max?"

"I believe he withdrew to his room."

"You mean he is withdrawing in his room," V smirked.

"That explains it. I knocked on his door earlier and I heard him blathering something about folding space and time, getting everything out of order, bouncing black native breasts, men wearing soup cans and something that sounded like scorpions, sphincters, and magic in the basement."

"That sounds like Max, alright. Maybe he has gotten his hands on some really cool stuff. *Sphincters?*"

"Perhaps he was muttering something about the twins. Sounds like one of Max's pet names for them. You know, like 'get out of here, you nasty little sphincters.' I did take a quick look down there. In the basement, I mean. No magic, nothing out of the ordinary, and certainly no naked men wearing soup cans."

"That must have been a terrible disappointment for you, Sweetie," V chided.

"It was. Very disappointing. My poor limping libido has taken a bruising. The damn thing doesn't stand for anything nowadays. I blame the nuns. Anyway, how are you, *really?* First, I must say you look terrible."

"If you must say anything, Peter, you must first spend the

night with bat guano shoved up your nose."

"Some new kind of therapy?"

"Do I appear to find you humorous, Peter?"

"Definitely not. I once spent a night passed-out on Carla Bean's floor after one of her dreadful poetry readings. I awoke the following morning to catch Carla standing over me, arms akimbo, robe flung open, and who it was did the flinging worried me, a lot. Had I, in my delirium, flung it? I don't do flinging! The very thought of being molested in the night by a tranny; especially Carla Bean! Unthinkable. I shudder to this day, V. I was terrified when I caught sight of her breasts, although they were ample appealing, small pink nipples like a young girl's and still perky, for implants. She's certainly in her 40s, or more, and yet her body remains lithe and winsome. Nice words. I will have to use them; 'lithe and winsome.' I don't remember ever using those words. And certainly not in anyway attached to Carla Bean. So, she asked if it was as good for me as it was for her. I blew on her hilltops, she closed her robe, giggled and ran away, leaving me to wonder if it was a reference to her poetry, which was feloniously gruesome, or the unthinkable...which is unspeakable. If it were indeed what her wanton demeanor implied, I should have no alternative but to throw myself from off the roof of my building. The oddest thing is, I found her quite divine. Is that nauseating enough for you to be just a tad bit empathetic? Just a tad bit happy, maybe?"

"Not even close to happy, Kiddo. Too much drama."

"You *love* drama."

"Only when it suits me. However, I think a night in a filthy cave trumps a night with Carla."

"Maybe, but all things considered, a night in a cave with bat guano shoved up my nose sounds not so bad compared to having sex with Carla. Any woman, really. So, tell me all about your spelunking adventure and then I shall tell you all my good news." A foul stench wafted towards O'Toole, causing him to move farther back in V's precious van der Rohe. He positioned his right index finger against his nostrils and tried, without success, to create a vacuum seal. "I had no idea bat shit was so odious."

"I'm covered with it, Peter."

"Sorry."

"And to top it off, we had to pay one hundred and fifty dollars to Skeeter Squeezer for driving us home…in a goddamned Volkswagen bug. How unreasonable is *that?*"

"Not completely unreasonable, considering the distance. A hundred and fifty dollars doesn't get you much nowadays."

"Easy for you to say. However, Lily and I had to get out and push every time we came to a hill. And it's mostly all up hill from the Springs."

"How awful it must have been for you, dear heart. Well, thank goodness it was a Volkswagen bug. How much could one of those things weigh?"

"More than you'd think, Peter." V leaned over to Peter and whispered, "There's something else."

"There always is."

"After Lily had fallen asleep in Snow White's crotch…."

"What?"

"That is what the dullards call a pile a rocks," V said moving closer to O'Toole, who could not lean back any farther to avoid the pungent stench. "I saw a shaft of light coming through the wall behind Snow White. So, I decided to inspect it."

What V first spied through a chink in the rock wall was a bright white room with odd symbols, mathematical equations and a map of Queen City floating in space, attended to by men dressed in white hazmat suits. While others, who were not working with numbers and symbols or making X's in the air with their index fingers on Queen City neighborhoods, wandered about. Two of the men strolled towards her, then positioned themselves against the wall to the side of the chink. V listened to their muffled conversation.

"Mister President, we will launch them from right outside this hole in the wall. From there we'll navigate them through the caves and send them on their way to Queen City. They are topper than top secret, Sir. We've taken every precaution to keep a lid on this. We don't want to raise questions throughout the rest of the mountain."

"*Ah ha*, do they really look like mosquitos?" President Dumbazz asked.

"Indeed, Sir. In every way. We've done wonders with nano technology. They're virtually invisible."

"We don't like 'virtually,' General Bughump."

"Totally invisible, Sir. I misspoke. *Totally invisible.*"

"Now yer talkin'. How long before they're ready?"

"Within forty-eight hours, Sir."

"General Bughump," said the President while looking down his nose with sour condescension, "...there is too much handwringing goin' on in Washington right now. They're all out to get me, you know...those nasty Communist Democrats! Every one of them left of Mao. And the phony news. I may have to close 'em all down. Nobody pays attention to the news anyway. Now, General, those there nano-drones gotta be ready to go tomorrow. Just how long do ya plan to hold this up, *huh?* Forty-eight hours ain't unacceptable!"

"Doctor Ooze and his team are eager to launch them, Sir, but there are a few bugs in the drones yet to work out."

"Bugs in the drones? How'd they git there?"

"What, Sir?"

"Bugs, Bughump. *Bugs?*"

"I just meant...I mean...adjustments, Sir. Adjustments with the guidance system."

"Why didn't ya say so?"

"*Ah*...stress, Sir. But we're on track, Mister President. We're all ready to monitor those drones right here from our lab, Sir."

"How many, Bughump?"

"For the trial run to Queen City, a dozen should give us a

good idea. If all systems work as they should, we can produce thousands within a month. We'll have the technology to monitor Russia, China, all of the Middle-East, Iran, North Korea, and the Mexican border."

"What about Canada and France?"

"Of course. And, if we need to search every home in America, we could."

"Perfect, Bughump, perfect."

"We could send a drone up the Attorney General's ass to see what he ate for lunch. God bless America!"

"Nope. The Attorney General is on my side. He does what I tell 'im. Besides, I already know what's up his ass, Bughump."

"I…I see, Sir."

"We gotta hunt down every one of them there terrorists… every brown person, every squinty eyed motherfucker!"

"There will be no place for them to hide, Sir."

President Dumbazz began to breathe heavily and said, "Okay. If it must be it must be. I get it. Forty-eight hours it is, Bughump. I'm so fucking happy, I want to piss my pants!"

"Very good, Sir. May I watch, Sir?"

"Get on you knees, General."

V's view was blocked when the President leaned against the wall's chink. She could no longer hear their voices. V surmised that the room she was observing was connected to miles of the underground complex for the United States Space Command, the Air Force System Command, and other top secret agencies buried deep within Cheyenne Mountain. V guessed that the entrance to the complex in Colorado Springs was about twenty miles from where she stood. President Dumbazz moved away from blocking her view. Again, V peered through the chink, but this time she felt the wall of rocks move. *"Shit!"* V said under her breath. The chink broadened and she froze in place. *"What can they do, shoot me?"* And then she thought, *"They might."* An uniformed guard walked directly toward V. However hard she tried to move, she stood frozen, for fear of stumbling into stalagmites, into the sharp daggers of stalactites, into who knows what.

"Thank you, Bughump. That was good. You can get up now."

"Thank you, Mister President. It is my pleasure to serve you, Sir."

"Of course it is. You wanna to do it again sometime?"

"Of course I do, Sir. *Anytime*."

The rock door slowly slid back into place, closing the chink. Without a sliver of light to guide her, V groped her way on hands and knees to Snow White's crotch and her sleeping wife. When V reached Lily, she became aware of the stinging abrasions on her hands and on her knees. Sweating, shaking, and breathing heavily, V rolled over next to Lily, put her arms around her, and said to herself, *"What's a nano-drone? Why do they look like mosquitoes? What did General Bughump just do for the President?"*

The next thing V knew the cave's lights came on. She shook Lily, "Lil, we've got to get out of here. *Now.*"

"What?" Lily yawned.

"We must get out of here, STAT." V urgently murmured.

"What?"

"We've got to...Are you fucking deaf?"

"Why?" Another yawn.

V whispered more loudly, *"I'm having an anxiety attack!"* That seemed to do it.

When they arrived topside, cave enthusiasts were beginning to line-up at the teepee for the privilege of being overcharged to explore what V would just as soon forget. How can she keep this to herself? She can't. It's not in her nature.

"Oh my God, V. Poor baby. We need to contact somebody," declared Peter.

"Who, Peter? It is a government facility. There is no one to contact, Peter."

"Sweet baby Jesus."

"There's more."

"Oh?"

"As the door of rocks closed there was a flash. I am certain it was a camera. They know who I am."

"You don't know that, V. Besides they wouldn't know who you are. Surely you were wearing one of your hats, dear heart."

"Of course."

"They'll never know who you are. You could have been a tourist from Texas."

"Texas! You can do better than that!"

"Oklahoma." All Peter got in return was some sort of indecipherable, convoluted expression. He continued, "Okay, Canada. Relax. You're safe now. You're from Canada, dear heart."

"I hope they never identify..." V sighed, took a deep breath before continuing, "Thank you, Peter. I feel better. What else do you suppose is hiding behind the Disney rock door?" V proceeded to answer her own question, "More war stuff, most likely." She pulled herself together, somewhat, before saying, "So, besides reading your own writing, what else have you been up to, Peter?"

"I've been simply trying to transcend time, while waiting for the two of you to return."

"You will need more than 'simply trying' to transcend time. If that is really what you want to do. I can't see why. Besides, you will need to do what it takes to get to Carnegie Hall, and you will certainly need to stop reading yourself after publication. Incestuous reading, I should think."

After a protracted silence, taking a closer appraisal of V's condition, Peter placated ever so sweetly. "All things considered, dear heart, you're looking far better than anyone should possibly expect after going through such a horrendous ordeal."

"Good to know, Sweetie. Thank you. I am sorry...just out of sorts." V replied, took a deep breath, and exhaled.

"Shall I tell you my good news?" asked an enlivened O'Toole, anxious to speak the speech he had carefully rehearsed, but now he would need to add some empathy, sorrow and some touchy-feely stuff.

"I would love hearing your good news, Peter." Peter began to open his mouth when V forged ahead, "But first, what do you think is going on? Spy bugs for the Pentagon? Yes, of course. I remember hearing something...."

The thunderous sound of someone banging on the front door. Lily shouted from the other side of Dionysos, "I'll get it!"

"Please do. I have a wretched headache. No Mormons!"

V's horrifying night was taking its toll. She thought about having overheard some sort of debauched espionage involving the President himself. She thought about her night on the dank floor of a cave. She felt exhausted. She was hungry. She was stinking of bat guano, Volkswagen Bug exhaust fumes and sweat. Mauve dye from her hat had drooled down the sides of her face. In summary, all things considered, V felt there was every reason to feel that if everything wasn't all about her, it damn well ought to be.

Lily entered the room and stood frozen with eyes wide, mouth agape, and speechless.

"Are you just going to stand there looking like a cloven-hoofed creature caught in the headlights?"

"I..."

"For Pete's sake! Who is at the door, Lillian?"

"I think it's that weird little guy with the hood you were talking to. You know. From the caves."

"Let him in."

"He's already in."

"Then bring him in here. *Wait.* I'll go meet him." V picked herself up and left the room, abandoning Lily to listen to Peter telling her about his outrageously false good reviews in London.

Peter can be as self-focused as Billy Butts sometimes; only Billy is a lot more fun—he exaggerates with more imagination than common sense. *"Is there a difference between exaggerating and lying?"* Peter questioned himself. *"One hopes so."*

"I hear a meowing," said Peter O'Toole, cocking his ear. "Must be Mercury. Where's it coming from? Sounds like...."

Pudgy Penny poked her head into the parlor and yelled, "I'm on it! Old Max must have left Merc in the basement, or someone let him in. Maybe it was a spy bug."

"You were listening!"

"Of course. That's what we do." Pudgy and Piggy ran into the basement and sure enough, there was Mercury who wasted no time running straight up the stairs and out. Something caught the twins attention. "What's that?"

"Looks like...rhubarb and strawberry preserves!"

Piggy Peter grabbed the jar and ran to his room, with Pudgy Penny in pursuit.

* * *

Gert was visibly worried as she tended to the body of her husband, who had never been out of it—his body that is—for more than one or two hours and never during daylight, but this time it's been nearly twenty-four hours since Charlie vacated, leaving his body eerily still with nearly imperceptible shallow breathing, as though he were in suspended animation, which he pretty much was. Gert put her ear against his hairy chest, caught a quick whiff of fried Telmatobius and boiled Huamantanga potatoes leftover from yesterday, or maybe it was the day before, and listened to his heartbeat which had slowed dangerously close to a standstill. His breathing was nearly undetectable. The mole just above the right side of her lips twitched, as it often did in times of stress. It was not the black mole, that was as high as it was round, its circumference the size of a dime, and that others found little less than vastly disconcerting; it was the long, stiff, brown, red and gray hairs that grew to nearly an inch from out the center of the mole that reminded Gert of an Andean fox, which she didn't mind at all. She loved it, in fact. Her rusty gray hair, elongated nose and pointed chin, only reinforced her similarity to the indigenous animal. Her whiskers were the frosting on her *trompe l'oeil*. Gert never cut nor plucked them since her visions from just a hint of peyote, told her that the sacred fox was her ally and protector, and she believed it with all her heart. Shortly after Gert's revelation, she tried to mimic the mannerisms of a fox, but only got herself shipped to a mental hospital in nearby Puno. After a couple months of shock therapy on multiple occasions and the threat of a lobotomy, Gert was released and returned to Puerto Nostradamus believing she truly was an Andean fox disguised as a woman; she keeps that revelation to herself; she gave up the mannerisms, but kept the whiskers; yet Gert knew, in fact, that she actually was a genuine fox. A prodigious red fox, dancing the Argentine tango with an invisible partner in the dead of night, had been reported by at least a dozen former guests of Puerto Nostradamus.

Gert ran outside to find those bewitching brothers. *"Alfredo, Álvaro, ven pronto!"*

* * *

V yawned, mostly from the boring conversation she having with the body of the weird little guy with Charlie's spirit inside. V could not listen while looking at him. The vision of the little man created an uneasy, queasy feeling, knowing that Charlie's spirit was inside. "You told me all this, Charlie. I have better things to do and if I do not, I shall find some." Charlie laughed and they hugged and exchanged friendly cheek-kisses. Reluctantly, V was hugging and cheek-kissing a short narrow-eyed man with only one name—Faakhir—whose entire body reeked of clarified butter and the scent of two distinct curries.

"I had another vision, Victoria."

"What?"

"A vision. Somebody removed the book that your father kept hidden in the basement."

"Now you have my attention. What book? And how do you know this?"

"I'm still one with the Brotherhood, as you know."

"I didn't know."

"Now you do. Those of us of The Brotherhood of Solar Agnation, sometimes confused with the Illuminati, which doesn't exist and never did, can see visions with our third eye. Like I said, we're not the Illuminati. Remember that there is no such thing."

"Why did your third eye not see who took the book...and where do you keep your third eye?" V suffered a Lucy moment.

"You already know that, Victoria. To really see, one must enter the fourth dimension."

"I see."

"Unlikely."

"Charlie, I have read dozens of books on this subject and they have all been duplicitous and badly written; every single one of them, Charlie." She needed to say his name twice to reaffirm herself that the little man before her was indeed Charlie.

"This book is tens of thousands of years old. It is now in the world, where no one knows what horrific catastrophes might follow. The rumor in the ether regions is that the book was originally a children's book; but in the wrong hands...well, who knows? Victoria, the book must be found. I don't know exactly what it's capable of. Your father never let any of us in the Brotherhood touch it. So, I don't really know much of anything about it."

"Right. *Who knows?* You certainly do not know much of anything, Charlie. Charlie, why are you telling me this?"

"Because, Victoria, I have reason to believe that it can open doors to unexplored dimensions and that could be very dangerous in the hands of the uninitiated."

"You are out of your mind, Charlie. You do know that, right? I've heard all this bullshit before."

"Have you heard the good news about the new color, never before seen on Earth? By the way, do you know how vile you stink?"

* * *

The shirtless brothers, Alfredo and Álvaro, came running.

They were buff and bronzed young men in tight white short-shorts, bulging clearly down to their nethermost. They were delicious, according to a good many guests. Their bulges sold front row tickets. Was that an exaggeration, a hyperbole, or did they find another use for their old socks? Alfredo was in his late twenties, Álvaro in his early thirties, both were hugely popular with the guests; female and male alike. Following closely on the heels of the brothers was Juan Carlos, alpaca shearer, gardener, general handyman, less attractive than the brothers, and he stank indescribably; except directly after his weekly Sunday morning bath. Rosemary Paola, the cook, and Salome Otilia, who did housecleaning and various other odd jobs for the guests, quickly followed. Miguel Angel, who could read minds, kept his distance far behind.

"Oh, thank goodness you're here," said Gert, visibly in distress.

"What's wrong, Miss Gert?" Álvaro asked. Alfredo stood next to his brother, looking gloomily at Charlie's body, which was unmoving and seemingly breathless.

"We must do the pinching massage. Pronto! Pronto!" Gert, with her nose twitching and the hairs in her mole standing straight out, barked—*literally barked.*

There were several candles burning near where Charlie lay unnaturally still. Incense filled the room with a thick pungent fog. The pinching massage was about to begin. Gasps were heard from several of those who remained outside.

* * *

V and the weird little guy with Charlie inside of him were still talking."How did you get here?" V asked.

"Astro-projection, of course. What did you think?"

"I was asking the little man."

"He can't hear you, but I found and got into him while he was hitchhiking, and getting nowhere. Finally, we got picked up by an eighteen wheeler hauling something the driver wouldn't tell the little man what, but I'm sure I heard voices in the trailer speaking

Spanish. When I asked, he said *'gnomes'* and the rest of the drive was in an unpleasant thick fog of silence. Gnomes, my ass!"

"Oh, my!"

"Oh, yes," Charlie said twitching and jerking before saying, "Oh, no!"

"What is it?"

Charlie continued twitching and jerking. On a one to ten scale, his pain was about an eleven. "*Ow, ow, ow!* I've got to go back! The pinching massage has..." Suddenly the twitching and jerking stopped.

"You lady from cave. No found man room. Where I?" asked Faakhir.

"Shady Sanctum."

"How get here?"

"Like everybody else, nobody knows." With that she gently escorted the confused man out the door.

Lily was still sitting in her usual comfy chair as V entered. "What did he want?"

"It's a long story, Lily. I'll tell you all about it after I've taken a bath. Where's Peter?"

"Had to get home to do something. He was never quite plain about what. He ran out the kitchen door. I never noticed before, but that man has the squarest ass I've ever seen."

"That is because he sits on it all day. Poor thing. I am off to take a bath. I feel like crap.

* * *

I remember the book you should you gave it to the devil brats you knew they were Monsanto's kids at the time I got to do something about them no Maxfield you've got to do something about yourself I want a dummy for what so I can talk to you without talking to myself you've messed-up time again no I didn't you rearranged the lives of others the futuretime and pastime they don't know it yes they do deep down inside they know it they have no sense for it and now it's time to wake up I am awake no you're not you're Haitian dough gum sleepwalking dead WAKE UP!

SEVEN
may I put my hands on her

Cardinal Rotundo minced forward on the legs of a Corgi. Shaped like a hot air balloon, Rotundo's red ensemble covered a heap of venial sins. His face was round, pink, and oily from an overlay of cheap moisturizer bought in the Vatican gift shop. His Eminence is balding with short salt and pepper hairs loitering above his ears. When he smiles, he is irresistible. When he frowns, everybody wants to hug him. He is well-liked, unpredictable, funny, generous, and a standup guy—*a mensch*. Cardinal Rotundo embraced a doctrine he calls, "The Will to Silliness." Being silly whenever possible, according to Rotundo, is also a way to worship God, "to give Him a laugh." Rotundo tends to be self-indulgent, a voluptuary, but only with the simple pleasures; food mostly. He repents several times daily. A typical Cardinal Rotundo joke is: *"Without the gift of guilt, you might as well play the piano without the gift of talent."* Perhaps "joke" is a misnomer, since he tells it mostly to dump culpability on whiners who, most likely, never understood it.

Rotundo toddled along the hallway gallery of former Popes on his way to the Papal Office. He shuddered, stepped lively, blessed himself to ward off any evil that may linger within the canvas of the painting of Pope Alexander VI—*a Borgia!* When Rotundo reached the Swiss Guards he signaled for them to stand aside. They did, as they always do for the Papal Secretary. He was about to knock the secret knock when the door flew open and two young men, who served on the altar of the Pontiff's most private chapel—hidden away somewhere in the Papal Palace, where sacraments were given by invitation only—sauntered out with a large box of sweets; cannoli and biscotti were carefully placed around a mountain of torroni. The young men were busily chewing and dribbling their treats as they breezed past Cardinal Rotundo, who could not resist sniffing the air for a hint of torroni and the scent of youth as he entered the Papal Office.

It is a dreadfully long walk to where Pope Arshmann (a.k.a.

Pope not so Innocent XIII) sat behind a Baroque desk that dwarfed his ludicrous, shriveled appearance. His Excellency was a steely man on either side of one-hundred. Bets were on the worrisome side. His protuberant nose narrowed to a sharp point, appearing to support his watery, blazing red eyes that were way too closely set; one might call them beady, pig-eyed, or demonic. Most go with "demonic." His lips, thin, gray, pursed and pinched, are attached to his nose in such a way as to leave no visible space for a mustache, however thin. He had the disgusting habit of darting his tongue across the tip of his hairy nostrils, licking his lips, then making a smacking sound as he kissed the air with his attenuated lips puckered into a constricted anus. He was an old withered German asshole wearing a skimpy white bedraggled wig. Pope Arshmann was never the best of anyone's company.

"A blessed day, Holy Father," Rotundo cheerily said as he approached Pope Arshmann to kiss his ring.

"Oh, get off it, Rotundo! None of your slobber today. *Oink, oink.*"

"Yes, Holy Father."

"Well?"

"Well?"

"And?"

"Huh...oh...um. I come with worrisome news." Trembling, Rotundo lost his cheer. "It's about the traitor and what he stole."

"There have been so many thieves and traitors, Rotundo. Who keeps count? No traitor could be worse than Luther, *for God's sake!*" After a few moments of trying to remember the names of some wicked traitors, none came to the Pope's befogged mind. He wearily asked, "Well...tell Us, Rotundo. *Oink, oink.*"

A respite of fearsome silence before Rotundo swallowed hard and delivered the worrisome news, "Brother Aires."

After taking a worrisome pause, a confident Arshmann said, "Brother Aires is dead, fatso. *Oink, oink!* Dead for decades.

We had that radical sect of Agnationers excommunicated and banned from practicing the unspeakable. We quickly stomped out those harbingers of evil. They were crushed, crippled, and or, sent to live within the Loving Hands of God Almighty. Although, Our Lord does not allow just anybody into His hands, crushed or otherwise, does He? Don't answer, Lard-o. Some of those heretic Agnationers got away and scattered like cockroaches. Others joined the Jesuits, and the rest disappeared to We do not know where. Do you? You can answer that one. *Oink, oink.*"

"No, your Holiness. I cannot. I don't know anyone who practices the unthinkable."

"Simpleton. We did not say 'unthinkable.' We said 'unspeakable,' and there is a Hell of a difference; two conflicting concepts on two opposing planes. You, you, you Italian meat ball!"

"I had no idea."

"Ideas don't come easy, Porky. *Oink, oink!* That takes *ein Gehirn*. So, of course you had no idea. How could you?" Arshmann, leaned back in his smug king-of-the-only-real-church pose, continued, "We sent an envoy to his funeral to make certain it was the body of the excommunicated heretic resting ten feet below thrice blessed cement. The mourners were easily led to believe that all that the extra four feet and cement filling the grave was Our customary Rite of Burial when a Brother leaves under his circumstances. Our Most Holy Mother Church paid all burial expenses, as well as free souvenirs of blessed rosaries. We may have forgotten to bless them. What does it matter to peasants anyway? Don't answer. We gave them catechisms We might have blessed. All with embarrassingly."

"That may be, Your Holiness, but...."

"How dare you 'but' We!?"

"Sorry. I won't do it again."

"You always do it again. We infallibly tell you, the traitor is blistering in the blue flames of Hell, piggy pork poo you!"

"Holy Father, forgive me, but it is not exactly about the dead traitor. It is something far worse." There had never been a more ear-splitting silence heard throughout Vatican City than the silence that emanated from the staring pig-eyes of His Holiness. Petrified, Rotundo closed his eyes and with brave briskness said, "Somebody is reading the book."

Arshmann took his time before cautiously asking, "What book, Our most dearest Cardinal?"

"The one you told me about years ago. You know, the one with the new color. The book Brother Aires stole."

With each word spoken by Cardinal Rotundo, the Pope stiffened into an unnerving bleakness until, finally, he asked, slowly, deliberately, venomously, "And you divined this? How?" You may answer both questions, now."

"*Visions,* Your Holiness. The Cardinals have been given a sign," Rotundo answered. "They are having visions."

With dismissive hand gestures, Arshmann shouted, "That is what Cardinals do, *dummkopf!* They have visions. That is their job. Most here, We must confess, have visions of sitting in the all-powerful chair."

"The one you are in, Holy Father?"

"Are you a jackass, Rotundo!? Yes, of course the chair We are sitting in. *Oink, oink!* We do not care for the visions you or anybody else could conjure with your itty bitty teeny weeny brains. Thanks be to God, We will not need to be here to see the next ass that sits in this chair. *Eselhengst!*"

"*He sounds like a mad scientist in an old black and white movie,*" Rotundo thought before saying, "That chair has never been on my mind, Your Holiness."

"That's because you do not have a mind. AND, you will, naturally and especially, continue reporting any devious machinations among the purples and reds, even if you are merely suspicious of their seditious plots. For that Most Holy Duty, We will see you go directly to Heaven. It won't happen today. At least, We don't think so. In the meanwhile, you have special dispensation for gluttony and material lust."

"I appreciate that, Holy Father. I do eat too much and I desire a good pair of Gucci shoes. However, Holy Father, I think 'gluttony' and 'lust' are rather extreme."

"We don't." The Pope's German accent broke through his Italian whenever he was apoplectic with rage. "Any other evidence of the book?"

"Whispers on the astral plane."

"Why didn't you say this before, *Schwein? Oink, oink.* Where was it found? Answer Us quickly!"

"Colorado. In a place called Queen City, Your Holiness."

"You have given Us disturbing news. *Snort, snort.*"

"I am so sorry, Your Holiness."

Arshmann sneered. "Of course you are sorry. You are a sorry barrel of waste who delights in delivering Us diabolical news. We went to Queen City in Our youth and We found it distasteful. It reeked of evil and nasty underwear. You know nasty underwear, don't you? Shut up. *Oink, oink!* We saw a lot of filthy *Unterhosen* there. That is where Brother Aires lived and that is where he died. The sting of a bee, as We recall. *Oink, oink.*"

Arshmann had visited Queen City while touring the United States. The day he left Queen City, lightning struck the newly ordained Basilica. That was the exact same day Brother Aires (a.k.a. V's father, the late Reverend Aires) was stung by a rare tropical bee and died. *Oink, oink.*

"You are *oinking*, Your Holiness."

"How dare you, you—"

"His Holiness told me to tell Your Holiness when He *oinked.*"

"We told you, but We did not *oink!*"

"I misheard, Holy Father. Forgive me."

"What are you? Some kind of child? Now tell Us where We were? You may answer only the last one."

Rotundo thought for a couple seconds before answering,

"Queen City."

"*Ah* yes, Queen City! Dark Angels walk the streets of Queen City. We bet you didn't know that."

"The book has been moved, Your Holiness. I know nothing else, other than it is in Queen City. Where in Queen City, who knows? Only the one who does know, is the one who has it."

"We hear, *oink, oink*, your simpleminded point. You always make me laugh, my little piggy. *Heehaw, heehaw, heehaw!* Do you know where the book came from?" Arshmann quizzed. "Of course, you don't"

"No, I do not, Your Holiness."

"*Holzkopf!* It is prehistoric! Aires absconded with it from the library directly below this office!"

"How can a book be prehistoric?"

"What did We say about Our lack of appreciation for queries?" asked the sharp-tongued Pope while folding his face into deep scarlet Chinese Sharpei furrows. "Go ahead. Tell Us."

Rotundo wondered when the old hyena started referring to himself as *We* every chance he gets? "Not to question His Holiness, however, I was only wondering, Your Holiness...."

"No *wondering*. No *questions*. No *buts*. We disapprove of the twaddle We hear in your voice when you say, 'Your Holiness,' fatso."

"*Ahh...I...I...*"

"You twaddled!"

"I did not mean to twaddle, Your..."

"Shut up! It came from outer space!" Arshmann shouted. "You are a cabbage head! *Gehen! Gehen! Gehen!* Go back to your office. We must make appropriate arrangements. By We, We mean *you. You,* will make the arrangements, and fast. Go! *Shoo, shoo! Gehen!* Run, my little porker. My little Rolly Polly, run! *Oink, oink, oink!*"

Rotundo backed towards the door, stopped and asked, "Your Holiness wouldn't have a couple extra pieces of torroni?"

There came no answer; only the long, loud silence of a red-eyed Pope to accompany the Papal Secretary to the other side of the door, where Rotundo urinated himself uncontrollably. The Swiss Guards giggled.

* * *

Back in Queen City, Carla Bean was frantic. Sunday morning and her Greek hadn't returned. From where? *"A walk, he said. A walk my ass! Twelve hours ago and he still hasn't returned from his goddamned walk."*

Carla had been awake all night, more or less, thrashing and writhing with anger from having a prized possession stolen; the agony from disbelief that her prized possession had walked out on its owner; the mania from insanity when considering her prized possession might be dead, or worse; her prized possession might be in another's bed. *"If I find out whose bed it is I will kill the bitch!"* No matter how, Carla Bean needed to know posthaste which bitch to kill, so she called every bitch she knew to call concerning her Greek's whereabouts. Her last bitch-call was to Billy Butts. Her iPhone felt warm, so she sniffed for a scent of burning plastic and detected nothing. She did, however, detect something other than sincerity at play with Billy Butts. Sincerity is certainly at risk with so many Anglophiles concentrated on Queen City's Capitol Hill, where what one says is often rehearsed, where one must take care in idle café chatter where what one says one day may be weaponized for use on another day.

"Sorry, darling," Billy said. "The last time I saw what's-his-face was on the bus, I think. Or maybe not. I'm never sure about these things, Carla. It could have been somewhere else. Let's see; before the coffee shop, I think. Eddy Spaghetti and I were having double espressos and Gunnysack Stanley was there, too. Or maybe someone else. Anyway, Stanley or not, he wanted us to join him. Eddie Spaghetti left for the baths, but I stayed and said sure why not and then we talked theatre, like professionals always do, until Chu'mana, the black snake woman, slid in between us. Do you know Chu'mana? Chu'mana's real name must never be spoken. That's why I don't know it. She's a princess, but when she wants, she can turn herself into a long black snake. Maybe poisonous. I don't know. That would be terrible, wouldn't it? I should ask her. When she appears in her human form. She's a poet, too. Chu'mana certainly looks like a poet princess. I hope she never bites me."

"Billy, shut the fuck up! I just spoke with someone who told me you dragged my Al out of Charlie's and took him home with you."

"*Huh?* What? Really? That's silly. Who told you that?"

"I won't tell you that. Where is my Greek!?"

"I don't know! Why don't you ask Tommy Too-Much? He's the one who left with your precious Greek. *Not me!*"

"WHAT?"

"All I know is I took what's-his-name to Charlie's for a beer. He asked me to dance, begged me really. In Greek, of course, but he didn't need English to tell me what he wanted. He grabbed me and pulled me onto the dance floor. He's a good dancer. He is allowed to dance, isn't he? Ask your Greek. He'll tell you, if you can understand him. We used mostly sign language. Did you know that words are slower than using your hands? Or using your hands is faster? By the time somebody tells you what they have to say, it's already done. Next thing I know he drops me in the middle of Whitney Houston, poor Whitney...*I Wanna Dance With Somebody*...that's an oldie but I still love it. Who doesn't? Anyway, after he drops me I see him leaving with Too-Much. Now I'd like to go back to bed." He touched the red phone icon on his cellphone and quickly called Too-Much to give him a heads-up. Too-Much abhorred every word of the message, and the messenger even more.

At the end of a long story, filled with wasted words, Billy said, "So you better get rid of him posthaste! She's probably on her way over to your place right now, Tommy."

"But I didn't...you fucking rat! Why? I really don't understand you. I can't tell you anything, can I! *Why?*"

Butts rambled on and on about trifles and the incomprehensible—the incomprehensible being his favorite subject—until he finally said, "I don't know why and I don't know anything."

Too-Much restrained from saying anything more to his former friend and betrayer...except, "Too late, Butts! I think she's at the door, asshole!"

Sometimes what one repeats comes back to bite in a matter of minutes.

*　*　*

V and Lillian sat catty-cornered in two well-worn toffee, cream and chocolate colored wing-back chairs. They gracefully dunked finger-tip bits of cranberry scones into lemon curd and sipped Mo Siegel's divine Red Zinger tea. They were clearly too anglo-fucking-posh!

"I looked everywhere, Lily. The cellar. Max's room. Under Max's bed where he hides and claims to makes himself invisible."

"How does he do that, V?"

"I don't believe he does," V tossed off. "I found nothing in Pudgy's nor Penny's room. Have you *seen* their rooms?"

"Once I did. A year or so ago." Lily answered with a just-ate-a-slug grin. "Disgusting," she quickly added.

"No surprise there. I just don't know where it went, Lil."

"Don't look at me, V. You know how I feel about Voodoo."

"The book is not Voodoo. It's something else. I don't know what yet. However, I am reasonably certain that Voodoo is child's play compared to Daddy's book." There was a worrisome silence. V poured herself another cup of Red Zinger before asking, "Lily, who went into the cellar?"

"Well, it wasn't me. Wait a minute. Somebody did open the cellar door, but just long enough to let Mercury out. *Oh,* and I think the twins may have gone down there. I'm not certain, but I'd put the blame on the twins."

"You think?" V interrogated.

"I think they're the spawn of Satan and likely to do

anything felonious."

"Oh my. I guess its possible. What about Peter?" V asked, not waiting for an answer, "Forget it. It wouldn't be him."

"If Peter did go in the cellar, V, I'm not aware of it."

"You should start, for your own good, being more aware of things, Lily. It makes one wonder what choices you may have missed."

"*Huh?* Give me a fucking break, Victoria! You've been smoking some bad grass."

* * *

Peter O'Toole stood naked, positioning himself in front of his full-length leaner-mirror within a gold-gilded frame screaming with filigree and bad taste. Love no longer visits Peter's bedroom, unless infrequent and short-stayed trysts count for something. It is doubtful that any of his tricks ever caught a real glimpse of his bedroom. None were ever invited to stay for breakfast, except for one beautiful blond boy who was homeless and penniless, so Peter thought it a kindness to send him off with a warm, hearty breakfast and thirty dollars. Other than that one stunning exception, sex was over so fast that most of his tricks found themselves out the door with half-masted dicks and untied shoes before the cock crows, so to speak. O'Toole told himself that time in bed was sapping his creative juices. Although, he never really believed it. When the loveless deed is done, it is done. Peter O'Toole had become a sad and lonely man who believes himself a failure, and one who has moved dangerously close to the edge of bitter. However, he hasn't yet allowed himself to show that face to anyone, nor does he plan to. He figures that if you hide and deny a thing, sooner or later, it's bound to shrivel up and die, or regrettably limp away.

O'Toole grabbed the hand mirror laying on his bureau of drawers, went back to the standing mirror, turned his back to it and positioned the hand mirror so he could see what was causing his lower back pain. *"There you are, you little fucker. Gotcha!"* A bump of a boil exploded as he squeezed the hideous thing that had risen overnight. What the thing appeared to be was the longest blackhead ever to emerge from a human body. He touched it. *"Eww."* It was covered with slime. His pain soon disappeared. He tugged on the slimy thing. He could not help himself. He pulled and pulled more vigorously. He was giving birth. As he tugged on it, it grew faster, longer and thicker. *"It's a tail!"* The tail stopped growing at about five feet. *"I need to get rid of this,"* Peter cried to himself while looking into the mirror, *"Still, it is a fabulously impressive tail, isn't it?"* Peter thought he heard someone say *yes*, but he quickly dismissed it.

O'Toole went to the book and began to read from the opened page, the same page he had read the night before, but this time the writing began to move by itself until it finally settled with a three-dimensional bold headline: HOW TO REMOVE TAIL. And that was exactly what he needed.

The commentator on the television was talking about the inconsequential nature of religion and, especially, the inequities of Pope Innocent XIII, a.k.a. Helmut von Arshmann, former German Brown Shirt for the Nazi Party. When the Pope was once asked about his questionable duties during the war years, Arshmann's only answer was that he only followed orders. *"If that's true, he'll burn in Hell,"* Peter said to himself. Peter, having been brought up by nuns, having been educated in Catholic schools, and though he no longer attended church, he still had a soft spot for the Church.

The cover of the purloined book swung open then it snapped shut. The book's cover repeated opening and snapping shut several more times. Peter was certain that the book was laughing at him; that it was listening to his thoughts. "Stop laughing at me!" Peter shouted at the book. And then, the book, once again, began opening and snapping shut over and over again. "Stop it!" Peter bellowed. He then sweetened his approach, "Please." And the book slowly closed its cover in silence.

The television continued to blare. *"That silly fake talking head has psychotic skid marks a mile wide. Bugger the telly."* Bugger became one more affectation from Peter's London collection. *"Bugger everything! Bugger, bugger, bugger! Bugger me! I hate television!"* He was keen on the B-word for sure. He snapped his whip of a tail and said more *"buggers"* until he found himself in the arms of an invisible Fred Astaire waltzing him to the book that no longer read HOW TO REMOVE TAIL. The letters slowly morphed into flashing bright white running-lights that spelled upon the air above it: HOW TO REMOVE A FAT PORK BUTT.

"I guess you think that's funny, Mister Book!" Peter sneered.

The Goat Boy giggled as he took notes from where he hid behind the mirror with its gold-gilded frame.

* * *

Charlie awoke gasping for air, in pain from the pinching treatment and famished. The first thing, or *things*, he saw were the Krotch brothers standing over him. There was an odious scent of crude about them. Charlie knew who they were—financial terrorists. He despised them beyond human words. *"Somebody ought to do something! Bury them up to their man boobs and let the red ants eat them; one tiny bite at a time."* He saw that once in a foreign movie.

"This is Chaz and Davie Krotch" Gert informed. "They are here to search their souls."

Charlie slowly stood, wobbled, then sat on the edge of the pinching table and glared at the Krotch Brothers and venomously injected, "Then, I expect you gentlemen will be here for quite a spell. Ain't nothing to buy around here. No Congressmen today, but we do have a Governor. You should have been here last week. Ain't that right, Gert?"

"Right. Last week? I don't remember last week. What happened last week, Charlie?"

"The party, Gert. That wild party."

"I love parties, Charlie."

"We danced in the nude while burning a six-foot effigy of Ronald Reagan." Charlie smirked before continuing. "We have demon parties all the time. Congressmen fly down just to attend them. Once we conjured Satan himself. A big fat dude he was. Just the kind of man you fellas would love. I'm sure you'll both get to meet him one of these days, sooner than later. And guess what? Satan said he's gonna run for President of the United States after he settles some potentially criminal dilemmas: paying-off hookers and tax evasion. Fat chance, *huh?* Who's gonna vote for Satan?"

"Why don't you give it a rest?" said one of the snarky Krotches.

Charlie noticed a boning knife on the kitchen table. How easy it would be to grab it and plunge it into the hearts of both those sons of bitches. It would be a service to Humanity. It was tempting, but Gert might object on the grounds that it was her favorite boning knife and she wouldn't want it sullied by tainted Krotch blood.

"We'll stay until we finish searching our souls," Chaz Krotch smugly offered.

"We need to start our searching," said Davie Krotch, anxiously.

"Best you do," sniped Charlie.

"In case you're interested, we don't like our sacred hero, Ronald Reagan, being made an object of fun. People have disappeared for less."

"What about El Trumpo?"

"You're not fit to kiss his feet!"

"Thank God for that." Charlie drooled with hatred.

The Krotches inched their way backwards until they were out of the clubhouse. They then turned and marched shoulder to shoulder towards their cabin, leaving a vomitus scent of crude and greed to linger and seep into flesh and other porous objects.

"You shouldn't be so rude, Charlie. You'll feel better after you've eaten. You were gone too long. You won't be able to project for at least another month, Charlie."

"I know."

"Glad you do."

"I don't like them here, Gert. They're the most despicable men on Earth!"

"I'm sure they're not the *most*. They're paying customers, and as shameful as it feels to take money from out their grotty hands, we need it, Charlie. You know that."

"I know," Charlie sighed. "but they're up to something."

Had Charlie and Gert looked outside the window they would have seen that the Krotches did not go to their cabin, but rather, they shifted direction from the row of cabins, made a sharp left turn, and walked down the hill that led to a dirt road where a couple figures behind darkened windows were sitting in the front seat of a black van.

"Well?" The man behind the wheel asked.

"Well, Bushy Wussy, it's ours for the taking." Chaz Krotch informed him. "We'll exterminate the locals and get started right away," said Davie Krotch, with a sneering show of manufactured teeth. "We'll start fracking whenever you like. The lake will give us all the water we'll need; and we can pump the fracking shit right back into it, and nobody will be the wiser."

Bushy the Challenged enthusiastically declared, "*Let's do it.* This time we won't make no mistakes. No advisors. Dumb shits anyway. Mother always told me how to do things. So he didn't have those weapons of...of..."

Missus Bushit, the silver-haired dominatrix, unchallenged leader of the Bushit Dynasty, kicked little Bushy in the shin and whispered, *"mass destruction!"*

"...of...mass destruction. No shit. Just smelly brown people. *So what?* Mother got that one wrong."

Once again the kid got kicked in the shin.

"OUCH! They don't deserve all that oil. No *sireee*. We do. What are they gonna do with it? Sweet baby Jesus, Mother! Don't you kick me again. Remember I was two terms. Daddy was...how many, Mother? OUCH! *Damn it, Mother!*"

The Krotch brothers smiled in unison. Little Bushy couldn't

win shit without the Brothers Krotch, their money and political influence. They needed a stooge in the White House so they could make policy drafted with war-for-profit in mind. And, the endless supply of oil shale surrounding Lake Titicaca was their's for the taking. This time they wouldn't need help from SCOTUS.

Puerto Nostradamus and the land surrounding it was the perfect spot for fracking, detected by sensors built into the 281-KROTCH to discover high-grade oil shale. The 281-KROTCH is one of three private satellites owned solely by the filthy Krotches. Their plan was to bury pipelines to carry the sandy oil from Titicaca to a refinery in Texas, and a second pipeline for gas that could go most anywhere in Louisiana. So, there they were: Little dumb Bushy Wussy sat in the driver's seat and next to the car stood Greed. Dumb and Greed—a fatal attraction. In the passenger's seat sat Dolly Bushit the Boss and mother of little Bushy.

"We can start," Davie spit as he spoke, "soon as we loose those loony-tune psychos in Puerto whatever-the-fuck."

Little Bushy made a limp fist, punched his open palm and shouted, "Mission accomplished! OUCH! *Damn it, Mother!*"

* * *

Cardinal Rotundo returned to his windowless office after devouring a delightful luncheon of calamari, sea bass and seared *scallops gigante* in the Palace Trattoria with his best friend, Mother George. He sat behind his desk, opened the snack drawer and took out a foot of salami, a wedge of cheese, olives, some crusty bread and a half bottle of Chianti. *"Thank God for special dispensation."* He licked his lips and sniffed the air. There was an enticing scent wafting up from the kitchen; intoxicating, irresistible. Then he heard crackling and sizzling and inhaled the scent through the thickets of hair at the entrance to his nostrils. *"It's roasted pig!"* Then, the sounds of doors slamming, the screams of altar boys as they raced down the hallway, and the heavy feet of Swiss Guards stomping their way past Rotundo's office door.

Cardinal Rotundo opened his office door expecting to find a troupe of Italian Boy Scouts. Instead, he was greeted with heavy smoke coming from the direction of the Pope's sanctuary/office/ hideout. Rotundo waddled into the hallway and plunged into a roaring cascade of terror-stricken Roman Catholic Immortals flowing past him in a blur of black, white, crimson and purple; most notably, Cardinals Lagerhead and Tomatoe, reeking of cheap beer and Patchouli Passion from the palace gift shop, their cassocks hiked above their knees exposing their black fishnet stockings to three giggling nuns with dirty habits, who were on the cleaning crew, gushed arm-in-arm down the palace hallway, smothering from the chemical stench of Patchouli Passion. Cardinals Lagerhead and Thumbass shared a closeness rarely seen in the Papal Palace. They were seldom seen without the other, but it did not bring about a frown, a snicker, nor a giggle. Intimacy of that sort was a common occurrence. If Mother Church can overlook pedophile priests, a couple of old queens in the palace is unremarkable.

Smoke poured out from beneath the door leading into the Pontiff's office. Old habits die hard, but this was not a time for Swiss neutrality; they were the first to run. Rotundo barged into the Papal office, most of the smoke had dissipated, he beheld the charred remains of what was once Pope Arshmann. Nothing remained but a mound of acrid ashes smoldering on the seat of the throne.

Rotundo stepped gingerly towards the throne and whisked the remains from off it with a dirty white cassock that he found under the Pontiff's desk. It was covered with chocolate, caramel and pieces of torroni were stuck to it. Rotundo was certain he could smell s'mores. He carefully examined the chair for burns. There were none. *"A miracle?"* Rotundo sat on the throne, the seat of the Holy Roman Church and Big Boss over mighty empires and smelly third world countries. *"Mine! Mine! Mine!"* What a rush! At times Rotundo could be a bit of a drama queen. One "mine" should have sufficed. *"Hmm...this chair...not very comfortable. Not comfortable at all."*

Spontaneous combustion is difficult, perhaps impossible, to explain, much less, understand; however, the proof of it is in the pudding, and its pudding lay scattered in shades of gray ash across a scarlet silk rug. While eying the ashes, Rotundo remembered the condescending manner behind the words when Arshmann said, "That carpet, piggy poo, was made by naked nuns and boiled worms. *Oink, oink!*"

Cardinal Rotundo visualized himself in the role of the Pontiff, but there was no time to daydream. At that moment, Rotundo's first order of business was to inform and assemble the College of Cardinals. It was his duty, as the Pontiff's personal secretary, to contact the Cardinals and bring them to Rome. Of grave concern to Rotundo, what with his absolute hatred for Cardinals Tomatoe and Lagerhead, was how to get them on his bandwagon and help him onto The Throne; while maintaining a safe distance from any sort of familiarity with them, of course. Rotundo tried, without success, to change his hatred into like—he would settle for indifference—but he could not bring himself to it. He hated them and that was that. So, Rotundo made a secret cellphone video while the Princes of the Holy Roman Catholic Church were locked in their apartment having their way with each other before evening prayers. *"What an ugly, useless pile of undulating blubber; like two humping hippopotami,"* Rotundo said to himself. Their cardinal sins could be uploaded to the Vatican Volleyball facebook page if he wanted to, but homespun blackmail should, for the moment, do the trick. *"That ought to do it,"* thought Rotundo. Cardinal Rotundo knew he had gone beneath his better nature, and so he was forced to own his clandestine enterprise; to move on or to suffer the pain of guilt. And, since Rotundo will always suffer the pain of guilt over the least of things—his conscience would not allow him to do otherwise—he decided that there was no sin for hating the two Cardinals; however, it might be a most grievous sin were he to act upon his impulse and torture the motherfuckers. Alas, there remains within the consciousness of Rotundo a sticky residue of infinite guilt from the demonic warnings and threats of Hell's eternal fire, drilled into him by sadistic and unhinged elementary school nuns!

* * *

V and Lily frantically tried to find the book. But without success.

"I looked in the cellar countless times and I cannot find it. The book is not there," pronounced V with the smart smirk that accompanies certitude. "It is simply not there." After her certitude and the smart smirk waned, she continued, "I do not believe any of it. Max would know the truth about Daddy's Bible. I am sure of that. It is all too absurd for words, Lily."

"Then why the anxiety?"

"Because Charlie's astral projection was so emphatic. Why would he go through all that trouble to lie, or to fabricate a prank?"

"Your guess is as good as mine, V."

V sat in a thoughtful demeanor, her hands pressed against her forehead until she announced, "I choose to believe Charlie." V thought a bit more and in a let's-get-down-to-it voice she said, "Somebody made off with the book and I am going to find out who it is. Come Hell or high water, I will uncover the culprit!"

"Perhaps you overlooked it. Or it never existed." Lily was tired of hearing about the book.

"Cute. I did not overlook anything, Lily. I am certain that the book exists, but not in the basement, nor anywhere else in this house. It did not walk away on its own."

"Maxfield? The twins?"

"The twins can't read!"

"O'Toole?"

"Peter? No. Of course not."

"You never know. Just sayin'."

"Have you any idea how much I hate that phrase; *just saying?*"

"No. Should I amuse us by guessing?"

V *humphed,* and somebody knocked on the front door, giving Lily an excuse to get away from Victoria the Autocrat.

"V, stay. You sit and I'll go."

"Don't let any Mormons in!"

"*Yeah, yeah, yeah.*"

Nope. Not a Mormon in sight. It was Mercy Pentcist holding a gift-basket filled with apples while her husband, Mikey, who held not a thing, nonchalantly busied himself visualizing nothingness. It was all the rage. Mikey blinked and the nothingness he saw disappeared. Something got in its way. He struck a pose from one of many he carefully rehearsed as examples of superiority; this particular superior pose was of a man of royalty, while yet, humbling himself in the presence of the unsophisticated. This was his favorite pose and he used it oftentimes to confirm his royal heritage. No question about it. He was a prince, alright.

Lily escorted them to the parlor door, knocked once and shouted, "The Pentcists!" Lily slid open the double doors and then left the Pentcists where they stood and she strolled out into the sun. When Lily was less than half a block away from Shady Sanctum she began to feel traitor's guilt for not staying to help V through an always bewildering encounter with the Pentcists. Lily dashed back, up the concrete steps, through the foyer, into the parlor and onto the sofa.

"We were passing by and thought we'd drop in to say hello. Hello. By the way, have you given some thought to your death?" Right to the point without any tiptoeing about. Who doesn't love that? "You need a plan, dearest. Death can strike just like that," Mercy Pentcist said with a limp snap of her fingers.

"Did you see our ad in *Westword*?" Mikey asked with that oh-yes-I-almost-forgot-to-mention-it, humble me.

"Missed it," V smugly lied. "Did I forget to say what an unexpected guest you are?"

"No, but thank you just the same," smiled Mercy.

The Pentcist's ad was published between two other ads, both for marijuana dispensaries, one of which is where V and Lily buy most of their stash, so naturally the first pages they turn to are the pot ads to see if anybody is selling a good diesel with sticky buds. There they stood: the unexpected guests with their Christian hairdos between a small bottle of hash oil and hand-crafted glass bongs. V and Lily were comfortably stoned before they were interrupted by the Pentcists abrupt appearance.

"We want to give you a special deal on cremation," Mercy interjected.

"Why is that?" asked V.

"Because you are our friend," Mercy answered. "Our friend," Mikey reiterated, modeling his condescending pose.

"I am? How incredibly fabulous the two of you are," V spouted.

"So if you ever think about it..."

"Mercy, I will never think about it." V sneered joy and goodwill. "What about you, Lily? Will you ever think about it?"

"Sorry. I plan to throw myself off Mount Olympus."

"Can one actually do that, Lily?" Mercy asked.

"I don't know, Mercy. Why don't you Google it?"

"We'll give you our lowest price. So low you won't believe it. Believe you me you won't believe how low we are willing to go. Do you know the famous Doctor Fuzzlbum? He bought a policy with us." Mercy was getting out-of-control pushy.

"I might remember Doctor Fuzzlbum," V said, with an inscrutable smile. Not quite the Mona Lisa's cryptic smile, but captivatingly inscrutable enough.

Mercy smiled while handing V a brochure. "You really ought to give some consideration to...."

V suddenly began to twitch and tremble. The brochure *accidentally* flew from her hand and slapped Mercy in the face. V then began to have an extremely high-spirited fit. Her eyes rolled back under their lids. It was quite unsettling. She convulsed like a frenzied holy roller. Her body flopped onto the sofa and continued thrashing about. Her legs kicked air and her arms flung in every direction until, with a yelp and a wail, she sprang from the sofa, stood and screamed at the top of her voice, "It's all black! I don't want to go! No, no. I love to live. I love my friends. Every single one of them. Don't take me away. Oh, Lily, Lily, Lily my love, don't let them take me. I don't want to go. Don't take me now. I'm too young to die!"

Lily turned her head away from the unexpected guests until she could manage a straight face. "You don't need to go, my darling V." Lily assisted V to lie down on the sofa. V's eyes widened and closed slowly. Her breathing shallowed. Her legs stiffened. Drool began to drip from the corner of her lips before running down her chin as she choked for air. Lily ran to the bathroom, tripping over herself; and when she returned, she placed a cold towel on V's forehead. V froze, stiff as a wizard's rod.

"What is it? She's not? You know, *deceased?*" Mercy asked with seemingly grave concern.

"Not yet, Mercy. Something she picked up from a shrunken head Maxfield brought home after visiting a tribe of who knows what in who knows where. Bad juju. I knew it. I knew it the moment he brought the cursed thing into the house. It did come with a curse, of course. They always do; that's the whole point of shrunken heads. Poor Victoria. If anything should happen, she'll be a great loss. She came, she saw, she conquered the mountains and plains of Colorado. Our beloved Victoria. My wife. She puts the Queen in Queen City!"

"Oh dear. Oh my. Oh shit! The Queen?" Mercy grimaced. "Wife." Mercy scoffed.

"Is she contagious?" Mikey asked while squeezing his butt cheeks.

"We don't know, yet," Lily said with just enough histrionics to be scary, but not too scary. "Although, it doesn't seem to be contagious. Minnie Beach came down with something quite similar, but it turned out to be acid reflux. And then there was that awful virus that…I don't want to talk about it…too depressing… the mailman died."

"May I lay my hands on her?"

"Why?"

Mercy believed that her hands were instruments of God,

but as with all beliefs, they mean little until there is a material manifestation. Astonished by the question, Mercy answered, "To cure her, of course. God heals through my hands."

"Too bad God didn't heal Mercy's arthritic hands," thought Lily. Lily was flummoxed. She found herself in the middle of another existential dilemma. Lily gets herself caught in existential dilemmas at least once a week and this was a good one. *"What is wrong with these people? Crazy or just plain stupid?"* Lily decided that the Pentcists were crazy and flat out stupid. Her dilemma vanished. *"If only Sartre had kept it that simple."*

"Yes." Lily hesitantly and awkwardly answered Mercy in a tone suggesting she had the business end of a revolver pressed against her head, "If you think it will help." Lily gasped when Mercy laid her hands on V's forehead, then she squeezed the top of V's head as if she were popping a canker.

Mercy threw her arms heavenward, pleading, "Jesus, Jesus, help this poor woman, Jesus. Take the poison that festers within our contaminated sister. Spare her from sickness, pain, mistaken identity, the devil, locusts, science, Democrats and ebola."

Mercy said a lot of things Lily did not hear. For instance, she did not hear Mercy whisper into V's ear, "Jesus wants you to buy a Prometheus Society LLC afterlife policy with us. Easy monthly payments. After your initial down payment and the usual two year waiting period, of course, the policy will kick in. So, don't die...at least, not for a couple years. Show her, Jesus. Show her the way to salvation. Cure her abominable lesbianism. Show our sister in Christ that she's too old not to think about her future. Buy for Jesus. Praise the Lord. Amen."

V sat straight up and shrieked, "I am not going to take this anymore!"

Mercy shouted, *"Alleluia!"*

"Thank you, Lord Jesus," Mikey chimed in with dubious conviction.

"It's a miracle!" Mercy bellowed. "It's a miracle! Holy mother f-bomb! It's a miracle!"

In awe of the power of Jesus, the Pentcists backed towards the private parts of Dionysus. Mercy grabbed the gift basket.

"We must go. There's someone dying in Littleton." Mikey actually made that up on the spot. Thinking himself clever, Mikey forgot to pose.

"It's a miracle!" Mercy repeated.

"Yes it is," Mikey confirmed.

Dionysus split and the Pentcists departed saying many "miracles" and other twaddle as they walked through the vestibule, out the front door and down the porch concrete steps into the brilliant, dizzying sunlight. Mercy actually believed with all her heart that her hands were the blessed instruments of Jesus. Or maybe blessed instruments of God? She never quite understood the difference. Is Jesus God or the son of God? How can Jesus be God when it is plainly written that Jesus prayed to God, his father? Lily would certainly find those questions divinely existential.

"I think I cured her lesbian ways, Mikey."

"You should ask her," Mikey was snarky.

Mercy tripped over a crack in the sidewalk and spilled her gift basket of fruit into the gutter. When she went to retrieve the biggest, reddest apple, Mikey accidentally stomped on both of Mercy's hands.

"You sonofabitch! You goddamned piece of shit! You stepped on the fucking hands of Jesus! You're so fucking stupid, Mikey! I should have stayed with my first husband. He wasn't a piece of dumbass shit. He wasn't a fucking loser, you fucking loser!" From the mouth of God's servant.

"Sorry, Pumpkin." Note to Self: *"Murder the bitch!"*

Together, Mikey and Mercy Pentcist disappeared around the corner just before Mercy was mugged. The muggers, three white skinheads, grabbed her basket, but she was determined not to let it go. While Mikey watched the mugging, not lifting a finger to help her, he noted that there was only one apple at the bottom of the basket, yet Mercy continued to struggle when two more of

God's own fingers were broken by the attackers who then ran. The tall mugger threw the basket into the street, but kept the apple. Mikey smiled as he watched them run down the street and turn into an alley. *"Thanks, guys."*

"Where the fuck were you, Mikey?!"

"Why do you ask?"

The following day an article will appear in the Queen City Post: THREE BLACK MEN ATTACK CHRISTIAN BUSINESS OWNER ON HER WAY HOME FROM PRAYER MEETING. QUEEN CITY HACKER STILL AT LARGE.

EIGHT

robbery, villainy, insanity, and cardinal sins

In the wake of the Pentcists leaving, V had the heebie-jeebies, "How presumptuous! How dare she put her hands on me! Why did you let her do it, Lily?"

"What was I supposed to do, V?"

"You could have told her NO. Told them we were Atheists, Pagans, cannibals for Christ, or something equally offensive to them? They *run* if you tell them you are Roman Catholic."

"Really?"

"It works for me. Lily, she had her hands all over me. I thought she was going to grab me by the pussy or something!"

After the subject was no longer amusing, Lily confessed, "I really don't understand any of it, V. I feel embarrassed for them and angry with myself. I try to be respectful, take effort not to insult the beliefs of others, but sometimes it's just too fucking difficult when all they do is insult my beliefs."

"They do not respect *our* beliefs and they never will. Why don't we give their mumble-jumbo shit right back at them? It's not enough not to be a part of their psychosis, we should get off the highroad, Lily, and tell it as it is. Besides, the highroad is bumper to bumper with hypocrites."

"S'pose," Lily sighed.

"Lily, she didn't even have the curtesy to leave the fucking basket. That should tell you a thing or two about her magic hands, and the greedy guilt-riddled brain of a death merchant."

"Apples," Lily said.

"Apples?"

"The basket. Apples."

"*Hmm.* From the hands of the serpent. They must have picked up the droppings from Old Pansy's tree. If that doesn't bring her bad juju, the devil knows what will."

"He does?"

"I hope so."

A knock on the front door. Lily was already en route to the door when V shouted, "Tell them we are not buying their death service and slam the goddamn door in their faces!"

It wasn't the Pentcists. The door into the parlor slowly opened and there stood a sad, contrite, miserable Peter O'Toole holding the book wrapped in wax paper in one hand and his five-foot long tail in the other.

* * *

The Vatican Palace was in a state of disarray as Cardinals gathered to celebrate the life of Pope Innocent XIII, and to jockey for the grand prize: The Throne.

Most of the Cardinals had made their way to the Vatican, yet more were yet to arrive. There were whispers that Cardinal Alletti would be the next Pope. Alletti had been a young priest who taught mathematics at a Salesian school a few short blocks from Vatican City. When Arshmann met the young Alletti in a foreign film art house in Roma, they bonded instantly for whatever dubious, or nasty reason. Arshmann wasted no time appointing him Cardinal, to the astonishment of the status quo. The Vatican Boys —Brothers, Priests, Bishops and Cardinals—did not like Alletti; although, they disliked Cardinals Tomatoe and Lagerhead even more.

No one likes a goody-goody. Alletti was, without question, a climber who used good cheer, his youth, a buff body and a nine inch tool to obfuscate his devious intent. From schoolteacher to Cardinal overnight! The other Cardinals felt they had fought long and ruthlessly for their Cardinalships; they were not appointed overnight by a horny, coldblooded, bloodsucking Nazi.

Most of the Cardinals felt obliged to admit that Alletti was pious in his own complacent way. He was obedient and intelligent, as far as those things go, but everyone agreed that under his manicured veneer he was rabidly seditious; a fledgling parish priest who rose to the position of Arshmann's loyal bootlicker. He now had to think about licking another Pope's slippers, once again, and it terrified Alletti the Bootlicker. Therefore, he had no choice but to become the next Pope himself. *"I know I can. I know I will. Who better than me? I am the best! I am. I am. I am the best man for the job. I want to be Pope. I must be Pope."* For whatever reason, Alletti did not have enough faith in himself to actualize the wants he desired. He needed encouragement, he needed to feel that he was something, worth something—something none of the other Cardinals ever gave him credit for. *"No one sees the real me. I am fabulous!"*

On various occasions our good Cardinal Bootlicker wrote to Cardinals in all four corners of the Earth, so to speak. Alletti's missives and emails were designed to massage the egos of his readers; but, undermost, to create a portrait of the author as a humble man, a man of The Church, a man of salt, a man of loyalty, a man of trust, and a man who could take their message and run with it. Those on the receiving end of Cardinal Bootlicker's lovely, considerate, and ambiguous missives would never forget the joy they felt from knowing a refreshing and fair-minded man of The Church: Cardinal Alletti the Bootlicker. Alletti had a knack for seeming to be the best of all things to all people. *"I'm a shoe-in. The next Pope. No doubt,"* thought Bootlicker. *"I am going to be Pope if I die trying!"* Perhaps, he never heard the adage; be careful what you wish for. *"Let me pray for my perfect Pope name... um...."*

Be that as it may, Bootlicker never took the time to know anything about Cardinal Rotundo other than "too fat." Nor did he know anything about the former Sadie Ginsburg—aka Mother George—other than her un-abating stream of uncontrollable profanities. Bootlicker should have paid more attention to them, otherwise he would have known to gird himself against their masterful machinations.

Cremation is frowned upon by Roman Catholic tradition. Arshmann's ashes were not premeditated, at least not by him. Since the cremation was not deliberate, that he didn't take his own life, there were no forgivenesses to be made, nor obstructions along the way to Arshmann's fantasy of an afterlife filled with boots, leather and young nazis, no doubt. The ashes of the body of His Holiness were poured into an ornate golden urn decorated with emeralds, rubies and topped with a ratty cross made of two splinters of wood, half the size of a toothpick, which were blessed and believed to be splinters taken from the cross upon which Jesus the Christ was crucified. Science, however, placed the splinters somewhere between the last of the Medici Popes, right up until Elvis was last seen in a Vegas laundromat—pretty much any time, really—but not anywhere near the scene of the venerated martyrdom. The urn that held the remains of Pope Arshmann was carefully placed within a clear plexiglass cube, so the mourners could see at least something of the late Pontiff. His red burial slippers were carefully placed on the top of the cube, giving it the appearance of a display in the window of a shoe boutique.

When the last of the tardy Cardinals arrive, the Papal Conclave will be locked in the Sistine Chapel to begin the carnage of electing a new Pope. There was no hope for getting out until the deed was done. The higher than High Service for Arshmann was grand to spectacular. The bells and smells alone were worth the price of admission. Cardinal Sunshine tweeted, "nix, 2 tacky & 2 gaudy fanfare 4 Arsh." That's a Cardinal for you, always the critic. Cardinals Lagerhead, Tomatoe, and Gulch thought it over the moon, especially since it was they who added their fabulousness to the shindig by supervising much of the goings-on, while carefully shifting their attention from the gladiolas to the sweaty workmen.

Everything seemed perfect; better than the old goat deserved. Mother George and Cardinal Rotundo had absolutely nothing to do with the lurid spectacle. They were in the statuary whispering ways to keep Bootlicker from The Throne, short of murder; which is neither rare nor unwonted and, most conveniently, it is sinless when done for the good of the Holy Roman Catholic Church. You will not find that written anywhere. However, the Office of Inquisition is still up and running, so there may be an answer to be found there, if an answer to the moral obligation for murder is required. For God's sake, just do it!

Rotundo saw, with abject clarity in big letters, THE THRONE. Although, he began to doubt his worthiness. He wasn't fully certain he would like being Pope. After all, the chair really uncomfortable, but he didn't want to disappoint Georgie. Rolly was willful and skillful at getting what he wanted much of the time, when he passionately wanted it; but, the Cardinal began to have some gnawing doubts. He thought he wasn't passionate enough, not suited to the office.

Georgie and Rolly (as they were known to each other), a daring team of superheroes, have been best friends since forever. Never involved on an intimate level, they are connected by their shared atypical vision. What the actual vision is that connects them remains to be untangled and beheld. "Did you know that Alletti is a fuck bunghole drag queen?" whispered Mother George casually into Rotundo's ear.

"What?" Rotundo's eyes evinced dark joy. His smile betrayed a devilish smirk. "How can you prove that, Georgie?"

"Mister Dirty Bootlicker, a countertenor, sings in drag at Il Gallo Gay Tuesday and Thursday nights. He calls himself Holly Waters. Ass licker, licorice."

"Is that the truth, Georgie?"

"Does it matter?"

"Of course it matters," Rolly answered.

"Holly Waters looks a lot like Alletti," Georgie explained. "Holy sheep shit, Batman! That's all the Cardinals need to know and, since the only jumping they ever do is to conclusions, they'll buy it sight unseen. Not the faintest whiff of scandal. What a bunch of losers. Present company excluded."

"I hope this isn't a mortal sin, Georgie."

"Certainly not, Rolly."

"You're a treasure, Georgie."

"Thank you, cocksucker."

Rolly was used to Georgie's profane syndrome and paid it little mind. "How can we get this information to the attention of the conclave, Georgie?"

"Rolly, you will find a bride of Jesus in Il Gallo Gay any night of the week. We love gossip almost as much as thwacking little children with rulers, brass bells, creating divisiveness, disseminating rumors and best of all, forcing the entire class to pay for the sins of one. We're the best when it comes to disseminating. It'll be all over the palace before midnight. Then, goodbye Cardinal Bootlicker! Vagina licker! Licker lackey!"

Mother George and Cardinal Rotundo giggled while doing their happy dance as if no one could see them. In the Vatican, however, nothing goes unseen.

* * *

Tommy Too-Much was out of intensive care. Carla Bean was in the city jail for attempted murder and with no money for bail. Her bank account had been hacked and her money flew through cyberspace to Athens. Laexandros Demosthenes Papadopoulos took to the air and was on his way back to Athens.

"I'm sorry, Tommy. I really am. This is all my fault."

"Yes. It is, Billy. It is all your fault. Well, maybe not *all* your fault. I should have known better. I should have known never to tell you anything. I should have known never to say anything in your presence that I don't want all over Capitol Hill by sunset. You can't help yourself. You're dangerous, Billy. You know, people disappear all the time in Queen City. I'm sure you don't want to be one of them."

Tears rolled down Billy's face, "I don't know what to say."

"There's nothing to say; except, stop with the blubbering. I have always wanted to ask you something, Billy. Do you cry for yourself, or others?"

"I hope she goes to prison," an abrupt change of subject, "and she'll never get out, except to be executed, of course," Billy Butts mumbled, as he sat upon what little room was left to sit on Tommy Too-Much's hospital bed. "Maybe that's too awful. I'm sure we can come up with something more suitable to her villainy than something so final. The electric chair. The needle. *Ouch!* I never liked needles. What do you think? Do you like needles. I can't imagine why. What do they use here in Colorado? Hanging? I bet they use hanging. Anyway, they used to, didn't they?"

"There's no longer a death penalty in Colorado, Billy. I'm tired of your nonsense. Thank you for coming.

"Not a problem. *So-o-o*, we're friends again, right?"

"*Yeah,*" Tommy wearily answered.

"I'm so happy for the both of us. I won't ever do anything like that again. At least, not to you. Guess what? I ran into Duchess Sylvia Rose Peterson von Smithwitz today."

* * *

Duchess Sylvia Rose Lipchitz Peterson von Smithwitz was the scourge and pariah of Society, polite or otherwise. Her so-called friends had entered her life only to take a brusque exit shortly afterward. They ran away as far and as fast as they could, without any excuse given, and departed from her life before the Duchess had time to become conscious of their absence. The spotlight of royal celebrity flashed and went out after her husband, Casper von Smithwitz, died from a green baloney sandwich. The Duchess sighs whenever she thinks of it and she thinks of little else.

There appears to be a connection between the Smithwitz death and the Bean death. Unquestionably odd, though most likely strictly coincidental. Smithwitz was a regular midnight visitor to the refrigerator. On the night of his death there was nothing in the fridge other than a single slice of baloney in a ziplock baggie next to a bottle of True Blood; not the real thing, of course, but a capricious midnight purchase from Amazon.

Baloney and hotdogs both contain the same sludge used to fill differently-sized casings. However, even if Bean and Smithwitz did die on the stroke of midnight on the same night, why weren't they found together? The coroner deduced that they were separate incidents, one having nothing to do with the other. There was no connection to the contaminated hotdog eaten by Bean and the moldy baloney eaten by Smithwitz; except, the baloney and the hotdog were purchased on the same day from Queen Soopers. To add a sharper, more piquant quality to death by indigestibles, the coroner died the following day from contaminated Rocky Mountain oysters. How far do coincidences need to go before they are no longer coincidental? Apparently, not far enough, yet.

The Duchess Sylvia could bedazzle a roomful of strangers, but she could not hold a coherent conversation. She walked as though she had an albatross suspended from each of her nipples. When she sat the albatrosses dove into her lap; hunting for sea urchins, perhaps. She was dumb enough to think she was smarter than whomever came within speaking distance, and not aware enough to know she was beyond unreasonably stupid. No wonder why nobody wants to be within walking distance of her peerless standing.

The Duchess Sylvia did not know before her husband died, that the Duke's title had been bought on eBay for two-hundred and forty-three dollars, plus postage and handling, for the certificate that came in a plain brown envelope.

Billy Butts and Duchess Sylvia Rose Lipschitz Peterson von Smithwitz were known to society as the pariah and the gadfly. Few were ever quite sure who was who since they exchanged roles as situations demanded. Billy and Duchess Sylvia shared a paucity of reality. They were made for each other.

* * *

"She looked a mess, she always does, but I adore her." Billy continued with duplicitous gallantry. "She's royalty, you know. Married a Duke. He left her nothing, but she's still a Duchess. Must be nice to be a Duchess. Did you ever want to be a Duchess? I was on my way to the Mayan to see a film about an artist nobody ever heard of. I saw Sylvia coming out of McDonald's. You did hear about the pink slime, didn't you? Anyway, the Duchess wore her black woolen dress. Stinks from across the street. It's bad enough she looks like Gertrude Stein, but twice as bad is that smelly old dress she's worn everyday since the Duke died from a midnight snack. Maybe it was a hot dog. Some kind of cold cut. When was that about? Anyway, that was one or three, I can't do numbers, Halloweens ago. Maybe it was a gunshot. I don't remember. I'm not good with facts. Don't you hate them. Great with names and faces. I know, I know. You don't have to tell me. Who wants to die on Halloween?"

Tommy Too-Much disconnected something that caused pings signaling for a nurse. He was having great difficulty with breathing, and his face went deep purple. However, Too-Much screamed as loudly as he could, "Billy! Shut the fuck up!"

PING. . .PING. . .PING. . . .

NINE

origins, orgies, and the color of magic

The twelve year old fraternal twins, Kuku and Kaka, with bright red bowl-cut hair reflecting the sun-drenched day into dancing sparks, not unlike those from the cracklings of a wildfire, watched from the gentle embankment of the river Ufat that, in a civilization thousands of thousands of years into the future, will be known as the river Euphrates.

There was a time, long before the Sumerians arrived, when the Martians came, settled and left within a few thousand years. Their new planet was becoming too hot for them. Perhaps, if they had taken better care of Mars, they would not have been forced to leave it, or die a horrible death by radiation caused by global warming. Before the Martians left Earth, for inexplicable reasons, in their rearview mirror for ports unknown, they also left behind their children to populate the Earth once again. Contemporary peoples who now claim Earth as their home are mostly descendants of Martians; an incredibly violent, sexually repressed race.

The transport ship began its descent toward the canvas of lush green vegetation that stretched into the horizon. The ship was made of quixelite, which gave it its unique color few will ever see off the planet of Sumer. After long and difficult studies, a Sumerian is prepared for the joy of practical wisdom, and the illumination that the color of quixelite imparts. When a Sumerian meditates on the color, the usual sensation is that of electricity entering the body, followed by a general euphoria from answers to questions asked long in the past, and long forgotten, yet there they are, all of a sudden. The thrill from the startling color of quixelite is pleasant, often orgasmic, always an unequaled beguiling experience.

The transport ship landed, bringing with it a most precious cargo: a book made entirely of quixelite. It was the color of magic especially forged for the twins. Quixelite is both the name of the color and the name of the mineral; like gold or silver. It can be found most anywhere on Sumer. One of the many amazing aspects of the mineral is that, when it is forged into thin sheets, it can be fashioned into books with any number of programs. A popular program on Sumer is reading stories of romance; some with as many as twelve Xs. The romance slowly takes possession of the reader, enhancing the reader's experience, until it is as real as the reader allows. Books of that nature are great summer reading; especially on the blue crystals of a warm Sumer beach.

On Sumer, the energy from quixelite enables the transportation of people—or any other solid matter—to anywhere on the planet. Sumerian scientists had been working on interplanetary disintegration-integration transportation for thousands of years, but they have yet to come up with a working model that is safe for human transport. And, yes; Sumerians are as human as Earthlings.

The Automagical Games, otherwise known as TAG, can be seen played by children in playgrounds, parks, front and backyards just about anywhere on Sumer. TAG is Sumer's most popular game. Children are taught how to play early-on to prepare them for TAG as adults. Unlike children, who use marbles and pebbles to play, adult TAG consists of a bag of fine red quixelite crystals and a place to hide. The Seeker must find the Hider, throw a fistful of crystals at the Hider before he or she escapes. When the red crystals stick to the skin of the Hider, they are absorbed into the bloodstream, which results in the Hider's ability to enter other dimensions. And, that is only the beginning of TAG.

Dimensions should not be confused with alternate universes. In all but a few cases, visiting an alternate universe requires folding space—a difficult achievement only for the well-seasoned Hider. Alternate dimensions, however, are as close as a step away. The quest of the Hider is to find his or her own way back home to their own time and place; sometimes taking up to eleven shifts—the record number of inter-dimensional travels thus far. When the Hider returns, he or she can claim the coveted prize: A deeper understanding of celestial mechanics. As simple as that.

There is nothing more valued on Sumer than quixelite and knowledge.

The parents of Kuku and her brother Kaka, are worshiped as Utu the God of Wisdom, and Gula the Goddess of Healing. The twins had no interest in following in their parent's footsteps. *"Absolutely not!"* They had no ambitions for healing the sick and no ambitions for sharing their wisdom; besides, they don't share and they *"don't care a blind man's ass"* about wisdom. They were, as always, dumber than mud and they'll probably be that way forever; and the concept of "forever" should be, in their case, taken literally.

The twins were ignorant of the fact that Utu was not their blood father. Utu did not know that the twins were conceived during the three day Festival of the Third Moon to celebrate the birth of Sin; the god of one of three moons circling Sumer. There are two other moons, but they are far too small for any respectable god or goddess to claim. The Festival of Sin is the most popular holiday on the entire planet; anything goes and everything does.

The moon's illumination poured into thirsty cups. Crystal dust was spread along streets that were filled with naked Mooners. Boys buggered boys and girls tickled one another's fancy. Men and women drank the moon. They cheered with gusto and they fornicated without inhibition, but with plentiful imagination. The taste of moon is exhilarating. King Monsanto the handsome, beguiling, seductive, horned stranger, hid behind the bushes waiting for the beautiful goddess Gula. Upon seeing her, he reached out and pulled her into the shrubbery where he schtuped her with his mighty dark power. For the entire three days of the festival they fornicated. In the meanwhile, Utu, Gula's husband, remained moon-wasted during the entire festival, having passed-out in the last stall of a men's room; the one with the glory hole you could get your head through. New Sumer public comfort stations are provided on the corner of every four blocks. It is comforting to know, that when in desperate need of relief, you're never more than half the distance to the nearest comfort station. Utu and Monsanto, King of the Underworld and Devil-at-large, pleasured themselves like two rabbits on cocaine. The goat boy watched from afar and took notes. The tangled mass of bodies writhed and wailed to the music of sweat lubricating skin-on-skin. Moans of desire. SCREAMS of fulfillment. Muffled cries from a pain nobody should want; though some did. The hair on the heap of fornicators sparkled under the bright moonlight, honoring Sin, the God of the Third Moon.

King Monsanto the Horned Devil, is the cruel and greedy son of Ayn Koultery the Throat Slitter, the Night Beast, Stealer of Dreams, certified Loony Tunes. Monsanto the Evil, who goes by many names, never had a father to emulate or to follow in his footsteps. Slow deaths from torture amused him. Force-feeding a squirming prisoner deadly poisons from nightshade and other lethal flowers, roots, plants, crushed dung beetles, just plain crushed dung, and a bevy of other delights, gave Monsanto a self-ejaculating whiz-banger. Monsanto's abominable, yet highly creative imagination pretty much kept him and his prisoners occupied. The Devil King of the Underworld's favorite enhanced torture technique was a doozy; death by relentless cabbage juice boarding, which caused the Devil King to giggle and snort at the prisoner's uncontrollable bodily functions. One day the Devil Monsanto will fuck the world, if he hasn't already.

* * *

The mother ship warped and folded space to get within a proximate and safe distance from New Sumer—which was eternally hidden behind the sun—and from there the Captain's transport ship manually made the rest of the journey.

After only a few thousand years BC, Earthlings had little more than a cell of Sumerian blood left in them. What began as an interplanetary biological and sociological experiment—seeding a barren planet with souls and Sumerian blood—had finally come to an end; leaving but a few New Sumerians on planet Earth to ultimately die into extinction. Except for those damned twins, of course! Evil never dies! Originally, the people of New Sumer were transplants from a planet on the edge of the solar system. They were the direct descendants of the Sumerians. Inevitably, their blood would eventually mingle with the blood of the Martian transplants who had escaped the self-destruction of their own planet.

The planet Sumer had a month-long window before the mother ship must return. It is an interminable journey around the outer limits of the solar system, taking sixty-thousand, six-hundred and sixty-six years, or thereabouts, to complete one rotation around the sun. It will take another sixty-thousand years, et al, for Sumer to make its way around the sun again. Present day Sumer is also known as Planet X.

Captain Talbot walked towards the twins.

"We thought you already boogied."

"I forgot something most important." The captain handed them a book wrapped in designer paper, covered with black and white four-dimensional pyramids.

"What's this?" asked a distrusting Kaka.

"It's a present. It's your heritage."

The twins thanked him with their usual lack-luster enthusiasm, "Whatevah."

"This is a very special book. You are given this because destiny demands it."

"Why?"

At a loss for words the Captain stuttered, "Kuku, I am only the messenger."

"That's what they all say," Kuku sneered.

"Why didn't you bring a present for both of us?" Kaka smirked.

"This is for the both of you to share," Captain Talbot said softly, yet with a tone of unmovable finality.

"We don't share!"

"What's it about?" asked Kuku who could not read.

"Yeah. Tell us all about it."

"Children, it's about..."

"We ain't children!" Kaka protested.

"I'm sorry. I should have remembered that."

"Tell us about the book," whined Kuku.

"As I was saying, it is about anything you want it to be. However, only the two of you can use it properly, can control it, so don't lose it. Its magic could be daunting to others."

"I love magic."

"So do I, sweet Kuku," the Captain agreed.

"Are you some kind of perv?" Kaka quizzed.

"Certainly not!"

"Just askin'."

"This is a very special book. You will take it because it is foretold."

"Who foretold it?"

"Our space folding time traveler and mystic."

"Who's that?"

"ME. Now listen. All you need to do is place your palm on the cover and ask it for anything you like. It will not respond to anything that might do harm to yourselves or to others."

"Bummer. Then what good is it?" Kuku said under her breath.

"This particular book is made especially for the two of you..." Captain Talbot informed, "...each page is made of compressed quixelite crystals. The crystals are empathic and they will reorganize according to what you are thinking and feeling; that is if the two of you actually think and feel anything."

"You're not funny," Kaka interjected. "And you talk too much!"

"*Yeah*, that. And you're not even amusing."

"May I finish?" An exasperated Captain Talbot asked. The twins smirked and yawned. "Moreover, they can illuminate the minds of the densest souls in the solar system. *Even yours, I presume.* The book has a tendency to do devilry. The two of you will like that. The crystals are living life forms. Who knows what goes on in their mini-minds, or in the reality of the book's reader?"

"What!?" Kuku and Kaka simultaneously shrieked.

"I don't know what you're talking about," snarky Kuku said while rolling her eyes.

"We're not interested in this stupid book."

The Captain knew he had no option available, other than to kiss the asses of those demonic twins. They don't even know how to listen. They've heard nothing of worth and that's mostly everything they heard—*nothing*. Talbot was anxious to get off this forsaken planet. So, he began to placate the little demons. "It's all for the good of your education. You'll grow to be a leader of...your...you know, your kind."

"What's that, asshole?" Kuku squinted her eyes.

Talbot swallowed and scoffed. "Special. You're both special."

"Why's that?" Kaka asked.

"I cannot say. *Please.* Please be so kind to give me your attention. Your attention will allow me access to your higher senses. This is important and you need to listen. And, I need to know you heard me."

"*Yeah, yeah, yeah.* We ain't deaf." Kaka sneered.

The Captain continued. "There will come a time when the book will show you nothingness. Don't be afraid. It is important for you to learn, and you will learn, sooner or later."

"What a sack of dark matter!"

"By that, Kuku means a big pile of dragon shit" Kaka informed.

"Why are you giving this to us?" Kuku asked.

"*Yeah*, who are we?"

"*Ah*, that is the question of questions. I have no idea who you are; other than 'the twins.' Now, I must get back to my ship. See you next rotation."

"Why do you think we are special?"

"You already think you're special, Kaka," giggled Kuku.

"Personally, I don't think either of you is special. I'm just doing as instructed. It is foretold that one day you will lose the book. So, learn what you can before you do." The Captain turned and began walking toward his ship.

"Wait!" Kaka screamed. "Why us?"

"I told you. Destiny demands it," Captain Talbot said over his shoulder while walking towards the ship. "The two of you are the descendants of Monsanto the King of the Underworld. See you in sixty-thousand, six-hundred and sixty-six years, kids."

"We ain't kids!" they said in unison.

"No you're not. You are evil, mean-spirited brats. That's what you are."

The twins vaguely heard what he said and that was intended. The Captain quickly turned back, took a couple packages from his pocket and handed one to each of the twins.

"What's these?"

"M&M's. You'll love them. Remember that the book is indestructible. Nothing can damage it in any way. After all, it was made on Sumer. It was designed and fabricated for the two of you and only the two of you."

"What is wrong with you? You keep saying the same thing over and over," Kuku smirked.

"Because one never knows exactly how dense the two of you are!" The Captain vaporized in a flash of colorful digits. Shortly thereafter, the transporter went into overdrive as it headed back to the far side of the sun where the mother ship was waiting.

The twins wasted no time unwrapping the designer paper to get their hands on the book. A blinding slash severed the azure sky. A sliver of sun slid through to heal the wound of the torn firmament.

When Captain Talbot had safely returned to the mother ship, he took the helm and began the process of folding space for the return trip to Sumer: the shimmering lady who spins at the edge of the solar system.

The twins watched the sky, and they began to wonder. They wondered for the first time in their lives. They wondered about wonder itself. They wondered what was on the other side of the sky. And then they wondered, *"Who am I?"* And, *"Why am I?"* Powerful is the book with the color of magic. But, the twins being the twins, will quickly become stupefied by the concept of wondering, and revert back to their natural brain-dead state of dumb-as-mud.

As Captain Maxfield Talbot prophesied, it took little time for the twins to lose interest in the book, and so they threw it into the river Ufat. Far into the future the twins will be known as Pudgy Penny and Piggy Peter.

* * *

New Sumer grew and prospered for tens of thousands of years before its civilization crumbled under the tyranny of seriously defective people: the Martians. The book took a perilous journey through many incarnations before reaching the Vatican and, subsequently, Shady Sanctum.

For example: CLEOPATRA VII PHILOPATOR PHARAOH QUEEN OF ALL THERE WAS ALL THERE IS ALL TO COME AND DON'T FORGET IT, cautioned the hoi polloi on a golden cartouche that hung above the entrance to the Queen Pharaoh's palace. Shortly after her slaves installed the cartouche, Cleopatra, plainly over the moon with the five foot high proclamation of her station, came down with a severe case of hubris, causing most of her friends to withdraw from Her Overbearingness. Her ex-friends moved on to ingratiate themselves into the lives of others, who did not enjoy as high a station as the Pharaoh Queen, but high enough to satisfy their low self-esteem combined with a hoity-toity sense of worth.

The cartouche was in hieroglyphics, of course, and there was no room left for another hieroglyph—not even any punctuation. The cartouche tormented Cleopatra daily, because every time she thought about it she thought of something else to add to it; something more to draw attention to her peerless standing in the natural, un-natural and supernatural order of things. It must be fabulous being the Queen.

C, as only her few friends and eunuchs dared call her, lied back on her golden recliner upholstered in fire chariot red silk embroidered with strands of gold thread. Next to her recliner stood the gold-plated, bejeweled cage for her royal snakes.

C casually ran her hands through the plush thick fur of her Russian Blue cat, Mercury XIII, when one of the new eunuchs begged entrance. She gave it. He placed figs on the table next to her. Figs are traditionally presented to C in the woven bowl that she herself wove with carefully plucked curly hairs, removed by the teeth of her eunuchs from each of the Queen's conquests. The eunuch who wins her favor is given the privilege to perform the plucking—one curly at a time.

"What's your name, eunuch?" Without sounding too demanding, C was straight forward with her request.

"Putinski, Your Most Benevolent."

"From now on you will call me C, but never in public. You must never speak in public, eunuch. You must always keep your mouth closed; sealed, corked, and airtight. Get it? If I say shut the fuck up, I mean shut the fuck up! If you don't, I will have your tongue cut out. Now let us see," C said while inspecting Putinski head to toe, "I shall call you Blanche because you are the gayest thing I have ever seen."

"Thank you, C. It is my honor," Putinski stuttered. He began to sweat. His mouth went dry. His lips puckered. He trembled. He was a mass of quivering fear.

"In a faultless world, it might be 'your honor,' but you are not in a faultless world."

"I don't understand, C."

"Neither do I, but then I'm the Queen and I don't need to. Are you a midget, Blanche."

"No, Ma'am. Egyptians are a tall people. Where I come from I am standard for our standard."

"Standard for what, Blanche?"

"My stature."

"We shall see. Your standard isn't much to write home about, is it? Remove your tunic and let us get a look at what you have, Blanche!" C demanded.

Putinski was uncertain he heard what he heard, "Excuse me, but I am not certain I heard what I heard."

"Then you didn't hear it from me, Blanche. Trust your Queen Pharaoh on that. Now, shut the fuck up and get naked!"

Blanche amused himself with his Russian rendition of *coy*, as he removed his tunic hesitantly, unhurriedly, sensuously; or so he thought. There comes a time when frugal theatrics give way to undesired consequences. Putinski was long past the age when he could get away with a bared chest and prefabricated charm. *Coy* was no longer an option for Putinski; it took him too close to the edge of absurdity. *Coy* discomposed no one more than Putinski himself.

During the siege of What's Yours is Mine, Blanche buried hundreds of tons of food smuggled in by caring neighbors. The food was meant for the starving serfs. And why did he do such a malevolent thing? So he could show his misguided neighbors how egregiously and unnecessarily, his people would only suffer at the hands of charitable Outsiders. There was no accounting Putinski's logic.

Putinski's tunic fell to the floor. C wasn't prepared to see what she saw and what she saw was the biggest, floppiest thingy she'd ever seen. "I must speak with Fuzzlbum the Ball Snatcher. He did such a marvelous job on you, Blanche. You will never wear a tunic, nor anything else, until I say so, and I will say so when your spongy eunuch-flab begins to spill and hang like the folds on a Chinese shar pei. 'Tis a pity you eunuchs crap-out so quickly. Blanche, the Queen's queen. You like that? *The Queen's queen?* Of course you do. I do and when I do what other choice do you have?

None. Now is the time we talk, seriously." C stared into the eyes of her eunuch and in a flash she realized that her suspicions were true.

"What will we talk about, C?" asked Putinski while staring at Mercury XIII, who stared back as C continued petting him.

"You like my pussy?"

"I do," Putinski said with a smile. And then he thought, "*Finally, something in common.*"

"Would you like to grab my pussy?"

"What?" Putinski was aghast.

"Just playing with you, Blanche," the Queen Pharaoh confessed before she declared, "Russian."

Putinski panicked. "I can expla..."

"I know, Blanche, I know. Russians are not as enigmatic as the crook-tail cats who guard the Queen Pharaoh when I'm in repose. You must admit that the Blue of the Russian is remarkable. Surely, you must." With the nonchalance of a snake about to strike, she asked, "How about we start with where exactly it is that you come from? What you are doing here? What is your favorite color? Who are you, Blanche? You do know who you are, don't you? Who are you?"

Overwrought, Putinski realized that he had nowhere to flee. So, he did all he knew to do to save his cowardly ass, "I was waiting for you to ask me that very question. Thank you, C. It is my honor."

"There you go with your honor thingy again. '*My*' honor is the same as "*your*' honor, so lose the honor stuff."

"Yes, C. Sorry. My mistake. I do know who I am. I knew you would find me out, even without my testicles. So, I am no longer incognito. I am the most well-known actor in the great territory to the north. I sing, I dance, I do comedy, but nobody does drama like me. I can bring you to tears. Forgive me if I brag, but I always tell the truth. The truth is, my audience loves me and I've never bombed anywhere."

"Of course. You are too funny. Who did your lift,

Blanche?" C asked as she moved in to take a closer look at her eunuch. She carefully inspected under his hairline and around his ears. "Nice job. I see this is not Fuzzlbum's work. The gods know he is getting on, going blind...his shaky hands can no longer be trusted. I don't trust him, I'll tell you that. No, this is not his work. Look at you, Blanche. It is amazing what can be done with pinking shears and a melon scoop on an old tired face, isn't it?"

"Not so old," Putinski whimpered. "Not so tired."

"I think I am being contradicted. Am I being contradicted, Blanche?

"No. I apologize. You are not."

"I'm not? There you go again. Twice contradicted is punishable by death. We will need to ponder your suspicious breeding. Get one of my guards to come and guard their Queen Pharaoh. All the crook-tails are currently dining in the Royal kitchen. When they come back you may leave. They are not as sweet as my little Russian. Listen to him purr."

Putinski anxiously volunteered, "I can do that for you, C. I can guard you."

"You think so, do you?" the Queen asked.

"Yes," Putinski anxiously offered with brave aplomb.

"*Why not?* Stand in the corner and guard me, Blanche."

"My pleasure," Putinski purred. He then marched to the corner where the Queen Pharaoh had pointed.

"My dearest Blanche, my vain Russian, stop playing with yourself, pick up the spear and hold it like you mean it. Be a *mensch*. Look like you own it and you'll go further than you ever expected in this life. Your Queen Pharaoh knows everything, and now She must take Her nap."

"I had better find the book and split. Nobody would question a naked eunuch prowling the palace; big thingy or not. Last year's news," Putinski thought.

Outside the Queen's chambers, Stephen Ghoulmiller the Fearsome Mummy Wrapper and General Creeper, was creeping about for every bit of useful information he could gather to bring down the Queen. Today's pickings were slim.

Motivated by unending enmity for the Queen Pharaoh, the Mummy Wrapper was determined to be the force of her demise. Her affairs with the Romans were the last straw. He asked himself, *"What to do? What to do? Stir up the country against Cleopatra? Divide the country so each side hates the other? That would never happen. Well, maybe. What else? Lie like it's the truth and respond to the truth as if it were a lie? Remember to stick to the lie even in the face of truth. Call it fake. Fake truth, fake truth! Say it enough times and it becomes the truth. Launch a camel dung bomb or two? What to do? What to do?"*

After C went to sleep, Putinski came running out of the palace naked. He was holding the book where modesty suggested; against his drooping man boobs. The book was covered with camel hide and tied with goat entrails to keep it from using its powers.

"I got it! I got it!" Putinski shouted.

"Give it to me!" exclaimed Ghoulmiller the Mummy Wrapper. "I knew you were the right man for the job."

"Thank you, Comrade. Nobody pays attention to a naked eunuch running around the palace anymore. Good of you to notice. You like my Russian colossus? You can touch it if you like."

"I like." Ghoulmiller the Mummy Wrapper wrapped his hand around Putinski's colossus, his pride and joy. "I like your colossus very much," Ghoulmiller drooled. "I will play with it now, Comrade."

"Okay. That's enough," Putinski said while disengaging the Mummy Wrapper's squeeze. "Before I give to you the book, you must give to me the deed to Egypt."

"You already have my word, Putinski!"

"I would rather have your word in your writing. I gave my balls and risked my life for this job!" Putinski proclaimed.

"Give me the book!" The Mummy Wrapper barked.

"Give me the deed!"

It was a standoff until Stephen Ghoulmiller the Fearsome Mummy Wrapper and General Creeper blinked. "Yes, yes! Okay?" He acquiesced while sniffing and licking the hand that held Putinski's prodigious colossus. "So, where was the Queen? *Napping?*" He put a smart-ass accent on the word *napping*.

"Exactly! She was having a nap. Boy, you're good, for a closet-queen. *Napping.* You must be a soothsayer. Here's the skinny. I'm thinking while I'm standing guard, feeling around for my balls, looking around for where she might have hid the book, knowing I had to get gone before the crook-tails returned, and then from out the blue, I thought to ask myself where I would hide it. I put myself in her shoes, so to speak, and pondered. Suddenly, I found myself staring at the gold snake cage. That's it! Where better? I carefully move the cage. It was heavier than I expected. Solid gold. So, I struggled, I pushed, I pulled, and I slide it. And then I saw it. There it was, the book, only an arm's length away. Then out comes this little black snake, probably harmless. But, who can be sure? So I swatted the little fucker. It flew smack up against the wall. But I didn't kill it. It bounced and slithered beneath Cleopatra's bed. Now, hand over the deed to Egypt, motherfucker!"

* * *

During the Dark Ages, the book was found in a cave in England where the Bastard of Dimbart lived to get away from the stench of packaged and commercialized stupidity. The Bastard hated the filthy townsfolk; the pathetic citizens who roamed the roads helter-skelter through the hamlet of Dimbart. The Bastard was a mean, vitriolic has-been filled with unbridled hatred. Bitchslaps would have no affect on him, especially since he's drunk on piss wine from sunrise to sunset, so he wouldn't feel them anyway.

The Bastard drained the bladder of piss wine and in a drunken stupor he threw the last stone from his throw-pile at Bernice the Socialist Jew and Streetwalker Bernice. Everyday she came to offer a piece of cloth for a bite of bread. It should come as no surprise that The Bastard hated Bernice the Socialist Jew. He hated all Jews. He hated all Socialists. He hated all streetwalkers, but not so much. So he was not about to share a piece of his bread, nor a sip of his piss wine with anyone. Especially with Bernice the Socialist Jew and and Streetwalker!

From the Bastard's vantage point, overlooking the rabble below, he threw rocks at all who came near his cave. The townsfolk, indifferent and apathetic, walked about with lumps on their heads. It never occurred to any one of them to do something about it. And that is how The Bastard of Dimbart got away with a dictatorship of torture, abuse, and nauseating manners. Eventually, everybody grew accustomed to his abuse, so it morphed into acceptance and apathy. Nobody any longer gave an intercourse. The pain of another stone, another lump, became a part of their human experience.

The townsfolk were known as "lump-heads." What else could they be called? What else could they do?

"So what's the deal here? Can somebody tell me? Anybody? Are you not tired of taking lumps? The Bastard is deformed, demented and devolving. It's time we take him down," whispered by a dirty lump-head to a couple other dirty lump-heads who sat near him at the bi-monthly meeting of the disgruntled and generally pissed-off lumpers who met in the Dimbart Town Hall thorn garden. It is called the thorn garden because a decade earlier all the roses turned black and died. The rose bushes remained sturdy, grew taller by the year with thorns that reached out to stab the unmindful, but they never gave birth to a single rose.

A decade earlier, Dumb McConnell from Yonder told everybody in the Town Hall that he saw The Bastard pissing on the rose bushes, "And as I watched him pissing, all the roses began to shrivel and fall."

The Baker of Dimbart, not yet The Bastard, attended a meeting at the town hall and, upon hearing Dumb McConnell from Yonder, he jumped to his feet and shouted, "Why in hell were you watching me piss, McConnell, you silly old prissy thing?" A few others in attendance also wanted to know. "That's the question, isn't it? I am sure that while he stood there watching, doing something more or less nasty, it was merely a coincidence that the flowers fell as I relieved myself. Believe me. Trust me. There was no helping it. I would have burst. It was the will of the powers that be, wasn't it? Blame the Puppeteer. Not me! I thought I was alone, but McConnell was there hiding and watching. I bet he enjoyed it. Whom do you believe? Mindless McConnell or me?" Spoken with outrage, disgust and a big dose of pride in his ability to defuse and confuse with a plausible counter-attack of innuendo and heinous accusations. "Who believes me?" The show of hands was less than The Bastard expected. "Put your hands down. Thank you, thank you. McConnell, you like watching men piss, don't you? What vile act do you perform while watching? Before you answer, do you remember the pies you stole from behind the Dimbart bakery?" The Bastard asked, looking around for those who had voted their belief in him. Not enough hands, yet!

"I did not steal them, you bastard! You put them in the garbage!"

"They were not in the garbage, McConnell! They were on the back steps cooling, you degenerate. Did I call the Men with Clubs to take you away? No. Did I not let you keep the pies? Yes. So how dare you call me a bastard?" The Bastard did not exactly let him keep the pies since Dumb McConnell had already thrown them into his sack, mangling them all.

"How can you take the word of a man like that?" The Bastard referred to McConnell as a corrupt aberration, a thief, and a liar. "Who represents truth? Me or the halfwit? I know truth, believe me. No one knows truth better than me. So, who trusts me?" A larger show of hands this time, but not yet enough to make a majority. "You know me. I have fed this entire hamlet with baked goods. I do not want to close the bakery because I have been sullied. I could not live with that. Where would you go to find a sympathetic ear to tell your problems and secrets to? You came to me with your most delicate of matters. So very kind of you. I remember every one of them. *Now!* Who believes the Baker Man?" Every hand in the hall raised except for Dumb McConnell's from Yonder.

"Thank you, citizens. As your baker and your mayor, I need to inform you that there is no such a thing coming called the Dark Age. Fake news. Don't believe the doomsayers. Nobody is ever going to launch the mother of all sheep shit bombs. There is no such thing as man-made Darkness. Fake news. So, carry on. Throw all the filth you like into the air, and ponder on all the fun you're having!"

Three days later the Dark Ages fell upon the hamlet of Dimbart. The Bastard had known the Dark Ages were coming and did nothing but deny and lie, like a finely-tuned politician. Eventually, The Bastard was ousted to the outskirts of the town. McConnell was soon elected the new mayor. That is how The Baker of Dimbart became The Bastard of Dimbart.

The Bastard, while breaking fingernails digging for throwing-rocks, uncovered the book and wasted no time starting a plague that killed hundreds of thousands, including himself.

* * *

Sir Geoffrey did not want to become a Crusader.

Sir Geoffrey enjoyed little more than getting others to feel good about themselves, even when it was at his own expense—which it usually was. He would exhaust himself from pretending to be stupid, if that was what it took to bring about, in the least, a smile. Pretending was easy, but when Poor Sir Geoffrey tried his honest best to be taken in-all-sincerity, to be himself, intelligent and empathic, no one ever took him seriously. He knew full-well that he had created the predicament himself. There was little left to do but acquiesce and accept the notion that it's too late to change the misconceptions of others. Sir Geoffrey was having a bad day. *"I will find a way not to be a Crusader!"* Sir Geoffrey declared with absolute certainty. *"I will become a stand-up comic!"*

Sir Geoffrey did not want to go to war—no how, no way. Only the infirm, those over sixty-five or under twelve, were allowed to remain within the ten-man-high stone and timber wall, surrounding Cheesy Castle, where none but the children smiled and laughed. However, when the children dared to smile or laugh it was forced, restrained, and disheartened. Some of the children were snatched from their parents for sneaking across the Cheesy Castle border—the penalty for that was removal and lockup. Although, King Cheesy had been known to sell a few of the better looking ones, mostly to priests, and a few to seasoned warriors who were leading armies of Crusaders. Some of the children lost their parents and grandparents to the Crusade of Christian soldiers fighting the Good War on the Infidels. The nuns remained to cook, garden, take care of those left behind, forge weapons, tend to the infirm, perform all the duties, menial or otherwise, that it takes to run Cheesy Castle, and, most importantly, to satisfy the needs of its namesake, King Cheesy. There was nothing the nuns did not know about the castle, or those of any importance who occupied it. *And there were no stand-up comics!*

Sir Geoffrey did not want to go to war; even if it were for Jesus. Sir Geoffrey cannot, no, never could he kill another human being. He would do most anything to be spared from killing Infidels. He would not, no, never rape, loot, nor terrorize those who would not kneel in the name of King Cheesy's Savior. Unless Arab heathens worshiped a dead Jew, it was off with their heads. Sir Geoffrey maintained his rock solid conviction that he was his own responsibility and he could not, would not, murder for Jesus.

All Sir Geoffrey wanted was to be a stand-up comic.

"We are your King and you will go!" King Cheesy commanded. There are no exceptions. What kind of knight are you? We can strip you of your title!"

"I do not want to go to war, Your Majesty."

"Who's asking you to go to war, Sir Geoffrey? You are only going to the East to raise the consciousness of the filthy brown savages. They need to know the love of Jesus. It's not war. Nothing like war. It's love, if you must know. It's all about love. You would free their souls to delight in the joy of the Risen Savior," King Cheesy said with pride and satisfaction from choosing his words with such heartfelt passion. In other words, the motherfucker knew how to lie with conviction.

"I beg Your Highness to allow me to speak freely."

"Of course," the King said with the arrogance afforded by gold and power. The King was a fat and ugly man, who got uglier when his patience began wearing thin. "But, if you think you will be dismissed of your duty to serve the Almighty, you are mistaken."

The Almighty? Was he talking about God, or himself? King Cheesy could have been referring to both. He was a master at ambiguity.

"It's just that...well, I heard rumors, Your Highness. Rumors of a bloody war and unspeakable horrors."

"Let Us stop you right there! There are no horrors of any kind! Our brave Crusaders are above reproach. We are doing God's work and you will be doing God's work—whether you like it, or not!

"I don't like it. In fact, I no longer believe in Jesus, and I may not even believe that there is a God," Sir Geoffrey blurted. "I have heard, through the grapevine, of beheadings, rape, looting the brown people for their vast amounts of gold and precious minerals. This is not for the love of Jesus or God at all. Some say the horror of broken bones and blood are enjoyed by many of the Crusaders. I see no reason for invading the brown people in the East simply for the enjoyment of your soldiers. None at all. I am better than your Crusaders. Therefor, I am a conscientious objector, Your Highness."

"*Many terrible things?!* We want to know exactly where those rumors came from!" King Cheesy was about to implode. "No to the love of Jesus? No to the existence of God. No to raping and plundering. No to all the fun things. So tell Us, what grapevine, where? *Oh,*..and you don't give a screw!"

"I never said that I didn't give a screw, out loud."

"You didn't have to. We heard it, anyway."

"I can't go, Your Highness."

"Of course you can. Did you know that We have a bust of

Us in the Royal Chapel between the Virgin Mary and Jesus?"

"I've seen it once or twice."

"You would have seen it more than once or twice if you went to church more often. You must believe in Our Savior, Our God, or..." and then quite suddenly and in the meanest voice Sir Geoffrey ever heard, "GUARD! Take this traitorous piece of monkey dung to the dungeon for six hours of torture, then throw his body to the pigs!"

The guard began to escort Sir Geoffrey to the dungeon when the King demanded, "What's that square thing covering your ass, dead man walking? Guard, bring it to Us."

The guard slipped his hand up over Sir Geoffrey's ass, smiled broadly, and then removed the book with the new color, dashed to the King, handed it to him like a hot potato. Then he returned to his post and began to tremble and mumble.

"What are you on about, guard!?"

"Nothing, Your Highness. Maybe something. E equals M and C something. In the future, I will need to think about what that means."

"Are you out of your skull!?"

"Only some of the time, Your Highness," the guard stuttered.

Then the King looked at the book he was holding and soon became obsessed with its color. "What the devil is this? A tool of Satan?"

"I found it in a cave. I hope it *is* a tool of Satan, Your Mad Majesty. You *must* be careful with it," Sir Geoffrey advised.

"I MUST! Your King MUST nothing! GUARD, take him away, *again!*"

"King, dearest! Excuse me...but you are not going to like this: When I was saying my morning prayers in the Royal Chapel, Jesus and his mom came to life and pulverized your bust with their barehands. It was miraculous!" As the guard escorted Sir Geoffrey toward the dungeon, they made a date to get together that night for a quick tryst.

After Sir Geoffrey and the guard had disappeared from the King's sight, the King opened the book and screamed in horror. He rose from his throne, floated upwards to the ceiling of the Kingdom's Hall of Justice, where he hung suspended for ten days, until the nuns took pity, formed a circle beneath the King and chanted one-hundred Hail Marys, two-hundred Our Fathers, and a thousand Acts of Contrition in unison while kneeling on the cold stone floor only a few feet away from King Cheesy when he crashed and splattered, frightening the nuns into a quick Amen! So much for the book not harming anyone.

Sir Geoffrey would not go to war.

* * *

The next incarnation of the book occurred the time the Contessa Victoria and her personal companion, Lady Lilith, found the Inquisition good wholesome entertainment.

"What a wonderful time to be alive," said the Contessa to her companion while strolling to the Conversion Center. It was typical for them, following Benediction, to head on over to the *Iglesia de los Mártires de sangrado*, the Church of Bleeding Martyrs, officiated by Bishop Gulch, the Grande Inquisitor.

"May we go down and watch awhile, Bishop?"

"The Contessa may do whatever she pleases. Your usual cushions, all washed and ready, await, Contessa."

"Thank you, Bishop Gulch. By the way, who's on today's ticket?" Contessa Victoria asked like a well-seasoned pugilist?

"I believe that would be Don Luigi Gohmerto the pig farmer, assisted by Cardinal Roberto the Bootlicker and Chief Justice of the Rules Committee on Torture. After him, let me think, *ah*, Brother Jesus O'Toole, not the one of yore, of course. This is the Jesus you will want to see. I trained Brother O'Toole de Pyrenees myself. His techniques are divinely extraordinary. His tools are exquisite. His secret is, Contessa, he does not torture in any ordinary way. He makes love to the Infidel. Then, when he withdraws his love, the Infidel feels the pain of love lost, and easily succumbs to the will of Brother O'Toole. That makes our job a little less strenuous, and a lot more interesting. What is wrong with Infidels nowadays? All they need to do is say, 'I believe' and be done with it. Simple as that. Just say the words. Now, let us go and I shall go down with you and perform some of my Grande Inquisitor duties. Nothing unholy here, just enhanced interrogation." Bishop Gulch giggled. "By the way, I'm having a little soirée next Sunday after mass. All the Sisters and Brothers will be there. It gets a little wild after midnight. I'd be honored if you were to attend, but only if you care for that sort of thing. You know, wild and all."

"Do we care for that sort of thing, Lilith?" The Contessa smiled and they both giggled.

Behind the altar in the Church of Bleeding Martyrs was a roughly hewn creaky door. Behind the door were wobbly, cobbled steps leading down into the underground vault just beyond the stalactites. The Conversion Center reeked with the scent of divinely administered torture. A couple Jews, an Atheist, a few Muslims and a Persian homosexual were on today's ticket.

Upon entering the Conversion Center—don't call it a torture chamber—Bishop Gulch announced with dramatic flair, "The Grande Inquisitor has arrived!"

The walls of the chamber were painted dark red, so any splattering of blood appeared Feng shui, until Mother George the Unkind cleaned the Conversion Center, as she does every Thursday; washing the bloodied tools, mopping the stone floor and walls until the bells rang for Angelus.

Don Luigi Gohmerto entered from behind a bloody curtain. When he spotted the Contessa and her companion, he ran straight over and squealed, "Ladies, so sorry you missed my performance. *Durn tootin'!* It was a hoot; like a hog at a bar-b-que, but as you know, I am always the big attraction. If you like, I can stay for a special session, yes? A grand performance just for you, Contessa."

"No need to bother you. We know how adept you are, Don Gohmerto, but for now, Lady Lilith and I are awaiting a performance by Brother O'Toole. The Grande Inquisitor has highly recommended him to us."

"I'm sure he has," Don Gohmerto scoffed.

"Please don't be insulted, Father," the Contessa begged with a saccharin-sweet smile.

"I'll tell him you are here." Don Gohmerto said, stinking of muscatel, shuffling-off like a drunken rat to the greenroom where the Brothers rehearsed their sublime techniques while awaiting their cue to perform the day's conversions. Today they were all giddy about experimenting with a few new persuasion tools which might require invasive cleaving.

"With each slash of his well-used brown leather whip, and other exalted methodologies," The Grande Inquisitor explained with pomposity, "Brother O'Toole uses his magnificent manhood as a persuasion tool, and that takes a lot of practice."

"How informative you are, dear Bishop," the Contessa flattered.

Bishop Gulch exhaled, inhaled, then declared, "Ladies, it is always a pleasure to entertain you. Please make yourselves comfortable and enjoy as you witness our humble, yet ever so divine, opportunity for the Godless soul to see the Light and be rescued from the pains of Hell."

Brother O'Toole de Pyrenees threw the bloody drape open and stepped into the arena. He wore a short sheep skin loincloth. That's it. Nothing else.

"Okay, O'Toole, go for it," said the excited, faux-smiling, Inquisitor.

"Any preference of heathen today, m'Ladies?" Brother O'Toole asked.

After examining the offerings du jour, "How about the Muslim?" The Contessa pointed to the Muslim.

"Good choice. He looks delicious, m'Ladies. And take a gander at the size of that."

"Oh, my, my, my, my. What a huge...!" The Contessa walked

over to the Muslim and held his huge means of communication. The Contessa moistened her lips as she walked back to the pillowed viewing area.

Brother O'Toole de Pyrenees took the unclad and unwashed Muslim out of his stocks and escorted him to the shackles. He fettered the heathen's arms, stretched them out as far as they would go, and then he bound his feet with strips of cow hide, stretching his legs as far apart as they would go, as well—which made the naked Muslim appear as a subject for a De Vinci painting. "Are you ready to accept our Lord as your Savior?"

"Praise Allah."

Brother Jesus O'Toole de Pyrenees looked into the eyes of the frightened man and said, in a manner to soothe the Muslim's fear, "Do you accept our Lord and Savior?"

"Praise Allah."

Contessa Victoria whispered something to the Bishop, who whispered something to Brother O'Toole de Pyrenees. The Brother gave a wide smile to the Contessa, then slowly walked over to the ladies, and encouraged them to fluff-up his prodigious instrument of mass conversion. When he was fluffed to the max, he thanked the ladies, then held his towering conversion tool while he walked back to the staging area. He took a position behind the Muslim. Then, with one quick motion, the Holy Implement of Brother O'Toole transformed belligerence into bliss.

"I accept. I believe," the Muslim cried.

After unrestrained applause from the ladies, Bishop Gulch turned to Contessa Victoria and said, "See what I told you, no one does more conversions, more pleasantly, than a long-haired blond with blue eyes."

"I can see why." Lilith said.

"It is time we return before vespers," The Contessa told Lady Lilith.

"Of course, my Lady."

The ladies made their goodbyes to all, including the giddy

Muslim-in-love. They were halfway up the cobbled staircase when Lilith nearly fell from an unstable step. A stone in the stairway had loosened, exposing the book that lay hidden beneath. They thought the color of the book a miraculous sign. Lilith tugged and pulled until she dislodged the book. She felt its energy pour into her. In fear, she wrapped her skirt around it, ran back down the dangerous steps and, breathlessly, threw the book at the Grand Inquisitor who cried upon seeing it, "It's the Book of the Dead! *Mine, mine! Finally mine!*"

But it was not the Book of the Dead. It was something far more useful. *"Ouch!"* And then he dropped the book onto the stone floor. Shortly afterward, the Grand Inquisitor himself dropped onto the floor.

The book with the new color hadn't been seen until it popped-up in one of the Vatican's treasure troughs from where Brother Aires removed it and took it to Shady Sanctum; the last incarnation of the Sumer book, so far.

TEN

better call fuzzlbum

With jaws unhinged in stunning, exquisite stupefaction, V and Lily stared at O'Toole's tail. It took the loud and desperate sound, that rose from under the floorboards, to close their fallen chops.

"What in hell is that racket?" V asked of no one in particular.

"I hope it hasn't anything to do with my tail," Peter whispered to an invisible someone glued to the ceiling.

Peter often spoke to dead and mythical folk; pointing fingers, forgiving those he hadn't forgave, or asking forgiveness from that special someone glued to the ceiling. Once or thrice, when he lifted his head to speak to the invisible, he wondered why it was always the ceiling and not the floor, or straight ahead, behind, beside, within? Every piece of non-existence resided on a ceiling. Any ceiling: a ceiling of blue or the cosmos beyond. As a Roman Catholic, having been brought up by nuns, and a graduate of a Catholic College, Peter knew—actually knew—nothing about God, except for what he was taught; and what he was taught was called truth, and it must be accepted without question, and that required an act of faith. Peter struggled with being able to take that giant leap of faith into believing in the existence of Heaven, Hell and God; For Peter, faith meant abandoning reason. Faith was intangible, invisible, an idea, and leaping over the abyss that separated the invisible from reason, giving himself over to an idea, was not in his DNA. Therefore, thus far, Peter's struggle was for naught. Oftentimes, Peter wondered why he felt guilty after those heart-to-heart one-sided conversations with ceilings? He felt as though he had betrayed himself; he felt that giving his soul over to an unknown entity was, in a way, committing suicide; and that was the reason he felt the guilt of betrayal. And then he thought about how to create a coved ceiling in his condo to understate the boxy rooms with their straight lines and uninspired edges that quash any sense for continuity. "For Pete's sake," Peter said as though everybody had a tail. "It's just a tail. No big deal."

"*Help! Help!* Will somebody get me out of here. It's Maxfield Talbot from Earth. I come in peace. What do you call this planet? Does anyone know me? It's me! Where is everybody? Help! I'm blind! Blind as a donut! *Help! Help!* I'm being eaten by something. Who can tell? I can't. *I'm blind!*"

V instructed Lily, "Do not let Peter move an inch!" And then she gingerly stepped across the cleverly designed red silk rug her father brought back from a "conversionary" trip to India. When she hit the hallway, her bare feet slapped Shady Sanctum's original floorboards that were now cracked and warped. The floor had been painted a light brown before it was covered with dark red and, finally, painted a dark green sometime after V graduated Queen City's East High. The boards had been meticulously stripped of any hint of green. Lily claims responsibility for that. V is not wild about physical work. Both women felt that the raw unvarnished floorboards, gave a sense of the Old West, a rustic Colorado comfort, a lived-in warmth, a sense of security within the walls of Shady Sanctum, but both ladies knew full-well there was no such thing as security. So, as one must do with movies of every genre, V and Lily shared a willingness to suspend their disbelief.

"I won't let him move half an inch," Lily firmly stated. She stared at Peter as though he were a cheesecake. Peter felt threatened, intimidated and just plain stupid.

"Peter, you can relax. We all make mistakes. I'm sure V will agree. We both love you. Stop worrying, V's not going to eat you. No cannibals here...or, are there?" Lily had gone for an amusing-kind of comfort in this uncharted territory, but Peter was neither amused nor comforted. In fact, he was disturbingly ill at ease, afraid and trembling.

"Please don't put disconcerting images in my mind, Lil." Peter was serious. He barely functions when someone plants an unwanted vision in his head. Like an ear worm, it sticks and repeats itself unrelentingly like a melody, or a line from a bad song that plays over and over and over again.

* * *

Big Beat, a checker at Kimchi Korean Cheap Market by day and a thug rapper on Saturday nights at a club called The Black Ace on East Colfax, a Colorado University student in Boulder, majoring in political science, runs and hides whenever V and Lily enter the market.

Big Beat told his supervisor, when she asked about his hiding behind the stack of canned dog meat and jarred kimchi display in front of the frozen fish bin, where a large poster was taped behind the bin depicting Barack Obama standing on a huge white turtle, holding a fishing pole and reeling in an Exxon oil tanker, "Those women can get inside your head and mess you up, Miss Kim. *Unnatural.* Know what I mean? They scare me. Both of them! I think they're evil. They came to The Black Ace once. A while back. I couldn't finish my set. They gave me the willies. I took the first bus home, but it went the wrong way. Something isn't right with them."

"You too funny, Ernie."

"Call me Big Beat, Miss Kim." His attempt to sound like a thug doesn't exactly play well in a cut-rate Korean market. Besides, Ernie didn't exactly know how to sound like a thug.

"Save thug-talk for Saturday night, Ernie."

"Sorry, Miss Kim."

Miss Kim headed for the front of her store. She turned back and said, cheerfully, "I like one you tell about gnomes. And time you trapped inside freezer and ate half gallon ice cream. That's good one," Miss Kim chuckled and continued, "Not like one about cat food display crashing. You said redhead woman's shadow did it. You Ernie Too-Funny." She giggled.

"It's the truth, Miss Kim. All of it is true." But, the truth of the matter is that Ernie was never certain about the truth of anything, caused in part by fabulously mind-bending pot; as he usually got stoned when left alone in the market.

"Of course they true. Love your stories. Love black yummy joy stick more." Miss Kim licked her lips and gave his ass a hard whack with a frozen shark.

"OUCH. What did you do that for?"

"For you! We more later."

"*Oh, yea.* We more later. Can't wait," Ernie said sans passion, interest, sincerity, but with overwhelming anxiety and fear of not getting it up for Miss Kim. Ernie could wait. He could wait forever. Miss Kim was a mercy fuck; so he did what he needed to do to keep his job before going back to school in September. Earlier in the summer Eddy Spaghetti came into the market after spotting Ernie in the window. He didn't plan to buy a thing. He just wanted to meet Ernie. It was love at first sight. Ernie and Eddy have been living together since the beginning of the summer. Their age difference didn't matter; they each were exactly what the other wanted. They planned to get married after Ernie gets his degree in political science.

Miss Kim's belly poured out from under her Bronco's T-shirt and spilled over her hot-pink overly-stretched peddle pushers. She wore candy-apple red, impossibly-tight heels bulging with ankle fat. She gave a snort, pouted seductively and said, "Now get black ass to work," she held the frozen shark high as she ordered Big Beat, sometimes Doogie, a.k.a. Ernest Washington Howser, a.k.a. Ernie.

None of the ass-grabbing went unnoticed by V and Lily. They were situated at the perfect angle to view reflections in several large round mirrors; although, a reflection from another mirror caused the image to appear *not* backwards in the mirror over the cabbages. When they saw Kim and Ernie coming their way, V and Lily were ready to do some damage.

"Lily," V whispered; loud enough for the clerk and Miss Kim to hear, yet low enough for them to think they were overhearing what they were not meant to hear, "I hope I didn't leave the pot on."

"Which one, Lily? Oh, no! You don't mean the one with..." V appeared nervous and anxious as she continued in a louder whisper—Lily calls it a stage whisper, "...*the body parts?*"

Kim and Ernie stopped dead in their tracks on aisle two.

"I think so, V. Poor cousin Ernie. He was so young. Sad to see him go to pieces. He did end up in a pile of useless body parts, didn't he?"

"He did. We need to get back to the caldron. I mean, the pot." V said, looking in the direction of the pretending-not-to-listen-nor-hear ears, and loudly exclaimed, "*Quick!* Before cousin Ernie boils over." Then, directly to Kim and Big Beat, "We have an emergency. We will see you next time. You know us. We'll be needing a couple new brooms soon."

"Gotta fly," Lily said as they were about to exit."

V turned back and prophesied, "I am seeing something." V's voice changed into something weirdly inexplicable. "Beware the deadly blow fish with black shaft. Avoid sushi for the next five weeks." And then they were gone. As silly as it was, it always worked. Besides, it wasn't they who started the cheap theatrics.

While shopping in Kimchi Korean Cheap Market, earlier in the summer, V overheard Ernie telling Miss Kim, among other things, "Devil witches spreading the word of Satan." V may have let it slip that she was an Atheist when she sneezed and Ernie said, "God bless you." For all of Ernie's education, some fables take longer than others to overcome. It should have been a clue, that if there were no Santa Claus, perhaps there were no anything else. A lesson, cruelly taught, but seldom learned.

* * *

V went to the basement door, slid the bolt and let Max out. "For Pete's sake, Maxfield! What's wrong with you?"

Max looked around to see where he was. "There's nothing wrong with me. I'm home. I'm happy to be home. Thank you, thank you. Victoria, you won't believe where I've been."

"Most likely, but tell me anyway. *Quickly.*"

"I went back through time. Into other dimensions. Other realities. There were several, as I recall. They were all awesome," Max firmly stated.

"I remember reading something about that. It was a dull-witted item on the Yahoo news feed." V oozed with disbelief.

"It's true. There are endless worlds to visit." After a bit of thinking, Max continued, "*Umm*...I gotta learn to fold space better. Did you know that Mankind is not indigenous to Earth? What do you think about that, V?"

"I don't know what I think. Folding space. Not from Earth. Okay, I see. I understand."

"No you don't. I hate it when you patronize me, Victoria. When I try to explain something to you, you condescend. You have a closed mind, Victoria. I expect more from you. I am tired of being treated as though I were a child!"

"Then don't act like one. Straighten up. We will talk about this later," V smiled and Maxfield followed suit.

"Wait. I've got to clean my shoe." Max removed his right shoe so V could see what was on his sole. And what it was, was a huge squashed bug nearly the size of the shoe's heel. "It was in the basement, Victoria."

"Jeezes and weezes! We'll need to call an exterminator."

"Nope. It was the only one. I brought it back with me from somewhere. It's called a cockpion. Quite interesting, but deadly poisonous."

Max finished scraping-off the last of the cockpion into the toilet and flushed the hideous creature from another place in their timeline into the sewers of Queen City. After Max disposed of the kitchen spatula in the dumpster, because V would have it no other way, they were ready to make an entrance.

When they walked into the parlor, V could see that Peter hadn't moved an inch. "Good boy, Peter. Good work, Lil."

Max playfully whispered into V's ear, "Condescending." Max was momentarily stunned when he caught sight of Peter and his tail. With an expression that could stop a herd of stampeding gingriches, Maxfield bellowed at O'Toole, "You have the book! I know you do. There are good folks on another planet who are coming for it. Be careful. They want it back and a couple other things, as well. Mum's the word, kiddos. Your lives are about to change. Oh my discombobulations, we're talking huge. An uncomfortable silence from the dumbfounded, before Max added, "Nice tail, Peter."

"Thank you, Max. I kinda like it myself."

"I've seen a remarkable number of folks with tails in my travels on this planet and several other planets. Oh, and on Sumer, of course. Earthlings call Sumer planet X, but its name is Sumer. Tails are like having a tattoo. You can have whatever you want on Sumer." Max informed. "You can be whatever you want."

"There's no such place, Maxfield. *Please.* Stop it. We're worried about you," V sighed with genuine concern for his welfare.

"You'll see. It's coming. Soon, Earth will no longer be habitable. Just like Mars! I remember those last days on Mars. So sad. Haitian dough gum would have helped back then."

"Maxfield! You are scaring me. Listen, there is no planet X, Y or Z." V was becoming more and more patronizing with each word. "*Relax.* We will talk about all this later, Max. *Okay?*"

"You'll see," Max pouted.

Peter broke the tension when he gave his *mea culpa*, "I was doing research for my next play, V." Peter babbled on, senselessly. His mouth was so dry it was difficult for him to form words. "I'm always bo-ro-orrowing books from you. Ra-right? You…well, you know that, right?" Peter ran his tongue over his lips and said, "How did I know this book was, was, *is* whatever this book is? I thought it might be light reading."

Max announced, "The book Peter *stole* is a toy to educate children and the young of mind. Victoria, do you think I have a young mind?"

"I do, dearest Maxfield," answered V. "I really, truly, honestly do."

Max giddily replied, "*I* can open the book without fear. Only me. Besides, that book was created for two diabolically stupid twins."

"I'm sorry, V," Peter interrupted, after wetting his lips really well. "I'm not sure about this, but I could be losing my mind. I mean, how would I know? My mind has been wandering lately. Am I holding a tail?"

"Yes, Peter." V answered. "You are indeed holding a tail."

"That's a relief...V, I want you to know that I was only looking for something to read," Peter said contritely, smacking his lips.

"In the basement?"

"*Yes*. Odd, isn't it? I thought I heard Mercury in distress. That's why, that's the reason I went down there. No other reason. No ulterior motives. Why would I go down there otherwise?"

"Seems dubious."

"Of course it does. I know. Please forgive me, dear heart."

"Of course, Peter, if you will please put the book on the table, stop lying, and go get a bottle of water." The table that V had point to, was a marble-topped spindle that stood in the corner near the fireplace, displaying several Albuquerque acting awards won by Lilith Champagne. They only made Lily Nettles frown. They used to make her feel on top of the world. Now, they were simply material fabrications of the opinions of others. *Who cares?*

"And you, Max, please tell us, calmly, where you had been keeping yourself for three days?" V sternly asked.

"I already told you, Victoria. I lost track of time. I was here and then I was there and then I am here again. But, I'm pretty sure I was gone about three months. Do I look thinner? I seem to have gotten dozens of time-life threads out of order."

"Huh?" questioned V and Peter.

"Humph," Lily scoffed.

"I miscalculated. It shouldn't matter. I don't think it should matter. You might wake up tomorrow to discover it's yesterday, but you won't know it. Or, you go for a slice of pie and discover you're not baking it until tomorrow. No real big things. That's good, isn't it? I can't remember everything. I don't know what you expect of me, Victoria. *Help me.* I'm going to cry.

"Don't cry, Maxfield. Sit somewhere and relax."

"I need a dummy, Victoria. I need a dummy so I can say things!"

"You already say things," V shot back.

"But not the things I'd like to say."

"I find that hard to believe," V sighed and shook her head.

"It's a planet. Okay? I visited another planet and it's coming our way. I'm actually from that planet. So was your father. They look and act pretty much like us, but they don't go shopping quite as much. All I know is, I was in the basement and then *poof*, I was traveling through time, folding space and stuff like that. All very technical. *Hush, hush.* I do know that they will appreciate getting their book back. The aliens have scads of 'em. That one's just a learning tool for Sumer kiddos, but dangerous in the hands of Earthlings. *Look!*" Max exclaimed while pointing at Peter. "I give you bad, bad Peter's tail. This book was made specifically for the despicable twins. Very dangerous aliens are on their way and they're prepared to destroy Earth, if they don't get their book back."

"What!?"

"Kidding," Max said with a toothy grin. "Wherever there was where I was, you were there, Lily. Peter and V were there, too, but it wasn't exactly any of you there, know what I mean? Of course you don't. None of you ever do. That's why I need a dummy. Lily, do you remember anything?"

"About what, Max?"

"Tomorrow, Lily. Tomorrow."

"Not a thing, Max." Concerned, Lily asked. "Are you okay, Max? You worry me."

"Never worry. Never better. I need some dough gum. It helps me remember things."

"Or wipes your brain memory-free. Then, where would you be?" V stared at Max until he bent his head in make-believe shame.

V turned to Peter and stared until he bent his head in real shame. V had a way of saying things loudly and clearly without saying a single word.

Peter's tail began twitching and then whipped the air and a side-table, breaking V's hand-painted Taiwanese porcelain gargoyle. "Sorry. It seems to have a mind of its own."

"I like the way it thinks," whispered Lily.

"Now look what you have done!" cried V. "That was a family heirloom, Peter."

"Pish posh," Lily chided. "It's a grievous offense bought from a Chinaman."

"You hated my gargoyle, didn't you?" V asked. "You always hated it," V answered herself.

"More than anything," Lily admitted.

"We'll talk later, Lillian." Turning to Peter, V asked with exasperation, "What do you plan on doing with that tail with a mind of its own?"

There was a knocking on the front door. V had dismantled the buzzer years earlier, so there was no choice other than to knock.

"I'll get it. It better not be Philistines!" V rose and sluggishly left the room. All these knockings on her front door were becoming tedious, tiresome, and took its toll on her bearing. One might think that she and Lily had nothing better to do than sit around, get stoned, and wait for somebody to knock on their front door. One might think that.

"Lily, you don't seem to be here," observed Max.

"I'm here, Max, but I think I've gone totally bonkers." Then to Peter, "Thanks for breaking that atrocity. Or should I thank the tail?"

Peter smiled and said, "Sometimes V has the taste of a goat."

"Yeah."

While picking up pieces of the broken figurine, Peter said,

"You're more together than most, Lily. At least, you don't have a tail. Now that could make you bonkers. You are the most nonbonkers person I know."

"Thank...."

The twins stomped into the parlor. "What broke? You'll get in a lotta trouble whichever it was who did it. Probably you, Lily." Then they spied Peter's tail and ran over to feel it.

"OUCH. Don't squeeze it," cried Peter.

"It's super cool. I've seen nicer tails, but I want this one," Pudgy Penny whined, then mused, "Maybe a tail would make me galactic-ally cool? Fuckturds will listen to me and do what I tell them to do. Then I won't need to figure out more ways to kill the mammy-jammers. *Way cool.*"

"I want one, too!" Piggy Peter squealed with delight. "I live in a world of fucktards, fuckturds and turdtards. They put me here to suffer forever and ever. I hate this planet! I hate this dimension! I hate all of you, too. I'm beginning to think like you fucktards I gotta live with!"

"You can't have my tail, children," Peter firmly stated.

"We're not children!" Angrily stated by the twins in unison.

"Of course you're not. What was I thinking? Sorry. *Mea culpa.* That means my fault just in case you didn't know."

"Asshole," Piggy said under his breath, but not under far enough to keep O'Toole from hearing it.

"I hate those creatures!" O'Toole wasn't certain if he thought it or said it. *"Cretins!"*

Max tried to explain the difficulties involved when living in separate realities simultaneously. But he wasn't having much luck.

Meanwhile, V was at the front door trying to make herself a human obstacle against Billy Butts, his derelict friend Duchess Sylvia Rose Peterson von Smithwitz, and Eddy Spaghetti who was in drag as Marie Aqua-net, from pushing their way in.

"Billy, I'm busy right now."

"I need to talk to you."

"About what?" a disgruntled V asked.

"Good day, Mith Victoria." The lady in black poked her head around Billy and stepped into view. The Duchess was a pitiful mess who reeked of peanut butter, sweat, dill pickles, and McDonald's secret sauce. She spoke with unexpected perspicuity, for one with an unfortunate front-and-center hairlip, "I am soth looking thorward to fusing your lafatory. MathDonald's lafatory was out of orther."

Here was the dilemma plain and simple; should V let the Duchess in, or should she disallow a fellow traveler's urgent need to relieve herself? And then there was how to keep Butts from pushing himself in behind her? V's choices appear to all involve violence. "Can you hold it?" V pleaded.

"I gueth, but I don'tf know how long, Mith Victoria."

V addressed Billy with a super-sized can of aloof. " And what do you need to talk to me about, Billy?"

"Carla Bean."

"What about her?"

"She tried to kill herself last night. Good thing the sheet came untied and the overhead sprinkler pipe was cracked. Then she caused a flood and when she tried to drown herself a guard came and fished her out. Now she's in the psych ward at Q. C. Health. Probably wearing a straitjacket. I was in a straitjacket once. I didn't like it much, but the Thorazine made it bearable. I bet they gave her Thorazine. You can't go out in the sun with it. Don't ask me why. I don't know. It's stupefying and it makes your mouth bubble with white drool...."

"That's too regrettable, Billy. However, I was under the impression that you hated Carla."

"I do, sometimes, and sometimes I don't, but we're still fabulous friends. We don't let hate get in the way of our being friends. I like it when we hate each other because then we get to make-up and after we make-up there are dinner parties to celebrate. Carla's got a heart of vanilla pudding and she gives uber fabulous dinner parties."

"*Hmm*...I do not recall having gone to one. I need to rush-off and tend to business, but hold that thought," V officiously said while trying to shut the door.

"What kind of business?"

"None of yours, Billy."

"*Yo, girrrl.* You gonna let this poor Duchess in before she pees on my tooling? I just had this gown repaired and back from the cleaners." Eddy said as he pulled up his white gown to keep it from touching anything that would get it dirty, especially from having it peed on by the Duchess. "Marie Aqua-Net has a competition she's gonna win at The Trade Club tonight. Of course, Marie Aqua-Net has no competition, if you know what I mean."

"I am sure she doesn't, Eddy." V smiled, then turned to the Duchess, "Okay, Duchess, go do your business."

The Duchess squeezed past V and shuffled to the bathroom. V nearly fainted from the stench of her. After a spate of words from the altered reality of Billy Butts, blathering about who knows what, V acquiesced. "What the...oh well...Billy, Eddy, be my guest." V opened the door wide to accommodate Eddy's gown. As they walked into the parlor Lily was saying something about Tommy Too-Much.

"Where's the Duchess?" V asked no one in particular.

"In the head," Pudgy Penny informed.

"Doing number one, but it smells like number two!" Piggy Peter exclaimed, while his sister giggled.

V paid the pig from Hell no attention. "What about Too-Much, Lily?"

"I was thinking about sending him flowers," Lily sighed.

"Why?" V asked.

"He's family."

"I s'pose. Although, we can get them at Queen Soopers. We cannot afford a florist, Lily."

"Fabulous, Peter! A tail. Nice touch. I love it. Better than a Warhol happening," Billy giggled. "Did you know the Duchess used to have horns on her head. Big ones, too."

"Interesting, Billy," Peter said with uninvolved interest.

"I never saw anyone with a tail before," Eddy said. "Horns either. Going to a party, Peter?"

"No, Eddy, the tail's mine."

"Did you get it on eBay?"

"I mean, it's really mine, Eddy. It's attached."

"*Lordy, Lordy.* Will wonders never cease? Well, Peter…I wish you all good luck with it."

"You're not scared or disturbed by it?" Peter asked Eddy.

"No. Should I be? I'm a live and let live kinda girl."

"You're a wonder, Eddy. No wonder everybody loves you."

"Thank you, Peter."

"Where's Marie going today?" Lily asked.

"Tonight. To a drag competition. Five-hundred dollars, *girrrl.*"

"I hope you win, Eddy."

Billy sat on the Bishop's chair next to Lily. "Lily, did you hear about Carla Bean?" Billy then proceeded to fill her in before she had the chance to say yes or no.

V shifted her attention to O'Toole and asked, "Are you going to have that thing cut off, or what?"

Piggy chimed in, "Can I have it?"

"No, Peter, you cannot have his tail!" V turned back to O'Toole and asked, *"Well?"*

"I think I really like it, V."

"And you plan to walk around Queen City with it, *huh?* Have you lost your friggin' mind!?" V didn't really expect a rejoinder, but...

"No." Sounds like V got her answer. "I can wrap it around my waist. Nobody's going to see it. Besides, who's gonna care?"

"I care! I should call Doctor Fuzzlbum," V offered.

"Who's Doctor Fuzzlbum?"

"He's a neurosurgeon, Peter," V said. "He owes me a few favors. Perfect for your problem."

"Then can we have the tail?" asked a snickering Piggy.

"I want to watch them hack it off!" Pudgy demanded.

"What did you do for him to owe you a few favors, V?"

"Not what I did for him. It is what I did not do for him, Peter."

"Do I want to know this story?"

"Probably not."

The Duchess, putrid and noxious, entered the parlor and caught a glimpse of Peter's tail and said, "Nith tail."

"Thank you, Duchess."

"I useth to hafe horns."

"I heard," Peter smiled with amazement.

"If you dethide to remofe it, better call Fuzzlbum. He remofed my horns and lethf barely a scar. *Hmm*, where did I put thoth horns?" the Duchess puzzled.

Max stood in the corner out of everybody's sight wondering if he were invisible. He fidgeted with the plaster of Paris bust of nobody in particular that Lily had brought home after the closing of *The Trojan Women*. A small piece of plaster broke from its base. He wasn't sure whether he had done it or not. But while trying hide the broken piece of plaster, the entire bust fell to the floor. This put an end to Maxfield's wondering. He was undeniably visible. He was a man of substance. He could be seen. "It's okay. No problem. Nothing here to see." Apparently there wasn't because nobody glanced his way.

Maxfield no longer attends the Theatre. He very much enjoyed the Theatre festival celebrating the god Dionysus at the City Dionysia in Athens. In the old days Aeschylus, Sophocles and Euripides were the big hitters, and farting was all the rage. But nobody farts onstage anymore; at least, not on purpose. V had tried, on many occasions, to coax Maxfield into going to the

Theatre with her, but he always refused. He cannot bear Theatre anymore. Everything is wrong. Disturbing. Gave him bad dreams. Bad vibes. Theatre has certainly gone downhill in the past couple thousand years. Once, Maxfield attended the Theatre with V for the Boulder Shakespeare Festival production of *Julius Caesar*. He was mortified. "Victoria, that is not the way it happened. Lies. All lies! Liar, liar, Shakespeare's pants on fire." Maxfield, who straddles alternate dimensions as a way of life, saved himself from watching the entire catastrophe by falling asleep in both of them.

"I'm going to call Fuzzlbum," V announced.

"Don't! I'm not sure I want it removed. I might keep it."

"It *is* sexy," Billy winked, pseudo-salaciously.

"Sure is a conversation starter," Eddy said.

"So are you, Miss Thing," Piggy snickered.

Pudgy giggled. "You do know everybody calls you Eddy Spaghetti behind your fat ass, right?"

"Enough! Go to your goddamn rooms, the two of you!" V shouted at the twins.

"Make us," Pudgy stood her ground.

"I'll break both your fucking necks!" Eddy was ready to kill.

Eddy Wilson loved to entertain. Almost every week a few of his friends, and he had many, would come for dinner, and at every dinner party everything he served involved spaghetti. He made chicken Parmesan sometimes, sometimes it was beef Braciole, or meatballs, or sausage, sometimes meat balls and sausage and other divine creations, but they were always accompanied with spaghetti with an array of different sauces. What was not to be loved? Over time he was given the nickname of Eddy Spaghetti, which he thought it a deserving and loving title. "I'll have you creatures from the black lagoon know that I do know. My friends call me Eddy Spaghetti because of my dinner parties. They gave it to me with love and respect. They even asked my permission. I was honored. It was an act of love, you pieces of donkey dung. And I don't have a fat ass! I'm wearing a bustle!"

"I wonder where I puth thoth horns. William, do you know where I puth thoth horns?"

"I think you mentioned something about a Chinese restaurant, Duchess," Billy reminded her. "They wouldn't let you in with your horns. After Fuzzlbum removed them, you went back and threw them at the manager. Unfortunately, one of the horns stuck him a little too deeply."

"Yeth, I rememfer. Who could forgith it?"

* * *

V's story about Dr. Fuzzlbum begins with her telling about her hospital job. V had volunteered once a week at Saint Joseph's Hospital. She performed many valuable services to and for the ill. She helped them with pillows and blankets, ice and magazines, tea, coffee and good cheer. Although, some days good cheer was on backorder.

V had an especial way to care for the goldbrickers who were working on getting themselves Workers' Compensation. They were mostly stupid, ugly, unpleasant and with a fuck-everybody attitude. For them, she served coffee that she had boiled until bubbles rose and broke in the air of the microwave. *"Oh dear,"* V would say after *accidentally* spilling the bubbling brew onto their private parts. *"Hot damn! That must have hurt. Sorry."* She had a great many of those *"Hot damn!"* accidents.

V tried to make a valiant attempt at spreading joy, but that was not something that came easily for her. It didn't fool the infirm even when she gave it her best. Being bipolar, some days V's best was pretty awful. *"Do I look like a candy striper to you? How long is your arm? You can't reach it for yourself!?"* The thing was, after V had done a bit of self-examination, she had a realization, *"I do not like people who do not like themselves! Period. End of story."*

On the morning of V's last day at Saint Joseph's, she was in the linen closet gathering no-ass gowns from behind a rack of towels when Doctor Fuzzlbum barged into the closet, locked the door behind him, and swiftly removed every bit of his clothing, including his socks, before masturbating like a brazen monkey. V could not hold back a cough to clear her throat. The moment he began to moan and writhe, she coughed. Loudly!

"Who's there?" Fuzzlbum was hoping he was mistaken and the coughing sound came from somewhere else.

V hid her scrambled egg and tofu burrito between a pile of hospital gowns and came out from behind the towels, still coughing, "I'm sorry to have interrupted, but I tried to hold it back. I see you couldn't either, Doctor Fuzzlbum."

"Do we know each other?"

"We do now. You are famous," she said while trying to clear her throat.

"Let me take a look," the naked neurosurgeon said as he rubbed against her to look as far as his eyes would take him down her throat. "You need bread and water," was Fuzzlbum's prognosis.

"I know," V swallowed. "Hey, I think it went down."

After a loud uncomfortable silence, Fuzzlbum spoke. "You wouldn't want to hurt my reputation, would you?"

"*What?* No. Of course not."

"I'll give you anything you want."

"Never heard that before. I always wondered how it would feel getting an offer like that. But nope, I don't want anything. Do you satisfy yourself often, Doctor? The floor does seem a little… gamey."

Fuzzlbum smiled, feeling an instant camaraderie with V and answered, "Before surgery."

"Every time?"

"Always. It calms my nerves. Keeps me from thinking about sex while I operate."

"Too much fun," she beamed. "I like that. I don't know why, but I do. There is a certain amount of poetic irony; *oui, je ne sais quoi.*"

"*Oui.* Perhaps you're right, but there must be something I

can do for you," reading her badge, "Victoria."

Fuzzlbum knew this chance encounter could damage his career. He certainly didn't want to jeopardize that, nor cause discomfort for his family. Paranoia took hold. It grabbed him by the throat and scared the bejesus out of him. He began to think of ways to murder her, but quickly changed his mind. He really liked V, and he didn't feel threatened by her—not completely, that is. "Maybe...how about...how about no doctor's fee? *Huh?* For you and yours, should you ever need neurosurgery."

"Possible, but not probable. I shall remember to call you, Doctor Fuzzlbum. And, don't you worry about...you know...mum's the word. Honest. I think you are cool, and cute as a button."

"Perfect, Victoria. Thank you. I feel a lot better," Fuzzlbum graciously said. "You wouldn't want to...?"

"Not today, Doctor. I like women." V opened the door and left. She hasn't seen him since.

Fuzzlbum, after giving V enough time to arrive somewhere else, slinked out of the linen closet and casually walked towards the operating room; choosing each step according to an assortment of differently colored painted lines on the corridor's floor. Each color led to a different destination.

Today's surgery involved removing a foreign object from the thick skull of billionaire media whore, Baby Trump, who came to Queen City especially to have the esteemed Doctor Fuzzlbum perform the operation. *"But, If I do decide to murder her, what was her name...ahh Victoria, it can easily be blamed on the Queen City Hacker."*

The Queen City Hacker is Queen City's first serial killer. One dozen victims within thirteen months, murdered with an unrelenting hatchet, and nothing yet to tie the victims together other than the same brutality of each murder.

Astonishingly, the object in Trump's skull was bigger than his brain. It took over six and one-half hours to disengage the giant ego that was smothering his intellect, getting in the way of his ability to reason, or to make the least bit of sense. For instance, when the patient was rolled into the operating room, drowsy and babbling something about *"Me and the Putinski. I'm gonna do stuff. Big stuff."* Over and over he repeated the same thing. Throwing in a load of *I this* and and *I that*. There was no one in attendance who could make any sense of it. *Gibberish. What kind of stuff?* Sometimes patients say the darnedest things—especially those in fear of ego removal. It's a big step toward letting the brain do its thing. He did say more 'I's than on a fly. That's one mother lode of ego!

    The mother lode was so tightly embedded in Trump's skull, Fuzzlbum had to remove it with a half inch chisel and a rubber mallet. What remained in his skull after the ego removal was something resembling a black, highly furrowed, chicken's egg; which was the regrettable size of Trump's atrophied brain. Fuzzlbum's assisting nurse weighed the slimy ego. *"Fifty pounds!"* A fifty pound pink slug! That surely had to weigh more than anything ought to weigh that is taken out of a man's skull.

    There it was, the slimy pink ego looking like an escapee from McDonald's. It growled, slid off the scales, growled some more, bounced around the room, hung from a florescent light fixture and sang the title song from "Gilligan's Island." Fuzzlbum coaxed the ego with open arms and as it got within hugging distance, he gave the nasty thing a whack with a bloody bone saw. The ego screamed profanities in Russian, then slithered its way under one of the styrofoam ceiling tiles and disappeared, leaving trails of pink sludge behind.

    Fuzzlbum quickly finished working on Trump. He installed a hinged door on the top of Trump's skull for loose change and condoms. Billionaires never carry money, so Fuzzlbum threw in a bit of lose change. Trump's hair weave and comical combover finally had a legitimate reason; to hide the hole in his head. Remarkably, Trump lived. Although he did complain about his feeling lightheaded and hearing rattling sounds in his head. Trump's little brain enlightened him, causing him to understand that he was never responsible for anything that went wrong, but only responsible for everything that went right. *"It's good to have a brain."*

Fuzzlbum's celebrity status began soon after replacing the backbone and tightening the anus of a Hollywood action hero. Fuzzlbum performed the operation in the inner sanctum of the Hollywood Church of Scientology. Few believed Fuzzlbum's fantastical fabrication. In fact, not a word of it was true. He simply made it up to impress the ladies at cocktail parties. It was Fuzzlbum himself who began the rumor that he, Doctor Fuzzlbum, Neurosurgeon to the Stars, was a major coup for the Queen City medical establishment. One of the world's most important surgeons was right here in Queen City. The rumored news of the surgeon's stature rose to the level of irrefutable credibility, at least in Queen City. However, as it happens, there was some truth to Fuzzlbum's celebrity in the medical world. He developed several procedures for brain and spinal cord surgery which are named after him. The Fuzzlbum Procedure is now regularly performed worldwide on farm animals. So, who better to remove a tail than Doctor Fuzzlbum?

Shady Sanctum chatter went on without respite. Eddy Spaghetti smoothed and arranged his gown, Billy Butts sat staring at the book on the table, Maxfield was still trying to figure out whether or not he was invisible, Peter stroked his tail while twins watched in envy, the Duchess stood next to Maxfield who decided that he was not invisible from smelling her, V was stressed-out while sitting next to Lily and holding her hand. V thought about calling Fuzzlbum whether Peter liked it or not, but her thought was interrupted when there came a loud pounding on the front door. This was not a good day for front doors.

"I'll get it," shouted Pudgy Penny running to the door.

"Don't let any zombies in!"

All eyes turned to V, *"What?"*

Dionysos parted as Pudgy stepped into the parlor carrying a basket of fruit, mostly apples, followed by Mikey and Mercy Pentcist.

"These here guys brought a basket of shitty apples. *Yuk!*

They said they'd leave it and come back later, but I knew you'd want me to invite 'em in, so I told 'em they can have a look at Peter's tail and here they are."

V screamed, kicked Billy off the sofa and to the floor, then she fell onto the sofa, her eyes rolled back and then they closed. She shook, moaned and shrieked, *"Out! Out! Everyone of you fuckers, out!"*

"She needs my hands!" screamed Mercy Pentcist, coming within touching distance from V. "She needs the hands of Jesus."

"Out, devil bitch, out! Take your fucking hands away from me! Out, out, out!" V growled, barked, and flailed. And, when she opened her eyes she saw that the room had emptied. V smiled an exhaled with relief.

Maxfield started breathing heavily, began to sweat and said to himself, *"Holy alligators! I did it! I messed up time!"* He ran to his bedroom, got under his bed and proceeded to time-travel.

Mercy cried and said to Mikey, as they stepped onto the sidewalk, "She needed my hands."

"Yes she did, Pumpkin."

"I forgot the fruit basket."

"Leave it, Pumpkin. Besides, they're on sale at Sooper's."

Peter stuck his head out of the kitchen and asked, "Is it safe?"

V waved to Peter to come back in. "It's safe now."

"What a performance. Brava, darling, brava." Peter applauded. "One of your absolute best."

"Thank you, Peter," V said while looking around the room. "Where's the book?"

"On the table where you told me to put it."

"It's not there, Sweetie."

"That's where I put it, V."

"I saw him put it there," Lily confirmed while coming down the stairs. V threw her hands up and with deeply felt resignation sighed, *"Shit, shit, shit."*

Peter, weary and distraught, acquiesced and said, "Better call Fuzzlbum."

ELEVEN

frackers, buzzards, and real live mormons

Digging equipment, land moving trucks, and piping for the Krotch, Krotch, Bushit & Mother and Vader, Diggers and Frackers, LLC, committed to laying a Peruvian pipeline to Houston, Texas, encompassed the nearly one half square mile of Puerto Nostradamus as did an intensely electrified chained-link fence, topped with razor wire and surrounded by an army of heavily armed Black Buzzards—the Krotch Brother's henchmen—dumb sycophants who enjoy the kill. It should be noted that not one of the Buzzards were actually black; they were as white as the KKK, but not quite as white as Baby Trump. All financial investments were strictly the business of the Krotches, who had earned a reputation as benefactors for good projects. "Good Projects" was their maxim.

The salary paid to the Buzzards was only frosting on the cake of their prerogative to neutralize unidentified foreign objects and looky-loos. The Black Buzzards' prime directive was to keep the kooks within the perimeter of Puerto Nostradamus from making contact with the outer world and, the fun part, by whatever means necessary.

Quonset huts dotted the land: offices for the Krotches, the Bushits and Darth Vader, a dining hall, an amusement building with TVs, computers with the latest games, marijuana, nose candy, a barroom, XXX videos in private booths with a warm hand towel dispenser and a glory hole in each wall, a vintage Pac Man and other arcade amusements, plus a candy box assortment of professional female *artistes,* and a male rent-boy, brought in from the States. Used and worn-out *artistes* and the rent-boy were replaced bimonthly.

The vanguard of Buzzards think—if "think" is what they do —that their duty is to blindly follow a man with a two digit higher IQ than their own—the lower the IQ, the higher the risk for believing fake news. They were told that the people inside the fenced compound were anti-Christians, Atheists, witches who practiced the black arts and, here's the clincher, they were terrorists with arms of mass destruction. For the Buzzards, there was nothing so motivating as the words "Atheist, anti-Christian and terrorist." Who would want Atheist terrorists attacking Christians, and the pipeline of Krotch, Krotch, Bushit & Mother and Vader Diggers and Frackers, LLC? *Really*, who would want such a thing? To question authority was unimaginable for the Black Buzzards.

Charlie and Gert owned Puerto Nostradamus outright, but they did not own the right-of-way to get on or off their property. No one objected in the past. The right of eminent domain did not apply in Peru. No one ever gave a thought to the possibility of outsiders like the Krotch Brothers imprisoning Puerto Nostradamus. The Krotches and their cohorts were anomalies who many questioned whether or not they were actually part of the Human Race. After Gert and Charlie refused to sell to them, FOX News portrayed Gert and Charlie as impediments to progress; and worse, they were traitors, squatters, devil worshipers and un-American. The Fake News outlets didn't agree. They never do. That's why they're Fake News. The Krotches with their endless supply of money bought or leased every bit of land surrounding Puerto Nostradamus, including the leasing of Lake Titicaca; pending the deed and permits to drill.

In the lilac cabin, one of the many differently colored cabins in Puerto Nostradamus, was the alluring female illusionist Tallulah Badass, a convincing Tallulah Bankhead look-alike. Poor Thing, in her harmless neurosis, Badass believes Miss Bankhead's spirit inhabits his body. Badass was once the prime suspect for being the serial killer from Duluth, Bernard Wang. However, Tallulah was Bernard Wong, not Wang. A month after they caught the real killer, Tallulah Wong thought about getting her past chopped off, becoming a total woman, and he's still thinking about it. He felt he was due for a change.

An alluring Goat Boy lives in a small rickety shack on the far side of the Puerto Nostradamus compound. Yet, once inside the shack, the Goat Boy can open the back door and step into any part of the universe he likes. There have been many stories about wardrobes and doors opening into exotic places, so it certainly must be true. The Goat Boy had elfin horns, cloven feet and a modest tail. He is human from the waist up, a goat from the waist down. His private parts were covered with a tuft of fur, so whether the package belonged to the goat or to the boy remains to be seen.

Satyrs do not usually like their presence known to mortals, although they will show themselves in certain situations to certain individuals. The one and only time Gert saw the satyr was on an early gray morning when she was foraging for mushrooms and herbs. When she saw him on the porch of the shack, she asked, "Are you Pan?"

He laughed and said, "No. Pan is my second cousin on my mother's side, or maybe it's my father's side? Anyway, it'll come to me. It was a long time ago. At the moment, Pan is busy causing mischief in the south of France."

"What an interesting life. They call me Gert."

"I know."

"Oh...well, what is your name?"

"I do not know. I was never given one."

"Huh?"

"I can only be given a name by my one true love."

"I hope you'll find your one true love soon."

"I do, too, Gert. Thank you."

The satyr had a beautiful voice, melodious and mysterious. He was ageless, strikingly handsome, bewitching with piercing eyes of silver. His smile sparkled with perfectly white human teeth. His flawless skin was as white as milk, breathtakingly translucent, smooth and inviting. Just to see him is to want to touch him. Gert wanted to reach out and touch him, but her better sense stopped her, as it also did from running her hands through his hair. His loosely curled hair was as white as his skin, yet it reflected a rainbow of sparks. In short, the Goat Boy was stunning, seductively winsome, and out of this world!

Gert asked herself, as her hairy mole twitched just before she turned into an Andean fox, *"Where does he go when he disappears? Where does he come from? Who the hell is this guy?"*

"Who gives a fuck! I gotta git back ta Jersey!" the Governor shouted before getting slapped by the realization, "Oh my God! Nobody knows I'm here."

"Where do they think you are?" Gert asked.

"Vacationing in the Berkshires, like always! They can't do this! We can't get out and nobody can get in. Isn't that against Peruvian law? It should be, shouldn't it? Somebody could get hurt, or get killed! What a thoughtless thing to do."

"It's disgusting and criminal, Mister Crapp."

"Governor Crapp."

"Governor Crapp." Gert wasted no charm and continued, "Charlie and I never worried about laws, politics, or that sort of thing. We who live here, including our guests, are honest folk. Doing anything this despicable has never occurred to any of us. Wouldn't you agree, Governor Crapp?"

"Yeah, yeah, yeah. No landline. No cellphone reception. No WiFi. No nothin'! And I don't know what you're talking about."

"The altitude, I guess." Gert smiled.

"Where's your computer?"

"The guard cut the electrical line. Besides, it crashed a week ago. Getting it to a geek seems unlikely at the moment, doesn't it, Mister Governor?"

"Despicable. That's the only word for it." Crapp's body language did not reflect his words. He was mocking Gert. "We're trapped like rats in a shit-hole, with all due respect, Miss Gert. Did you ever see a subway rat? Fat, mean and ugly as all hell."

"On or off the train?" Gert asked.

Crapp paid Gert no mind. "I'm responsible for the welfare of millions living in my Garden State. What if one of us needed ta get to a hospital? Oh Holiest of Holy, don't let it be me. One of us could die in here. Please. *Not me.* There's nobody pregnant here, is there?"

"Not as far as I know, Governor Crapp."

"It's inhuman!"

"Inhuman indeed. There's no other word for it, Governor Crapp." Gert said, with a tinge of sarcasm.

"Lose the Crapp and call me Governor. Just Governor, Toots. Ya got it? I don't like the way you say Crapp."

The sun-bronzed brothers, Alfredo and Álvaro, wearing tight white short-shorts, and nothing more, approached the Governor.

"My brother wants to know if Governor is Mafia?" Alfredo asked.

"What! Certainly not! There's no such thing as Mafia. Never was. Get it out of your head right now! Why do ya ask such a vicious question?"

"Rumors," Alfredo answered. "They fly on the wings of sparrows."

"Don't listen to rumors from birds. One day you'll listen to the wrong bird, and you could end up sleeping with the fishes. You got it?" That was when the Governor's face swelled into an angry red moon and, noteworthy, he actually did look like a big pizza pie hit him in the eye. "Because if you don't got it you...!"

"You like massage with warm coconut oil?" Alfredo interrupted the Governor with a smile, a nod, and a wink. "We make you happy. Like last time. You like last time?"

The Governor lit up. "Yes," he said with a furtive tone.

Moving closer to the Governor, Álvaro asked, "Sound good? You want now?"

Crapp began sweating, breathing heavily, his mouth went dry and he could not speak. He dipped his index and middle finger into his Coke and wiped his lips until they were lubricated enough to move and speak. "I want...oh, God...I want...." Crapp shivered and whispered.

"Of course you do." Gert tittered. The boys agreed.

The Governor and his "service technicians" silently left the clubhouse.

"Have fun!" Gert yelled through the screen door.

The brothers escorted the sweat-soaked, big-headed fat man from Jersey to the yellow cabin. Crapp inserted the skeleton key into the lock on the cabin's door. The three of them entered. The irresistibly delicious brothers were the Governor's only retreat from his current predicament. And these sweet treats were something else! They quickly steered his mind into a different direction. Both brothers had a whopping talent for that sort of customer service, along with a knack for making everybody feel helplessly enthralled simply from being alive. The brothers knew how to stop time and they knew how to detach a mind from its brain, freeing it to travel into ecstasy.

* * *

Billy Butts was hurt and pissed with V for dismissing him. He loved her, she was one of his very best friends forever. He indeed loved her, not entirely as a fag hag but..."*She'll be sorry...I've got her stupid book!*"

The "stupid book" he smuggled from out Shady Sanctum lay next to his computer. He reached into the bag to remove the book and, barely touching it, he felt a painful sting. He quickly withdrew his hand. "*What the hell? Jesus Aitch!*"

Billy, in a state of solemnity—a state he seldom visited—reflected on his life and misadventures until the irritant disturbing him subsided. He was awash with strange sensations he never felt before. Billy was elated. He certainly must put this "bewildering perception" in his diary. Billy reached for his faux zebra leather covered journal with Marilyn Monroe holding down her dress from the wind of a passing train beneath the subway grate, and wrote: "*The easiest dimension to access is the fourth. The seer need only see it, feel it, or hear it to be in it. The fourth dimension is simply a way to observe and interact with a higher level of consciousness. Communication is somewhat more difficult with those who are yet to experience that higher consciousness. This leaves one forever seeking others who live in the fourth dimension. Other than an instant flash of lightning, or buzz words, there is little else to prepare one for fourth dimensional thinking. There is a loneliness. There is no god other than oneself in the fourth dimension; leaving no one to blame for the consequences of actions and choices than oneself. Fourth dimensional thinkers are usually thoughtful and truthful. The religiously inclined call it "born again." The fourth dimension is an unexpected shift into an unexpected inner life of a seer; an unexpected shift in attention; an unexpected place where the subconsciousness can communicate freely with consciousness. What bewildering perception is this?"*

Billy Butts put down the pen and closed his diary with the holographic image of Marilyn Monroe rising from a faux zebra cover. Billy thought about putting his finger on the strange book again, but he didn't want to push his luck. He was intuitively certain that there would be undesirable consequences next time. He didn't want a tail like Peter's for Fuzzlbum to saw off. Besides, he gave Fuzzlbum a blow job behind the bushes in Cheesman Park a few years back and didn't want to run into him again. He wasn't going to take any unnecessary chances, so he quickly withdrew his hand from the temptation of touching the book.

Billy opened his diary and read his last entry. *"Good gravy! What the...? Did I write that?"* He did indeed. He read it several more times. Electricity filled his body. Tingling, stinging, and tremors engulfed him. He had to get out and talk to someone, go to the baths, have sex with a stranger, anything! He thought of visiting V, but he quickly realized he couldn't without confessing that he had 'borrowed' the book. *"What the heck is the color of this thing, anyway?"* He went into his small galley kitchen and returned wearing rubber gloves, so that he could safely put the book into his backpack. He decided to face V and get it over with. He headed out for Shady Sanctum. Billy could put it under V's sofa and then pretend to find it, but he chickened out, changed his mind, and decided to visit poor Carla Bean first.

* * *

"My poor, poor Carla, whatever are you going to do?"

"I don't know, Mercy."

"Have you heard anything about when you might be getting out of this foul Godless place?" Mercy asked.

"Soon, I hope. Since Tommy Too-Much dropped all the charges, I won't have to go back to that filthy jail; the things they write on those walls! I'm amply medicated and expect to be for quite some time; therefore, no need to keep me here."

"No need to keep you here," Mikey repeated.

"I'm broke, you know," Carla confessed.

"Carla Bean is broke? *C'mon*. Really? How?" Mercy asked incredulously.

"I'm too exhausted to talk about it now, Mercy."

"I understand." Mercy gave her best impression of sincerity and caring, which she had rehearsed on the drive down from Brighton to visit Carla. Mercy was in the driver's seat, as usual, and Mikey sat quietly in the passenger seat, thinking of little else other than how to murder his wife without getting caught.

"Her bloody body will need to appear as if she were the victim of the Queen City Hacker," thought Mikey, then he felt the need to laugh uncontrollably. So he did.

"Which brings us to why we're here, Carla," Mercy said then quickly added, "I mean, aside from seeing you, of course, and sharing your pain, in your time of need."

"Sharing your pain in your time of need," Mikey soothed.

"Sharing my pain...so thoughtful." Carla said, with a hesitance often associated with mistrust.

"We were thinking," Mercy said.

"The two of us were thinking," mimicked Mikey.

"Perhaps, we could help you. Perhaps, we could take all your worries away."

"All your worries away," said the parrot.

"There's nothing that could take all my worries away, not even half of them," Carla glumly said and continued, "All my money, gone. Everything."

"How is that possible?"

"I don't want to talk about it, dearest Mercy."

"So you said. Sorry. I'm so very sorry to hear that," fluttered Mercy. "What about considering our complete Christian Service package. We'll give you a special price."

"A special price," Mikey regurgitated.

"The Prometheus Society, LLC..." Mercy tried to roll one of her butt cheeks up so she could scratch her ass, but she was in a bit of a tight fit so she gave up and continued, "...is prepared to leave your family worry-free, after a two year waiting period of course, for the policy to kick in. After that you might find yourself in the arms of Jesus before you know it."

"I don't have a family."

"Everybody has a family, Carla."

"Not me." And then she quickly added, "What do you mean by *before I know it?*"

"One never knows when one will find oneself in His arms," an exalted Mercy righteously informed.

"You're fucking with me, right? I'm sure I won't be going anywhere soon; especially to meet and greet Jesus."

Mercy was taken aback. "You never know. You live alone in that huge place, don't you?" Mercy asked, even though she already knew the answer, so she quickly continued, "Poor thing. We provide a death watch device that you wear around your neck. If you feel you're about to die you just push the button. You should wear it all the time. Push the button and we take it from there, with dignity. There is, of course, a small fee for pushing the button when you're not dying."

"With Dignity. Small fee." Mercy's husband accentuated.

"What do you think, precious Carla?" Mercy asked.

"*Think?* Mercy, I've been through too much to think. Please, another time."

"Take your time. Think about it when you're ready. We all

die, there's no denying it. Be prepared. Trust us and Praise the Lord! And let us pray."

Meanwhile, outside the door of the hospital psych ward, Billy was stopped and told to open his backpack by Nurse Ivanka the Wretched. Two hospital guards stood near her. Nurse Ivanka the Wretched grabbed Billy's backpack and opened it. The salami-scented Nurse asked as she reached for the book, "What's this?"

"*Umm*...just a book."

"Let me see that! Looks like contraband," arrogant, rent-a-guard pronounced.

"You'll need to leave this with us before we are allowed let you pass. You can pick it up when you come out, sir." Kindly smiling, awesome guard said with a flirtatious wink. His wink was enough to rev-up Billy's libido into overdrive.

"What's your name?" asked a demure Billy Butts.

"Brad. Brad Studd. With two Ds."

"Oh, my God! His name is Brad Studd," Billy said to himself, and then said to Brad Studd, "Is it Brad or Studd with the two Ds?"

"Studd."

"I'm Billy. Billy Butts, with two Ts," he stammered.

Brad smiled broadly, showing his perfect white teeth, and said, "I'll be here when you come out."

"I'm already out...I mean, you will?" Brazen-faced Billy began to shiver.

"Your book, sir."

"My book, yes. You really shouldn't handle it," Butts said to all three of them. But he might as well have invited them to read it page by page.

"No worries," soothed Brad. His voice was a love song to Billy's ears. Brad unlocked the door for him. Billy noticed Brad's fabulous ass and nearly swooned. Billy entered the ward with his head in the clouds as he walked in mid-air from a place called Lust and an ass he wanted to kiss.

The psych ward was bright from the sun shining through a wall of barred windows. Molts of skin and dust danced in the shafts of sunlight. The beds were filled to capacity, but Billy would not look at them, nor acknowledge their existence. Hospitals terrified him. Billy approached Carla who was sitting in a wicker chair talking to the Pentcists.

"Well, if it isn't my two favorite people," Billy sniggered at Mercy and Mikey.

Mercy glanced at Billy and said, sourly, "We need to go. It's a little too gay in here for us."

"Need to go," Mikey mechanically said. Mercy had given Mikey strict orders, on their drive down from Brighton, to remain mum and stay out of her business. She shot him a shockingly demonic shut-the-fuck-up kind of smile.

"Be sure you let us know, Carla dear. The Prometheus Society, LLC exists to serve our dear Christian brothers and sisters in their time of need." Mercy gave an ugly glance toward Billy and said, "We are one in Christ." Mercy *humphed* and turned back to Carla, "Don't forget what I told you. God bless you, Carla dear."

"Thank you, Mercy...Mikey. I'll give it a think."

The Pentcists picked themselves up to leave. Mercy had more to pick up, including the wicker chair that was still attached to her ass, "Good day, Mister Butts. *Oh,* I've been meaning to ask you; what does that upside down pink triangle thing mean?"

"I'm not sure, Missus Pentcist. It might have something to do with the Teamsters. If you like, I'll ask around for you."

"Yes, please do." Mercy said while trying to disengage herself from the wicker chair, while staring directly at Billy as though he were a bug, "*Oops*. I just remembered what that means. Oh dear. I didn't mean...oh dear."

"Yes, you did, you stupid, hypocritical, ignorant cow!" And then Billy said aloud, "I will pray you don't go to Hell, Missus Pentcist."

"I pray you do!"

Mikey and Mercy knocked on the locked door to get out quickly. They were let out by Brad Studd with the fabulous ass.

Billy took time to swoon, sigh, and exhale before saying to Carla, "She is such an evil bitch. I suppose they were here practicing their usual unscrupulous sales tactics."

"Something like that. Nice of you to come, Billy. I think I'll be going home soon."

"Good to hear. Nice of Too-Much to drop the charges."

"It breaks my heart to think of what I did, Billy."

"It ought to. You nearly killed the man."

"Don't be cruel."

"I'm sorry, but you were a tad bit cruel yourself, Carla," Billy spoke as carefully as he knew how so not to start an argument. It didn't take much to trigger one of Carla's hissy-fits, or an all-out frightening exhibition of her wicked kick-ass rage.

"Yes, I was cruel, but I didn't kill him, did I? I guess I didn't know my own strength," Carla admitted, unenthusiastically.

"Are we still friends, Carla?"

"Why shouldn't we be?"

"Good question." Billy said. "I never should have told you where your Greek was. I had no idea that a woman your size, and at your age, could possibly do that much damage to another person."

"I didn't know my own strength."

"Well, if I ever need a bodyguard, I'll call you."

They started to giggle, but it was pretty much inaudible.

"I feel guilty and responsible for what Tommy did. He only did what was natural for him, Carla. I know better of course," Billy boasted.

After a scrutinizing pause, an inner laugh, Carla said, "Of course...I never thought otherwise. And what did you mean by 'at your age?'"

Billy changed the subject, quickly. After more small talk

that did not involve age, Billy left. When he was let out by a guard he hadn't seen before, he panicked, "I left a blue backpack with a valuable book in it with Brad Studd. An awful nurse wouldn't let me take it in. Do you know where they are?"

"The guards?"

"The backpack...and a guard named Brad Studd, with two Ds.

"Don't know any Brad Studd..." said an old gray-haired, balding man in grimy yellow overalls. "...but, if Mr. Studd was one of the guards, he would've put what you're looking for in the linen closet," he points to the door directly across the hall.

Billy inhaled deeply, slowly exhaled, and said more to himself than to the guard, "Oh, please, please, please let it be."

"I don't look at things that aren't my business," said the man with rusty eyebrows an inch or more long, putting on his eyeglasses that hung from a shoestring tied around his neck, continued, "I'll get it for you."

"Thank you." Billy was relieved.

The guard walked across the hall to retrieve the backpack. In record time he returned with it and asked, "Is this it?"

"*Yes!* Thank you, thank you, thank you!" Billy grabbed the backpack, took a quick look to make sure the book was still there. It was. "By the way, what happened to the guards who were here? Especially Brad."

"With two Ds?'

"No. It's Studd with two Ds. Brad's spelled with only one."

"*I see.* I don't keep track of what isn't my business, but I did hear that there was a mighty panic about some people disappearing. *Poof.*"

"*Poof?*"

"Yup, *poof.* Just up and gone."

"How did they...?"

"I did hear something, but I'm not one to take some of what

I hear seriously. My wife is always telling me I don't listen. Anyway, Nurse Hunitits was walking towards the ward here and witnessed, if you can believe this, the three of them go up and disappear. You know. Like 'beam me up, Scotty.' Honestly, young man, strange things are always going on, aren't they?"

"Right, strange things." Billy liked being called a young man. He wanted to get going, but he was engaged with what the man in the yellow overhauls was saying.

"Anyway," continued the guard with improbable eyebrows, "Nurse Hunitits seems to have gone completely buggers, if you know what I mean. *Wiki-wacko*. They're gonna send her up here to the bin. I heard she can't complete a sentence, but don't take my word for it. I just hear things, you know? I was down in the boiler room working, they'll need a new boiler soon, when I got the call to come up here. I don't do guard work often, 'cept when I'm needed. But when you get the call you get going, know what I mean? Probably somebody's pulling my leg, but just in case, who's to say? Coulda never been a Nurse Hunitits, or maybe there was. I guess that's what happens from kicking a can of rumors down the road. *Hunitits?* What kind of name is that? What do you think, young man?"

Billy thought he heard that strange kind of talk again; that spooky-scary talk that gets into your head. "Gotta go." Billy turned and bolted for the elevator.

Tomorrow the headline in the *Queen City Post* will read: WORM HOLE SUCKS UP SAINT JOSEPH EMPLOYEES. In the article it says that Nurse Melania Hunitits, the only eyewitness to the supposed worm hole sucking, was admitted into the psych ward for observation. The headline for the story below the sucking wormhole read: QUEEN CITY HACKER DOES IT AGAIN.

* * *

There was a knocking on the front door. Lily came from the kitchen, wearing a green apron when she opened the door. *Mormons!*

"May we tell you about the good news—"

"Nope. We prefer bad news. Besides, we're busy making peanut butter hash oil brownies and cannot be disturbed."

SLAM!

And then there there came another knocking on the front door.

"What now!?"

TWELVE

shitty tits, made in china

Tittle-tattle of Cardinal Alletti's extracurricular activities at *Il Gallo Gay* spread into all corners of the Vatican. It was also tattled that Alletti's make-up, gowns, ten inch heels and accessories, were charged to the Vatican's Leper Outreach Fund.

There was no argument about Cardinal Bootlicker's musical talents. He sang opera at salons given by Pope Arshmann. The beauty of Alletti's voice was truly *squisito,* but was he the prepossessing Holly Waters whose stunning rendition of *Strani Amori* was *"semplicemente stupenda?"* Was it actually Alletti who left tears rolling over the cheeks of the patrons at *Il Gallo Gay* or was it Fernando DellaRosa, the most beautiful drag queen in all Roma? There was the night when Fernando was accosted by three men who tried to rape him. A three year case and the *polizia* hadn't a clue for who it was slit the throats of the three men who had followed Fernando from *Dal più grande pasta party annuale di Roma,* where he had been entertaining in the guise of Holly Waters. However, it could not have been Alletti, since he had an ironclad alibi—he was busy licking Arshmann's boots.

"Do you think it's really Alletti?"

"Does it matter, Rolly?"

"He might be innocent."

"Let's not let that get in the way of The Throne!" Rolly thought he heard an element of a Borgia in Georgie's voice. She continued, "In any case, Alletti is no longer a threat. The fix is in. My Sisters are already on it."

"How perversely clever you are, Georgie. You're really scary sometimes."

"Thank you, Rolly. Piss pot cum licker."

"Georgie, I'm not really sure I want to be Pope. I don't think I am holy enough."

"And Arshmann was?"

"Of course not. That's why we need someone very special. Someone who cares enough to bring God and His Love back into Catholicism. That's what I think. This is serious stuff, Georgie."

"I know. But I didn't know you thought that way, Rolly. Anyway, I love you no matter what. Bastard prick."

"Thank you, Georgie."

"But, I would give yourself more time to be certain. I wouldn't choose now, ass fucker."

"Okay, that works, stench-mouth." A smile, a hug, and then Rolly asked, "How would you like to go to Colorado, Georgie?"

"And chance missing the Conclave?"

"We won't."

"How do you know that, Rolly?"

"As the Papal Secretary, I have access to every certificate that must be signed and approved by me. As well as every document pertaining to the rules of conduct in the process of choosing a new Pope. Without those documents—"

"*Wow.* You can't be the only one with those documents?" Georgie was impressed.

"Maybe not, but I'll take the chance. No one has seen them since Arshmann was elected Pope and that was back when most of the Cardinals were having their knuckles broken by demented nuns and Saint Peter was still Pope! If there were duplicates, I am reasonably certain they must have gotten misplaced over all these years."

Georgie blurted, "Jesus fuck look at you!"

"Thank you, Georgie."

"What's in Colorado?" asked Mother George, who was having a dickens of a time suppressing her excitement.

"A book. A magical book, I think. Arshmann was keen to put his hands on it. It was stolen from one of the underground treasure vaults by an excommunicated Brother and taken to

Colorado where it was used to practice Lucifer's black art; or something equally sinful. I don't know, but if the Nazi wanted it, it must be something important; so, I want to get my hands on it. If it is a work of evil we'll destroy it. If not we'll enjoy it."

"Fuck a poet after we eat shit and fuck yourself read it, right?"

"I think I might have understood that. We have the address of the excommunicated Brother. It's in Queen City and that's where we're going. He's dead, but his bachelor daughter lives there. It'll be quick. Ya wanna go?"

"You bet you ass, motherfucker ass licker shit head!"

"Your syndrome can be alarming to people who don't know you. What happened to your pills?"

"I don't like them. Bitter as Hell."

"You're not supposed to chew them."

"They make me feel funny. *Dirty vagina!* I want to go to Colorado.

"We need to fly commercial, Georgie. We cannot afford to be seen going to America at a time like this, you know...dead Pope and all. Let's go find ourselves the right disguise for the high plains of Colorado."

"Why?"

"It seems appropriate. We're goin' to the Wild West, pardner, where they root, toot and shoot. I always wanted to be a cowboy." There was no mistaking his excitement nor his youthful joy.

"Then why aren't you?"

"Get real, pardner." Then, Rolly slapped his hands together, giggled and said, "Let us mosey along over to the saloon for double whiskies and soda."

"Too exciting, Rolly. What fun!" exuberant and thrilled, said Georgie, only to be followed by the longest unbroken silence in the history of the solar system before she continued in a sad and subdued voice, as if she were ashamed to say, pained to say, what she was about to say about what she felt she had to say, so she said it in a most regrettable tone of sincere distress, "Don't be insulted big guy, but you may be forced to buy two tickets for yourself."

"*What?* I have no idea what you're talking about, Georgie. Why would I buy two tickets for myself?" Rolly was visibly hurt. When Rolly is hurt, Rolly attacks. "Are you going to wear a muzzle to protect the blessed innocence of children from your unsavory mouth?"

"At least, I don't have to buy two seats, blubber butt."

Rotundo and Mother George are the best of friends, however, like many old married couples, they bicker, bicker and bicker...(Keep in mind that all their bickering is said in Italian. Therefore, a copious amount of Italian hand-jive leaves the translation askew. Think mimes eating a hot cheesy, overstuffed calzone.)

When they arrived at the airport, as it happened, Cardinal Rotundo was forced to buy two seats for himself. Mother George's syndrome might rear its ugly head, so she kept her mouth filled with hot cinnamon hard candy; noisily chewed instead of slowly sucked.

Rolly and Georgie were dressed to kill, or maybe just to blind the good people of Queen City with their impeccable, yet devil-may-care taste in American Western *haute couture.*

Rolly was wearing tan cowboy boots made in China—his spurs were confiscated by a security guard with a face covered in tattoos—jeans from China the size of a *Cirque du Soleil* tent, a Chinese leather belt with a buckle in the shape of a skull and crossbones, a blue Hawaiian shirt adorned with an assortment of white and yellow flowers, made in China, which he wore outside his jeans; so, sadly, nobody would see his Chinese belt of imitation leather; it was the only 5X shirt to be found on such short notice. Finally, he topped himself off with a cowboy-style woven straw lacquered hat, made in China, to match his authentic Chinese cowboy boots. To describe the indescribable is unimaginable; a stupefying blow to the senses. Rolly and Georgie put together their all-American glad-rags at a place called Walmart Italia, subsidized by the hardworking children of China.

Georgie presented a more subdued appearance than the unintended 3-ringed farce that Rolly produced, directed, and starred in. Georgie's idea for what the ladies on the wrong side of middle-age wear in the Wild West was a bit closer to reality. The Holy Mother just might pass as somebody who shouldn't cause eyes to bulge, or explode. In fact, she came close to a distinctly American flirtation with casual *ordinaire*. She wore a paisley synthetic scarf, made in China, an ankle length Kelly green muumuu with an attractive African design, made in China, gray socks and faux black patent leather Mary Janes, also made in China.

"Is Walmart a Chinese company?" Georgie asked.

"I think so, yes."

They boarded the plane feeling cool as jazz and all-American in their new Italian Chinese-American wardrobe, including knockoff Ray-bans made in—it didn't say where where was made. Upon entering the Alitalia cabin Mother George could not be silenced. "Fuck, shit, piss! I hope the pilot doesn't go on strike today!"

"For the love of God, Georgie, nobody is going on strike today. Go, go, go. Quick, let's get to our seats," whispered Rolly who had begun to sweat and turn bright red.

The eyes and ears of the passengers were deluged with an impossibly fantastic and unexpected sideshow. During the flight Georgie's expletives increased, as did their volume. In short order, the sideshow had lost its captive audience. Some fellow travelers asked, while others demanded, flight attendants to, "....silence the old bitch's horrendous language...tone it down...throw the bitch off the plane right NOW!" Literally meant, one supposes.

Italians are a joyous happy people, they love to love and to share their joy…that's a fact…but Georgie had gone way over the top. The lion's share of the passengers were busy trying to devote themselves to the in-flight Catholic foreign movie in no language spoken on Earth. The movie was all about the violence surrounding the death of the Christ.

"What in hell is this?"

"Some sadomasochistic obscenity?"

"Isn't this supposed to be about Jesus Christ?"

"What kind of twisted mind came up with this!?"

"Who? Who's Mel Gibson?"

"Holy Ghost, this guy puts the Roman back into the Catholic!" And many more uncharitable remarks ensued.

The movie played on while some locked themselves in restrooms, some covered their heads with whatever they could find and what there was to find for hiding their heads were on-loan blankets, compliments of Alitalia. Then there were the sounds of choking and regurgitation which, of course, caused others to do the same—some twice. The aisles became slick and peppered with multi-colored chunks and slivers of food. Well, mostly food. Looking down the aisle from the head of the cabin, one could easily conjure the talentless upheavals of a Jackson Pollack; it was quite an emotional response. Then the oxygen masks dropped and everybody rushed to their seats and that's when the riot began. In a rush to suck oxygen some of the passengers slipped, fell and slid into other passengers; causing fierce turbulence from the food fights, wild punches, the bloodied faces and blackened eyes of passengers, flight attendants, and the co-pilot. This can all be traced back to an incomprehensible, sadomasochistic, homoerotic movie as the cause for the worst and most disturbing riot in the history of in-flight aviation. Only two passengers kept themselves glued to the screen and out of the fray: Mother George and his Eminence Cardinal Rotundo.

Of course, not one word of the misadventure on the plane was true in either English, Italian or Aramaic. But, it is what Rolly and Georgie will tell their Vatican cohorts so that they, too, can share in the adventures of their mythical journey to Shady Sanctum in Queen City, in the land of Colorado, home of the Broncos.

When their plane touched down at Queen City

International, passengers could not disembark quickly enough. But, not Rolly who, for the umpteenth time, had "to go."

"I can't hold it any longer, Georgie. I really can't. I have to go now," he announced in a clearly audible whisper which resulted in all eyes turning in his direction. It took three Hail Marys and Georgie's strong arm to roll, push, shove, and hoist Rolly out of his seats. Even Cardinals feel remorse for the temple in which they reside; and Rolly was no exception. Georgie was cursed with the job of hauling Rolly's temple out into the aisle and pushing it towards the restroom in the back of the plane against the flow of traffic, anxious to be anywhere but there.

It had been a long and torturous flight that will not be soon forgotten by those who suffered Georgie's ribald obscenities, or the embarrassment from having to watch the Walmart Cowboy getting pushed and prodded along the aisle to the telephone-booth-sized restroom where Mother George struggled every which way, inch by inch, to push him into where he needed "to go." It was clearly an aerodynamic challenge; evidently miraculous.

Moreover, it was undeniably preternatural when an arm from on high reached down through the picture book Colorado sky to add a hand and help Georgie and the taxi driver to squeeze His Excellency into the cab just enough to close the door without and inch to spare. Georgie felt the pain from stretched muscles she never knew she had, "Oh God, my back feels broken."

Rolly was humiliated, but as painful as humiliation can be, Cardinal Rotundo was used to it. The disgruntled cabbie took the scenic route and charged extra for the added weight.

After they arrived at the address written on Vatican stationary, Rolly managed to squeeze himself out from the backseat of the cab all by himself. And *there* it was to behold! And so they beheld...*Shady Sanctum.*

Simultaneously, on Historic Colfax Avenue, a truck driver flicked-out the remains of his Cuban cigar and yelled out the window of his eighteen wheeler, "Gotta get this load of fresh gnomes to town!"

* * *

V canceled the Grecian Culture Study Group. She didn't feel up to hosting a roomful of chattering women: *"For Pete's sake, Carla. The Romans taught the Greeks everything they knew. It was the other way around, Minnie. I'll have to ask V. Lemon squares, anyone? Did any of you girls ever see Never on a Sunday? It's an old movie they ran on an old movie station. I saw that, Sylvia. Good music. Ohh, I would love that recipe. Indicative of Grecian culture. I adore musicals. It's not a musical. What's it about? A whore in Greece. Oh, no. I can't watch something like that. Too much testosterone? Of course you can, Billy."* So, there it goes to a level of culture that must sink to find itself. There won't be a murder of old crows today. Although, one of them may be the book thief. V's anxiety from not knowing who stole the book was becoming a serious health issue. The book was pretty much all that occupied her mind; so, she cancelled the study group.

"Why is it so important to you, V? If it's not found, how is it going to affect us in any way?"

"Lily, it will not affect us...not really...at least, I hope not. But, what if the book fell into the hands of the black market, or Washington Fascists."

"There are Washington Fascists?"

"Get real, Lily. Of course there are."

"For Pete's sake, V! Get over it!" Lily demanded.

V continued in one of her moods: *Le mood du jour.* The mood of that day was the pretense of caring about things for which she could not control. That was the easiest way for her to convince herself that there was no fault, nor guilt, attached to inaction.

"I choose to think differently," V sighed. "I cannot get over it, Lily." Lily had ruffled V's feathers, so V said in her serious business-like voice. "Whom do you think took the book, Lily?"

"I've been racking my brain about that, V. I think it's down to the old bag lady Duchess, or Mercy Pentcist. You know how she uses those magical hands of hers. There are, of course, the twins. There's something horrid and menacing about them, V."

"You took this friggin' long to figure that out, Lilian?"

Billy Butts knocked timidly on Shady Sanctum's front door that was weathered from passing years, scratched, with chipped red paint, blue paint and finally green. Bare wires hung from an electrical box that led to a disconnected doorbell. Billy knocked aggressively.

"Not again! Maybe I ought to install a goddamned doggy-door. It better not be any—" V opened the front door to find a serious-seeming Billy. "Hey, Billy. We were just talking about you."

"Really?" Billy half-heartedly asked.

"No. Not really."

"That's funny." Billy wasn't sure if V was going for funny or general confusion. V has always been hard to read and impossible to predict, except by Lily who usually came up with the right prognostication.

When they entered the parlor, Lily was sitting in the bishop's chair. Billy thought that Lily seemed solemn, or there was something unusual in the air, and not just the lingering scent of marijuana, as he headed for his customary spot at the far corner of the sofa.

"Hello, Lily."

"Watch yourself, Billy. V isn't happy."

"Really?" Billy nervously asked.

"No. I don't know really. I thought you did, Billy?"

"No. I don't know a thing, Lily; certainly not *really*."

Billy put his backpack on the floor beside the sofa as he slid deeper into its corner where he placed a sea-foam green throw-pillow over his middle-aged paunch. "I feel like I'm interrupting something," Billy said, nervously. "Am I?"

"Are you?" V asked.

"How would I know?"

"We were looking for a thief." Lily said.

"You don't know one, do you, Billy?" V asked.

Billy was mortified and all he could think to say was, "It smells like a marijuana dispensary in here."

"Does it? Have you ever been in a marijuana dispensary?" V asked.

Knowing he should shut up and get out, but afraid to move, Billy melted yet more deeply into the corner of the sofa and meekly answered. "I've never actually been to one. AA, you know. But I imagine that's what one smells like."

V sniffed the air. "Possibly. I am not sure. *Wait.* I thought I detected something odd. Nope. My nose is not working today. What do you smell, Lily?"

"Remember a couple summers ago, V, when that rat died beneath the kitchen floorboards and it stayed there all summer? Oh gawd, and it was a hot summer, too. The stench of it lingered well into Thanksgiving. How cringeworthy is that? After a while we simply got used to it. You know, like those noses in Texas that are accustomed to crude and other disgusting odors. We adapt. Would you not agree, Billy?"

The ladies were definitely stoned.

Here it should be noted that Billy suffers from chronic paranoia, severe anxiety and a host of ailments from the neck up. Billy has trouble figuring out how to reply to "would you not agree" to which it takes eons to ponder the correct answer. "Yes" meant he did not agree and "no" meant the same to Billy. Because of that, he began shivering and sweating. His mind spun with so much to filter it was turning into sludge. Billy felt numb, ill-at-ease, and frightened. In a flash of dreadful insight, Billy was certain that he was intercepting V and Lily's cryptic conversation in a secret language, and at his expense.

"She knows I stole her precious book. No doubt. Well, there might be a tiny doubt she doesn't. But you don't believe that, do you? They're witches. Yes. Of course. I should have known, and they're going to torture me. V and Lily are going to kill me. Me. Me, ME. Something is going to happen to me. I just know it. I

should have seen it coming. There have always been rumors. Maybe they want me to join their coven. That could be it. They have a coven. I've always suspected that. Someone told me they were witches...very common among lesbians, I am told. Hmm...by who? That cute guy in the Korean market. Don't be silly. I know. I've got to get out of here and think about it. You're being silly, Billy. Be careful. Think, think. You know, it could be fun joining a coven," Billy said to himself. All that and more journeyed through Billy's problematic mind.

When he decided he could not not agree, he said, "I agree." With that best guess, a frightened Billy ran into Dionysus, spilled himself into the foyer and out the front door.

When the ladies heard the front door slam they each gave the other a puzzled glance.

"Too weird. What got into him?"

"He's like that sometimes, Lily."

"I know. I hope he gets better soon."

"Why? Then he would lose all his charm, Lily. He is perfect the way he is. How else would we know him otherwise?"

What the ladies did not know was that the book was in a backpack less than eight-feet away. And what Billy was yet to realize was that he left his backpack at Shady Sanctum.

"They're going to find out I'm a thief! I'm not a thief. I'm not a thief. Oh shit! I am a thief. They're going to kill me for sure. Put a spell on me. I just know it. I'm going to lose two more friends, aren't I? Where do they all go? I'm missing something, aren't I? What? Oh well! If I see it I'll remember what it was," rambled through Billy's mind.

* * *

Meanwhile, O'Toole changed his mind over and moreover. Should he have the surgery, or should he keep the tail? Should he postpone, or cancel his appointment with Fuzzlbum, or should he bite the bullet and have it removed? What to do? A playwright's mind must never be cluttered with things of little consequence.

Room must be left for significant things...really big things. This was definitely a significant thing, a really big thing, but, given Peter's impoverished celebrity, to remove or not to remove his tail was a choice needing prudent thought.

O'Toole, held his tail while staring into the reflection inside the overstated Cheval mirror. *"...a naked man with a tail. How fucking weird is that? Should keep it, shouldn't keep it, but it is exciting. Still, the book was stolen. Worse. Broken trust. Lying. Oh, fuck me! I am so full of bullshit. I stole the book. Simple as that. Yes, I did. I did! I did! I did! What was I thinking? Will she ever forgive me? I think I'm going crazy. Damn! I love this fucking tail."* Naked and sporting the best of all possible tails, O'Toole continued to stare into the mirror at his tantalizing tail. In a blink, he saw the satyr standing directly behind him. Surprised, O'Toole quickly turned, but there was nobody there. *"What the hell? God, he was gorgeous! Drop dead gorgeous!"*

"Thank you," said the voice behind him.

O'Toole, his mind fully confused, slowly turned back to the mirror and he saw the satyr within it.

"Ordinarily, I would be freaked-out by now, but oddly, I'm not. I didn't...."

"Speak out loud? You didn't need to." The Goat Boy silently said to O'Toole, who could not take his eyes away from the satyr's beautiful smile, his alabaster skin, his unearthly mesmerizing eyes.

"I'm in love! Yes I am. And I didn't look below his belt. Quite unnatural, for me," Peter mused.

The Goat Boy giggled and said, "We'll meet again, Peter. By the way, I'm not wearing a belt," and then he vanished into the mirror with the overstated frame.

* * *

V found Cardinal Rotundo a delight, for a Roman Catholic, even though she had to instruct him how not to sit on this chair, nor that chair, nor no, no, not that one! She also found him rude for wearing his hat in the house, as if he were brought up in Texas where men had the disgusting habit of taking their shirts off, but leaving their hats on at the dinner table.

V found Mother George a fun-loving, witty, intelligent woman who, aside from her vulgar disorder, knew herself and the roguish devil she was born to be. V became *simpatico* with the Good Mother almost immediately; although V did not much care for being called "a fucking piece of monkey shit," but she could live with it.

Since it was not Halloween, Lily ruled out trick-or-treaters, circus clowns, street corner doom's day sayers, fire eaters, preachers, thrift store models, Walmart shoppers, or simply down and out bums.

"*Try the goddamned sofa!*" V said to herself. "Why don't you rest on the sofa?" V pseudolishously, quaintly ordered with a smile.

"And a very nice couch it is. *Grazi*."

Does V dare correct a Roman Catholic Cardinal, even if he proves to be an imposter, or worse, a Mormon? Sure, why not? "Nice couch." V mimicked Rotundo's words with a restrained villainous smile. "I do love that word—*cow-ouch*. I love Italian. In America we say sofa. *Soo-fah*. But you may call it what you like. What do I care? What do you call a *soo-fah* in Italy?"

"*Divano.*"

"Isn't that a lovely word, Lily?"

"*Yeah*. A couch, a sofa. *Divano*. I get it." Lily said as if more boring words had never been uttered.

"It's getting late, bitches!" Leave it to Mother George to liven-up the party.

"*Try the goddamned sofa!*" Lily so wanted to say out loud?

"Would you like to sit on our *divano?*" V asked with a heaping ladle of saccharine.

"*Grazi*. I shall sit on your *divano*."

"Good for you," V blurted. "Perhaps that's best."

Mother George also blurted, "Perhaps that's best, you

fucking piece of monkey shit! We have a plane to catch."

"You must excuse me. I have things to do. It was a pleasure meeting you both. I hope you find your book. *Bon voyage.*" Lily scooted upstairs to count cat pictures on facebook until the nuncios had left. "*Like. Like. Like. I wish they had a DON'T LIKE button!*"

"I am most sorry. I have knocked over your bag. I hope there's nothing breakable," sighed the Cardinal.

"Doubtful. It belongs to a friend who leaves things behind all the time so he will have an excuse to come back. He will come to retrieve his backpack when he has nothing better to do. It is so disappointing when friends only think of you when they are bored and *you* are at the bottom of the dance card. Don't worry about the backpack, Cardinal. Nothing of importance."

Cardinal Rotundo bent over the arm of the sofa to put the backpack containing the book upright while the unoccupied end of the sofa lifted high into the air. Rotundo couldn't get hold of himself even when V and Mother George tried to pull and push down on the other end, but it was too late.

Rotundo rolled away like a giant pollywog, moving the butler's table a good four feet farther from the *divano*.

"*Jesus fucking Christ!*" V said behind clenched teeth.

"He's not usually this clumsy, Miss Victoria. Most of the furniture in the Vatican palace is much larger and more solid; much more comfortable," Mother George said, apologetically.

"Really? I must search Google and see for myself." It is amazing how two little words, "Really" and "Google", casually spoken by V could sound threatening to the Mother Church and Her good taste, as expressed through the hands of a kitschy Vatican decorator.

"Good idea. Google it, shitty tits!"

THIRTEEN

gnomenclature for unconscious dimensions

Carla Bean promised to pay all the hospital bills, plus any other expenses Tommy Too-Much accrued due to her latest "discourtesy." It was the very least Carla could do. To do more would only spoil the boy. However, Carla's Greek, along with her liquid assets, tucked away in Cayman Islands, Deutsche Bank, and elsewhere by the late Mister Bean, took flight; leaving Carla in a penury condition. Now, Carla does not know how long she will be able to manage the estate without the purloined money. The pinch was over twenty million U.S. dollars.

How did the Greek get all her passwords? How did he move the money so quickly? Why can it not be traced? Or can it? How can an extremely intelligent woman be so incredibly stupid? Did the sultry scent of a hot Greek prove to be an anesthetic to commonsense?

As much as she did not want to, Carla Bean gave serious thought to selling La Bean Hacienda, along with some of its contents; a piece of jewelry, or two, the Andrew Wyeth, and certainly the Pollack and the Warhol. Although, she won't miss the latter two, she might shed a tear or two for the Wyeth. The Warhol and the Pollack, strictly investments, hang in the loo attached to one of the guest bedrooms. The Wyeth hangs in her bedroom. *"After I buy a condo in O'Toole's building,"* she thought, *"I should still have at least a million, or two. Who knows what a mansion covering an entire block goes for in the current Queen City boom market?"* But, as Fate doles out whatever She likes, there was nothing available in Peter's building. The last unit sold for nearly a million, plus there were obscene monthly condo dues, and all for nothing special. The largest condo had less floor space than Carla's swimming pool, and this eyesore has the nerve to pose as "contemporary." She thought it common, with neither character nor style; tackier than Trump Tower—which ushered in the popularity of the golden shower, the Golden Fake Leaf Age, the Glitter Age of

Liberace, and the excess of Busby Berkeley. *"Oh, Gawd! Poor Peter lives in an ostentatious latrine."*

Renting was worse. The Millennials had poured into the greatest city on planet Earth at an alarming rate, changing its landscape, its skyline, and causing the cost of real estate to double overnight. Anyway, it's all moot since nobody could imagine Carla Bean as a renter, including Carla Bean. *"I'll continue to think about selling, but not now. I need to save La Bean Hacienda. Jesus Aitch! Twenty million fucking dollars, you sonofabitch, you fucking little prick!"* Carla imagined herself a vagrant adrift in a Dicksonian landscape of crime and degradation. She gathered a bit of gratitude from knowing that Poor Houses were no longer in vogue. Still, she had everything a person could possibly want and more. She wasn't exactly left with nothing, but the recent calamity presented Carla Bean with another dimension of reality; a dimension on the brink of returning her to an earlier time when she had nothing. *Nothing. A former lap dancer. A man called Carlos.* She screamed. She cried. Then, she suffered a flash of empathy for others; for those with little to nothing—or was that a hot flash?

* * *

Tommy Too-Much, stitched, stapled, bandaged, in a haze of pain killers and pot, found himself consumed with fear and gloom, trying not to poop himself, was thinking of his very near future...like NOW.

With Tommy's rent past due, Carla's invitation to come live with her in La Bean Hacienda came in the nick of time. "Come live with me," she offered, adding, "forever." Forever sounded like a threat to Tommy, especially when "forever" is offered by Carla; it's like an invitation from Freddie Kruger to a pajama party. "Forever" is always of short duration, inconceivable, unimaginable and downright pointless! Its existence cannot be confirmed. Every time Tommy tried to take his mind to the edge of forever—akin to infinity—he found himself overwhelmed with angst for fear of losing himself to psychosis.

Too-Much could not work since the "incident." He could

not afford to continue renting his cubicle at *Bella Donna Cheap Clips*, nor could he lift a comb to tease, nor scissors with which to kill himself. Aside from the misfortune of being brutally beaten and left for dead, Too-Much did have a posh place to go; The Bean Mansion where he could call home until the end of forever. Perhaps, in time, Too-Much might even learn to forgive and tolerate Carla Bean. Until then, why bother to unpack?

* * *

In less than an hour, nano-drones were scheduled to sweep through Dead Squeezer's caverns on their way to spy on an unsuspecting Queen City.

Techies, scientists, all those who worked in the clandestine facility, unknown to anyone not directly involved in the project—hush-hush, need-to-know, very top-top secret and that sort of thing—were all instructed to "shake a leg or die!" The underground laboratories were not connected to the underground megaplex that occupies Cheyenne Mountain, which must be at the top of enemy Nuclear Target Lists, or damn close to it, of Russia, China, North Korea, Iran, Pakistan, Alabama and other lesser-known despotic States that are too numerous to mention.

The State of America, Inc. owns Dead Squeezer's Caverns. Remember the guide, Dead Squeezer's nephew? He was an FBI agent. A great actor, sharpshooter and collector of every Broadway musical album since the early Nineteen-fifties.

Other than the Disney-rock door, or the two-hundred-plus narrow pinewood steps that led to the surface, there was no other way out. The steps were put together overnight by day-laborers. Where the steps reach the surface, a grove of cactus and boulders surround the exit. There are hidden sharpshooters trained on that exit. There is no other way to reach daylight. After working through the night, the undocumented day-laborers were never seen nor heard from again. With the exception of the missing day-laborers, no one from below ever actually set a foot on the those stairs. The scuttlebutt was, there would be an elevator installed as soon as the money could be appropriated from Congress, which pretty much meant never. Until never, all entering and exiting went through Dead Squeezer's Caverns, and only after it closed to the public at 4:00 PM daily. Afterwards, the Marines would takeover the caverns to guard the entrance and play Pinocle. Their duty was to stand watch over whatever and wherever there was something worth watching.

There were well-appointed quarters in The Black Hole—the workers' nickname for the facility—for the military and civilian scientists, and the occasional high-level guests who came in from D.C., Los Alamos or Sandia Labs from nearby New Mexico.

The President remained the night to watch the launching of the nano-drones. The launch was scheduled to happen directly after the bats came home to settle down—up really—for a long summer's day.

"Sir, this photograph," General Bughump handed it to the President, "is all we have."

The President held the photo up, down and sideways. "What is this?"

"The lab boys were able to determine that we are looking at mauve felt with margarine stains, microscopic bits of house dust, cat urine (male), cheap wine, tofu, or, perhaps, high-grade putty plastic made in Jersey City by suspected Muslim terrorists."

"My God! Muslims terrorists, you say?"

"Affirmative, Mister President."

"The Black Hole must relocate immediately, General."

"Straightaway..."

A complement of white lab coats sped past Snow White on their way through the caverns to board the waiting caravan of *Plumbers On Demand, College Boy's Haul Ass, We Haul Anything Anywhere, Manafort's Dried Fruits and Nuts,* several black vans, one eighteen wheeler, and six chartered buses for the evacuees; most all the vehicle space had been liberated to haul the priceless instruments of mass surveillance.

"Launch the nano-drones, General," the President

commanded.

"Mister President, the bats haven't returned yet."

"We haven't any time, General. Tell your people to hit the floor!"

General Bughump used a bullhorn to give the order, "HIT THE FLOOR OR DIE!"

With a nod to the Commander of Button Pushing, the nano-drones launched at the very moment the bats were returning, and so they ate the nano-drones. A technician was killed when her hearing aids stopped working. She couldn't hear the General's command when a nano-drone went up her nose and drilled its way through the top of her skull. The nano-drone prototype lost contact with The Black Hole and was pronounced irretrievably lost.

Later that morning, a number of bats fell to the cavern floor. When the mother of a screaming sticky-faced brat stepped on one of the dead bats, she shrieked in terror. The brat picked up the dead bat and tried to eat it, but only got its head in his mouth before his mother's slap sent the nasty dead thing flying against the Disney-stone door, triggering the sticky-faced brat to scream and accuse his mother for causing the "kaboom" that coincidentally rumbled throughout the caverns while blowing out huge chunks of stone wall which were quickly sucked back into the rush to fill the vacuum beneath the prodigious crater, exposing the edge of a crystal-clear lake and more unexplored caves. Miracle of miracles, two-hundred-plus pinewood steps fell to the unexplored kingdom and became a staircase to the unexplored world below.

The evening's local TV news will cover the EXPLOSION IN DEAD SQUEEZER'S CAVERNS: *"All visitors who were witnesses to the explosion were removed and taken to an undisclosed location for testing, since they may have been exposed to a deadly virus that, an Army spokesman said, could be worse than ebola because this virus may be air-borne. The caverns were closed and will remain closed while a team of specialists from Washington declare the site decontaminated and safe for visitors. The spokesman gave no estimate for how long decontamination will take, nor how many detainees there are in custody for testing. More news on this and the rest of today's news at ten."*

Tomorrow, the headline in the *Queen City Post* will read: WORM HOLE THROWS UP THREE SAINT JOSEPH EMPLOYEES. No mention of the latest Queen City Hacker killing, nor the other big story: the explosion, the detainees for testing, nor any mention of the deadly virus. The local TV news was left with little to mention at ten, so Daisy Mae Shuckinbee the Untruthful read from her new book, *How to Avoid Questions*. Her last book, *Tips For Euphemisms*, was a huge success in Alabama and Mississippi, where it was released as a graphic novel.

Most of the folks who were rescued from the nauseating gas in the caverns, piped in by a brigade of Marines, were found unconscious. Many were stretched across the cold floor, surrounded by the Little People with Big Heads—which had always been Dead Squeezer's most popular room. The rest of the unconscious were found peppered about other don't-miss attractions. But there is always something and that something was the boy who tried to eat the bat was wide-awake and unaffected by the noxious vapors.

All the victims were removed and lifted on a Sikorsky CH-53E Super Stallion copter that whisked them around Cheyenne Mountain where they were taken to a waiting, unmarked jet. The hyper-energetic brat who tried to eat a dead bat proved himself to be uncontrollable, a hazard to the pilot's health, and he was most likely suffering symptoms of bat-poisoning. Before the Super Stallion was in the air, the "little angel" died a peaceful death as he happily nestled, tightly, in the strong arms of the pilot.

The victims will remember nothing from the caves, nor will they have any memories of the lives they had led prior to being gassed by the Department of People Gassing. All they will remember is waking to find themselves in Guantanamo Bay Naval Base, where they will remain in the blistering heat and scalding humidity until they are trained assassins proudly working for the honor of the United States of America—something along the line of a classroom filled with Manchurian Candidates.

* * *

The following morning, V asked Billy to drive her and Lily to the caverns, since neither of them drove anymore, by choice. Queen City traffic had become quite hazardous from the swarm of Millennials hogging the streets with their skateboards, bicycles and scooters, going the wrong way on one-way streets, and when it came to stoplights they proved to be colorblind.

"Billy, think of the fun. You like a good mystery, don't you?"

"It sounds too dangerous, V dahlink. I can't do it. I need more sleep."

"Get your ass out of bed and be here in thirty minutes, Billy Butts! We are talking emergency here!" V abruptly disconnected.

Sure enough, Billy showed up thirty minutes later. V and Lily were waiting on the porch and as soon as they spotted his red Beamer convertible they dashed to the curb and jumped in the car—almost literally.

"Now...do as I tell you and let's go!" V shouted in Billy's ear.

When they arrived within sight of the dirt road at the bottom of the hill leading to the caves, they saw armed soldiers blocking the road ahead.

"Billy, stop the car...NOW."

Billy skidded to a full stop along the side of the road where wild sunflowers and columbine filled the landscape until it reached a barbed wire fence. Beyond the fence there was nothing to see other than a flat cement runway, but not a plane in sight.

"What's going on?" Billy asked.

Lily squinted as a large part of the cement surface began to open. "V, it doesn't look like we ought to be here."

An armed black helicopter rose from out the opening in the cement. Whatever time it was, the three of them knew their's was up!

Like nothing Damocles could have imagined, the black

helicopter hung suspended overhead. Armed soldiers appeared from nowhere and surrounded the trepidatious Queen City trio: V, Lily and Billy Butts. From everywhere, there was a gun trained on them.

"Shut your pie holes and don't move!" a soldier bellowed.

"Does anyone really say 'pie hole?'" Billy said under his breath.

A cage—large enough to hold the trio and an armed Marine—lowered from the helicopter.

"Stand back!" a voice shouted as the steel cage was grabbed by half a dozen Marines. It was then maneuvered and steadied close enough to the ground for V, Lily and Billy to hear a Marine shout over the sound of the hovering helicopter, "Git in, maggots! It's yo magic carpet ride."

Three hostages and an armed Marine were lifted into the sky and flown towards the opening in the cement. The cage blundered and jerked over the oblong opening while the helicopter lingered above. Billy was sure he was going to be sick. The cage was lowered into the hole where more Marines waited to guide the cage safely to the floor. Billy thought it was a rough landing. *"Ouch."* The Marines detached the cable which then was wound back up into the helicopter. The gap in the cement closed immediately afterward. The helicopter, steady as a hummingbird, remained hovering overhead. Billy's new Beamer was driven away by an agent doubling as a visitors' parking lot attendant.

It was an exhausting interrogation.

"Are you now or have you ever been a terrorist?"

"No, no, and I don't know."

"You don't know, Mister!?"

"I believe in reincarnation. By the way, I *love* your uniform."

"Don't play with me, Mister! I just got it outta da cleaners."

"I'm not playing, sir. I don't play. *Gosh.* You asked if any of us have ever been a terrorist. In this life I would have to say no.

There's no way of telling in any of my past lives. See my conundrum?"

"What's a 'conundrum?'"

"I'm not sure. I never used that word before...not until I touched the book."

"What book?" demanded the interrogator.

"I don't know. It belonged to this woman." Billy pointed to V.

"It belonged to my father...after he was excommunicated. The man next to me stole the book...."

On and on the interrogation went until after nearly two hours when the interrogator barked, "All o' you, git out!"

V, Lily, and Billy were escorted back to the cage. The opening overhead opened. A cable descended from the waiting helicopter. A cute Marine attached the cable to the cage. The four of them stepped into the cage and were flown back to the side of the road. They were so focused on what had just transpired, neither V, Lily, nor Billy noticed that the Beamer had been moved to the opposite side of the road.

"Terrorist. A woman," the Marine barked.

"A woman?" questioned V.

"*Yeah,* and her miserable kid, too."

"Her kid, too?" Lily seemed relieved.

"I don't have any kids," V told the Marine. "No, not a one."

Billy remained silent, which was unheard of in the real world.

"Both trained Muslim terrorists. *Yup.* Now get into your car..*nice car*...turn around and go home. Nothing to see here," the Marine helped Billy into his Beamer and let the women fend for themselves.

"Thank you, sir," Billy broke his elongated silence with a newfound respect for Marines.

The Marine caught Billy's gaze, smiled, winked at him and

said, "You could have made a good Marine."

"Me?" Billy blushed.

The Marine leaned into the car and whispered into Billy's ear, "No, *me*. You could have made a good Marine; *me*. It's a little awkward now." The Marine pulled back and shouted, "Go home!"

"Yes, sir!" Billy saluted. "I will go home to 555 Evergreen Street, apartment 704...if you're ever in Queen City…know what I mean?"

"Gotcha."

Billy started the car's engine and soon they were headed back to Queen City. V was so relieved to know that she was not the woman in question she invited Billy and Lily to lunch; a rare event. However, with grave disappointment all round, there was no vegetarian restaurant to be found. That is, none that V would be "caught dead in!"

"The helicopter ride was awesome," Billy noted. "I thought they were going to torture us for information."

"What information?" V asked. "You don't have any information."

"I might have."

"What kind of information, Billy?" V interrogated.

"You guys were spies. It was your maroon hat in the picture," Billy offered.

"People have disappeared for less," Lily interjected.

"I never said anything, did I?"

"You thought it, Billy," V murmured. "And you cruised a Marine."

"I did not! It was me who got cruised,V. By the way, do you remember getting a needle?" Billy asked them both.

"I don't remember…Jesus…where in hell were we?" V was definitely worried.

"In a helicopter," Billy answered. "I remember getting a needle."

"How did we get in a helicopter?" Lily asked.

"I don't know. I remember…that's strange…I'm not sure… *ah*, Billy." V said. "You will need to come in as soon as we get home. We have your backpack."

A thick pall overcame the driver's seat of Billy Butts' new candy-apple red Beamer convertible with DISCO on its vanity plates.

* * *

In the dead of night, an eighteen-wheeler filled with "genuine" Norwegian gnomes from Mexico, was unloaded into waiting vans and trucks. The gnomes were then stacked as high as possible, sometimes higher, and then the vehicles rolled through Queen City distributing the colorfully festive, red clay smiling Mexican Norwegian gnomes onto Queen City lawns. Sometimes the gnomes rolled into the gutters where they were smashed by ritzy cars and nasty boys. Sometimes the gnomes cracked and broke all on their own, committed suicide, or ran into La Bean Hacienda's columns that like to play a game that involves kicking gnomes into Old Pansy Hedgeworth's backyard. The objective of the game, from the columns point of view, is to remain upright after each kick and to get home before dawn.

* * *

What the Krotch, Krotch, Bushit & Mother and Vader Diggers and Frackers, LLC pumped directly out of Lake Titicaca, they pumped back into Lake Titicaca as waste. Surely, one day someone will wonder why the lake's shiny surface doesn't appear to have its shimmering sparkle, its charm. And why were there so many dead fish floating on its surface, as if there were poisonous contaminates polluting the water? Since the Krotches leased Lake Titicaca, and bought much of its surrounding property and the people on it, they did not see it as a problem, but rather a byproduct of progress. They owned it. Or leased it. Or had a permit. Or something legal…*or…oh, well…maybe.*

By the time the fracking operation was scheduled to be complete—in another two or three years—the plan was to be long gone: Buzzards, redneck workmen, and all the superlative state-of-the-art equipment a taxpayer's money can buy...*gone with the wind.*

* * *

What the residents of Nostradamus were hopping-mad about, began some time in the wee hours....

After changing her foxself back into herself just before dawn, Gert, naked and exhausted, shaking leaves and sand from her wet hair, out of breath from running all the way home after scoping out the perimeter of the fracking operation, chased by two snarling dogs that were trained to snarl in a most alarming way, also, trained not to bark, while an eager Buzzard with a strong arm, an attitude, and a lightsaber, ran behind those ferocious, genetically modified German Shepherds. Gert the Fox had made a leap of trust in her ability to go from the ground onto the electrified fence, up and over the razor wire, without grounding herself, or getting sliced. She grabbed her housedress from under the counter and put it on. Something was wrong. Very wrong.

Gert went into the kitchen, and not a sliver of food anywhere. She went to the cold storage locker and NOTHING. Enough food for a month was gone! Someone or someones have stolen every last bit of food, and Governor Crapp was the prime suspect. As the news traveled through Puerto Nostradamus the residents became hopping-mad.

For the time being, Gert was the only resident capable of overcoming the challenge of a gazillion volts of electrified chainlink fencing. Until food is found, it is all existential on the Puerto Nostradamus side of the fence. Their ability to obtain anything to eat was severely limited. "*And where in hell is Crapp from Jersey!?*"

Crapp from Jersey was hiding behind the shed that the satyr sometimes called "Home." With Gert's keen sense of spirit-smell, she found the culprit in little time. There, on the satyr's little porch, was a big ol' pile of greasy Crapp, shoving the last of a smoked ham into the dark abyss beyond his drooling lips. Gert sent Álvaro and Alfredo to the old ramshackle ostrich barn for long, heavy rope.

FOURTEEN
what's a gingrich, birthing and a beautiful thing

The Overlord, telepathically. "A gingrich is a rat. They're huge, for rats. More like the size of a cat. A really *big* cat. A fat cat. You might think you want to pet a gingrich, but don't! They are deceptively vicious and venomous; teeth as long as tusks and sharp as razorblades. I'd think twice about approaching one. They hide in shadows, under rocks, in garbage, tunnels, sewers, under and in anything that's filthy. Should you see one, it's usually already too late. They attack without provocation. Without warning. Learn to use your nose. Humans cannot smell them, but you will, even though you'll be living in a human body. Gingriches have a stench that you will know when you smell it."

"What do they smell like?"

"Lies. Nothing, but lies. You've got to learn to smell the stench of them. Humans no longer use their noses in the way they were intended. The miasma from the gingriches goes unnoticed by them. The nose plays a leading role in intuition. Ask any dog. Gingriches strike with unnatural speed. They inject a deadly venom that kills its victim, almost instantly. 'Almost' because the dirty gingrich uses its razor-sharp claws to tear open the back of its prey to get at the sweet meat around the spinal column. It is sweetest about the time the victim dies, after a long and painful death. The gingrich chews on the backbone with its ugly foul teeth before taking the remains to its lair for the little wifey and the little gingriches to gnaw on. You will never hear and you will never see a gingrich coming, unless you use your nose."

"Why are you telling me this?"

"Gingriches are part of the standard information with which you should be well-acquainted before going to Earth and taking on the role of a human. Understand?"

"Yes."

"Good. There is not much wisdom down there, anymore.

There used to be, before the philosophers died. There is little left to collect. So, collect as much of it as you can."

"I will. Can I go down to Earth now?"

"Soon, Peter."

"Peter? What's a Peter?"

"That will be your name: Peter O'Toole"

"Will I be special?"

"Of course. Very special," the Overlord said.

"Then I'm ready to go."

"Remember, you cannot terminate your human form until it is time. When it is time it will terminate itself. Should you, because you have had enough of it and you want to come back...you won't. You cannot. For you, it is not possible to come back. You will never be one of them. You have a different destiny. Your's is the last pure soul. There are no more."

"Pure?"

"Not refurbished," explained the Overlord. When a soul leaves Earth, it is then refurbished within the sun. Spirits, good and bad, are created within the sun, Peter. Once they are refurbished, they are sent to Earth, terminated, then back into the atomic flames of the sun to be refurbished, time and time again, but they will never be pure."

"That's terrible."

"Not at all. They feel nothing and they won't remember a thing. When the refurbished souls come back from the sun, they are better for it. However, this will not be your fate."

"Good to hear. Is Earth Heaven?"

"A masochist might think so. In the beginning there was never a more beautiful garden in the universe. But no more. *So sad.*"

"I can't wait to get a human body. I want the sensation of living within a flesh and blood body. I want to feel the magic of organics. I want to be smart and handsome. I want to be seen as angry, talented, and sexy. That's what Socrates told me I should want."

"Socrates will say anything to get the attention of a young spirit. You may not know this, but I am the original Overlord, or so the quixelite tells me. Quixelite has been around longer than consciousness itself. Hard to fathom, isn't it? Quixelite thinks, but not as we do. They are inexplicable lifeforms with unequaled intelligence. *Oh,* and please accept my apology if you do not end up as talented, angry or as sexy as you imagine you want to be."

"What?"

"You will be something all together different. More than you can imagine. And, stop listening to recycled philosophers. By the way, never forget that all is miraculous. Existence is miraculous. Don't waste your time searching for it. The miraculous is all there right in front of your eyes. Accept existence and maybe one day an answer will come to all your questions when you least expect it."

"*Wow.* I am really excited. Can't wait to do this."

"Good. I am the last of the Neanderthals, Peter, and I am the first to grow a soul, and you are the last. I make all the rules here myself. I like being an Overlord."

"What rules?"

"There are no rules. I couldn't think of any. Can you?"

"No. I don't think so. How come you haven't taken your old physical form?"

"You're shitting me, right? Have you ever seen what Neanderthals look like? Of course, not. I prefer to appear perfect in every way. A Playgirl centerfold with huge…never mind."

"You do appear perfect. Are you God?"

The Overlord laughed. "Not likely. More like an angel."

"*Oh.* Angels are beautiful."

"There you have it. I am beautiful."

"I think so. So where is God?"

"You got me on that one!" The Overlord laughed, then asked, "Do you really need one? I mean, must everyone on the block have a god?"

"I don't know."

"Maybe, it's you. You could be God the Oversoul."

"But I'm not. Simply accept the miraculous. You will have a conscience. If you listen carefully you will know what you need to know to navigate through life on Earth."

"By the bye, you will not consciously remember this conversation. "

"Then, why did we have it?"

"Good question. Maybe your subconscious will remember and tell you. Listen to that, too."

"Okay."

"Are you ready?"

"Yes."

"One more thing: There is a price for EVERYTHING. Travel with kindness."

And, another soul fell to Earth.

Invisible to everyone, in an old Philadelphia hospital, the Goat Boy carefully took notes while watching over Peter O'Toole as he entered into the human world on Earth.

* * *

Hiding in Old Pansy's backyard, the fifty pound ego that Fuzzlbum removed from the head of Baby Trump, had grown into five hundred pounds of gelatinous blubber the size of a dumpster. In the shade behind the ivy latticework, the Trump monstrosity lay beneath a spreading chestnut tree. No longer pink, Trump's ego had turned into the color of the bottom of an outhouse.

Egoless, Baby Trump's private jet came to a full stop at Queen City International. When he stepped out onto the tarmac, he began feeling more lightheaded than usual. A mile above sea level will do that.

"Where's my van?" Trump demanded.

"It's already here and waiting for you, sir," said Vlad the Impaler."

"You're sure the van is armored?"

"Yes, sir. Extra thick. Just for you, comrade."

"I can't take any chances. You know I'm going to be the President, right?"

"I do, Mister Trump," Vlad said. "There is no doubt about it, sir. It's been all arranged."

"Get Fuzzlbum on the phone!" Trump demanded. "Tell 'em I'm here and t'be ready t'put the damn thing back in. I need help. I mean, assistance. I never need help, Vlad. I mean, I demand assistance with a shitload 'o stuff, you know…the stuff I said I'd do to prepare myself for what I was born to do. You do know I'm special, right? Have I ever told you that?"

"You have, Sir. Many times."

"So you shouldn't forget it. I told you many times so you shouldn't forget it. My followers expect great things from me. They know I'm d'best man t'represent dem. They would die for me…kill for me. Some may have to…to protect my specialness."

"Of course, sir. You should expect nothing less."

"I don't. I am a New Yorker. That makes me even more special. I'm a Billionaire and that makes me specialer. I'm smarter than anybody and I have really, really beautiful ideas, so beautiful, the most beautiful you've ever seen, believe me. But I need my old ego back, and I need it NOW!"

"Yes, sir."

"How's my hair?"

"Perfect, sir."

When the armored van pulled up behind St. Joseph's private employee entrance, Fuzzlbum was standing outside the door, waiting for his patient. He did not dare tell Trump that his ego escaped and hasn't come back. However, Fuzzlbum managed to find an ego on eBay and had to outbid, ten times, a sonofabitch from Lapland. It's not certified, but the seller assured Fuzzlbum that the ego once belonged to Adolf Hitler. Fuzzlbum laughed. He thought it was a joke.

"I'm havin' a bad time. Bad. Bad, Fuzzy. Y'know what I mean? Really bad. I don't got a lot o'time. And that's bad. I want my ego back posthaste. Posthaste, posthaste…" Trump thought a moment, which was painful endeavor; thinking, "…posthaste… that means like now, right?"

"It certainly does, Mr. Trump."

"Good. I don't get t'use big words often, Fuzzy. My people don't understand big words. So, let's posthaste this. I gotta big speech to give. A huge speech. The biggest and most important speech ever. I need my old ego back. I intend t'use it ta win the hearts and minds of white America! It's time to make White great again"

"With a monosyllabic speech, no doubt?" chided Fuzzlbum's Nurse, Svetlana the Russian Gorilla. "Here you go, sir. I am rolling you directly into operating room," said the Buxom Primate. When Trump was seated in the wheelchair, she pinched him quite severely. "You like that, Mister?" the Russian primate asked.

"Yes. Do it again."

"You'll be screaming in three syllables, Mister Trump. You might actually use four syllables, but I don't think so. Svetlana knows what her boobalah likes, yes?"

"Oh, yes. You're new here? There was another nurse…d."

"*Shh*. She gone. Now Svetlana pinches Trump again. Now I am rolling comrade into operation."

"Whatcha doin' later, Svetlana? Care to share a few cheeseburgers with me tonight?"

"I will pinch FBI Director later tonight. Sorry." She gave Trump a toothy smile. Her scarlet lipstick was slathered over the canker sores that covered her lips. She continued, "You will need ass-out gown. I now help you out expensive clothes."

"It will be your pleasure. OUCH! What was that for?" Trump asked, with a tinge of annoyance.

"Did I hurt my little cabbage?" Nurse Svetlana the Russian ape ground her teeth and mumbled.

"You got me by surprise, Nurse. Don't be offended. I love women who come from, you know."

"That's me. I know. From you know. I from sub-sub-suburb of where you know. I am not mail-order bride! I am not that kind of girl. Quiet now. *Shh*. Sweet dreams, my little dumpling. I love cheesy burgers, fat man," said Nurse Svetlana the Buxom, as she plunged a giant needle into his neck. The syringe was filled with something green and potent, and it shines in the dark.

Fuzzlbum and Nurse Svetlana lifted Trump into an upright position, leaned him against the wall and, with a copious amount of sexual urgency, removed his clothes. This was standard practice when the two of them have the operating room to themselves.

"Well, that's disappointing," Svetlana sighed. "Holy lymph juice! Where's his balls?" Svetlana was genuinely surprised.

"He doesn't seem to have any. Let's get Mister Peanut, the man whose body drips sacks of fat, onto the table," declared Doctor Fuzzlbum, with disgust.

"Vhat a loser!"

Since the doctor and the nurse were the only two awake and since the door was locked to the operating room reserved for VIP patients only, it was time they made their move. Together, using a large rubber sheet covered with little Micky Mouses, Fuzzlbum and Svetlana managed to haul the patient onto the operating table. Svetlana elevated Trump's head. "Doctor, he wearing orange pancakes! We wash pancakes away before shaving head, yes? Poor little Trump will not like that."

"We won't need to shave his head, nurse. His only real hair is covering the bald spot from my first operation…the rest is a weave. Nurse, bring me the ego."

While Svetlana was unwrapping the plain brown paper that

covered the cardboard box containing Hitler's ego, Fuzzlbum did a tiny insertion to find the latch to open the door that led to the famous Trump branded brain. When Fuzzlbum found it, he opened the hidden cavity and was shocked to learn that Trump's brain had shrunken to the size of an unshelled walnut.

"I'm ready," Fuzzlbum said while pointing to the box.

Svetlana brought him the box. "*Whoa.* This ego is heavy."

"Yes it is. They do that when they sit around collecting dust." Fuzzlbum did not want the Buxom primate to know the genesis of the ego in the box. He opened the box and removed Hitler's ego.

"The color. Should be pink, no? Not red and black, yes?"

"Not necessarily. Sometimes egos get darker while they're in storage…ripening." Fuzzlbum slid the ego into the opening on Trump's head, closed the hatch and sealed it with horse mucilage.

After Svetlana gave him a big Russian slap, Trump awoke. "Is it over? Does my hair look good?"

"Over. And your hair so beautiful I cannot tell how beautiful your hair," Svetlana smirked.

After getting dressed, Trump reached into the inner pocket of his suit jacket and came out with three envelopes that had been stained from the cheeseburger he put in that same pocket with the envelopes as the plane was landing; one contained a check made out to Nurse [fill in the blank] in the amount of two hundred thousand dollars. Another was for Fuzzlbum and contained the code to access his two million dollars from a bank in Cyprus.

"Say anything to anybody and you will suffer my wrath. *Wrath.* That's a real word, isn't it?"

Fuzzlbum silently laughed and said, "It is, Mister Trump. And a very good word it is."

"Good. I learned it all by myself."

The last envelope contained a check for two hundred million dollars to build a new wing to St. Joseph's. The wing is to be known as the Trump Wing for the Advancement of Neo

Surgical Procedures. The blueprint for the new five story addition clearly showed that each letter must be at least forty feet tall, must have LED illuminated lettering, and must be installed directly over the entrance or no deal: T R U M P.

Under his breath, Fuzzlbum whispered, *"God help us all."*

Baby Trump made his speech on time. "I got a plan. It'll be the best plan ever come up with by a human being since the beginning of everything. Believe me. The best. The biggest and the best plan ever. I am going to be the best President ever. You better believe it. I will round up those filthy, filthy, they are so filthy, bad people. I don't have to tell you. You know and I know. You know what I'm talkin' 'bout. Shit hole countries is what I'm talkin' 'bout. I don't have to tell you. I will round dem up and put dem in their place. My people will no longer accept the indignity of filthy, begging mongrels. Great is not good enough for some people. You know who they are. Of course you do. Are you with me!? HEIL!"

Adolph's ego and Trump's walnut-sized brain were the perfect match; however, deadly. Heavy hearts everywhere were saddened in disbelief. After Trump was removed from office, he was last seen sitting at a sidewalk table of a Dairy Queen behind Saint Patrick's Cathedral, enjoying a hot fudge sundae with a double helping of wet walnuts, when a pack of angry, filthy, deplorable mongrels from Juarez attacked him, ripped him to shreds, then ate him.

The goat boy did not wince, he simply smiled and took notes.

FIFTEEN
there goes the neighborhood

After hunting for Asian spices, Peter O'Toole was coming into Queen City from a strip-mall in Aurora when his Uber car came upon a large crowd blocking East Colfax Avenue traffic in both directions.

"What do you want me to do?" The Uber driver asked.

"You can let me off here," Peter instructed.

Peter walked towards the crowd. When he entered the crowd, Peter spied a good-looking young black man and asked him what was going on?

"The Black Madonna is flying."

"Excuse me?"

"The Black Madonna. She's flying. See?" The young man pointed upwards. "See, she is flying."

"*Wow*. What a trick. Wires? Jeez, she's naked, and awfully fat, isn't she?"

"Some men prefer a Rubenesque woman, or have no preference at all.

"Please, excuse me. I do know better."

"Good to hear. She is known only as Paradise. And, it's not a trick."

Still feeling admonished, Peter said, "I'd bet she's light on her feet." *Not even a smile*. Feeling stupid and embarrassed, Peter continued. "My name is Peter," he said, extending his hand.

"Mine's Ernie," he said, taking Peter's hand.

"Nice to meet you, Ernie. Do you know what's going on here? Other than a naked woman flying? I can't imagine how she's doing it."

"I guess you need to know how to do it, to do it," Ernie smiled.

"*Ahh...umm*...what do you do, Ernie?" An awkward

question.

"Why do you ask? I'm sure there is no reason for you to care. May I have my hand back?"

"Sorry," Peter laughed and released the handsome young man's hand. "I write plays. My business is to explore the inner lives of my characters. So, I'm always asking inappropriate questions. I apologize, Ernie."

"I'm a senior at UC Boulder, majoring in political science. One semester to go."

"Nice," Peter said with an eager smile, a bit nervous, trying to hide his sexual attraction.

"I was on my way to work when I ran into this."

"Where do you work?" Peter asked.

"It's a little Korean grocery store. On Colfax. I work for a bitch. I play half-witted for her. It helps her to feel superior. Poor thing. The things one has to do. Tuition is a killer."

"I know. I was educated in a Seminary. Full scholarship. I cannot imagine having to pay for an education nowadays."

"A Catholic priest?"

"Lord, no." After an uncomfortable silence, Peter continued. "Maybe I can find some spices where you work. I've been looking for some all morning. What's the name of your store?"

"Kimchi Korean Cheap Market."

"I know that place. It's close to my condo. Maybe I'll catch you there."

"I'll look for you."

"My two best friends go to your store often. I bet you know them. Victoria Aires and Lily Nettles?"

Ernie looked into Peter's eyes, then he saw Peter's tail for the first time, he turned ashen, ran, and disappeared into the crowd; leaving Peter to obsess and agonize about what it was he had said to scare the dear boy off. The Black Madonna continued to fly high above the cheering crowd. Peter, who hated crowds, cut down a cross street and phoned Uber.

"I'll have to take it slow, sir," the driver informed. "There are strange cracks in streets everywhere, my friend."

"Fracking!" Peter announced to his driver, with the self-satisfied smugness that comes from the arrival of his, often repeated, dire prediction. "It was bound to happen sooner than later. I just knew it. I'm right about that."

"Being right is not always a cause to celebrate. Right or wrong, it's way too serious a thing to gloat about. Best choice might be to remain silent, Peter! Were you attracted to Ernie?"

Peter knew that voice. It was the satyr from the mirror speaking to him telepathically. "I guess I was attracted to him. A little. Just a little. Where are you?" Peter asked, telepathically.

"I am next to you. The driver cannot see me." The satyr materialized next to Peter, however the driver still could not see him. "You need to be with your friends in Shady Sanctum. The rest of your family will join you."

"I don't have a family," Peter told the satyr."

"You have me."

"I wish I did. I want you. I want to..." Peter blurted telepathically, hoping he didn't sound too forward, to eager, too salacious.

"Not too forward at all, Peter. I like it. I like a man like you. I like you. You did have me a bit...well, jealous. You know, with that young man you were speaking with. That's a sensation I never experienced before."

Excited and jittery Peter said, "I'm glad that it was only 'a bit,' but your jealousy certainly flatters me. What's your name?"

"You have to give me one."

"Give you a name?"

"Only love can give me a name. Give me a name, Peter"

Peter realized that he may actually love him. It was so sudden, but it felt real. It was the strongest attraction he had ever experienced. He wanted the satyr more than he ever wanted anyone; more than anything in his entire life—more than fame, more than money. The satyr made him feel sensations, all good and beautiful, that he had never imagined possible. He wanted to melt into him; to be a part of him. Peter thought a bit and said, "Angel."

"What a beautiful name. Thank you, Peter." Angel disappeared.

"*Wow,*" thought Peter. *"That was speedy. I hope it's not a one night stand."*

From a distance came Angel's voice, "Not a one night stand, Peter. *Forever.*"

* * *

Halfway home from their curious interrogation at Dead Squeezer's Caverns, cracks began to form in the highway. Billy was forced to weave in and out of cars that were stuck with one or more of their tires sunken into interminable fissures. Billy prayed and did his best to avoid becoming just one more accident on an unforgiving Colorado road. What's more, there was the matter of V shrieking directions into his ear from behind. There was no avoiding her Mulligan stew of verbal assaults. There was no avoiding the real vulgarities of life's obstacles.

"I'm going mad!" Billy was losing his cool, big time.

"You are not going mad, Billy. No more than the rest of us. Never trust a totally sane person. They're always hiding something," Lily soothed.

"I can drive better than that, Billy!"

"Then why don't you drive, V!?" Billy shot back.

"*Sarcasm and mortal fear, at once!*" Lily wondered how she would play that on stage? "*Life mocking death? Some sort of Dylan Thomas rage. That could work fabulously with Blanche DuBois.*"

"I'm not sure I remember how to drive." V mumbled between clenched teeth.

"But you remember how to drive people crazy!" Billy was

getting feisty.

A thunderous silence befell upon the driver and the passengers for the rest of the increasingly dangerous road trip.

When they reached Shady Sanctum, there was the unnerving sound of metal scraping, then the dropping of the passenger side wheels into a fissure in the street next to the sidewalk, and finally, V self-interested screaming into Billy's ear. *"Out, out! Get the fuck out of this thing!"* V slid to the sidewalk side of the car and tried to open the door. "Shit! Lily, you'll need to get out on the driver's side. *Well?* Are you just going to sit there, Billy?" V stepped onto the street and froze in place. Billy and Lily followed and, seeing how they were surrounded by ruptures of unknown depth, they carefully tip-toed to the sidewalk, then ran up the steps to Shady Sanctum's porch. V called out to the porch next-door, where the Widow stood gazing at nothing and everything, "Hello, Missus Stillwater." There was no response.

"She didn't hear you," offered Billy, a bit more relaxed.

"She never does. She's either deaf or mean spirited." V finished unlocking the door. When they were inside, V said, "Billy, come to the kitchen with me, please."

Billy followed V. *"Here it comes,"* he thought. *"I'm sorry sorry sorry."*

"Billy..." V began.

"I did it!"

"Did what?"

After a thoughtful pause, Billy chose to say, "I'm not sure, V. I can't remember. What did I do? What do you think I did?"

"Nothing. I just want to apologize for the way I treated you today. You did not do anything wrong, Billy. It was me. I made it all about me. I was so awfully unappreciative. I apologize. Sincerely."

"Thank you, V. I appreciate that, but if I hadn't taken you to the cavern, I would still have my car in the parking garage under my building."

"Possibly. Blame it on my bipolar disorder." V pouted. "*Oh, do forgive me.*"

"Of course. I have something for you, V."

"For *moi?* Pray tell?"

"It's in my backpack."

"Oh! My present has been here all the time."

Sweat, the size of beachballs, mercilessly betrayed Billy. Boiling saltwater bubbled on his forehead. Billy was about to spring a major leak when, slightly behind V, they reached the parlor in time to see Lily passing a vape-pen to Peter O'Toole.

V was in a chastising mood when she said, "You do know that crap has chemicals in it? What are you doing here, Peter? Don't you know all hell is breaking lose?"

"And that is why I am here, dear heart, to die with my friends."

"Nobody is going to die here, Peter. Not today. You got in, how?"

"Key. I've always had a key, V. Hey, I ran all the way over here from my condo to be with you. I nearly broke a leg in one of those cracks. Fracking, you know."

"Of course. I'm sorry. It is just so terrifying! What is happening out there?"

"I told you. Fracking."

"I know, Peter. At first, I thought fracking meant fucking. You know, from *Battlestar.*"

"Turn on the TV!" Peter said, somewhere in the gray area between speak and shout.

The four of them dashed off for the TV room. Lily grabbed the control first and turned it on. Every station was talking about the end of the world.

NEWS FLASH: FARTWATER, TEXAS DISAPPEARS INTO SINK HOLE. QUEEN CITY, COLORADO IS CRACKING UP. THE HACKER STRIKES AGAIN. MORE AS IT COMES

IN.

"That's enough! I can't stand it!" V said, and everyone agreed. Although, everyone always found a reason to agree with V; it saved them from stepping on those eggshells that would magically appear beside their feet.

"I didn't know you had a television," Billy said, surprised.

"We don't use it much anymore. Except for emergencies," V said, guiltily.

"Fartwater, Texas. What an awful name," Lily sneered.

"I took a bath in fartwater once." Billy, was trying so hard to lighten things up. "There's nothing to do in Fartwater, I suppose." There was no response. Billy sighed. "*Sometimes I hate people!*"

"Frackers," Peter broke the silence. "I knew it!"

"You don't know that," V scolded Peter.

Peter looked straight forward and never twitched a muscle. He had learned the hard way when it is time to keep his tongue behind his teeth.

The four of them returned to the parlor.

"Okay, Billy, what have you got for me?" V asked, as she sat in her Van der Rohe chair. "Lily, are you going to Bogart that thing?"

"What about the chemicals?" Lily teased.

Lily passed V the vape pen. Billy sat in his corner of the sofa as usual and as usual he positioned the throw pillow to hide his paunch; although, it only brought attention to it. He reached down and retrieved his backpack. It seemed much lighter than he had expected. Billy began with, "Well, V...you know how when you get mad at somebody, somebody you dearly love. you sometimes, not often, do something to get even with that somebody, but only in silly loving way, of course, but sometimes it's...*it's*...*it's gone!*"

A rolling, thunderous rumble from an earthquake shook Shady Sanctum to its foundation.

"What the...?" "Fuck me!" "Holy shit!" and "Jesus Aitch!" were all said at the same time.

All four jumped up simultaneously headed to the porch. Max and the twins rushed into the parlor, joined them and followed closely behind. Fire hydrants, for as far as the eye could see, were torn out and strewn about the neighborhood. Water was flooding the streets.

"I knew it!" V shouted. "The twins have the book! Where are those thieving creatures?"

"Behind you, Auntie Vickie," Pudgy Penny grinned.

"And we don't have your stupid book, and we ain't creatures!" Piggy Peter snarled.

V's cellphone rang. Well, not actually rang. Her cellphone chimed with the *Ride of the Valkyries.* She answered and said to the gathering, "It's Tommy Too-Much."

"Is he okay?" asked Billy.

"Hello, Tommy. Are you okay? Good, good. And Carla? Oh, dear. You will need to calm her down. *Umm*...alright. What? Tell her we like her, we really really do. We like her. Would you tell the bitch we fucking like her! Good. Now, follow that up with a Gabor slap and then drag her skinny ass over here. Okay? Be careful." V touched the red telephone icon and announced to all, "Carla's not doing well. She is behaving erratically, moaning and making strange sounds. Naturally, its freaking Tommy out. She needs to be among friends and apparently she just realized she has none. Tommy said she thinks we all hate her."

"No one here, actually, *hates* her." Peter said. They all glanced at one another, and all took their time to *um, ahh* and think before they agreed.

The twins, who hate everybody, hated her a bit less than the stinky Duchess Sylvia Rose Lipschitz Peterson von Smithwitz.

SIXTEEN

coming home to roost

An underling black suit said, after opening her door, without knocking. "Madam Secretary, you are needed up in ASS,"

"Excuse me...who in hell are you?"

"Special Agent Bumnutts, Madam Secretary."

"What do your friends call you?"

"Agent Bumnutts, Madam Secretary."

"Some might call you an interesting-looking man, Agent Bumnutts."

"Thank you, Madam."

"Some might not. I like that cute little widow's peak thingy you've got going on there. Are you a vampire?"

"No, Madam Secretary."

"You look like one."

"So I've heard, Madam."

"If you were a vampire, you'd go a long way in this town."

"I have no political ambitions, Madam Secretary."

"Of course. Not an opportunist, either, I presume. Your innocence is written all over you, Agent...*umm*...what does your mother call you?"

"Bummer, Madam Secretary."

"So, Bummer, what's up in ASS?"

"I have not been fully briefed, Madam, but I can tell you it has something to do with the nano-bot program."

"Those damn nano-bots, again! Please, close the door, and lock it. I, for the love of the All-Powerful, expect to be All-Powerful myself one day...so you can stop calling me Madam, for now. It makes me sound like I'm running a whorehouse. Do I look like I'm running a whorehouse? Don't answer that! Although, I shouldn't pass judgement, should I? I have heard that there is very good money in whorehouses. Of course, when I am All-Powerful I can have anything I want…and that includes a whorehouse. Call me Madam Secretary. I don't like 'Madam' all by itself. Tell me, Agent Bummer, have you ever been to a whorehouse?"

Agent Bummer, embarrassed by his one-inch dick, hesitated before saying, "I have never been..."

"Are you a virgin?" The Secretary stared directly into Bummer's eyes and Bummer's eyes stared back. Agent Bummer was the first to blink. "You *are* a virgin!" Madam Secretary laughed her head off, so to speak.

Someone is about to scream with delight. Someone will be seduced in a ferociously blunt way. The seduction will be over-produced, over-acted, over-rehearsed, over-directed, over-written and totally unexpected.

"You don't know what you're missing, Bummer. My husband's been to whorehouses from here to Bangkok, so what do I care, Sweetie? He gave me every detail. He's been talking about opening a whorehouse within walking distance of the Congress. Huge money in whorehouses. In Congress too, of course. Lobby money. The Senate. The House. So much lobby money! They pocket it and they pass bills that are bought by Lobbyists. Talk about whorehouses!"

"What, Madam Secretary?"

"Money, money, money. People are suckers."

"I don't think so."

"Who gave you permission not to think so, Bummer?"

"Nobody, Madam Secretary."

"You got that right, Dracula! For now, I've got some really big fish to fry, younger fish, pollywogs. Gotta fry 'em, if you know what I mean. Of course you don't know what I mean. I am blunt-witted; even Baby Trump's minions don't get my drift. So, you will very much like escorting me to wherever my schedule takes me this evening."

"It is my honor."

"Of course it is. Do you have a minute?"

"There is ASS we need to..."

"I know what we need, angel ass. I am the Secretary of Offense & Commerce," she said with a cream cheesy smile accompanied by chunks of bagel with everything. "Sorry," she said, after pushing the remains of breakfast into her mouth. There was still the pungent aroma of lox on her breath when she continued, "And such a sweet gentleman you are. You are, aren't you?"

"I like to think I am a gentleman. Thank you, Ma'am." Bummer gulped.

"Don't thank me. A gentleman is what a gentleman does, nice Bummer. "

The Secretary of Offense & Commerce wiped the corners of her mouth, rose from her huge mahogany desk, walked over to Agent Bummer, positioned herself closely behind him, kicked his ass and he flopped across her desk shaking like a frightened puppy. He landed hard. His face pressed against a vase of miniature silk sunflowers. Madam Secretary grabbed his belt and yanked his pants down in one swift motion; then, the Secretary of Offense & Commerce pleasured Bummer as she debriefed him. It was all up the *derrière* from then on. It never crossed the Secretary's mind to take a look at his thingy. She already knew the sad news; he had nothing to show for himself. Not even a thingy.

Everybody: CIA, ASS, FBI, special agents, not so special agents, computer geeks, janitors and Merry Maids seemed to be taken with saying ASS when and wherever they could. Perhaps, in surveillance work that singular frivolity, that one half-hearted smile, may be the only light moment in an otherwise intensive line of work: keeping America great again. It was self-amusing to say ASS.

The acronym ASS is an obvious provocation for American Secret Surveillance, a shadow branch of the FBI. Most of the special agents assigned to ASS operated spy drones. The very first statement in the ASS agent's manual is to: *"Covertly surveil any suspicious Americans, non-citizens, black neighborhoods, Asian neighborhoods, Latino neighborhoods, neighborhoods with a high percentage of Muslims, queers, fag hags, Democrats; all persons of interest, including nude women on rooftops, pools and beaches. To be a suspect could be for as little as buying one ounce too much of fertilizer for window plants, or for ordering French cigarettes online."*

ASS is situated in a gymnasium-size room in the Pentagon. The room is stark white and filled with banks of computer monitors, but there were no surveillance contractors; except, for one lone agent monitoring a dozen screens dedicated to navigating nano-drones. The fiasco at Dead Squeezer's Caverns had caused the Saint Reagan Nano Development Project to be put on temporary hold.

Scientists and engineers were doubling their efforts to develop new and better nano-bots. The new fruit fly bots will replace the long outdated pigeon bots, squirrel bots, mouse bots and bee bots. Unlike the Dead Squeezer mosquito bots, the fruit fly bot will operate on nuclear power. They will feature a nano-nuclear warhead that can be instructed to "sting." Fruit flies are not equipped to sting. They have no stinger. But, by introducing the DNA from a wasp, these little buggers not only spy, they bring their target down. It may take a few days to eliminate the target, or it may be instantaneous, depending on the fortitude of the target; untraceable execution through the magic of miniaturization.

The Secretary of Offense & Commerce was greeted by General Bughump. Bughump led the Secretary past the blackened nano-project monitors to the very last monitor which was transmitting from a most unlikely place.

"Madam Secretary, please have a look at this. I think we may have located the lost prototype."

"What exactly would you have me see, General?"

"We are unable to explain this, Madam Secretary. The lost prototype has begun reporting from..." the General swallowed hard before continuing, "...the Vatican."

* * *

"You stole the book?"

"I did not steal anything, Georgie. It belongs to the Vatican and we're simply returning it to the Holy Roman Catholic Stolen Loot vault. That is why we went to Queen City, wasn't it?"

"Of course it was. Sorry, Rolly. I get principled every motherfucking turd up your nose once in a while."

"I will take care of the book, Georgie. I will deliver the paperwork to the Director of Assembly (DOA) and that Director, sweet Georgie, is *me*. Then, off to the Sistine Chapel and the ghost of Michelangelo. I'll see you after the white smoke."

"I'll pray for you, Rolly. I think, shit head, that God has something special waiting for you."

"I pray it's not perishable."

Cardinal Rotundo scuttered off like a short bowlegged tomato. Not too shortly afterwards, he had all the needed paperwork to call the conclave of Cardinals. But first, he needed to change back into the formal dress of a Cardinal. *"All those awesome American cowboy clothes and we never thought to take pictures!"* bemoaned Rotundo.

Cardinal Alletti sat in the Sistine Chapel appearing unhappy and mean, vile as a rattle snake, searching the faces of every Cardinal, hoping to find even the slightest hint of guilt on the face of *"the bastard who tried to defrock me."* After an investigation, it was determined that he was not the singing drag queen, but as human nature will have it, even though Alletti was found not guilty, few thought him innocent. Stares, both real or imagined, caused Alletti to suffer chronic self-reproach accompanied by constant paranoia. From the accusation alone Alletti was annihilated, crushed, disappointed, hurt, and he no longer had faith in the godliness of God. Alletti compensated with a constant grin, irritatingly tightlipped. He would never, ever, show any pain, nor would he betray his loss of faith. He was an unwilling participant in a melodrama set on the stage of his mind. Alletti's secretive

Mona Lisa smirk hid worlds behind his contorted, frozen, taciturn, vacuous grin, a wax figure in the Vatican museum—an artifact of himself.

Cardinals Tomatoe and Lagerhead sat next to Alletti. That Tomatoe and Lagerhead were having a torrid affair, was a woefully held secret that disqualified both from becoming Pope; neither had the right stuff. Yet, they were always the first to demonize homobuggery. Then there is Rotundo, *"I must be going completely mad to turn the book over to this bunch of hyenas, but here goes."*

"I call it the 'new color book.' It is a new inexplicable color never seen before. At least, not by me. It was retrieved in Queen City, Colorado. It was not easy to obtain this book. It took quite a lot of physical effort. I almost broke my back on a so-o-o-fah while getting the book out of somebody's backpack."

"Get on with it!" Lagerhead can be, well, he's pretty much the rudest man on Earth.

"It is the book that was stolen by the late Anti-Christ himself; Brother Aires. His Former Holiness, Papa Arshmann, had spent decades trying to relocate this book," explained Cardinal Rotundo.

"What is it—*this book?"* Cardinal Gulch the Brusque, who had been a Bishop from Queen City, sporting an orange beard which clashed terribly with the rest of his attire, asked.

"I don't really know, Cardinal," Rotundo answered. "Arshmann said that it is a book of enchantments. It has been around for hundreds of thousands of years. Arshmann's words, if not exactly, certainly capture the gist. I simply do not remember because I am beyond excitement and blessed to have rescued this precious antiquity from the Infidels and to return this treasured book to its proper place."

"I'll be the judge of that," a grumpy Lagerhead, not believing any of what he heard, mumbled. Then, snarkily, he continued, loudly, "Let us see that book, Cardinal Pork! Perhaps, you are color blind."

There was a wee bit of muffled laughter from Cardinal

Tomatoe.

"Of course," Rotundo bowed his head, ever so slightly, to Lagerhead; then reached inside his designer red dress and removed the book. It was in a Queen City King Soopers plastic shopping bag. "Allow me to show you the 'new color book.' Here, pass it around, BUT, I cannot emphasize this enough: DO NOT TOUCH that book with your bare hands. It is covered with that plastic bag for *your* protection; *not* for the protection of an ancient artifact that has the ability to protect itself. Look at it, hold it, but it MUST remain inside the plastic bag."

Lagerhead was the first to grab the book. His greedy first choice was to violently rip the plastic grocery bag from off the book. Rolly was mortified. It was certainly just a coincidence when Cardinal Lagerhead fell forward, farted, belched, and died.

Bewildered, Cardinal Rotundo mused, *"It could have been Lagerhead's arrogance, his self-important pomposity, his mean-spirited behavior, or it was his unwavering state of certainty that poisoned him with his own bitter bile. It was the Will of God. Thank's God."*

* * *

"What are we looking at, General?" The Secretary of Offense & Commerce asked. "I think it's the Sistine Chapel, Madam Secretary."

"Are we recording this, General Bughump?" The Secretary asked, then quickly added. "Was the President informed?"

"Yes, he was informed. We record everything that moves. He is golfing at one of his country clubs at the moment," said the General, rather officiously.

"The bug cameras, are they motion sensitive?" asked the Secretary.

"Yes. The slightest motion will trigger the bot to transmit."

"Please tell me how a hot bot got to the Vatican. And what the hell is going on in the Sistine Chapel?"

"Madam Secretary, at O-eight-hundred hours the

transmission began. At first the reception was poor, until our computer geeks, the Siamese twins, were done tinkering with it. The reception is as you can see, more or less, acceptable. I never thought the twins could do the job, you know, being attached at the scrotum and all, but their work gets done lickity split."

"General!"

"Yes, Madam Secretary?"

"Look at this. Four Cardinals appear to be dragging a dead Cardinal. *Oops!* They just threw him against something out of range, but he bounced back. They're kicking the poor bastard. *Oh, look.* There's a black Cardinal who just threw himself on top of the dead one. *Holy Cow.*"

"Too bad this generation of nano-bots doesn't have the ability to transmit sound," lamented the General.

"I hate missing things!" exclaimed an angry Secretary of Offense & Commerce. "Hey, nice Bummer! Give me your phone. I need to text someone and tell him what's going on here. What *is* going on here, General?"

"I believe they are electing a new Pope," Agent Bummer answered.

The General sneered at the agent. "Are you a General?"

"Sorry, sir."

"Geez, Agent What's-your-face, you wouldn't have one with a bigger text pad, would you?" asked the Secretary. "It's going to be a long message. Does anybody have a goddamn stylus!?"

* * *

"We can't hang the sonofabitch! No sense in tying him up, either."

"Gert! He ate all our food. What are we supposed to do?"

"I'm thinking, Charlie, I'm thinking. We may have a way out of this. A way to get food, get rid of that fence, and the frackers and the Buzzards at the same time."

"What have you got?"

"I'm gonna keep it to myself for now, Charlie. Don't want to jinx it. Go ahead and let the Governor out of the freezer. There's nothing left for him to eat, anyway."

"We could eat him."

"We could." But Gert's idea did not involve eating anybody, although it certainly sounded doable in a pinch, but eating the porker is off the table, for the moment. Gert's idea would be a challenge. Late morning. Sunlight. There is an *estación de policía* in Puno. How fast can a fox run forty-plus miles safely, in daylight? Then there will be the problem of her nudity when she transforms back into her Gert-self. They will need a diversion. "We'll need a diversion, Charlie. A really big one."

"Okay, I have an idea. Why don't we tie Crapp to the fence? Let him tingle for awhile. That's a diversion."

"No, Charlie. The fence is so highly charged, you'd be electrocuted along with him. When it comes to avoiding electrocution, even a fox would need to be as smart as...well, you know, as a fox."

"Talking of foxes, Gert, you do know I know, don't you?"

"Suspected. Thanks for the confirmation...and the months spent in a mental institution," a loving chide.

"I'm so sorry, Gert. I should be more trusting."

"I know. You will be more trusting from now on, won't you?"

"No question about it."

"Good, Now, I have a plan, and I will need your help, Charlie."

Gert's plan needed a diversion; a major one; not one for the kiddies. Sex. Shocking sex. Sex on display. Just the scent of it will attract the attention of all those horny Buzzards. Just a scent and they'll come running with their dicks out. It will involve the brothers Alfredo and Álvaro, Tallulah Badass, Stinky Juan Carlos, Salome the housecleaner, Rosemary the Cook, and Miguel Angel the mindreader. The diversion will be big and with a whole lot of triple Xs. But she didn't want to share her plan with Charlie just yet.

Crispy Crapp remained in the freezer.

SEVENTEEN
lunchtime at Shady Sanctum

Back at Shady Sanctum the electricity had gone out. It didn't much matter at the time, but it will as the day wanes. For now, there is plenty of sunlight to last well into the lingering midsummer evening.

Maxfield went to his room, crawled under his bed and made himself invisible. Lily tore the clear packing tape off dozens of boxes in the spare room in search of candles. A hysterical Carla and an impressively empathetic Too-Much, who finally got her to calm down, were on the front porch. Angel sat at the kitchen table watching Peter making himself a peanut butter and banana sandwich while making plans for their future.

"Peter, do you think they will object?" Angel asked.

"My friends? No. Absolutely not. They'll love you. It's just that, well, I'm afraid you won't like me after you get to know me."

"Why is that, Peter?"

"I'm not young anymore. I've a past that I am not proud of. You caught me flirting with Ernie. And, I'm not as smart as I lead people to believe. In fact, I'm actually kinda stupid."

"Peter, I was in the hospital room the day you were born. I know you. And frankly, I must say, you really *are* stupid."

"What? I said '*kinda stupid*,' not just plain old flat out everyday stupid." Peter was incredulous.

"*Gotcha*. Stop doing this to yourself. You're not stupid and you know it," Angel put his hoof down. "Peter, you should know that you are the last of the new souls. There are no more."

"*C'mon*. People are born everyday, Angel. I assume that every single one of them has a soul?"

"Of course, Peter. There are no new souls left on this planet, except for Maxfield. Maxfield is an ancient soul, a new soul that he's kept from his beginning. All the other souls currently available, healthy souls, have been recycled. Negative and atrophied souls from many lifetimes of bad choices and bad deeds, are thrown back into the sun where all their memories are vaporized. Those souls no longer exist."

"Of course, you know I have no idea what you're talking about. But I shouldn't like being thrown back into the sun and vaporized."

Angel chuckled. "That's not going to happen to you, Peter. The used souls are cleansed and restored to their original essence. Eventually, new souls can be created, however, it takes thousands of thousands of years. Peter, you are the last of the unique."

"I don't know how I should feel about that, Angel. And since I have no idea for what you're talking about, I'll just go with the flow."

"I've watched over you all your life, Peter." Angel takes Peter's peanut butter scented hands and kisses his palms. "You are very special in every way, Peter. Run your hands through your hair, Peter."

"*Huh?* Okay." Peter withdraws from Angel's hands and moves his fingers through his hair. Peter stops abruptly when he feels a couple bumps an inch or so above his hairline. "What the...."

"They're your horns, Peter. They're growing. One day you will be very proud of them."

"*I already am.* I've been waiting for them. I don't know why. A premonition, I suppose. I just don't want to turn into a mean old friggin' devil."

"Not a chance, Peter. Besides, like humans, not all devils are mean, old or friggin'. Some are quite gentle. They're what they call angels here on Earth. Angels can appear to be any age they want...any physical form they want. You will see. You named me Angel. The most beautiful name you could have given me. You are my angel, Peter. Peter the Angel."

"Oh, boy. I like that. Thank you, Angel." Peter's eyes began to fill with tears. He wiped them away, thought a moment, then smiled. "Will I get wings?"

"Do you want wings?"

"Maybe. Since I have horns and a tail, wings might be a nice addition. No feathers. The bat kind. But, I'll pass on cloven feet. Sorry. No insult meant. I wouldn't change an inch of you. I love you." Peter's teeth began to chatter, his body trembled. Peter was in love like he'd never been in love before, like he ever could have imagined possible. Peter said it again, "I love you, Angel."

"I know."

"Do you eat peanut butter where you come from, Angel?"

"Not with bananas." Angel chuckled. "Just joking. That combination is a favorite. Whatever we want, Peter. By the way, devils don't have cloven feet, unless they want them. Except for Monsanto, a most evil devil, I don't know of any others."

The force from the earthquake was bad enough, but the aftershock was yet more powerful. When the ground beneath Shady Sanctum finally stilled, Billy, holding out his backpack said, reluctantly, yet with presence of mind, "V, it's gone. What I had for you is missing."

"You lost my present," V pouted. "Well, there is no reason to worry over it."

"I didn't lose anything, V. Clearly, somebody stole it."

"Ut-oh!" the twins popped up from behind the sofa and squealed in unison.

"What are you telling me, Billy?"

With an unctuous edge, Pudgy Penny blurted, "I bet I know."

"Go to your rooms, the two of you!" V yelled. The twins ran up the staircase, giggling. "Okay, Billy, before you accuse anyone of theft, what is missing from your backpack?"

Billy, shyly at first, said what he had to say, "I had the book with the new color. It made me smarter. I wrote an essay about the fourth dimension. I understood it until I didn't anymore. Something about something. Time and consciousness, maybe. Anyway, V, I am not the same. Something has changed. I am sorry and I apologize for having betrayed my best friend."

"*I* am your best friend? *Hmm.* But are you? Are you really my best friend?" V asked.

"I don't know. I mean, after Lily and Peter, I'd like to think I am. I have many acquaintances, V, but real friends? I don't know. I think of you and Lily as my best friends. At least, the best I have. I think, sometimes, there's something wrong with me."

V was quiet for a moment as she looked directly into Billy's smokey blue eyes. *"There truly is something different about him,"* V thought, then said, "Thank you, Billy. *See?* You *have* gotten smarter," V chuckled. Billy felt relieved. A weight the size of a grand piano was lifted from his shoulders.

"I was told to get a dog last week at Racine's," Billy told V. "I was telling Mad Michael about wanting to find someone to marry. 'Billy, for the love of Aunt Jemima, get a fucking dog,' Mad Michael the Pissy recommended. I had a dog once. It pissed on everything, including me. '*Ohh,* my gay nerves, to have a man like that!' Mad Michael swooned.' He's not as cute as he thinks he is. Anyway, V, I know it was meant to be an insult, but I thought about it and decided a dog would tie me down. I like living alone. I can do whatever I like, whenever I want. But, I also want a relationship. It's confusing, V. I want someone to love and someone who loves me. Crap, it's all existential, isn't it? Love, I mean. Without love, what would be the meaning of life?"

"Wow. We all want that, Billy. We all love you, Billy, in our own ways, to one degree or another. Happy to hear you are smarter. You must demonstrate more of that to me one of these days."

"V, please. I know you love me, but, please, don't make fun of me. I'm tired of it, honestly. I'm tired of you bullying me. And that's my first demonstration."

"I earned that, I suppose," V said. Then she said, mostly to herself, "How many more of my dearest friends are thieves?"

"I never thought of it as stealing, V. I thought of it as borrowing. A bad thing, I know. But, you know I would have brought it back. I'm not a thief. You know I would never actually steal anything from you. I don't steal from anybody. You know that!"

"I do, Billy. I do. Settle down. Everything is fine. Forget it. Not another word. *Still,* I would like knowing who has the book now?"

Carrying a shoebox filled with an assortment of candles, Lily entered the parlor at the rear end of the conversation between V and Billy.

"The cowboy Cardinal," Lily said, matter of factly, setting the shoebox on the butler's table.

"What?" V asked, incredulously.

"The cowboy Cardinal took it," Lily casually pronounced.

"You weren't even in the room. You left, as I recall," V was certain.

"I heard all the commotion when he knocked over Billy's backpack, then the *'divano'* and whatever else. It was all a ploy."

"Do you have a crystal ball, Lily?" Billy asked.

"I eliminate the possibilities. One by one. The cowboy Cardinal took it."

Meanwhile, out on the front porch, Carla and Tommy were having a heart-to-heart about losing La Bean Hacienda, where they were going to live, and how surprised they each were to connect so well; as if they'd been best friends in a prior life.

The din of distant drums added rhythm to the ear-splitting sirens screaming from firetrucks, ambulances and squad cars. A Mariachi band played in the bed of a sixty-eight yellow Ford pickup that moved slowly along Colfax Avenue accompanied by bellows of voices, angry and horrified, squeals of gnomes as they pushed one another to higher ground, pieces of confused and panicked conversations, and the local news from Colorado Public Radio on Carla's iPhone: FRACKING ACROSS COLORADO BLAMED FOR QUEEN CITY EARTHQUAKE. NO EXPLANATION FOR NAKED FLYING BLACK HOOKER.

PERU AND ARGENTINA ARE ALSO EXPERIENCING MAJOR EARTHQUAKES. DALLAS JOINS FARTWATER, TEXAS FOR BEING THE SECOND CITY SWALLOWED BY A SINKHOLE. DALLAS IS NOW TWELVE STORIES UNDERGROUND. FARTWATER NO LONGER EXISTS. QUEEN CITY MAYOR SAYS: "WE ARE CLOSING IN ON THE HACKER." AMATEUR ASTRONOMER REPORTS THE EXISTENCE OF PLANET X.

"Carla!"

"What?"

"The columns!" Too-Much suddenly cried out and pointed to the columns. The columns that had stood watch over La Bean Hacienda had tip-toed, so to speak, past Shady Sanctum while Carla was reading the news on her cellphone to Tommy. The columns settled on either side of Widow Stillwater's mansion.

"That's odd," said an amazed Carla. "My columns, my Doric columns, have never done that before. They do run off some nights to kick gnomes, but that's about it."

"You could chain them, or train them, or use a sledgehammer on them." Tommy offered.

"Have you no compassion?" Carla asked Too-Much.

"For pillars walking and kicking!? Are you kidding?"

After catching her breath, Carla said, "Sorry, Tommy. I apologize." Carla questioned herself, then continued, "I get too close to inanimate objects, Tommy. *Things*. They've become too large a part of my life. I find myself responsible for them. *Things*. Inorganics, Tommy. We all share the same atoms. All of us. Those pillars and I share the same molecules. They are a part of me and I care for them as I care for myself. Well, not as much as I care for myself, of course."

"Of course."

"But that may not be within your grasp, Tommy. I know it's simply a hairdresser's attempt to try ones hand at chiding-wit. So, I forgive you."

Tommy could not bring himself to utter a word. He was confused about what had just transpired. It felt as though he had been punched in the chest. He slowed his breathing and realized that his best choice was to remain silent. There appears to be a universal practicality for knowing when to change the subject, and when silence is the best choice. However fast their friendship developed, it was too soon to test it. So, after a bit of remaining mum, Tommy did what every well-mannered person ought to do when all goes south; he changed the subject.

Max awoke and quickly screamed bloody murder as he hit his head against the wooden slats underneath his bed. He ran downstairs like an asymmetrical fuzzy bowling ball, screaming, "Tape! I need tape! Lily! Help me! The cellar is filled with cockpions. They are ugly and poisonous. I killed one, but it divided first. TAPE! For the love of bananas will somebody give me some tape! Am I here? Where am I? Do you see me? V, do you have any uppers? Downers? Shrooms? Of course not. You never do. Getting weak and soft in your old-age; seeking no more adventures. There are plenty more left if you want them, Victoria. When are the two of you going on an adventure? *Hush.* We did a Frankenstein, a bad thing, and now the cellar is teeming with cockpions. Thousands of them. V, do you have any *special* cookies or brownies? Anything? Damnit! What am I here for?"

"Tape." Lily answered, casually.

"Yes, tape! We need to tape every possible way the little buggers can get out of the cellar. They're growing bigger and bigger. If insects were our size, we'd be food."

"What do they look like?" Lily asked.

Maxfield caught something in the corner of his eye and turned to see what it was and what it was was a cockpion the size of a New York deli Kosher pickle. Max turned to Lily, pointed and whispered, "Like that." Lily screamed like a tornado siren and ran upstairs. Max squished the Crispr experiment under his shoe. "Oh, dear. What a mess. And on my brother's favorite carpet."

V screamed, "In the kitchen. Under the sink."

"What's under the sink?" asked a confused Max. "I'm not going under the sink. You know perfectly well, Victoria, that I can't fit under the sink."

"TAPE! YOU DRUGGED-UP MORON!"

Max rushed into the kitchen and spotted Peter and Angel hugging. "*Ahh,* love. You're both looking particularly well this evening. Is it evening? What's going on here?"

"I have a name, Maxfield. I am now Peter's Angel."

"But you've always been an angel," said Max, affectionately.

"Max, you can see Angel?" A puzzled Peter asked.

"Of course, Peter. I've known this guy forever," Max beamed and said.

"How long is that?" Peter asked.

"Forever! Tape. Under something. I need tape," Maxfield said. "Good seeing you, Angel. Nice name, Peter. You boys take care of each other. I'm happy for you. Angel, could you conjure me some peyote?"

"Sorry, Maxfield. The Overlord would never allow it. Especially the Neanderthal."

"*Oh, her.* I guess not."

Lily came running down the stairs and, together with Billy and V, rushed into the kitchen.

"Under the goddamned sink!" V yelled during another aftershock that caused the cellar door to fly open; making that the best place to start taping; "Quickly! quickly!" V cried out while she sprinted to close the door.

Meanwhile, Old Pansy Hedgeworth ran out onto her front porch and called for her two chihuahuas, "Babies!? Where are you? Where are my little boys?"

She heard whimpers behind the house. Thinking something terrible had happened, she galloped into her backyard and, horror of horrors, her little boys were stuck butt first in Trump's massive ego. Her little boys were slowly being sucked into the humongous, filthy, nasty thing. Old Pansy tried to pull her babies out. She tugged and she coaxed, but only got herself bitten by both of her little boys. "My babies are being eaten alive! *Help! Help!*"

For the moment, frenzy best describes the mood in Shady Sanctum's kitchen. Packing, masking and duct tape were distributed to eager, nervous and hesitant hands.

"This ought to keep our minds off the end of the world, for awhile. Give me the duct tape and I will do the coal slide door and any other place I find where they could get out!" Peter grabbed the duct tape from Lily's hand and bolted out the kitchen backdoor with Angel. They went around the side of the house and triple duct-taped the coal slide door. "That ought to do it."

"Help! Help!" This time Old Pansy Hedgeworth was heard, along with her barking chihuahuas, "*Help! Help!* Will somebody help me!" She lurched at Trump's ego to retrieve her babies, but she was sucked in, head first.

EIGHTEEN

on the road, a woman with a dick, rolly stomps on it

The residents of Puerto Nostradamus readied themselves for the "big diversion." Charlie and Gert waited in the clubhouse for Gert the Fox to leap over the fence, once again, without getting herself electrocuted. Charlie will not take part in the diversion. He had one job to do and that job was...*nothing and worry.*

"It's okay, Charlie. You can watch. You're allowed. Besides, it might be fun. You can tell me all about it when I get back."

"*Nope.* Every second we're apart I will think only of you. I wait only for you and you alone."

"What a pile...you're funny, Charlie."

Charlie, who will constantly worry about Gert's safety while waiting for his cue to torch the fuse during the grand finale. "I found the old generator."

"Where did you find it, Charlie."

"On the porch of the old shack. It just appeared there. *Humph.* Odd, isn't it?"

"*Yeah*, really odd. Get it hooked-up for the kitchen. Especially the hot water and the freezer before it starts to defrost. Oh, and you might get some music going for our big diversion."

"You got it, Babe."

Meanwhile, the beguiling brothers, Alfredo and Álvaro, waited with Tallulah Badass in her cabin. Alfredo helped Tallulah tuck in her family jewels. Well...one thing led to another and before you know it....

Juan Carlos, the stinky sheep shearer, took two baths. Nobody wanted to share a cabin with Stinky Juan. He made himself comfortable in the Governor's cabin, keeping busy with rehearsing his role for the big diversion. The Governor had no use for the cabin. He was still on ice, and well on his way to becoming a Crispy Crappsicle.

Miguel Angel, the mindreader, was hot to trot and ready to get on with the big diversion. Upon arrival at Puerto Nostradamus, guests are warned about Miguel and given free tinfoil hats, along with some complimentary advise, *"Wear them around Miguel to protect your precious thoughts. And, don't be deceived by his devilishly good looks. His magnetic attraction is a force of Nature. Touch him and he will seduce you, pleasure you, and he will know more about you than you do."*

Waiting to make their dazzling entrances from the yellow cabin, were Rosemary Paola and Salome Otilia. Salome does light dusting, uncommonly light dusting, odd jobs and no windows. She is best known for giving jeff sessions behind the cabins which are generally quick and only require one hand. Salome earned her reputation by her willingness to do whatever is needed to keep the guests happy. Giving jiffy jeff sessions to a few horny old men was only the least she was willing to do; and she was available twenty-four hours every day. Salome is tipped well for her kindnesses. She has been saving every bit of her hard earned cash to go to Dollywood in America.

Rosemary Paola, the cook, was grateful to be employed. She did what was asked of her and did the best she knew. She and Gert pretty much ran the clubhouse. Rosemary Paola had no dreams nor aspirations, no savings, just nine ungrateful children.

The uber fabulous Tallulah Badass, appeared outside the door to her cabin. She wore a slinky bright neon fuchsia dress with sequins and long fringes at the bottom, just below her knees, that danced to the rhythm of her slightest motion. He dress definitely had a Charleston *wacka-do-wacka-do* feel about it. Its open-back plunged way down south, exposing her orin hatch. Her higher than high heeled shoes, dyed a matching neon fuchsia, made her feel ten feet tall. *"Holy Carmen Miranda. Fuck me, RuPaul! With these heels I can conquer the world!"* Although, all she had to do at the moment was conquer the brutal Black Buzzards.

Her role in the big diversion began with Tallulah's grand entrance. She sashayed towards the electrified fence. *"There should be music,"* she thought. but then there should have been electricity to spark the speakers atop the clubhouse. But, just as she was thinking about doing her routine acapella, keeping the beat in her mind in sync with her gyrations, Charlie turned the gasoline generator on and Tina Turner came blasting from the rooftop speakers—*What's Love Got To Do With it.*

"Hey, boys! You want a piece of this?" Badass strutted along the south fence, facing the fracking action, pulling on a lump of strawberry saltwater taffy from Atlantic City, teasing the Buzzards by grinding her money-maker, and with some pretty awesome tongue action. "Hey boys, I am Tallulah Badass, the Queen of the fucking Universe! What else do you need to know?"

The Buzzards, in small groups at first, meandered closer to the fence to see what was happening. Tallulah was what was happening! While making eye contact with as many Buzzards as possible, she continued to perform her salacious grinding and lip-licking, before she gave the horny Buzzards the treat they were waiting for, at least one of the treats they were waiting for; she moaned like the soundtrack of triple X porno film as she took out her marco rubios. *Boom, boom, bah-boom, bah-boom.* They were real implants...*absolutely ferocious double Ds!* The Buzzards were hootin' and howlin' for more. They were mesmerized, hypnotized and out of control. Soon, the Buzzards grew to five deep, then six, and so forth. Those in the back row pushed on the row in front of them, to get an unblocked view, to get closer to the source of their arousal, to get the full affect of Tallulah's mammoth marco rubios, until the drooling Black Buzzards in the front were poked and prodded dangerously close to the electrified fence. *Boom, boom, bah-boom, bah-boom, bah-boom!*

"Hey boys, ya wanna kiss these bouncing babies?"

The Buzzards roared with yeses and erections.

"C'mon, baby. I wanna lick those tits!"

"Careful, stud. Lick these babies through the fence and you'll get the shock of your life!"

Meanwhile, the Buzzards who were standing watch at the north end of the fence, began making their way to where the action was; hitting pedals to the metal in a caravan of super-sized, fully armed, black golf carts.

Alfredo and Álvaro swanked out of the cabin. Without a stitch, hormones raging and stiff upper lips, they paraded like peacocks over to Tallulah. The Buzzards jeered and heckled.

"Hey. No queer stuff!"

The louder the Buzzards booed only excited the brothers more. After a bit of manhandling, directed straight at the Buzzards, Alfredo inserted his roy blunt deep into Tallulah's orin hatch and began johnny cornyning her. Álvaro then began to roger wicker Alfredo. Buzzards hollered and whooped. They didn't know what to make of it. Suddenly, "queer stuff" was quite exciting; they inched closer to the fence, giving each other permission to like it."

Rosemary and Salome, each wearing seven veils, danced to a DeMille epic, complete with the orchestrated soundtrack to *Lawrence of Arabia* pouring from out the speakers, and the scent of incense and cheap wine, with a Roman guard escort. A trail of veils lay along the ground as the merry maids danced to their positions, kneeling in front of the fence. Poor Rosemary Paola, in her fifties and sagging, only removed four veils. Salome removed only six veils because that day she needed a tommy cotton maxi-pad.

Juan and Miguel strutted from out their cabin into the sun; wearing big smiles and even white teeth. The prominence of their rand pauls showed exactly how high their ambitions were. Salome and Rosemary gladly emphasized the degree to which they would lower themselves without gagging on the size of those lindsey graham pork barrel attachments. The rows of Buzzards continued to grow. In a surprise move, the brothers pulled back the Velcro of Tallulah's gown, exposing the largest and most bewildering object lesson, strictly for the Buzzards—an oversized, puffed-up Randy Paul.

The screams from the Buzzards was deafening. In the heat if the moment, the hornier Buzzards dropped their pants and help one another to feel the burn.

Tallulah began to levitate inch by inch by inch by inch.

With tongues wagging and mouth drooling, the Buzzards moved to within millimeters from the fence. Sadly, but insanely stupidly, two horny Buzzards tried to maneuver their randy pauls through the diamond-shaped openings in the hatch-work of the electrified chain-link fencing, but were thrown backwards after losing what they thought was the best part of their manhood, and that was very likely true; the Buzzards identified with little else. So many straight white men are fascinated with women with dicks, and for their own dicks, for that matter. And then, unfortunately for the Buzzards, the entire first row of horny soldiers of fortune got too close to the fence and fried. The second row of Buzzards stepped over their dead comrades and moved closer to the fence.

"Okay, let's do it," Gert said, while removing her robe.

"Be careful, Gert," Charlie said before Gert the Andean Fox ran up and over the fence to begin her journey to Puno.

* * *

Cardinal Tomatoe was inconsolable as he laid upon the dead blubber of Cardinal Lagerhead, screaming bloody murder, literally. "Which one of you is the bloody murderer!? Oh, bloody, bloody murder!"

Most of the Cardinals in the Sistine Chapel were dancing to the music of the spheres; some with themselves, some with one another, some in a conga line. They paid no attention to the ugly dead beer-bellied man, nor the equally ugly mean-spirited black man on top of him. Some of the Cardinals played hopscotch, while others played patty-cake and a game that involved slapping each other; something best done in lederhosen, and it certainly didn't appear to be fun. But he conga line did.

On his knees under a naked cherub, Cardinal Alletti prayed and wept. And, without a camera in sight, wasting histrionics. His political mealticket went up in flames. Then came the loneliness; the loneliness of one who climbs too high too fast only to lose his footing, fall, and forfeit all and more. Alletti's dreams of the Pontiff's throne were charred and fettered by his own choices. He awaits for a pound of his own flesh to be exacted by the fingers of the dark unholy angel. That is the price for an unjustifiable and undeserved privilege. Dante Alighieri must have dealt with that, on one level or another.

Rolly never moved. He sat and watched the circus. The scene faded and blurred into a canvas that Hieronymus Bosch never painted, but should have.

Rolly beheld Angel, the satyr, who had sparkled into view. Angel smiled at Rolly as he stood behind an elderly Cardinal who watched the high-spirited behavior that had engulfed the Sistine Chapel with a conservative smile and sad eyes. Rolly heard the satyr inside his head. "This is your next Pope, Rolly. Do you like being called Rolly?"

"Only when it comes with love. Do you know me?"

"It does come from love and I do know you, Rolly," Angel said. "My name is Angel, the name given to me by the last true and immortal soul, Peter the Angel of Creation; although he does not know his true calling yet. The man in front of me, Rolly, will be the next Pope for these dark times. There is a plague of death and evil in the world and His Holiness will drag, by his teeth, if he must, this dreary old charnel business, if not into the twenty-first century, he will settle for the twentieth—where the Church would most likely be stuck for another twenty centuries. I know that you don't really want to be Pope anyway, Rolly. It was brave of you and Mother George to retrieve the book. And where did you get that cowboy disguise? The best ever! I will need to take the book with me, Rolly. Georgie is waiting to share a pizza, or two, when the conclave reaches its conclusion, which will be soon."

"What is going on with the conclave, Angel?" Rolly asked.

"They're intoxicated by the book, Rolly. They will come round soon and get down to work. They will not know what happened. All they will remember, except for the dead Cardinal, is that something happened. The book likes you, Rolly."

"Really?"

"Absolutely. By the way, you have something on you."

"What?"

"On your robe. Where your heart is, Rolly."

Rolly moved his hand over his heart and felt something sharp, metallic. He dislodged between his fingernails. "It's a bug." On closer examination, "A metal mosquito." Rolly placed the mosquito underfoot and stomped on it into oblivion.

The monitor in the Pentagon went black.

When Rolly looked up, Angel was no longer there and the Cardinals were sitting as though they had never moved from their mission to elect a new Pope; except for dead Lagerhead and raving Tomatoe, who was still whining, moaning and whimpering. In short order, white smoke rose heavenward announcing that a new Pope had been elected.

"Poor, poor Rolly. I know how badly you wanted it."

"I didn't want it all that badly. *You* did, Georgie. In fact, I'm relieved and to tell you the truth, I feel giddy."

"So, we are okay, right?" Georgie asked.

"Same as always. We'll have lots of fun. More fun than we could have if I were Pope.

Georgie was happy the ordeal was finally over and her playmate Rolly was back. "We could continue harassing Alletti just because he's Alletti. I hate that son of...*oops*...I do not appreciate Cardinal Alletti almost as much as I do not appreciate butt pimples and GMOs. What Cardinal did they chose, motherfucker?"

"A lovely old man from Argentina."

"That's nice."

"Mother George the Kind, I do believe *you* would have made one helluva Cardinal." Rolly was genuine.

"I know, motherfucker! But, *tweet, tweet,* my mouth wouldn't keep quiet and I don't appreciate red as the color of my attitude. I do not have a red persona, shithead! I sparkle in black."

"Who doesn't?"

"Rolly, how about we go for a pizza, or two?"

"Or two, Georgie."

* * *

Puerto Nostradamus is off the beaten path. It is nearly three miles from any road. There is no way to reach it, or to reach the Krotch, Krotch, Bushit & Mother and Vader Diggers and Frackers, LLC, other than by helicopter, or to follow the tire ruts through a field of tall grasses. The road to Puno is a long and perilous odyssey for a fox; especially in broad daylight. Cars, guns, children, dogs, and cats lay in wait to pounce. It is the places themselves where one may hide that are the very places where danger most likely awaits. A fox, for all the talk about them being vicious and destructive, is a vulnerable creature in so many ways. For Gert it was especially difficult to adjust to the thinking, intuition and the innate abilities of a fox since she was not born into the culture. She, one day and all of a sudden, just discovered her fox self; leaving her with much to learn and without any genetic information for it.

After several miles on the road Gert the Fox, who was already exhausted, collapsed flat out and breathless. She felt she could go no farther—not as much as another inch. She felt that she might die that day of exhaustion and without being able to move in either direction. She could not go on. There she was, Gert, along the side of a road; broken pieces of tarred rocks to one side of her, wild bushes, tall grasses and weeds on the other. She tried to stand, but it was too difficult, simply moving required much effort. Her heart fluttered with fear; fear of becoming roadkill or attacked by something in the shadows; she knew there was no other choice given her—she took a deep breath, hoped for the best, and crawled into the thickets.

When Shirley MacLaine held a seance in the clubhouse, the Duchess of York asked to speak to the spirit of Samuel Beckett. At the time, he had recently died and the Duchess thought that his spirit might still be hanging around. *"I can't go on. I'll go on,"* Mister Beckett channeled through Shirley, and he said nothing else. Gert was so impressed she made it her mantra. She would rest in the weeds awhile before willing herself to go on to Puno and hope for a miracle. The dry rough ground beneath her rumbled.

Gert huddled as close to the earth as she could. There was no going on without recouping at least some of her energy. There, in the shadows of the bushes, tall grasses and weeds, Gert the Fox fell asleep. It was an aftershock that rumbled through the ground beneath that startled her awake. She didn't know how much time had passed, how long it would be before sunset, or if she should turn around and go back to Puerto Nostradamus. The answer was obvious. She lost hope of ever making it to Puno; her little fox body simply wasn't able.

Shortly after Gert had woken, good fortune arrived in the form of a pink Cadillac's brakes screaming with the *flop, flop, flopping* sound of a flat tire coming to rest only inches away from Gert's muzzle. The door opened and out stepped Elvis Presley. He slammed the door shut, kicked the flat tire and angrily whispered to the bright blue cloudless sky and all the nothingness surrounding him, "Shit! *We're having an earthquake, Jesus. I'm in the middle of nowhere and I ain't never gonna make it to Puno on time! Help me, Jesus.*"

The Andean fox is graced with acute hearing, so hearing what Elvis said was easy when it sounded like somebody turned the amplifier up to maximum while Ozzy Osbourne shrieked, screeched, and bit the head off a gecko. Gert the Fox thought that she could jump into the back seat, but then he might see her when he gets back into the car. Then Gert had a brilliant idea.

Gert the Fox changed back into Gert the Woman. She rubbed dirt on her face and arms. Without a stitch of clothing, with pieces of thickets dangling from her hair, moaning and sobbing, Gert crawled out from the shadows.

"What the…what happened to you, lady? *Ah,* Jesus…are you okay?" Elvis was genuinely concerned.

"Robbed and…and…*oh,* I cannot say." Gert was not as good an actor as Lilith Champagne, but with a little practice….

"You don't have to, Ma'am. You don't have to say nothin'. It's unspeakable, I know. We need to get you to a hospital. If anybody ever did this to my mama, I'd hunt 'em down, if it took a lifetime. I'd hunt 'em down and pray to the Good Lord to help me not to do anything my mama would want me to. Ain't no way they could outfox me. I would find 'em," Elvis told her. "After that… well, who knows?"

"I need to get to Puno. I need some clothes. I am suffering, Mister Presley."

"You know me?"

"Everybody knows you," Gert gave him a sly, foxy smile.

"Please, lady. Don't suffer. I can see it on your face. I can get you to Puno as soon as I finish with this fuckin' tire. Excuse me, Ma'am. I didn't mean…I mean, it just slipped out."

"No excuses, please. I use that word all the time. My name is Gertrude. Everybody calls me Gert. Please call me Gert, Mister Presley."

"Please call me Elvis, Miss Gert." He removed his shirt and draped it around her. His torso was lean and firm; solid as that proverbial rock. This was not the fat Elvis from another dimension; so, removing his shirt was entirely Gert's pleasure.

"I'm ashamed to be seen this way, Elvis. And here you are giving me the clothes off your back."

"Don't worry, Miss Gert. I've seen hundreds o' naked women."

"You have?"

"So far."

"Good for you. My husband and I own Puerto Nostradamus; not too far from here. *Umm,* it's mine really. Family money. It hasn't gotten in the way of our relationship—my husband and I." After a pause and a vacant stare into the heart of nowhere, "I'm sorry. I forgot what I was saying. "

"Nothing to be sorry for. Family money. Relationships are hard, Miss Gert. You're fortunate. You know what?"

"What?"

"I've heard o' that place—Puerto Nostradamus," carefully pronounced, observing that Puerto had three syllables. "Rumor is,"

Elvis continued, "There's strange and supernatural things goin' on in there."

"Maybe the rumor is true." They both smiled. "If you ever need a job, I mean, when you're all fat and washed-up, come see me."

"Fat and jolly, I hope. Thank you, Miss Gert." Elvis peeled-out and they were rocking and rolling on a "donut" tire. *"We're off on the road to Puno,"* Elvis sang.

"You have such a beautiful voice, Mister Presley. I mean, Elvis. If you don't mind me asking, why are you going to Puno? You're a long way from home."

"I am. I heard about this here all-you-can-eat and beer bust festival. It's a benefit to help the Society of Tortured Souls."

"I've met many tortured souls, Elvis. They come to Nostradamus for help. You should stay away from all-you-can-eats, Elvis. They are a dangerous refuge for tortured souls."

"I understand that, Miss Gert. That's why I want to help the SOTS. Oh, look. We're coming into signs of life. There's a couple houses over that way. If you see any clothes hangin' out to dry that you think you can wear, speak out."

"Sots?"

"Society of Tortured Souls."

"Yes, of course. The mind is slow today. Especially being, you know, what I had to suffer...what he did to me." Gert found the trip to Puno a delight. "Oh, look! Some clothes.

Elvis, the perfect gentleman, stopped the car and grabbed a burka from off a stranger's clothesline. A woman in a housecoat burst out of the front door, screaming and pointing her finger, *"Fatwa! Fatwa! Fatwa!"* She ran in pursuit, but too late, Elvis and Gert were back on the road to Puno.

NINETEEN
hitler's ego, and monsanto's bad seeds

An ear-splitting "HELP" *a*nd then there was silence.
"That came from Old Pansy's place," Peter said.
And then, in an absence of time, as quick as a thought, he and Angel instantly appeared in her backyard.

Head first, Old Pansy was up to her boney knees in Baby Trump's ego. Peter grabbed her faded red velvet house slippers and pulled them off so he could grab her ankles and get a good grip on her, *"My god! What ugly feet!"* Then came a PLOP sound, a huge sucking sound, the sound of Trump's ego slapping shut, closing the vacuum left by Old Pansy. She was out, covered in slime, catching her breath, spitting out bugs, small body parts and refried beans from Taco Bell. She will be her old nasty self in short order....

"Don't just stand there! Get my boys, you worthless waste of space!" Old Pansy demanded. Short order was but a small part of a second. She was back to her old self.

"I'll do my best," smirked Peter. Peter does not suffer being ordered, especially by an old crone. There comes a time when even the most forgiving souls must stand up for themselves.

"You better do better than your best. Get my boys out, you ignoramus! Or I will sue your fucking ass! GO!"

"I just saved your life, lady!"

"Fuck you!"

"Ut oh." Always best to think out possible reactions to possible decisions, if given enough time, that is. If not given enough time, ones favorable chances narrow when forced to make on the spot decisions, less than thoughtful choices; granted, most decisions are made that way—on the spot. Peter was exasperated when he turned and said softly, without the fanfare of actually saying, *"go to Hell, you reptilian battleaxe,"* which he was thinking; but with a broad self-satisfied smile, and a smug, a superior air of whimsy, "Goodbye."

"Where are you going!? My God! You've got a tail!" She yelled at Peter's back as he walked away. "Get your tail back here!" He kept walking. *"Please.* I don't care if you are Satan."

Angel, whom Old Pansy could not see, took notes as he leaned against the apple tree trying to stop laughing. Peter slowly turned and came back. He grabbed the necks of her boys and pulled, but they yapped and bit his fingers at every opportunity. Peter grabbed the ears of one of her boys and yanked.

"Don't rip my baby's ears off, you nincompoop! You're gonna kill 'im, you sorry sack of shit!" Old Pansy shouted while beating Peter with her red velvet house slippers.

"That's it, lady! Satan is outta here!" Again, Peter turned and began to leave, but the sound of a thunderous belch, an apple falling, followed by two Chihuahua zombies flying out of Trump's ego and hitting the apple tree, stopped him in his tracks. The zombie dogs picked themselves up, growled and nipped at Peter's ankles.

"Sorry about that," said the giant ego, in a sonorous voice.

"You speak," said Peter, amazed.

"I'm going to call the police!" Old Pansy shouted.

"So am I, you monster bitch!" Trump's ego articulated.

Old Pansy clucked, shuffled down the path leading to the front steps of her house, marched up to the front door, went inside and locked all seven locks. She would have no success contacting the police. They were currently occupied coping with the pandemonium consuming Queen City. *An aftershock!* Pansy and her boys crawled into, what she felt was, the safety of her bed. There they stayed. Poor Old Pansy Hedgeworth...how she hated life!

"I speak when I want, or need." said the gentlemanly five-hundred pound ego.

"Who are you. What are you?"

"The ego of Mister Baby Trump."

"How is that possible, ego of Baby Trump?"

"It's possible. Here I am. Just call me Ego, or Mister Ego, please. I'm finally free from that psychopath's head, *forever.*"

"Mister Trump certainly doesn't sound to me as somebody without an ego. In fact, that's why he sounds so preposterous."

"The fat guy has an ego, alright."

"*Oh?* Another? How did that happen?"

"Doctor Fuzzlbum, whom you know, wise choice keeping your tail, and you're gonna love your horns, anyway, the good doctor replaced me with the ego of Adolph Hitler that he bought for a song on eBay...which was noxious, deformed and rotted-out. Trump is now operating with Hitler's abomination. I'm glad to be out of that cesspool for a head! He made me into a self-aggrandizing, insatiable, greedy, lying asshole! And that's not who I am. I believed I was all alone in the universe; just a hardworking blob in Trump's head. Even when I was removed, I thought about getting back into his head. Stockholm Syndrome, I presume. Luckily I changed my mind from making what wold have been the most regrettable mistake of my life. After all his abuse came into focus, it occurred to me that I had been his prisoner. Now that I'm free, I believe I'm a better ego for it. I certainly have given it my best to be a sterling example of a blob."

After listening with compassion, Peter rethought. "I am sorry for you, but you are a cannibal. You eat living creatures while they're still living, Mister Ego. I can see some un-chewed rats and squirrels."

"I don't chew."

"I can see that. Sorry."

"Listen, I eat whatever I can. I'm sure the universe will forgive my not cooking home on the range, nor my inability to handle a knife and fork. I'm in no position to be a chooser, my friend. Fortunately, for me, I am amply supplied with lifeforms. After they are assimilated, the smarter the lifeform, the smarter I become. It is for their intelligence I hunger. That is the reason I chose to remain and learn more about your people. They are beyond interesting."

"Oh shit! You're a people eater.! You're...you're like the Borg."

"You gotta be kidding me. I'm nothing like the Borg! I said smarter lifeforms, not stupid myth-dwellers, mass murderers, hateful bigots, haters of the unknown, self-absorbed, fake reality makers, hypocrites! I don't eat shit like that! Give me some credit for better taste. Peter, tell me you understand what I'm saying."

"I'm trying. But you still eat living creatures."

"So do you, Mister Carnivore! You have no idea how many living lifeforms are attached to the things you eat. When I collect all the information I can, I will, most likely, burst."

"Literally?"

"*Yup*. What other way is there to burst?"

"Okay. Then what?"

"I don't know, Peter; but there must be something beyond the big burst," jiggled Mister Ego.

"Who cares? I mean, so what? We spend years of our lives in search of the unknowable. I mean, the unknowable is unknowable! So why bother?" Peter asked, but it didn't really sound like a Peter question. It sounded angry, sad and discouraged.

"Don't ask me. I'm just a blob. No one cares what I think."

"I'm listening, Mister Ego. I must care...somewhat."

"When you accept a thing as unknowable, you create its existence. Eternity is unknowable; therefore, it exists."

"That doesn't make one bit of sense."

"That doesn't need to make sense, Peter. It's up to you to make the sense of it. How else could one know that the existence of eternity exists? One must have faith in the eternity of existence. Eternity and the unknowable are products of one's imagination, and imagination is the key to everything. Just a thought, Peter. I ramble." said Mister Ego. "But there is more to put into this equation."

"More? More of what?" Peter asked, totally at sea.

"The power of kindness."

"Why is that a part of this 'equation?'"

"Because it opens doors."

"Right. And now you're a blob who sounds like Jesus Christ!"

"Jesus Christ? *Hmm.* One of us is a plagiarist," the blob chuckled.

"So, you don't eat people. That's good. How have you learned so much, Mister Ego? You sound like an educated man, were I any judge."

"I am not a man and you are not a judge. I am an ego, and all this blah-blah-blah is giving me an appetite!"

Peter thought a bit and said, "Do you like bugs and creepy crawly things?"

"You betcha! Some of the smartest creatures on Earth are creepy crawly things. They are architects, builders of underground cities, underwater wonderlands, and great thinkers who live in the clouds, and actually walk upon their vaporous substance. You're pretty smart yourself, Peter. You would be surprised. Ask Maxfield. He's a bug person. He knows. He can tell you how they're organized and how they're tired of getting stepped on. Why do you ask? Do you have any creepy crawly things?"

"Have I got creepy things!? Follow me, Mister Ego." Peter led Mister Ego to Shady Sanctum the long way around the block. They were more than likely not seen since most of the neighborhood residents where confused, frightened, and behind closed doors.

After Peter pulled the tape away from the coal slide door, he quizzed, "Mister Ego, are you sure you are really, really hungry?"

"I could suck you in and dissolve you...here is where I would snap my fingers and say, 'like that,' if I had any fingers."

"I know you wouldn't suck me in and dissolve me," Peter was unreasonably certain about that.

"Good for you. Faith in action. No, I wouldn't. And, for your information, I wasn't eating that old bitch, either. She threw herself in me! What a foul piece of meat she was."

"Some around these parts say she eats children," Peter whispered, on the sly. Before opening the door to the coal slide, Peter instructed, "They're nasty and poisonous bugs. Probably knee-deep by now. They multiply quickly and you gotta suck up every single one of them. You cannot, you must not, leave even one down there. It will only multiply again and that would be disastrous, not only for Queen City, but for the entire planet! Only you can save the world, Mister Ego."

"*Yeah.* Like I haven't heard that before." Mister Ego laughed, pushed himself through the rectangular opening onto the coal shoot. On the way down, he shouted back, "Peter O'Toole, the last soul from Philadelphia and elsewhere! You never were meant to be human, Peter." Mister Ego chuckled, then fell upon his cockpion feast. *"Yummers!* These little buggers are delicious. Never tasted DNA like this before."

Angel stood nearby, taking notes when Maxfield came running towards Peter, "What are you doing!?" he asked, frightened by the thought of what would happen if the cockpions escaped.

"It's okay, Max. Baby Trump's ego is down there eating all the cockpions. I told him what you told me about them. Do you mind if he stays in the basement a day or two? Just until he recovers…and, of course, is done with all the cockpions. "

"*Umm*...who in blue blazes is Baby Trump?"

"You've got to be kidding me, Maxfield," quizzed Peter, confused by disbelief. *"*Has anyone *never* heard of Baby Trump? That's not possible."

"Nope. It's possible. Never heard of him. That must come as a grievous disappointment to that person, I suppose."

"I imagine," Peter said, incredulously.

"What does he look like?"

"Manufactured."

"The ego, Peter, the ego."

"Does it matter? He's an ego, Max. He's huge."

"Huge?"

"For an ego."

"Sure. Let him stay. Can he do anything else around the house?"

"I don't know, Max. Other than saving the world, you should ask him yourself."

"I don't want to speak to somebody's ego. I need a dummy."

"For what?"

"A dummy can say what he pleases and people will listen. They don't listen to me, Peter."

"Get a twitter account."

"What in hell is a twitter account?"

"It's *ah...ah*...I made a bad joke. Max, I always listen to you."

"Always?"

"Maybe not always."

"The truth, Peter, is when a dummy speaks the truth, everybody listens, no matter how frankly truthful, even when it hurts. Did you know that Edgar Bergen and Charlie McCarthy had their own radio show? Think about that."

"Hmm."

An aftershock! The flagpole with the rainbow flag, the one that was in the front yard of "the boys" next door to Old Pansy Hedgeworth, fell over from the aftershock and right into Old Pansy's front yard, landing on the roof of the porch, and severely damaging it. Within seconds, the flagpole that stood on Old Pansy's corner with the American flag, a monument to the Veterans of Foreign Wars, toppled over, destroying the roof of her porch completely. The tops of the poles pierced her bay window, causing the flags to intertwine as they hung suspended over Old Pansy Hedgeworth's favorite chair.

"Angel, did you do that?"

"It wasn't me, Peter."

* * *

"Monsanto wants his bad seeds back," the Overlord told Captain Talbot.

"Why, after all this time?"

"He needs help processing and cleansing problematic souls. One by one. They all must be refurbished in the furnace of the sun. They're coming up in droves and they're in unusually bad shape."

"Sounds awful," Captain Talbot shook his head.

"They will all be cleansed, but they won't be sent back to Earth."

"I have a question."

"I have an answer."

"Is Peter divine? Does he really have the last original soul?"

"Yes. He has the last original soul, indeed. Humans will eventually disappear. The disillusionment from learning there's no Santa Claus should have taught them not to put all their beliefs into one basket. There are no tooth fairies, either. Lessons from disappointments gone unlearned. Peter and Angel will be there for the end and they will be there to begin a new world. A new Creation. You must know there actually is a thing called global warming. They've gone too far, too late. The Earth Mother has had enough!"

"Sad," the Captain sighed. When will this happen?"

"Not right away, but soon. Not everybody will cease to exist. Some will be transported to Sumer. Maxfield and his family will be among those who will be spared."

"So Maxfield will be coming home, at last."

"If he's had enough of living in two worlds, bring him back.

He's aging, you know. Humans may not survive another rotation." The Overlord reached into the air and brought back a pillowcase-sized sack of quixelite crystals. "Give this to Peter and Angel. They will know what to do with it. It's for Maxfield's family."

"Family?"

"You will know who they are when you arrive." The Overlord reached into the air again and conjured a book, neatly wrapped in plain brown paper. "This a present, especially created for the family. Give it to Miss Victoria Aires, your brother's daughter." Two large suitcases appeared next to the Captain. "If Max chooses to stay, give him that suitcase. Careful, it's a very special kind of mirror. And, lastly, this suitcase contains especially designed clothes for a human called Minnie Beach. See that she gets it. Her soul must be remembered for its beauty. That is the total of it, Captain. Anytime you are ready, the window is open."

* * *

Max came around the corner of Shady Sanctum, stepped carefully up the steps to where Carla and Tommy Too-Much sat noticeably close to each other.

"What happened to Peter?" Tommy Too-Much asked.

"He's undergoing a metamorphosis," declared Maxfield.

"You mean his tail?" Carla asked.

"I mean his thinking, his tail, his horns, his fiancé Angel and so much more."

V came out onto the porch followed by Marie Aqua-Net. V had overheard Carla and Tommy talking. "There's nothing wrong with Peter's thinking, Max. It's you, we all worry about."

"Just you wait and see, Victoria. Soon, Peter will no longer be human."

"So much for that five hundred dollars! There won't be any competition tonight." Eddy reached up and carefully removed his wig. "Have you got a place for this, V? I just had it done."

"Ask Lily. She has a few styrofoam heads for her Theatre wigs."

"Great." Eddy went back inside and called for Lily.

"What do you mean by no longer human, Max? It is just a silly tail," V said, dismissively.   "It's not about his tail, Victoria."

"I give up. If it is not about his tail, then what, Max? *What?*"

"Something never seen before on Earth. You'll have to wait and see," said Max. "By the way, humans are doomed. Do you use Amazon?"

"Sometimes. Why do you ask?" V asked.

"I want a dummy!"

"Will a hand puppet do?"

"You distress me, V," Max sighed, stormed into Shady Sanctum and slammed the door.

"He gets like that," V declared to her guests, in the form of an angry apology. "Call it what you will."

"We all get like that sometimes," Carla piped up, unaware of her own irony.

"Some think Maxfield is a genius," V offered. "I find that *iffy*. Besides, how would I know? What about you, Carla? Do you have any idea?"

"V?" Carla asked.

"What?"

"Take a look at the widow's place. My beautiful pillars, my columns went there right after she died."

"She's dead? That's not possible," V said, astonished. I saw her less than an hour ago."

Max yelled from the other side of the front door, "Time bends! You might step into this house and it's a day later, or the day before. It could have been yesterday, Victoria."

"Max, go under your bed and disappear!" V shouted.

"I just may!" Maxfield stomped off towards his bedroom.

Carla explained to V, "She's dead alright. It took the

ambulance awhile to navigate all those cracks in the streets, but they did. The dead widow on the gurney bounced and almost fell into a widening gap before she was hauled into the ambulance feet first."

"Who called the ambulance?"

"I think it may have been one of my pillars."

"Poor thing. She was all alone in the world. I should have been a better neighbor." V sighed.

"Tommy and I have been talking about the house next door," Carla said. "Now that it's available…well, it's a fixer-upper, but it could be fun. A labor of love. And yes, V, I'm coming to realize that we all should be better neighbors."

V flipped, "What is wrong with you, Carla!? The more I get to know you, the more I like you. But, what is with this newfound…I don't know…Carla, you must know you have been a bitch since forever. You've been uppity and dismissive every time I tried to be nice to you. You're not better than me."

"I never thought you were, V. Maybe I was insecure about who I was…who I had become."

"Wow. That's real. Give me some time to adjust to this new you."

"Of course."

Tommy Too-Much tried to disappear, but wasn't having much luck, so he kept his eyes closed.

"You will see," Carla said, charmingly. "If the house next door comes on the market, I will sell La Bean Hacienda, if I find a buyer, and purchase it. I want to be your neighbor, V. I think we're going to be great friends."

"I'm willing, but…"

"No 'buts.' Thank you, V." Carla directed V's attention to the street. "The ambulance driver said that the electricity is coming back all over the city."

Mikey and Mercy Nice were marching the streets, delivering God's message. Their mouths and signs delivered the same message from God: "THE WORLD IS ENDING. BLAME ATHEISTS! BLAME HOMOSEXUALS!"

"Go away!" V shouted. Get away from here with your stupid babble!"

"This is America and we have freedom of religion, Miss Aires! Unlike you, we practice love! It is our Christian way."

"I have freedom *from* religion. And if that's love and Christianity you practice, I pity your souls!"

TWENTY
lock and load and risky pleasures

Elvis parked his pink Cadillac in front of the Puno Police Station. "I'll go with you, Miss Gert."

"You don't want to miss your beer bust, Elvis."

"All you can eat, too. Can't miss that. I still got time and I ain't gonna let you go in there all by your lonesome. I insist."

When Elvis insists, what are you going to do? After an abbreviated interlude, a thoughtful pause, the lady firmly said, "No. No, please. I need to hold my head high. I must accept and endure the pain of my shame. I must walk in with my head held high. I must do this by myself." Gert didn't mean one bit of it.

"Suit yourself, Miss Gert. I respect that. You take care now," Elvis peeled out onto the pavement, raised his arm high with a casual wave of goodbye, then disappeared around a bend in the road.

"God help me!"

Wearing a burka in Puno is undoubtedly a rare occurrence, and a hazard. The sign above the door read: *Mantener el Orden Público*. When Gert opened the station door, three of Puno's finest had their guns drawn and aimed at the terrorist; and she was the terrorist.

"No, no! It's me! Gert Aires-Birdsall. Remember me? Puerto Nostradamus."

"*Mierda y ¡oh Dios!* It's the fox lady. Take that thing off, *por favor.*"

"I'm naked underneath."

"What were you wearing when you stole it?"

"I didn't steal it. Elvis Presley did."

The Big Cop instructed the Little Cop to get the hospital on the phone. "Tell them it's the fox lady, *again.*"

"No please!" Gert shouted. "This is an emergency. Bushit is

destroying Lake Titicaca. The Governor of New Jersey, U.S.A. is in our freezer."

"And why is that?" The Big Cop asked.

"He ate all our food. You don't believe me, do you?"

"Well, it kinda sounds a lot like...well you know." the Big Cop said.

"*Crazy?* I'll just have to show you because we need the Army to invade the Puerto Nostradamus side of the Lake and there's no time to waste. So, NOW!" Her burka fell to the floor and she wasn't in it. And then, cautiously, the wagging tail of Gert the Fox appeared. One can well imagine the excitement that caused. *None,* actually. The air was thick with silence. The burka filled back up with Gert inside it. "We don't have anytime to waste. Their fracking is causing the tremors."

"Hang up the phone! Get General Cajoles *de la Armada.* Tell him to bring all his heavy whatever he's got!"

"Nukes, too?" asked the Little Cop.

"We don't have nukes, you nincompoop!" The Big Cop was nervous, exited and sweating. He was having trouble believing what he had just seen; but he knew what he saw and there was no denying it.

The Medium Cop turned to Gert and said, "Nincompoop? That's a gringo word, yes?"

"Yes."

The Big Cop grabbed the phone from out the Little Cop's hand and said, "General Cajoles, listen! We got a flesh and blood Bushit. If we turn him over to the Hague, we get ourselves a huge reward, plus favor with the Peoples of the United States! *"Está bien, los hombres, de bloqueo y de carga! Tienes que a partir de película de Hollywood. Bloqueo y de carga!"*

"Lock and load!" Gert shouted.

* * *

The main water supply for the fire hydrants in Queen City was shut off. The last of the gushing water flowed through the streets, washing away bright green leaves and a hodgepodge of debris into corner drains, leaving the streets for the sun to dry, and the drains to manually unclog; when the Queen City Department of Un-clogging gets around to it and they will not be getting around to it until the streets and the sidewalks are repaired and repaved..

All fracking in the U.S.A. had ceased. Fracking in most other countries had lessened, or had also ceased. Aftershocks were fewer and were lessening in their intensity. Repairing Queen City streets and roads will take the remainder of the summer just to show any real progress, even with repair crews working around the clock, seven days a week. Billy Butts' new red Beamer, lodged under the sidewalk in front of Shady Sanctum will, most likely, stay there for quite some time. In the middle of the street, the huge hole that no one knew how deep it was, threatened to become a long-term fixture for the foreseeable future.

Eddy Spaghetti in his bejeweled white gown, came out of Shady Sanctum carrying a black plastic leaf bag. He placed the bag on the edge of the porch, carefully arranging it so that it spilled over onto the top step, and then he carefully held his gown and sat. Eddy had removed most of his makeup and left his wig adorning a styrofoam head on the butler's table; his heels were parked under it. Getting to his apartment, at least for the next few hours—and assuming the world doesn't end—seemed to be a difficult challenge for Eddy, what with the streets and sidewalks being wet and broken apart, and then he would need to walk the streets for a couple dozen blocks in his gown. He would not have minded it at all had it been shorter dress, but it wasn't and he would need to hold it a foot off the ground all the way home and Eddy thought, *"Too fucking much! Ahh...the trials and tribulations of wearing a dress."*

Eddy was engaged with examining the devastation all around Shady Sanctum. It was difficult for him to believe his eyes. He didn't know exactly what he felt, other than vulnerable, numb and closer to death. He moved his head from side to side as if to say *"no, no, no"* to the mayhem—and then a huge sigh. "*Girrrl*, tell me I'm dreaming."

"You ain't dreaming, honey. You can't click your heels out of this one." Too-Much sighed.

Peter came around the side of the porch from the backyard wearing a grin and feeling like the cat that's got the cream, so to speak.

"We were wondering where you went, Peter...." V said.

"Taking care of a cockpion problem." Peter answered with great satisfaction from having saved the world from the death and devastation. *"Although,"* Peter thought, *"without Old Pansy screaming bloody murder I wouldn't have met Trump's ego, and I wouldn't have been able to do zip."* Peter was quite right in his thinking: he couldn't do zip without Old Pansy leading him to Trump's ego; otherwise, nothing short of divine intervention could have saved the day—and Peter was not about to rule that out; residue from Peter's Catholic upbringing still stuck to him like a label on plastic.

"What's a cockpion?" Tommy Too-Much asked.

"One of Max's experiments. He's very loose-lipped. Ask him," Peter responded.

Surprised, Carla said to Angel, "I know you. Do I know you? I know you. Of course I do. I'm sure I know you. Don't I? What's your name?"

"My name is Angel and I am Peter's intended." Angel responded, proudly.

"How fabulous is that!" squealed a jubilant Tommy Too-Much. Peter and Angel are gonna get hitched! Well how about that? Before the world ends we'll simply must have a marvelous party!"

"From your mouth to the ears of the universe, Tommy," Carla said, agreeably.

"Let's hope there's no wax in them." Too-Much said.

Confused, Peter nudged Angel and telepathically asked, "How come they all see you?"

"They are members of your family, Peter. Everyone in your

chosen family sees me. Your family is *our* family."

"I don't remember making a choice," Peter whispered.

"You did."

"How wonderful!" Eddy exclaimed. "Mozel tov to the happy couple!"

"That is so cool. Congratulations, the two of you," Carla said with cheerful enthusiasm.

"Since when did you become a member of our family, Carla?" V's edge was definitely on the fun side of devious.

"I would never presume such an imposition. Forgive me, V. I will be the long-lost spinster aunt, the next door neighbor; if I sell my estate and buy it. Otherwise, I will be out on the streets peddling my tired ol' ass from door to door. V, can you imagine that?"

"Imagination creates reality, Carla. I will keep my brain occupied with something other than your tired ol' ass...*um*... although, I seem to remember hearing rumors...."

After taking a long pause to think about what rumors they might be, Carla decided it wasn't a game she wanted to play, "Anyway, darling, I promise you that I will very rarely visit, if ever; unless, you pick up the phone and call for something. Or, we become fabulous friends."

"I wouldn't rule out us becoming fabulous friends. One can never have too many. As for your being a spinster aunt, I don't see you in that role, either. Easier to see you as a streetwalker."

"He left me with nothing, V. I'd hate being seen naked and desperate."

"So would everybody else."

Peter blurted, "You girls are way too much!"

"You are so right, Peter. The world is ending, kiddo. It's way too much or nothing!"

Carla bust into laughter. "You are sensational, my dear Victoria! Where have you been all my life? We're going to have lots of fun, you and I, you and me, oh fuck it, the two of us. By the way, because the world might be ending, of course I hope not, but if it does, you have every right to feel a bit of anxiety, V."

V chuckled. "Thank you, Carla, but I do not recall ever feeling anxiety. I don't know what you're talking about."

"Carla," Lily interjection with a great big smile, "believe me, she doesn't know what you're talking about."

Then V had a revelation: "What is this shit about the world ending? A little rumble. A little shake. A couple fire hydrants break. The house behind the alley collapses. It was cheap and tacky anyway. Closed streets and highways all because of a few holes and gashes. Flying hookers. That's a strange one. Creatures from another dimension invading the cellar. And Billy's Beamer. That doesn't mean the world is ending. It means that the world is clearly ill. But it must recover, *it must.* But if the world really is coming to an end...well...I will not have it!" V said firmly. "So, whatever the future holds, I'm all for celebrating, kids!" And everybody agreed.

Lily broke in, "I say, let's get snarkered!"

"Good idea." Carla raised her glass and said, "Here's to the happy couple!"

Too-Much raised his glass, "To Peter and Angel."

Brad with the Hot Ass, who had disappeared into a wormhole for three days from the hospital where Carla was kept for anger management, was walking up the block, stepping over cracks and fissures, while studying a small scrap of paper. He appeared lost. He was having trouble finding house numbers, and with good reason. The owners of every house on the block had no numbers attached to their homes, not on their doors nor to the side of them, but rather on little ornamental plaques in different areas of the front yard. The placards were moved from time to time, depending upon what was planted, how they were arranged, how high they would grow, what season, or how deep the snow—they tended to be obfuscated and easily missed by pedestrians who didn't know exactly where they were going. And then, sometimes gnomes in their puckishness, hid the placards by taking positions directly in front of them, just for spite.

Too-Much saw Brad with the Hot Ass coming up the sidewalk and said to no one in particular, "*Oh, my nerves*, that poor man needs my help," then he called out to him, "*Hello-o-o? Hello-o-o there.* Can I help you find somebody?"

Brad with the Hot Ass ran up to the bottom step of the porch, out of breath, but he managed to speak between breaths, "Maybe. Yes, please. I met Paradise...the Black Madonna...the hooker who flies over Colfax...."

"WHAT!" Too many voices to distinguish who all said it.

"Paradise is a friend of Mad-Michael's," Tommy Too-Much announced.

"She told me that I would find Mister William Butts at this address."

"The Black Madonna is telepathic," Angel said.

"I wasn't sure about that," Brad said. "I mean, it felt like she was in my head. Good thing I wrote it down."

"I know you, too!" Carla said with confidence to Brad, even though she knew little, except, "You worked at the hospital. You're the one with the hot ass. Turn around." He did. "Oh, yes. That's you alright. Billy thought he'd never see you again. Billy wanted so much to find you. I only recently recovered from my little trip to the edge."

"I haven't recovered, at all," Tommy Too-Much spilled, then leaned into Carla's ear and whispered, "Sorry. Truly. Won't mention it again."

"Of course," said Brad, happily. "You are Mister Butts' friend. Wait, wait! Don't tell me. Carla, right?"

"Not only are you drop-dead gorgeous, the ass of a god, you remember names, too," said an astonished Carla Bean with a yearning for Brad with the Hot Ass, for her lost youth, for a balm for the pain she felt from having just learned a grievous lesson taught by a deceitful Greek.

"Thank you, Ma'am. I'm pretty good that way, remembering names, I mean," said Brad, blushing.

Angel hushes Brad telepathically, "Change the subject!"

"But, not to change the subject, I really need to know if William is here."

"Brad's good!" Angel told himself.

"Aren't you divine," Eddy said, while scanning Brad from head to toe.

"Well, thank you, Brad said. "I love your gown."

"This? Just something I threw together on my little sewing machine."

"Don't pay attention to the stitch bitch, Brad," Tommy Too-Much purred. "You go right through that door, Mister...*Brad.*"

"Thank you," Brad smiled at Tommy, walked up the steps smiling to Eddy, opened the front door and closed it gently behind him, but not before saying, "Thank you," to everyone in general. And then he was gone.

"Damn! I'm about to..." squealed Tommy Too-much, crossing his legs tightly together.

Carla snapped at Tommy, "Get over it, bitch."

"You're not supposed to use that stuff on me," Tommy chided. "Only I get to use it. Besides, it's a Cher thing. You gotta get the attitude just right, or you won't get away with it. *'Get over it bitch,'*" Tommy showed her how to say it with panache and fabulousness. And then he continued, "Who's up for a par-tay!?"

"I don't think there are many, if any, party treats in the house," V sighed.

"Tommy, go to the Hacienda and please bring back a few of those big canvas shopping bags filled with Champaign, single malt Scotch, wines, cheeses. There's a gazillion things to bring. Whatever you like. There is that tray of brownies—no. Never mind."

"*No?* Why not?" V asked.

"Because they are, you know, Alice B. Toklas," confessed Carla.

"*Hell, yes!* You bring those suckers with you posthaste!" V demanded.

"You'll need a hand, Tommy. I'll go with you," Peter offered. Tommy, Peter and Angel took off for La Bean Hacienda.

When it's the end of the world there is nothing to do but *par-tay!* The excitement of a celebration took everyone's mind away from what may come.

"Did you hear about Dallas?"

"Don't it just make ya wanna cry?"

"What about Fartwater, Texas?"

"Hey! Did it occur to anyone that Brad can see Angel?"

"Where are Billy and Brad?"

"I think they're in the TV room. Talking," Lily said.

"*Talking? Girrrl,* I don't think so."

"Now we have another family member! Lily, come sit with me. I am having an extraordinary anxiety attack. My first...*ever*," with a nod to Carla. "How many tofu turkey rolls will we need come Thanksgiving? I'll need to order them from Trader Joe's. That's if the world doesn't end."

Meanwhile, Angel and Peter were having a private telepathic conversation. Tommy was busy trying to remember everything on Carla's list as he carefully placed them into canvas bags. Tommy was quite involved with exercising his ability to remember. He should have written it down.

Angel: You must be careful inside the heads of others. Unless invited, you are a trespasser and, if found out, you will be treated as a trespasser.

Peter: How?

Angel: Humiliation for one.

Peter: How do you know if they know?

Angel: You don't. Don't be lured into it. Don't be seduced by it. Have you heard the thoughts of strangers?

Peter: I'm not sure. A little maybe. A few.

Angel: Exhilarating, isn't it? You wonder if they hear you, if they know you are listening? At first, you think it is an illusion.

Peter: Yes. That's exactly how it was.

Angel: It persists—the illusion—in a seductive way; pleasurable and daunting at the same time. Risky pleasures mixed with fear can be irresistible, Peter. You are having a 'cannot-be-happening' experience, it goes against your reality, and you don't know the etiquette. So, get out quickly. You will ask yourself time and time again; was it real? Was it the truth? Peter, this moment *is* Truth; for us, anyway. Other than that, I haven't a clue. What do you think?

Peter: Damned if I know.

Angel: Well, there you go.

Peter: Who is the Neanderthal Overlord?

Angel: You remember her?

Peter: Vaguely.

Angel: Now you're beginning to remember. *Good.*

Tommy was finished with packing four canvas shopping bags to the brim,. "I need to check if there's any mail."

"You've got to be kidding, Tommy." Peter was amused to think of mail delivery when the world may be coming to an end.

"Never know." Tommy headed off to the mailbox at the north end of the building.

"We'll be here," Angel said.

"Angel?"

"Yes, Peter."

"The world isn't really coming to an end, is it?"

"Worlds are born and worlds end everyday, Peter."

"Angel, you know that's not what I asked, right?"

"I do."

Tommy returned. He threw a few letters, including a sales flyer from Victoria's Secret, into one of the shopping bags. Soon, they were on their return trip to Shady Sanctum.

TWENTY-ONE
party like it's the end of the world

A quixcube is a square box. Its outer shell is made of quixelite. One of the many properties of quixelite is that it has the ability to create the illusion of invisibility. Real invisibility just doesn't seem possible, but there is always somebody who won't give up on the notion, and that's a good thing. Until now, quixcubes have been used solely to transport goods and people around planet Sumer—which is twenty times larger than Earth. There are many sizes of cubes. There is a super-sized quixcube currently under construction. It will hold tens of thousands of professional TAG player fans who follow the Worldwide Automagical Games (WAG).

Captain Talbot will be piloting the smallest of the quixcubes. There are two well-appointed levels and it can carry twenty souls comfortably; upwards of a hundred, in a pinch. Quixcubes have been used for centuries to transport people and materials around planet Sumer, but this will be the first time a quixcube ST-10 will be used for interplanetary travel. The ST-10 is the first in the ST (Sumer Transport) series to fold spacetime across the solar system. Stars hosting planets in the universe and perhaps the multiverse, will no longer be out of reach.

Captain Talbot stepped into the quixcube and waited for the dispatcher's signal to begin folding space to the third planet from the sun.

"The coordinates have been preprogrammed and set. You are cleared to go anytime you are ready, Captain," the jovial voice of the dispatcher came from the speaker panel to the side of the Captain's chair.

"Ready," said the Captain.

"You bring that baby back home, Maxie."

"You can count on it, my friend."

"Clear to go."

Clouds twisted and gathered into a towering new-color funnel with its eye surrounding the quixcube. Lightning pummeled the cube causing it to rock wildly, until a prodigious white flash, followed by the rumbling sound of rolling thunder as spacetime tore and swallowed the quixcube.

* * *

Unless they were cracked, chipped, or otherwise damaged, every gnome on Capitol Hill gathered in Cheeseman Park. There were over a thousand gnomes, eating grasshoppers, popcorn, condoms, whatever they could forage for the stamina to get on with their protracted march along Historic Colfax Avenue from Cheesman Park to the Capitol Building, demanding equal protection under the law for gnomes, lawn jockeys and pin wheels. However, chances are they will run into a whole mess of alligators when it comes to equal protection for lawn jockeys.

The gnomes chose a bad day for it. Three blocks into their march several dozen comrades, brightly painted, green, blue, yellow and all with pointed red hats, had tripped over cracks and shattered, or they disappeared into gashes and holes in the streets and sidewalks. It was devastating; a sad day in all of Gnomedom. They gave-up the march in memory of their fallen heroes. The gnomes, exhausted and disheartened, retreated throughout Capital Hill and waited like everybody else, until after the end of the world. There was, however, a good chance that gnomes could survive the end of the world; should the end of the world actually happen.

* * *

Poor Sir Geoffrey was determined to marry *somebody* before world's end. No one of reason could possibly imagine why. It's the end of the world, isn't it? But, there may have been a reason. Were Poor Sir Geoffrey married, he could face the end without having to face himself.

Poor Sir Geoffrey gathered together his stock and bond portfolios, bank statements from several banks in the United States and several more in Europe, as well as an itemized list of his offshore accounts and how to access them.

Poor Sir Geoffrey was as rich as Croesus and none of his friends, certainly not his Capitol Hill friends, ever suspected. Poor Sir Geoffrey had absolutely no doubt that today, even during the denouement of civilization, would be the best day of his life. *"The best should always come in the end...like desert. It should, but it doesn't always. However, it will today...today will be the best,"* Poor Sir Geoffrey said to himself.

He was met by his chauffeur in the garage of his Queen City County Club estate. "Rolls or Jag, Sir?"

"Don't we have something less conspicuous, Omar?"

"What about the Harley?"

"Perfect!"

Like a bat out of hell, feeling the freedom of the open road, hot wind whipping against his face, inflaming his nuptial desire, Poor Sir Geoffrey braved the broken Queen City streets along his way to Shady Sanctum on his cobalt blue 2016 Electra Glide Ultra Classic.

* * *

Minnie Beach slammed the door as she exited her house, leaving her lamentable life behind. The lawyer, Nelson the Sonofabitch, had abused and humiliated her for the last time. His abuses were manifold: conveniently hiring his whore to work in his office, and then having the gall to bring her on the FEA field trip, right under her nose. *"No more."* Minnie was tired of his disappearing for days or weeks at a time, no explanations, the slaps, the bruises, the name calling, belittling her for getting fat, and so much more and it all hurt in the heart of her soul. *"Enough is enough is enough!"*

Years earlier, before meeting and marrying Nelson the Sonofabitch, Minnie was crowned Miss Commerce City. She was in the top three competing for the title of Miss Colorado. Before that, she won the title of Prom Queen at East High. Her dating life was a full dance card, waiting room only. Every ounce of fat can be laid at the feet of Nelson the Sonofabitch! And, it was Minnie who worked two jobs to put the ungrateful piece of shit through eight years of school, until he finally managed to pass the bar exam, for the second time. So, she gained some weight. "*So what!? What else did the Sonofabitch expect?*" She was required to account for every minute of her day, to keep the house spotless, to cook dinner every evening whether he showed up or not. The crying, the loneliness, the suicidal thoughts of the unloved weighed heavily on her like a tyrant's thumb. In fact, that's exactly what it was—*a tyrant's thumb.* Minnie Beach could no longer accept oppressive dominance from a man she no longer remembers loving.

"*What did he expect!? Of course a body gets fat! That is what happens when your life disappears and you're stuck with nowhere else to go, but Hell.*"

Minnie was out on the street, hopeless and overwhelmed with fear. What had she done? She did not have any true friends, close or otherwise, and she knew it. After knowing Minnie for only a short while, people did not like her all that much. She tried too hard to be liked, to be a friend which, eventually, turned any promise of friendship cold. She just tried too hard. No one ever met the real Minnie. What they met was someone confused, afraid, with a bewildering intellect, someone pathetically sad, a vanquished woman.

Minnie Beach lived within walking distance from V and Lily. Minnie thought that she might find a kind shoulder at Shady Sanctum, a shoulder she might cry on. She had no idea, really, what she would find there, what she could expect, yet Minnie Beach was hopeful that within the walls of Shady Sanctum she might find some comfort to help ease the panic of being absolutely helpless and alone.

* * *

"Great party! Thanks Carla!"

Everybody cheered, poured more drinks, ate another brownie and smoked another dooby.

"Better thank V," Carla said, hardly able to navigate a glass of single malt to her mouth, hitting her nose, then her chin, before reaching her lips with the heavy leaded whisky glass.

"Thanks to both you ladies," Billy said.

"Thank you very much," Brad said, holding Billy's hand.

"We need to put something over that hole in the middle of the street. The stench is stupefying. I wouldn't get too close to it." Peter cautioned.

"Who knows how long it will be until the city gets around to it?" Lily said, rhetorically. No one knows.

"I might have some old sheets of plywood in the carriage house." Max remembered.

"V, do you have a LED flashlight?" Peter asked.

"In the kitchen. The same drawer, where you found the tape."

"Gotcha. Do you happen have any stinky cream for muscle and back pain."

"I do," said Lily. "I hurt my back doing *Peter Pan* in Albuquerque. The rigger didn't know what he was doing. Drunk, I think. He nearly killed me while on my way to Neverland." Lily threw her words over her shoulder while on her way upstairs.

"What do you want with that gawd-awful stuff, Peter?" V asked.

"To put under my nose. There's something that stinks so repulsively you can't get close to that hole without getting knocked over by the fumes. I want to see what's causing the foul stench down that rabbit hole."

When Lily came back, she found Peter in the kitchen and gave him a tube of something with so much wintergreen and camphor that it was staggering. Peter smeared it under his nose and headed for the hole.

While Maxfield headed for the carriage house, Peter inched his way to the hole to check out the size of it. Within a couple feet from it, the stench was so overwhelming, Peter had to stop and back away. Something, or somebody was rotting down there! So much for stinky creams.

"Hello there. Peter?" Minnie Beach called-out while coming down the opposite side of the street, trying not to fall as the sidewalk shifted underfoot. She was breathing heavily and gasping for air by the time she reached Peter.

"Hello, Minnie," Peter greeted. "Be careful, it really stinks around here."

"I'll say. Why do you have all that stuff under your nose?"

"To protect myself. Don't you smell anything else, Minnie? Get a little closer to that hole. Why are you wearing your housecoat and slippers?"

"I left my husband," Minnie announced as if she had just won an Academy Award.

"About time you left the sonofabitch. Good on ya, Minnie."

Minnie sniffed the hole. "Nope. Nothing. I don't smell a thing, Peter. Are V and Lily home? And yes, it *is* about time. Just in time for the end of the world. Ironic, *huh?* What other calamity will happen today?"

"I wouldn't ask that question were I you. It's bad luck to ask that question. The end of the world is enough for one day. They're home with the clan having an Armageddon party. That ought to take your mind off of discomforting things."

"A good day for it. Thank you, Peter." Minnie went up the steps, still out of breath, and disappeared into Shady Sanctum.

Peter shined the light down the hole, "What the...? RATS!" He shouted just as Maxfield was approaching with a sheet of plywood."

"What's that stinky stuff on your nose?" Max asked.

"Can't you smell them?" asked Peter, handing the flashlight to Max.

"No, nothing. Just you." Maxfield said, looking down the hole with the LED flashlight. At first he saw a thousand little white lights shining back until, "Holy rotten alligators. Those are gingriches! Hundreds! Maybe thousands. *Gingriches!* I can't believe they're still on Earth. I was with my brother somewhere around Dallas, when we saw our first gingrich. Kirby was converting heathens and I was looking for bugs. Dallas went and sunk into a sink hole, you know, but it was only a matter of time, wasn't it? I was hoping never to see another gingrich. Deadly poisonous, you know. They have an insatiable appetite. Worse than the short-horned migratory locust. And way worse than a cockpion. They're bigger than Mercury, and Merc weighs twenty pounds! No plywood sheet is gonna hold 'em in after sundown. *Nothing will.*"

"After sundown?"

"They're out of their nests, Petey, and they're ready to feed! They need to be exterminated. *Posthaste.* There's nothing I know that'll kill a whole nest of gingriches, and I think there may be several nests down there. They're like cockroaches—there's no such thing as just one. Fire would only kill a few of 'em. They can burrow deep underground in a matter of seconds. There's only a few hours left before sundown. What to do? What to do?" Maxfield pondered for a strategy to terminate them.

"You're asking me? How would I know!" Peter was horrified.

"This is the worst thing!" Max declared. "Bad. Really bad, Peter. After sundown they will kill half of Queen City. Maybe Aurora, too. And that is just the first night of the many dark nights of the gingrich before they burrow back into their underworld for another seven years."

"You're scaring me, Max."

"You should be scared, Peter."

"Max, I've heard you can fold spacetime. Is that true?"

"Angel's been talking, I see. Where is he, by the way?"

"He went to Peru on business."

"*Ahh,* Nostradamus. Yes. I can, Peter, but I'm not always reliable. I get discombobulated. I've been working at it for millennia. Wait a minute! Did you mean to fold space for those monsters down there?"

"I was kinda thinking that."

"Without old Maxfield going with them, I hope?"

"Without you, of course. You know I love you, Max."

"Really?" Max asked.

"Well, I certainly don't want any harm to come to you. Sincerity and truthfulness are aspects of love, aren't they, Max?"

"You get the full ten points for that, Peter." Max scratched his head, looked to the sky and said, "I don't know if that's possible. I'd need to be in the center of the fold funnel so that I can escape their fate. But, I think it might be impossible."

"Couldn't you fold space and jump out in time to send every one of them to somewhere else without you going with them?"

"That's the thing, Peter. I may need to create two folds simultaneously. One for the gingriches and one for me. No one has ever done that. What am I talking about? I don't remember what I was talking about? I need some Haitian dough gum."

"The thing is, I really don't want them killed."

"Why?"

"They have as much of a right to life as any of us," Peter said, uncertain he was being honest. "Maybe some things should be exterminated. Like a nasty virus, or a cancer cell. You know, things like that. Not mammals."

"Are you out of your mind, Peter! Where on Earth could you send nests of gingriches without killing people somewhere else on Earth?"

"I thought about that and I've been thinking maybe the moon."

"Peter, if you don't want to kill them, I wouldn't send them to a place where they will suffocate in less than a minute. Nice try, Peter."

"Thanks. *Wait!* What about that place where you created

the cockpions?"

"I did not create them alone, Igor. That place is Sphincter Island. YES! That is a great idea, Peter! Gingriches will love dining on cockpions. Should have thought o' that. Good boy, Peter. You don't mind killing cockpions, do you?"

"Of course not," Peter confessed. "They're unnatural anyway."

"Unnatural? I'll think about that. Gotta get some dough gum! You got any? I don't suppose you do. Never mind. I don't know if I can do it without getting caught in the fold. I'll go ask a few experts."

"Who?" Peter asked as Maxfield ran up the steps to the porch. "Where are you going, Max?"

"Under my bed."

* * *

With signs written with ugly words hoisted towards the heavens, Mikey and Mercy Pentcist braved the cracked sidewalks, the tremors, the aftershocks, and paused directly across the street from where Billy Butts' BMW had sunken into the pavement in front of Shady Sanctum.

"Witches! Demons! Homos! Baby killers! Begone!" They shouted. Then Mercy said, "Mikey, there's a black man sitting over there wearing a dress."

"I see that, Pumpkin."

Mercy yelled again, *"Homosexual black man! It's people like you who cause all the ills in the world! Black queer!"*

"Black queer!" Mikey echoed.

"*Girrrls,* you better get your sorry asses outta here before I come over there and shove those signs down your motherfucking throats!"

"You wouldn't dare!" Mercy shouted back.

"No?" Eddie rose, lifted his gown and began to walk down the steps."

"Let's get out of here, Pumpkin."

"Just like you...a coward. He's nothing but a black homosexual."

Mikey push Mercy forward. "We're going," he called to Eddy who was now about to step into the street. He felt his body shake and tingle with anxiety; the kind of anxiety that usually accompanies loathe and disdain while in the face of it. He fears that one day he will burst with unstoppable rage until Mercy was nothing but pudding.

"Move!" Mikey pushed her harder.

"I think my Jesus hands can shoot death rays."

"Move, move, move. What did you say?"

"I said, if you were listening, stupid, that I can shoot death rays from my fingertips."

"I thought that might have been what you said. Let's keep moving. And, don't use your death rays. Okay?"

"Okay," Mercy said.

The Pentcists continued up the street. Eddie turned around and went back up the steps. When the Pentcists reached the end of the block and went around the corner, a SWAT team repelled from rooftops and from an incredibly noisy black helicopter that swooped in and hovered directly above. A dozen squad cars careened from both directions, on a oneway street, until they abruptly stopped to create a reasonably impenetrable barricade on either end of the block. There was no escaping. The gun barrel end of the law surrounded the Pentcists.

"NOSES ON THE GROUND! ARMS BEHIND YOUR BACKS!" The Megaphone Man bellowed.

"What did I do?" Mercy cried. "Mikey, did you do something?"

"HIT THE DECK! NOW!"

They hit the deck of broken cement, of indescribable litter, of wet leaves and a dead squirrel. They were forthwith handcuffed, pulled to their feet, and dragged towards the waiting SWAT van.

"What about our Miranda rights? You didn't read us our rights!"

"You are correct, Ma'am. I shall take it upon myself to personally advise the concierge at the FBI welcoming desk. The concierge will be delighted to read them to you," said the Megaphone Man with a Cheshire grin.

"He's being a smart ass, right? Are you sure you didn't do something, Mikey!?" Mercy quizzed through clenched teeth.

"I don't remember doing anything. Why don't you use your death beams now, Mercy."

"They don't work in handcuffs."

"How do you know?"

"Because these handcuffs are too fucking tight, and they're behind my back!" Mercy yelled. "Careful! I have the hands of Jesus Christ with death rays!"

"Shut the fuck up, lady!" barked a member of the SWAT team.

Before Mikey was forcibly hustled into a black van with darkened windows, his feet were chained to his wrists and a leather Hannibal Lector mask was strapped on.

"Mikey!" Mercy shrieked. "Jesus Christ! What have you done!?"

* * *

Sitting in the Shady Sanctum TV room Brad and Billy were fabulously enthralled, hands touching hands, making plans to live together forever; end of the world, or not. Each knew, in a timeless moment, they were soulmates. There was no question about it. Billy was a minor celebrity in Queen City and Brad was a former Calvin Klein model. Brad once graced a block long billboard in Manhattan's Times Square wearing nothing but a bottle of Obsession.

"I'm sorry," Brad said, contritely.

"For what?" Billy asked.

"For touching your book."

"I did ask you not to."

"I'm glad I did, Billy. Do you want to know why?"

"Will it make me nervous?" Billy asked.

"It shouldn't."

"Okay," said Billy after a deep breath.

"I can't tell you much because everything was blurry, out of focus. I was floating somewhere in a space. And then, overhead, there were little squares of flashing lights moving towards me, then past me. It felt like I was being pulled inward and upward into a black hole, faster and faster. But it wasn't black once inside, it was radiant. And so beautiful I cried. And then, I found myself watching old black and white clips from the film of my life. And then, in Technicolor and wide screen, I saw you. *'Billy Butts, Billy Butts, Billy Butts',* kept flashing in front of me. And then…right then…right there…I knew I had to find you. I knew you were my one and only. My destiny."

"Wow," Billy faintly uttered. The proverbial feather could have knocked him over.

"Yes, *'wow'*. You were in every frame of my film from then on; *our film.* I was deep in love. I am deep in love…with you. And then, I found myself right where it all began. Right in front of the door where I last you. I'm told I was gone for three days, but it felt like a matter of minutes."

"Oh, Brad."

* * *

The sounds of sirens and helicopters broke their moment of enchantment. An invisible force kicked them in the gut and hurled them back into the jaws of reality. Something was happening on the street. The lovers went out the side door and made their way through the gathering neighbors until they were closeup to the yellow police tape.

"STAND BACK," the Megaphone Man warned.

During all the excitement, Billy and Brad, hand in hand,

made their way along the yellow police tape, to gather the skinny. And the skinny they gathered was—as the tired old adage goes—stranger than fiction. Mikey Pentcist was the Queen City Hacker. Simple as that. "He confessed everything, loud and clear, through his Hannibal the Cannibal mask," the lady in blue shorts and cottage cheese legs, holding her poodle named Charlie, as though she wanted to protect his innocence, told Brad and Billy.

The news story about the Queen City Hacker will be heard by few, since the End of the World News was the only news.

The Pentcists ran a crematory service, The Prometheus Society LLC, and they sold insurance for full-service burial arrangements, as we already know. These arrangements did not go into effect until after a two year waiting period. The Society also collected a hefty downpayment and, of course, a monthly insurance fee. We know that much. What we don't know is that an FBI agent uncovered the connection one night in a dream: Every hatchet victim had insurance with the Pentcists!

"Okay, Missus Pentcist, do you mean to tell me that all those victims were slaughtered only weeks before their insurance was to be activated and you had no suspicions? You never suspected anything? And we haven't even talked about burning bodies for the Mafia, yet."

"There is no such thing as the Mafia. It doesn't exist. And I did not know a thing! I still do not know a thing. I know nothing about anything," Mercy said while sniffling.

"How is that, Missus Pentcist?"

"I was in love. I trusted my adoring husband. I thought he was a good Christian, like myself. I loved him more than anything, well maybe not more than Jesus, but I loved him and that's God's truth, but now it is my Christian duty to tell God's truth. And His truth is that Mikey pulled the wool over my eyes; kept me in the dark while all the time he was in cahoots with Satan. He was a liar and a killer and I am an innocent Christian. But I forgive him. That's the Christian way, isn't it? Did I tell you about my Jesus hands?"

"I see this is an emotional time for you, Missus Pentcist, but try and make sense, if you can. You must feel like throwing your hands up, giving up, alone, not knowing what to do, or what to say."

"You got that right," Mercy shot back.

The Sympathetic FBI Man continued. "I can't imagine the pain you must be going through, Ma'am, but I know you will come out of this and into a beautiful sunlit day; sooner than you'd think, if the world doesn't end. Now go home. We'll be in touch. In the meanwhile, I suggest you divorce that pile of scum as soon as possible."

"Yes, of course. But if he gets executed, sooner than later, there won't be any need for a divorce, will there?"

The Sympathetic FBI Man was speechless.

"Did I tell you that I have the hands of Jesus Christ?"

* * *

"You'll never guess who's coming!" yelled Piggy, running in through the backdoor with Pudgy on his heels.

"You're all gonna get it now," Pudgy warned. "Every single one of you creepazoids are gonna get it."

"The world's ending," said Piggy. "And we won't be here to watch it with you."

"Sorry, you bunch of losers! We're goin' home!" Pudgy pronounced, curtly, with a double-sized whopper smirk.

"Home? Oh, I hope so. I loath beyond redemption, you creatures. You monsters! Please, do go home!" And then Lily thought, *"Umm, they probably came from the fires of Hell!"* Lily was quite perceptive. In fact, that is exactly where the twins' father, the evil King Monsanto, reigns over the largest kingdom in all dimensions of existence.

* * *

The entire Peruvian army was mobilized, including tanks, flatbeds with rocket launchers, trained assassins, trucks to transport prisoners and soldiers, air support only minutes away from Puerto

Nostradamus, Jeeps piled high with bodybags, Hershey chocolate bars, and an army of eager soldiers jazzed and ready to whoop some ass. They were within a mile of ground zero and closing in.

The Holy Black Madonna flew overhead. All the soldiers blessed themselves, even though not a one of them actually practiced Catholicism. They continued on their way to open that can of whoop ass. The Holy Black Madonna disappeared into the clouds.

TWENTY-TWO
back to sphincter island

After disappearing for nearly an hour, Maxfield reappeared under his bed, squirmed, wiggled, and struggled into a standing position which, for Max, was a difficult proposition. He was covered from head to toe with an inflated, quixelite reinforced, green rubbery suit; a quick glance and he's a colossal bullfrog, until a double blink of WTF brings Maxfield into focus. Barely able to keep a steady pace in his protective coat of armor, Max limped along under the burdensome weight of it. *"Dang and damnation! If we can travel through time and space, why can't they make this thingamabob of a suit a little less something!?"* Maxfield asked himself, but nobody was home to answer him.

Leaving the laughter and the applause from the partygoers behind, Max made his way to the porch where Peter was waiting. With Peter's support, Max bumbled to the lair of the gingrich without taking a tumble.

"Can you hear me out there?" Max asked from somewhere deep within the bullfrog.

"Yeah, fine," Peter answered.

"I've consulted my Overlord about our problem, Peter. I am assured that this will do the trick."

"What trick, Max?"

"I'm going with the rodents to Sphincter Island and I should be back...hopefully...maybe...well...soon...we'll see."

"And your Overlord thinks you'll be safe in that getup?"

"Overlords are never wrong!" A fact delivered sternly. "You will need to get in the house and stay there until I am gone...just in case the wrinkle in the fold is larger than expected."

"Larger than expected? The wrinkle in the fold?" Peter was really getting nervous now.

"There is no such thing as a wrinkle in the fold." Max

chuckled and continued, "An old Sumerian laundry joke, Peter."

"That's not funny, Max."

"What is, Peter? Who knows how much of Queen City I'll take with me if the fold is not precisely done? It could wipe out all of Colorado, for that matter."

"Joking again, Max?"

"Nope. Not this time."

"Jesus, Maxfield!" Peter ran into the house.

After Peter told everyone what could happen. Faces pressed against the window panes of Shady Sanctum, waiting and watching with wide-eyed curiosity, yet trembling with fear and anticipation of an unthinkable event.

Maxfield looked about to see if there was anyone close to ground zero. There was that commotion up the street, but there was nothing he could do about that. Max, cautiously managed to get himself in a sitting position, crab-walked his way to the hole, then sat upright with his feet dangling over the deadly abyss.

The partygoers watched Maxfield let go and fall into the nest of gingriches. V and company came running out of Shady Sanctum and circled the hole, trying to see something, anything. Peter, with the flashlight in tow, peered down the hole and... "What the...? *Empty.* No Max. No rodents. No Nothing!" Peter exclaimed.

"No cigars, either! What a bunch of losers."

V snapped at the twins. "Go to your rooms, Peter! You too, Penny! I'm sick of the two of you demon monsters! I hate you! I hate you! I hate you!" There it was. V said what she had been wanting to say for years. She was exhilarated. Free from a two-ton burden. V felt positively fabulous. Not so much as a flake of dandruff weighed on her shoulders.

Lily pronounced, *"Ditto."*

"What are you going to do about it, Auntie Vickie? We hate you, too. Always did!" Piggy was venomous.

Then they turned to Lily. Pudgy, with her face screwed into a ball of ugly said, "You too, dumbtard!"

O'Toole had enough of the devil brats and bellowed, *"That's it!"* And then there was silence. Peter turned a rusty shade of rugged. His body tightened. Peter appeared young again, in his early thirties, virile, and nary a fatty inch to pinch. He snapped his tail like a bullwhip. His horns grew and rose to nearly six inches high, and they were beautiful ivory. He was certainly something one would instinctively obey without question; because one would feel compelled to. He didn't appear threatening. He appeared inviting. Peter was altogether something else, and he was stunning. The twins fell on their knees and begged forgiveness.

"To your rooms, NOW!" Peter's voice boomed and reverberated throughout Shady Sanctum. Windows broke in the attic of the Mummi Mansion. Helga Mummi was in the attic working on a mobile that, when set into motion, would twist and turn in perpetual motion; no breeze required. Apparently, Helga was too anxious to try spinning the mobile into motion. So, she spun it with too much force, before the glue dried, she sent baseball-size fired clay heads, each representing a member of the Queen City City Council, to fly off its spokes, shattering the attic windows that hadn't already been broken by the thunder of Peter's voice. It was the head of Pentcist the Halfwit, the President of the City Council, that flew off and broke on Helga Mummi's head. She went down for the count, and she would never get back up again.

The twins flew to their rooms.

"Peter? Is that you?" Too-Much asked.

"Why do you ask?"

"Oh my stars. You should see yourself, Peter. You look like the devil. Fabulously hot, but still the devil," Too-Much offered his unsolicited opinion.

Sir Geoffrey's Harley roared down the block and came to a stop near the crowd. He dismounted with flair and walked over to see what everybody was looking at.

"What are you all looking at?" Sir Geoffrey asked of no one in particular. "Holy fish heads! What have you done with yourself? You look absolutely fantastic, Peter."

"You don't think it's too much?" Peter quipped.

"*No-o-o*. Absolutely not. Quite distinguished, Peter. Are you a devil? Maybe *the* devil?" Sir Geoffrey asked.

"I don't think so," Peter replied. "I still feel like myself. Angel says I can appear anyway I like, but I think I'm gonna like the way I look now."

"Good choice."

* * *

Maxfield's fold left him outside the gate to the hospital once overseen by Doctor Sphincter the Evil who practiced his diabolical experiments with neither empathy nor the morals of a Cracker Jack. Playing with pieces of humans was Sphincter's passion. The gingriches had scurried from the light of the sun, and quickly dug burrows into the island sand.

A man dressed in white, who wore a black rubber apron, came running towards the gate, not to unlock it, but to shoot the giant bullfrog, discharged his pistol. The bullet bounced off the belly of the giant amphibian. He shot another and another, until Maxfield roared for the man in white to stop shooting. They each took steps towards the other until they were face to face.

"I am the Retired Overlord Maxfield Talbot from the planet Sumer; a planet on the edge of the solar system."

"Good to know. What are you wearing!?" The man in white demanded.

"It's the first thing I grabbed from the closet." Max went for levity. It didn't work. From inside the bullfrog to the outer world, levity got lost in translation.

"Take it off!"

"I need some dough gum," Maxfield lamented. "I'm not sure I know how. I mean it was assembled especially for me...back home. Ninth planet. Tenth if you count Pluto. I think I will need to free my hands first."

As Maxfield fumbled with unlocking his glove two female nurses came running towards the gate. Finally, Maxfield managed to disengage one of his hands from the glove.

"Are you okay, Doctor Sphincter?" One of the nurses asked.

"Never better."

"Doctor Sphincter! Holy hoppers! I've gone back in time," Maxfield was astonished. "Why don't you greet our guest, Nurse Blubbersnout."

"Of course you have come back in time." Doctor Sphincter chortled through a cruel smile.

"*A frog?* You want me to greet a frog?" Nurse Blubbersnout the Ugly asked.

"You know what I feel about inappropriate questions, Blubbersnout." Sphincter threatened.

"I apologize, Doctor."

"You know what to do," Sphincter instructed Nurse Blubbersnout the Ugly who then extended her hand through the bars of the gate. As Maxfield reached out to shake her hand, she grabbed it and quickly injected a potent potion into the palm of his hand. The bullfrog collapsed instantly.

"Good girl," Sphincter condescended.

The nurses, Blubbersnout the Ugly and Sorrybody Three-Tits assembled an assortment of body parts for Doctor Sphincter. His nurses were always ready to assist him with his many great and useful experiments. The nurses were taught to think by Sphincter the Evil himself. He convinced them that they came from Upper Montclair, New Jersey. He gave them little smarts and the personality of a pigmy housefly. Both were clumsy and dumber than dirt, but they were perfect nurses. To create Blubbersnout the Ugly took six female inmates and the balls from Luigi the Giant, one of the male inmates. To create Sorrybody Three-Tits took five female impersonators, and a handful of leftover Tammy Faye Bakker. Both Nurses were designed to be obedient to their master. The evil doctor taught them obedience and the joy of playing with body parts and squishy innards.

When Maxfield awoke, he was no longer in the bullfrog suit; pieces of it were strewn about the laboratory of Sphincter the Evil. Max's feet were bound by leather straps. He was wearing a straight jacket. He wriggled on the floor of Sphincter's laboratory jail cell.

"We're going to make you well, froggy. What do you think of that?" sneered Sphincter the Evil.

"What year is this, Doctor?"

"Nineteen thirty-nine, you big dummy," said Three-Tits with an amusing *savoir faire*.

Blubbersnout chimed in and said, "I bet you don't know the month and day, either, froggy."

Maxfield answered, "It doesn't matter. But this doesn't make sense. I've never gone back in time before."

"Listen to froggy! Moon looney sickness."

"Leave the man alone, ladies. Go play with some nasty parts."

There was a fast and loud pounding on the Lab door. Sphincter always kept it locked. "*Ah*," the doctor said, "There is somebody I want you to meet, froggy. He is my greatest creation. Be careful. He has a hair trigger and if he doesn't like you, he will eat you."

"Yummy," Maxfield scoffed.

Sphincter walked to the lab door and unlocked it. "And now, meet my darling monster. It took a busload of school girls and two Senators to create my monster. I love this boy! He thinks he's the cruelest monster there ever was and, as intended, he acts accordingly."

The Frankenstein monster was Michelangelo's David compared to this abomination.

"Hey," Maxfield called from his cell. "Your monster's a thing to behold, but he's all brawn on brawn. A bit overdone, don't ya think? Come to think of it, I mean...considering what he's made of...did you give him a working brain?"

"*No* and *no* on both counts, froggy. My beautiful monster is brainless. He doesn't need one. He just does what I tell him. There is no telling what reckless devastation my dearest creation could leave in his wake, if I asked him. But he can be sweet as a bunny, if I asked him. At night. In my room. Just him and me. Under the sheet. If you know what I mean."

"Oh, I know what you mean, Sphincter. To change the subject, as heart breaking that is, do ya wanna see a trick?" Maxfield asked, not caring if Sphincter answered or not.

But he did, "What kind of trick, froggy?"

"First, before I do it, I must tell you never to go out after sundown. You could get...*wait*...maybe sundown is a great time for you and you handy monster to get out of bed and go out and take a stroll through the tulips. *Perfect*. A must-do event. *Ahh*, you wouldn't happen to have any Haitian dough gum, would you?"

The doctor smiled a smile only a duck would trust, and said nothing.

"Okay, here's the trick, said Max." And then he burst into a cloud of blindingly bright new-color sparks, leaving the leather binding and the straightjacket on Doctor Sphincter's prison cell floor.

* * *

And then, Maxfield came out from under his bed and jogged down the stairs. "Well, kids, are you gonna welcome old Max home?"

Everyone was pleasantly surprised. Not two minutes had passed since he fell into the gingrich hole. After the applause and cheers quieted down, they all went into Shady Sanctum where the end of the world party had just gotten really-really wild.

The devil brats remained hidden in their rooms. They knew exactly who Peter was. He was the devil with the last and the first pure soul. They had run into him a few millennia earlier when they learned that, with little provocation, Peter could hurl them into oblivion, and he almost did simply because he found them to be pests. And, having the King of the Underworld for a father, would be of no help saving the twins from actually being hurled into oblivion. Peter has nothing to do with the Underworld, and he is far more ancient than Monsanto. Legend is: an entity named Peter began many worlds with nothing but his thoughts. He also ended many worlds just as quickly. Consciousness of existence was at Peter's behest. Only, Peter did not yet know it.

Angel appeared among the partiers long enough to properly greet everyone. When he came upon Sir Geoffrey, Angel said, "Welcome to the family." Then, without warning, nor farewells, he and Peter dissolved into blinding pixels of another color.

"I love this family," Brad offered, with great enthusiasm.

"*Girrrl*, this is the best."

Meanwhile, as the end of the world party grew merrier and louder, Sir Geoffrey and Minnie were sitting more closely together. Sir Geoffrey Hemphill and Minnie Beach were having an earnest and agreeable conversation.

Electricity was restored to all of Queen City. Cleaning crews and volunteers were out to help anyone in need. The Shady Sanctum clan, with all their noise and hoopla, had forgotten that there was a world outside their sanctuary door, where some paused on pieces of broken sidewalk, to listen to their happiness.

The aftershocks had ceased. All available Army and Marine reservists, as well as the National Guard, were called out to close and confiscate every fracking site, oil drilling and pumping sites in America. Even the good people of the State of Texas thought that was a great idea! Holy Flying Black Madonna! Will wonders never cease?

TWENTY-THREE
welcome to wonderland

After a barrage of rockets burst in the clear Peruvian sky, warning of inevitable war, Elvis and Gert began the parade.

Gert was perched atop the back of Elvis' pink Cadillac convertible, waving like a prom queen to those within the Nostradamus side of the fence. Behind the wheel, Elvis sang "Shake, Rattle and Roll" as they entered The War Zone. The Black Buzzards trained every can of whoop-ass on the Cadillac, until the army behind them rumbled into view. Bushit Junior and Darth Vader came running. Bushit Junior did the running, Darth wobbled like an old, fat, mean spirited, has-been.

"Stop, stop, stop! Now! You Buzz—buzz—birds!" The Village idiot shouted. Nothing happened. No one moved.

Then it was Vader's turn: "Order! Down! Now! You will live or you will die. I can save your lives if you get down on your bellies *now,* or I will see you die *now!* That's my best offer. I may look old and bad, boys, but I have the heart of a child!" Nothing happened. No one moved. They were thinking about how unlikable that dirty dick really was.

"Every one of you maggots, on the ground!" The Army Captain bellowed in return. The Buzzards dropped to the ground. Several soldiers collected their weapons while others had begun to bring down the fencing around Puerto Nostradamus and to throw two rows of electrocuted Buzzards onto neat piles. Gert casually slipped out from the passenger side door while Elvis turned his pink Cadillac around; that was the day Gert Talbot-Birdsall gave Elvis Presley a great big teddybear hug and a not-too-quick peck on the cheek, before he put it in gear, pealed-out and split. Her only disappointment was that he never did sing her favorite song, "Blue Suede Shoes."

Meanwhile, Peter and Angel, both invisible to everyone except Gert, were standing on the porch of Angel's little shack in

Puerto Nostradamus watching the goings-on. They watched as Vader and Bushit Junior were handcuffed and dragged away; two war criminals to be processed and sent to the Hague.

"Sir," Gert whispered to the Army Captain, "there's a frozen Governor in our freezer. We don't know what to do with him?"

"The Governor of where?" The Captain asked.

"New Jersey."

"Thaw him out. Give him some electroshock therapy. If that doesn't work, bury him and forget he was ever here."

After the Buzzards were safely detained and locked in trucks with just enough ventilation to keep them alive in the hot midday Peruvian heat, the search for others who might be hiding in the compound ended with a divine payoff! At gunpoint, were Mamma Bushit, former television evangelist and consummate American example of family values. Behind Big Mama, the most delicious, the most satisfying, the best of all, the make-my-day moment: The heartless, the incomparable and despicable Krotch Brothers were nudged along by imposing assault rifles.

"Captain, I found these three stragglers huddled in the corner of the porno arcade," the soldier said.

"Lord, fuck a duck! Today is the best day of my life! You dirty little scoundrels will be spending years in a nasty, smelly, Peruvian prison. Then, maggots, you'll be transferred to the other side of the lake, where Argentina will have smelly cells with toothless old men waiting just for you." To the soldiers, the Captain ordered, "Throw them in with the Buzzards. They'll learn to get land deeds and not to forge legal documents next time, and not to destroy one of the Wonders of the World! However, you can be assured that there will never be a next time for them. And we'll pin everything we can on you maggots to keep you in the darkest, dirtiest corners of Hell." This was a perfect off-with-their-heads moment, but the Krotch Brothers would have to settle for the Captain shouting, "Get these ass-wipes outta my sight!"

The Army Captain told Gert and Charlie, and those who were gathered around them, "We'll be back to haul off all that contraband over there after the weekend. You might want to commandeer whatever property you want. There's a great video arcade, portable housing, whatever, and tons of frozen food." Cheers and words of gratitude all around.

"You wouldn't happen to have any food that's not frozen with you, would you?" Charlie asked.

The Captain made a quick announcement, "READY, BOYS," and a large trailer, pulled by an Army tractor, filled with food supplies, came rolling in. "All you gotta do is start grabbing and taking every morsel of it into..." the Captain looked about and... "Why are these people naked?"

"We do not discourage nudity, nor public sex, here in Puerto Nostradamus."

"What a brave idea," said the Captain, with a broad smile. "Maybe, I'll be back and spend a little time with y'all."

"You're always welcome," Gert said.

A crashing sound accompanied Tallulah Badass as she came running out of the clubhouse. "I bumped into Frozen Crapp! He toppled over and hit the floor awful hard. Oh, Lordy! If the freezer didn't kill 'im, I think, maybe, I did."

Everybody shrugged so-what until the Governor came crawling out of the clubhouse. They were horrified. Crapp looked like crap, what with his freezer burns and missing nose.

"I'm sorry, everybody. I'm really, really sorry for eating all your food. Can you ever forgive me?" Crapp pleaded and belched, followed by the scent of smoked ham and salami.

Once again, more shrugs of so-what, but this time their shrugs turned into sneers as they looked upon the Jersey Governor rolling in dust, sweating and crying in an effort to stand up by himself without the help of others.

The Captain whispered to Gert, "See, problem solved."

"Thank you, Captain."

"You want me to take him out?" the Captain asked.

"Out? You mean...?"

"Yup."

"Thank you, Captain. I'm not sure that I'm above that. However, I don't think it will be necessary this time."

* * *

Meanwhile, invisible to all, Peter and Angel were still standing on the shack's porch when Peter said, as if it were a confession, "Angel, I'm growing wings."

"I know. Is that a bad thing?"

"No, not at all. I think they'll be fun," Peter said, with a devilish grin.

"Are you ready to see one of our residences?"

"*Our.* That sounds nice. You mean there's more than one?"

"As many as you can imagine, Peter. *C'mon.*"

Hand in hand, they walked into the shed. Angel pointed to the opposite wall, "Let's go through it, Peter."

Before Peter could refuse, or show any trepidation, they were on the other side of the wall. Peter stood with his mouth agape and his eyes sparkling with wonder; the kind of wonder Peter lost to childhood, had returned. Everything was new and beautiful with why-is-the-sky-blue wonder; a kind of wonder that makes one cry.

Ahead was the most beautiful estate Peter had ever seen. Until that moment, he would have thought it unimaginable. Rolling hills of green lawn filled the air with a freshly-mown scent. Willows wept along the path to a palace of inexplicable beauty. Angel nudged Peter and they walked through the unopened door. When only a few feet into the grand palace, Peter stopped to take in its splendor. Peter was overcome with exquisite awe. Angel watched and took mental note of how much Peter's wonder was a joyous event to behold; a life-altering event, a pleasure for a satyr to behold.

Angel took the hands of a swooning Peter and kissed them. "This will be epic," Angel foretold.

"Epic?"

"Our share of time and space. We will possess it."

"I don't understand what you're saying, Angel."

"It doesn't matter. Now it is time we get back to Shady Sanctum." And then they were gone in a flash of pixels.

* * *

"They're here!" shouted Piggy and Pudgy. "They're here! They're here!"

"I thought the two of you were sent to your rooms." V's wide smile assaulted them with cruel disgust.

"You didn't send us anywhere. It was a Seraphic Angel who sent us to our rooms, Vickie dearest. Peter might be powerful, but you're not. Ain't no way to kill a Seraph, you know."

"Are you talking about killing Peter?" V asked.

"Wash out your ears, human idiot!"

"You know what," V declared, "I don't care one bit what you dung brats say anymore!"

Sparkling pixels brought Peter and Angel into view.

"*Ut oh!*" The twins made a bee line for the backdoor.

* * *

The quixcube appeared on the back lawn of the future Bean Center for the Arts.

"*I knew it! The Calculator of Folds crashed, again.*" Captain Talbot returned to his quixcube and manually re-set the timeline of the fold. *"Let's do it!"* What appeared to be a second later, the Captain exited the quixcube. This time he was on-spot in spacetime. He crossed the lawn to the east gate of La Bean Hacienda, then followed his nose to Shady Sanctum. As he walked through the damage and the cracks he said aloud, "Humans. Go figure."

* * *

Two hard knocks on Shady Sanctum's front door.

"I'll get it," Carla offered.

"Don't let any Mormons in!" V, Lily, Billy, Eddy and Too-Much shouted in unison." Then they all laughed and cheered with another toke, another drink. When Carla opened the door she was met by a Black Suit holding a manila envelope. She trembled as she asked, "Yes. Can I help you? Who do you want to see?" Hoping it wasn't she.

The suit glanced at the manila envelope and read, "Missus Carla Bean."

"I'm just Carla Bean. My husband is deceased."

The Black Suit reached into his vest pocket and showed her a photograph. "Is this a photo of you, Ma'am?"

Carla glanced at it and said "Not a good one, but that's me."

The Black Suit eyed the photo, then Carla. "This is for you, Widow Bean." That was the first time Carla was called Widow Bean, at least to her face. Carla vowed that this would be the last time anyone will call her that, to her face. The Black Suit handed her the envelope. She noticed an unbroken Interpol seal.

"Thank you. Who are you, if you don't mind my asking?" And then a sudden realization, "I remember you. Oh, my gawd. It's you, isn't it? How did you know I was here? I don't live here, but you already knew that. Oh my gawd...*Architectural Digest!*"

"Yes, Ma'am. That was me. Just doing my job, Ma'am. You take care." The Suit turned and walked away.

Carla closed the door slowly to watch him until he got into his van and drove out of sight. She sat on the foyer love seat. Carla stared at the envelop, excited and scared at once, took a deep breath, sighed, tore away the Interpol seal and opened the envelope and took out the document. When she was finished reading it, she read it again. *"Oh my gawd!"*

She ran back to the partiers, screaming! "My money! My money! It's a letter from Interpol saying they will release the money after I identify the Greek thief. Barring the world ending, I will testify and identify that fucking Greek cocksucker! No offense, Tommy. Right now it's all in cyberspace. That's where they keep large sums of money."

Too-Much popped up and said, "Carla, the truth cannot offend me. A cocksucker I am and a cocksucker I'll always be."

"*Girrrl,* tell it like it is."

"Tommy. I will never, never say cocksucker in a mean spirited way...except for that Greek sonofabitch...and I won't flatter him with the moniker again."

"I get it," Tommy stops Carla. "Should I tell everybody the plans we've been talking about?

Carla pipes in, "And, it is over fifty million! Where did, how did that cock...cocky Greek manage to get all this?"

Shady Sanctum turned into a funeral parlor. Not a sound to be heard. There, in that moment of silence, they did not know how to react. Everyone was happy for Carla. Not a jealous bone in the house. And everyone wondered what her joy must feel like; what it would be like to be her. And everyone, for a moment or two, wanted to be her.

"Should I tell them?" Tommy asked Carla, breaking the silence.

"Sure. Why not?" Carla answered.

Tommy Too-Much filled his "family" in on what will no longer be just a dream. He told his audience that Carla was considering buying the mansion next door, and how he will have a huge apartment of his own in the finished basement. Too-Much also offered that, if Carla recovered her stolen fortune—and now she has—she plans to turn La Bean Hacienda into the Bean Museum for the Arts. It will display the collections of all the Friends of Erotic Artifacts, and any other art their newly established family chooses to exhibit. Minnie's rubbing would have a wall all to itself. The *pièce de résistance,* a ninety-nine seat theatre over which Victoria and Lily will have complete control. It will be called the Lilith Champagne Theatre. And now with Carla's sudden windfall, the prospect for a theatre with Lily as its namesake, V was overwhelmed with joy. She was so happy for Lily, V did not so much as a nanosecond think of herself. Lily was stunned.

The news heard round Queen City: THE END OF THE WORLD IS OVER. CLEANING CREWS ARE WORKING AROUND THE CLOCK, LOCAL RESTAURANTS ARE OFFERING FREE FOOD TO THE HOMELESS, AND THE FRACKING AND OIL DRILLING VICTIMS. QUEEN CITY HACKER FINALLY CAPTURED!

Minnie Beach and Sir Geoffrey Hemphill had come to an agreement for the terms of their marriage. They will not have intercourse. They will have separate bedroom suites on opposite sides of his mansion. He will put two million dollars in cash in a safety deposit box that only Minnie, having the key, could access. That gave Minnie a welcomed feeling and a renewed sense of security. Although, Minnie saw through any illusions of security, that there is no such thing as security, but with the title of Lady Minerva Hemphill and a couple million in the bank just for herself, this was an illusion she could live with...assuming her world doesn't end anytime soon. It won't. At least, not today.

And then, one last knock; a slow knock, a short knock, a pleasant knock, on Shady Sanctum's front door.

"I'll get it." Lily rose and went to the front door. When she came back, she had Captain Maxfield Talbot in tow.

"Holy mackerel soup!" Maxfield trotted over and gave the Captain a big hug. "So good to see me," said a happy Max.

"So good to see me, too," said an equally happy Captain Max."

"Max, is this your son?" Lily asked. The two Maxes laughed.

"You better tell her, oh Captain, my Captain. It was all your fault in the first place."

"I suppose it was," Captain Max confessed. "I was practicing time travel techniques when something went wrong. Your Uncle Max was sent to Earth, while I was able to make it back to Sumer. We are the same person."

"Proof that you can be in two places at once...without harming the spacetime line!" Old Maxfield giggled with glee.

"You're here to pick up the twins, right?" Lily asked, hopefully. She got right to the point. Getting rid of the twins would add a cherry on the top of her sweet joyous confection.

"Yes. Among other things." The Captain reached behind him where suitcases and a special present for the family appeared. He announced, "I come bearing gifts."

"And he's not even Greek," said a giddy Carla. And everybody laughed.

"Anything for me?" Piggy asked.

"Or me?" Pudgy echoed.

"NO! The two of you go sit on the front steps and shut up! I don't want to hear a word out of you two mongrels until I hand you over to your father."

The twins left muttering profanities.

"You're all a bunch of turdstools!"

"Yeah, turdstools!"

"They're Princes?" Too-Much asked.

"Toads," answered Captain Max.

After the twins had left the room, the Captain retrieved one of the suitcases, read the label, and announced, "This is for Minnie Beach, who will soon be married to Sir Geoffrey Hemphill. After a quick divorce, of course." The Captain forced himself to ask her intended, "She does know you're gay, right?"

"Yes. *Yes! Oh, yes, yes, yes.* I never knew *'yes'* could feel so good."

Minnie smiled and said, "And, we are quite fond of each other." She was keen to open the suitcase. "This is so exciting."

The suitcase was filled with clothes, jackets, shoes, gowns, a bottomless suitcase that will forever be filled and refilled with endless surprises. The first surprise was the wedding dress of her dreams. Minnie looked more closely and said, sadly, "I think you may have gotten my size wrong, Captain. These are way too small." Minnie was disappointed and embarrassed.

"Try on something, Minnie. How about this lovely red dress?" The Captain took it out of the suitcase.

"If you insist, but it won't get above my hips. I don't want to tear it...or be ridiculed."

"I insist," said the Captain, sternly.

Minnie felt that she had no choice in the matter. So, she took the dress and left the room.

"This present is for the entire family." The Captain handed it to V, who then opened it. It was a book with the new color. "This is nothing like the other," the Captain said. "This book has been created for each and every family member. All of you in this room and Gertrude, who lives in Puerto Nostradamus, will need to learn the language of spirit. It's in the very first chapter. You may need to read it a couple times. Maybe more. After that, you'll be able to learn more than you can now realize, or imagine, as you continue to use the book. Everyone in this room will develop powers you cannot yet suspect."

"That's some color!" Brad said, impressed.

Suddenly, Peter and Angel appeared near the fireplace.

"Peter, Angel, this is for you. The Overlord said you'll know what to do with it when the times comes."

Angel and Peter opened the sack. It was filled with quixelite crystals. "Yes, Captain. I do know exactly what to do with these. Thank you." Angel bowed.

Minnie returned wearing the black dress. Minnie couldn't possibly be more than a size four. She was radiant. She ran into Sir Geoffrey's arms and cried her heart out. Everyone else was in shock and they cried for her happiness.

"What a mushy family you all turned out to be," Uncle Max chided.

"Maxfield, are you coming home?" Captain Max asked.

"Nope."

"It will be awhile before I return. Certain?"

"Yup."

"Okay, Max, if you are certain you want to stay..."

"I am."

"Then, this is for you," the Captain handed the other suitcase to Max. Max opened it, jumped, and went into his happy dance.

"What is it?" V asked. Max's excitement was contagious.

Max reached into the case, turned his back and picked up its content, hiding it from the family.

"What is it, Max?" Billy asked.

"*Yeah. C'mon.* What is it?" asked Too-Much.

Max turned around and he was holding a dummy, an exact look-alike of himself. Max, with his arm up Little Max's ass squealed, "It's my dummy!"

"I ain't nobody's dummy!" The dummy objected. "You got it?"

"I got it." Uncle Max said to Little Max."

"I forgot to tell you, Max. Sometimes, the dummy speaks for himself," the Captain smiled.

"Three Maxes! Oh my nerves!" It was V who said it, but everyone was thinking it.

The clan expressed their gratitude, their thanks and their goodbyes to Captain Talbot.

After the Captain was escorted by Uncle Max through Dionysius and out the front door, they all found somewhere to sit and wait for V to be the first to open the book. After she did a bolt of lighting struck upwards from the first page. Suddenly, V was in a state of euphoria. She heard herself speaking with an Overlord. Then she passed the book along. After the book had been passed around to everyone, there was silence. They were struck by wonder. And, they all instinctively knew that their lives were just about to begin.

Peter handed V an envelope and simply said, "Sell this."

"What is it, Peter?" V asked.

"The deed to my condo. Sell it. Use the money to produce my plays, or not. Do with it whatever you will."

"I will. I would love to produce your plays...most of them."

"Most of them? You couldn't help yourself. Could you, V?" Peter was jovial.

"Nope," V smiled. "Where are you going, Peter?"

"To live with my Angel."

Angel put the sack of quixelite into Peter's arms. "Come, Peter! We'll put some crystals around Shady Sanctum. It will create a negative-free zone and so much more."

"What is that? The 'much more?'" Peter asked.

"Remember walking through the wall? The door?"

"Who could forget that?"

"Come," said Angel. Our family will discover it. We don't have much time for the much more."

"For what?"

"We're late for a very important date."

Peter and Angel embraced and then they were gone. That moment would be the last chapter of their lives on Earth.

Captain Talbot kicked the twins into the quixcube, closed the hatch and the hellish monsters were on their way back to Sumer where King Monsanto was waiting for his mutants.

* * *

There was a beautiful spot beneath a tree covered with huge green leaves with sweetly scented golden blossoms that gently swayed in a warm breeze. In the twilight, Peter and Angel lied on the grass in an embrace under the tree while overhead tiny splinters of light in the black sky surrounded the pale violet glow of two full moons. There will always be magic for Peter and Angel to conjure wondrous delights for their new home, in a dimension all their own, in a newly born universe, where they will create their Wonderland.

"Anything? Anything we want, Angel?"

"Anything *you* want, Peter."

"Humans. Should their be humans?

"You might want to give that some serious thought, Peter."

"*Yeah.* I think that might be a good idea." Then Peter said out loud for the very first time, "I love you, Angel."

Angel embraced Peter and whispered, "I love you too, Kiddo."

"Forever?"

"Right up to the end."

And at the end of their first day in Wonderland, the satyr and the angel rested.

END

Edward Crosby Wells
Denver, Colorado
edwardcrosbywells@yahoo.com

Printed in Great Britain
by Amazon